Christine Schott
Canon Fanfiction

Research in Medieval
and Early Modern Culture XXXVI
Studies in Medieval
and Early Modern Culture LXXXV

Christine Schott

Canon Fanfiction

Reading, Writing, and Teaching with Adaptations of
Premodern and Early Modern Literature

DE GRUYTER

ISBN 978-1-5015-2361-8
e-ISBN (PDF) 978-1-5015-1597-2
e-ISBN (EPUB) 978-1-5015-1598-9

Library of Congress Control Number: 2022946068

Bibliographic information published by the Deutsche Nationalbibliothek
The Deutsche Nationalbibliothek lists this publication in the Deutsche Nationalbibliografie;
detailed bibliographic data are available on the internet at http://dnb.dnb.de.

www.degruyter.com

Acknowledgments

For the production of this book I am indebted to Shannon Cunningham from the Medieval Institute Publications, who first contacted me to see if I was working on anything new. Without her initial inquiry, this book would still be nothing but a plot bunny collecting dust in my head. I am ever grateful to my family for their unfailing support and enthusiasm for my weird academic pursuits. My sincerest thanks go to my beta reader, Sten Maulsby, for his careful and insightful feedback on a draft of this project, and to Dr. Leah Acosta Tenney for sharing her expertise on the causes and symptoms of aphasia.

I am also grateful to the Converse College MFA program, especially Sheila O'Connor, who oversaw the first iteration of this project as my critical paper for my MFA in creative writing. Sheila, I'm so sorry my twenty-page paper ended up being fifty pages long. But look where it got me! Additionally, I owe a debt of gratitude to John Kennerly at the Erskine College library, who, despite the interruptions caused by a global pandemic, went above and beyond to make sure I had the research material I needed to continue working.

But most of all, I am grateful to my students, even (perhaps especially) the ones who "don't like literature." You keep me on my toes, you don't let me get away with making assumptions and taking intellectual shortcuts, and you continuously give me reasons to share my love of literature with young people like you, for whom the past is brand new.

https://doi.org/10.1515/9781501515972-001

Contents

Introduction: To the Teacher

The Decline of Literature, the Rise of Cancel Culture, and the Problem of Canon

In a broad way, this book arose from my dismay as interest in literature among undergraduates has waned drastically in the last decade. In a 2018 study conducted by the Association of Departments of English, 66.3 percent of higher-education institutions surveyed reported a decline or a sharp decline in their number of majors between 2012 and 2017.[1] This drop-off has alarmed many institutions into repackaging their major "not just as a program in literature but more expansively as one in English studies, [... to include] media, composition, rhetoric, film, cultural studies, and other interests."[2] While I myself teach creative writing and composition and have a deep interest in many items in the above list, I remain troubled by the obvious diminution in undergraduates' passion for literature itself, which is what brought me into academia—first as a medievalist and then additionally as a creative writer. A majority of my own teaching load is general education literature courses for non-majors, so I am confronted every day with profound indifference toward the field to which I have dedicated my professional life. My daily challenge is to make literature of the past feel relevant, meaningful, and—at the very least—interesting to business majors and pre-med students who see my field as a useless distraction from what really matters in their lives. One way of addressing this problem is through canon fanfiction, the subject of this book.

I also came to this project through a question literary scholars have been wrestling with for decades: what do we do with the traditional literary canon? In the wake of the "canon wars" of the second half of the twentieth century, the shift away from primarily "dead white male" literature has been a welcome and a necessary one in an increasingly global, diverse, and self-aware literary community. But the problem remains that the likes of Chaucer, Shakespeare, and Milton were incredibly important in the history of English literature and continue to exert influence on readers, writers, and thinkers of today. Many high schools and institutions of higher education, like mine, continue to teach them as a matter of course. And, although the sentiment is not universal, many of us find them genuinely meaningful, even moving. Yet we would have

---

1 ADE, "A Changing Major," 32.
2 ADE, "A Changing Major," 15.

https://doi.org/10.1515/9781501515972-002

to be willfully ignorant to deny the existence of plenty of objectionable content in the traditional canon. *The Merchant of Venice* may be leagues ahead of *The Jew of Malta* in its portrayal of a Jewish person as a human being, but Shylock is still a villain, still an embodiment of antisemitic stereotypes. And that is to say nothing of the antisemitism at the heart of the *Prioress's Tale*, which is so horrifying that we often avoid teaching it at all.

But the ideologies of ethnocentrism, racism, misogyny, homophobia, xenophobia, and bigotry are not just problems on the pages of Norton anthologies. As white supremacists have laid claim to Western literature and history, and as the academy itself has descended into a storm of controversy over what we should do about it,[3] we have been forced to admit that such abhorrent content has real-world consequences, even today. If we were ever content to pretend that the authors of the traditional canon had universal appeal and held universal values, the skeptical faces of our students—who are increasingly not even *living* white males but female, trans, nonbinary, international, first-generation American, BIPOC, Muslim, Jewish, indeed every variety of human being—demand that we think again.

So what are we to do with those authors whom we love at their best but who repulse us, and our students, with the limitations of their worldviews? In the current environment of cancel culture, in which (usually online) commentators shame and withdraw support from public figures who have offended them, our students' instinct, if not ours, might simply be to stop reading them entirely. Cancel culture is a controversial movement, lauded by some as an expression of social justice and grassroots advocacy, and condemned by others as nothing more than censorship, a way to enforce "dogma or coercion," under a progressivist banner.[4] But the fact that there is more than one way to view the issue does not alleviate the difficulty of how to respond as an educator. I personally have avoided teaching the *Prioress's Tale* except to advanced English majors—in part because the antisemitism in the tale is offensive and in part because real-life antisemitism is on the rise,[5] and I cannot be certain that students in my class won't take the story at face value and use it to fuel prejudices they may already have. But this has never been a satisfactory approach in my own mind, nor can I imagine really "canceling" Chaucer, much less Shakespeare. To forget the past is perhaps the only thing worse than repeating it. One way

---

3 See, for instance, the public and contentious exchanges between Dorothy Kim and Rachel Fulton-Brown, summarized by Nick Roll in *Inside Higher Ed*, "A Schism in Medieval Studies."
4 "A Letter on Justice and Open Debate." For the supportive response, see Uprichard, "In Defence of Call-Out Culture."
5 See commentary by Greta Anderson, "Responding to Rise in Campus Anti-Semitism."

out of this dilemma is to give students a stake in the literature of the traditional canon, allowing them to address its failings by rewriting them in a fanfiction of their own making.

Why Call It "Fanfiction"?

I have coined the term "canon fanfiction" to describe artistic productions that use and specifically respond to traditionally canonical sources in the production of a new story. A full definition and defense of the theoretical and practical connections between "canon fanfiction" and what we might call "popular fanfiction" appear in chapter 1. However, an additional justification for the term "fanfiction" may be useful for the instructor here. It is simply the term's transparency for our target audience: undergraduate students.

When I describe this project in other, more standard terms to friends, students, and even my colleagues in other academic disciplines, I receive the classic knotted brow of concentration, the thoughtful nodding of the head that indicates they neither understand nor care what I mean. Then I say, "Basically, I'm talking about fanfiction," and if my conversation partner is of a certain age, immediately the brows unknot and I receive the gratifying, "Ohhh!" that tells me they get it. To outside observers—that is, to students, laypeople, and scholars who are not deeply imbued in the theory and practice of literary studies or fanfiction—the parallels I highlight in chapter 1 are often obvious. I could apply the terms "extradiegesis"[6] or "hypotext/hypertext intertextuality,"[7] and those would perhaps capture levels of subtlety that "canon fanfiction" does not, but I have published elsewhere on the importance of making what we do as scholars comprehensible to people who do not reside in the ivory tower.[8] I have no investment in using Greek-derived vocabulary to make my work sound esoteric, and I certainly have no interest in talking over the heads of the very students I hope to win over to the love of my field.

---

6 Turk, "Metalepsis," 86.
7 See Barta-Smith and DiMarco, "Introduction," 5.
8 Schott, "How to Save Literary Studies."

The Pedagogical Use of Canon Fanfiction

Any number of scholar-teachers have commented on the power of fanfiction as a pedagogical tool. Most have been invested either in its ability to engage students who might not otherwise find literature interesting or relevant, or in its potential to free students from the strictures of traditional composition and rhetoric, given that—although writing itself is a vital life skill—very few students will ever need to write a formal academic paper in the professional world.

This is fan culture scholar Henry Jenkins's characterization of how a student might experience a traditional lecture-and-paper approach to literary education: "the reader [i.e. student] is supposed to serve as the more-or-less passive percipient of authorial meaning while any deviation from [such] meanings [...] is viewed negatively, as a failure to successfully understand what the author was trying to say."[9] There immediately follows his characterization of the instructor's role: "[t]he teacher's red pen rewards those who 'correctly' decipher the text and penalizes those who 'get it wrong,' while the student's personal feelings and associations are rated 'irrelevant' to the task of literary analysis." Although much progress in active learning has been made since Jenkins wrote this in 1992, and although scholars ever since Barthes have made claims to have dismantled the idea of "authorial" or "authoritative" reading, in my experience Jenkins's characterizations are not far off the mark, even in my own classroom.

Although I, trained as I was in a post-deconstructionist academy, am happy in theory to entertain a multiplicity of meanings, in reality many of my comments on student papers do, indeed, attempt to "correct" errors in interpretation. These generally stem from students' lack of fluency in the cultural idioms of the literature they are studying. It is easy for students to think of the Wife of Bath as an unambiguous symbol of female liberation because she is irrepressible and gets in a good punch on Jenkin; they are unfamiliar with the medieval misogynistic stereotype of the shrew, which casts the Wife's actions in a more ambiguous light. So when they give me papers on Chaucer as proto-feminist, I find myself constantly reminding them of the context he was writing into. That historical context is important in a traditional academic analysis of the Wife of Bath, but most of my students are not going to be academics, and their grasp of historical distinctions tends to be minimal. They commonly see the Middle Ages as a benighted world in which "a woman who spoke her mind would be immediately punished." I am not sure where students get this idea about medieval England, but in my experience it is astoundingly widespread. I can—and do—

---

9 Jenkins, *Textual Poachers*, 25.

try to correct such sweeping and dismissive generalizations about a vibrant and complex historical period, but when it comes down to it, I am not a history professor; my job is to make literature come alive to my students. As such, I would rather see them experiment, for instance, with imagining the Wife of Bath living in their own hometown and deciding, once she is removed from that "benighted" medieval world, whether her behavior really represents female empowerment— or is just another way of dismissing "bad" women. Their answer may not, in fact, be immediately better, but they may discover they have more insight on the subject than they did when the Wife was stuck in a historical period they had no context for understanding.

This is where literature teachers can make use of canon fanfiction, and they can do so in two ways. First and perhaps most obviously, they can teach published canon fanfictions in relation to their sources. *Wide Sargasso Sea* is already taught next to *Jane Eyre*, for instance, to help students question the implicit colonialist attitudes underlying Rochester's relationship with his mad wife. Second, they can encourage or even assign students to write their own. Doing so gives students a different way to relate to literature as well as a new and often more amenable method for expressing a response to it. And perhaps just as helpfully for teachers as for students, responding through fanfiction helps break down the sense that there is a "right" and a "wrong" way to respond to a canonical text, policed by the infamous "teacher's red pen." As Wyn Kelley and her coauthors argue, "Rather than judging students' reading practices from the standpoint of a hierarchy, whereby students are taught to devalue the forms of reading that they do in their everyday lives, a participatory understanding of literacy recognizes that there are many ways of making meanings with a text and that all 'count' as valid forms of reading."[10] In my example of the Wife of Bath transported to twenty-first-century America, for instance, the question of how we interpret the Wife remains ambiguous, but suddenly the answer to the question matters: I once had a student tell me she was pretty sure she'd met the Wife of Bath at her church, and I still regret not asking her whether the congregation thought of that woman as a liberated free spirit or a loud-mouthed joke. If I had asked that student to write me a fanfiction using that scenario, I am certain I would have found out.

Scholars offer various reasons to teach fanfiction in the literary classroom. One argument I have not yet seen made for using a creative assignment over a traditional academic analysis is a very practical one: it's harder to cheat on it. With SparkNotes, GradeSaver, Bartleby, and a dozen other "homework help"

---

10 Kelley et al., "From Theory to Practice," 28.

sites encroaching on our intellectual territory, instructors are working harder and harder to give assignments that actually require students to think for themselves rather than simply googling an "answer" to a question. However, if students must write a story, there is nothing for them to google. Taking intellectual short-cuts would not be impossible, of course; having been assigned to write a canon fanfiction of *Taming of the Shrew*, a student might stumble upon *Vinegar Girl* or *Kiss Me, Kate* and patch-write an uninspired pastiche of someone else's work, but one could argue that there would be value even in that sort of cheating. First, they[11] would have to read an additional novel or play (or at least a good summary of it), and then they would have to process how the fanfiction respond-ed to the original in order to mimic its effects. More than that, though, as an in-structor of both literature and creative writing myself, I find that students don't *want* to take shortcuts in creative writing as much as they do in academic writ-ing. Because creativity is emotionally as well as intellectually engaging, I find students are less likely to try to find ways out of thinking about their own crea-tive work, and they tend to be more invested in doing it well.

Other arguments in favor of fanfiction are more far-reaching. Speaking of popular as opposed to canon fanfiction, Paul Booth makes an impassioned case for what is at stake in a broad sense. "[N]ew generations of fans will become future teachers, thinkers, and responsible media citizens," he says, and then adds an alarming but valid observation: "[i]ndeed, once formal schooling is complete, one's fandom may be one of the only places where one is encouraged to think critically, to write, to discuss deeply, and to make thoughtful and critical judgments about hegemonic culture."[12] Of course, our general education stu-dents may be unlikely to engage actively in Shakespeare or Chaucer fandom after they leave college, but the skills they learn in writing canon fanfiction will, one hopes, help them learn to talk meaningfully about literature and other arts of the popular kind in their later lives.

Jenkins highlights the so-called soft skills students gain by writing and dis-cussing fanfiction, including "the ability to share and compare value systems by evaluating ethical dramas" and "the ability to make connections across scattered pieces of information."[13] These seem very basic skills, but I can attest from a number of years in the classroom that they are not as basic as we want to think they are. Fanfiction can also draw out more nuanced aspects of the human experience; Rukmini Pande has used it to reveal to students the under-

---

11 Throughout this book, I consciously use "they" as a gender-neutral, third person singular pronoun.
12 Booth, "Fandom: The Classroom of the Future," 1.1.
13 Jenkins, *Convergence Culture*, 176.

lying racism they don't even realize they harbor.[14] Additionally, while for some students, college will be the first time they are asked to think critically about the arts, others are probably already doing literary criticism online within their own fandoms, discourse communities that Jenkins, following James Paul Gee, calls "affinity spaces."[15] There, fans can "debate gender representation in comic books, address the roles of Joseph Campbell's classic hero's narrative in young adult fiction [...], offer compelling Bechdellian analyses of the roles of women in media."[16] More generally, Melanie Kohnen points out that "through fannish practices, fans educate one another about identity formation, diversity, media representations, digital technology, and the media industry."[17] In other words, within their chosen affinity spaces, they already do the things we as literature teachers want them to do, and we simply want to invite them into the new affinity space of academic discourse where they can use those same skills.

While fans may already be doing literary criticism online, it is important to help them develop the tools to do it well. Booth's claim that "[c]ritical fans encourage civil discourse, even if it's a disagreement"[18] may be slightly idealistic. It is true that many fandoms put heavy emphasis on civility of discourse in message boards and commentaries within that fandom; Lori Kido Lopez argues, "Since fan communities spend so much time engaging in online discourse, there are often strict rules about the kinds of participation that are allowed and the kinds that are discouraged."[19] This may be particularly true of fan activists such as those Lopez studies, who hope to engage people outside of their fandoms. However, trolls exist even within fan communities, and even where the discourse is genuinely civil, there is no guarantee that students learning such discursive practices will transfer that civility into interactions with people outside their affinity space. In a literature classroom, they will likely encounter students who share very little with them in terms of worldview, and allowing them to talk about each other's response to literature through the medium of their own fanfiction will encourage them to bridge that gap between their fandom comfort zone and the "real world" of diversity and divergent beliefs.

Likewise, as Toby Miller points out, fans aren't *necessarily* engaging in the kinds of analysis online that we would like to see in a classroom. Speaking of the fandom surrounding the mid-century television series *The Avengers*, he ob-

---

14 Pande, "'You Do Realize *The Lion King* Is Set in Africa, Right?'" 105–8.
15 Jenkins, *Convergence Culture*, 177.
16 Booth, "Fandom: The Classroom of the Future," 1.7.
17 Kohnen, "Tumblr Pedagogies," 351.
18 Booth, "Fandom: The Classroom of the Future," 1.9.
19 Lopez, "Fan-Activists and the Politics of Race in *The Last Airbender*," 439.

serves, "Collective consciousness about the show does not lead to collective investigations of gender politics on TV, or postcolonialism."[20] Just because it didn't does not mean it can't, but as Trent Hergenrader points out, students "*need help doing it.* [...] It's the *instructor's* job to design an educational experience that can make use of an existing semiotic domain."[21] In fact, it often seems from discussions of the use of fanfiction in classrooms that the professors writing the article are much more aware of what the students are achieving than the students are themselves. For instance, Amanda Gilroy very smartly analyzes the methodology and guiding principles of her students' fanfics of Jane Austen,[22] but one wonders whether the students were capable of doing the same kind of analysis.

This is why, in my own literature classrooms, I ask students to submit an explanation or analysis of their own fanfics of pre- and early modern literature as a way of forcing them to think through their creative impulses. The results are not always impressive, but sometimes they are surprising. Several years ago, an Athletic Training (AT) student rewrote the opening of the *Canterbury Tales General Prologue* with the famous springtime setting changed to winter. Besides demonstrating a surprising ear for verse, she explained in her analysis, "I feel like the characters that are described in the general prologue are not those of happy new beginnings, but past times of corruptions that need to be frozen and forgotten until the spring returns in which the characters are then true and honest to their responsibilities."[23] Thus, changing the setting highlighted the hypocrisy that Chaucer pokes fun at in his estates satire but which the characters themselves (with the exception of the Pardoner) refuse to acknowledge. More recently, another AT major rewrote the Anglo-Saxon exile poem "The Seafarer" as being narrated by a veteran with post-traumatic stress disorder (PTSD). In his analysis, he said that the only kind of modern parallel that seemed to correspond to the Seafarer's profound sense of isolation was that of a soldier surrounded by a world that didn't understand survivor guilt. As a result, he rewrote the exile as "a solider documenting his emotions, in hopes to find rest in the dark of the night."[24]

A traditionalist scholar will look at these examples and say, "All well and good, but that's not literary analysis." And to an extent, that is true: the critical difference between traditional literary analysis and canon fanfiction is that the former is based on evidence in the text and the latter is based largely on free as-

---

20 Miller, "Trainspotting *The Avengers*,"193.
21 Hergenrader, "Genre Fiction, and Games, and Fanfiction! Oh My!," 144, emphasis original.
22 Gilroy, "Our Austen: Fan Fiction in the Classroom."
23 Jeffs, "Rewrite," 2.
24 Moody, "The Soldier," 5.

sociation and emotional response. I try to capture some of the evidence-based discussion in having students analyze their own work, and indeed encouraging students to probe *why* they respond with the emotions that they do can be a highly illuminating developmental experience. But even without that, I am not convinced that the activity would be useless. Rita Felski and other scholars of the last decade have newly underscored the importance of emotion in the realm of intellectual discourse.[25] In fact, I would posit that evoking an emotional response to literature may be the most important thing a literary class can achieve at the present moment in history. In a cultural climate that makes a virtue of dehumanizing whoever disagrees with us, I would say that an exercise in emotional connection, especially in response to a piece of literature that, unlike *Harry Potter* and other centers of popular fandom, does not immediately connect with students, is an essential exercise in learning empathy. For my AT student, no longer was the Seafarer a remote, self-pitying, dead white man: he was a neighbor, a countryman, and someone for whom the student had a deeply humane fellow-feeling. The activity may not have turned him into a budding professional academic, but should that really be our pedagogical goal in a general education course? I would rather turn students into fans than into scholars.[26]

I should note that this book is focused on Classical, medieval, and early modern literature of the traditional Western canon, in part due to its popularity in professionally published novel form and in part because that is the field in which I was trained. However, canon fanfiction can be successfully used to help students forge connections with cultures that may be very foreign to them. In my World Literature class, I have received a number of charming modern adaptations of Sei Shonagon's *Pillow Book*. Although a vast majority of my students have no immediate connection—cultural, historical, or emotional—to Heian Japan, the ingenious flexibility of Sei's list form, and the quirky subjects she writes about, have often delighted my students as they tried out her writing style for themselves. Sei's list of "Things that are distressing to see" includes items like "Someone wearing a robe with the back seam hitched over to one side" and "[T]he sight of some swarthy, slovenly-looking woman with a hairpiece, lying about in broad daylight with a scrawny man with hair sprouting from his face"[27]—all very aesthetic judgments. In response, one student cited such twenty-first century examples as "When you think you went unnoticed

---

25 See, for example, Felski, *The Limits of Critique*.

26 For an extensive study of how participatory reading practices like fanfiction have been used in the teaching of *Moby Dick*, a text students often find alienating, see "Part III: Learning Through Remixing" in Jenkins and Kelley, *Reading in a Participatory Culture*, 105–52.

27 Shonagon, *The Pillow Book*, section 104, p. 1151.

when you tripped or ran into something, only to have your friend text you and say that she saw your accident with laughing emojis" and "When you silence your phone for a movie but forget to turn your alarm off and it still goes off in the middle of the quietest part of the movie."[28] In her commentary, this student explained the connection she found between herself, a white American college student, with the attendant of a Japanese empress a thousand years ago:

> There are some connections to the original version [such as] the quip about a baby sitting next to you on an airplane, which was supposed to connect to the point in Pillow Book where she mentions a baby interrupting an important conversation. Through these connections to the original version, the reader is able to see that while technology and the social status quo have changed, human nature has stayed relatively the same over the centuries. People can always relate to simple social faux pas, such as tripping and falling, and other such embarrassing moments, as well as joyful and funny moments.[29]

This student is not making overly ambitious claims about a "universal human nature"; what she is responding to is that "fellow-feeling" that we find in learning to sympathize on a basic level with another human being. If my students leave my classroom with that sort of fellow-feeling toward people whose existence they neither knew nor cared about before they entered it, I consider my work, at least in part, successful.

Canon Fanfiction in the Diverse Classroom

The other way in which canon fanfiction can be useful in the classroom has not, to my knowledge, garnered significant attention, and yet it is perhaps the most important: it can allow students whose voices, perspectives, and sometimes even existence have been denied or erased by canon literature to write themselves back into the tradition. As Katie Clinton and her coauthors point out, "The movement toward multiculturalism has focused on expanding the canon, affecting *what* is read in the English classroom. It is equally important to bring alternative motives for reading into the English classroom in order to expand *how* the canon is read."[30] Fanfiction has long been a safe space for the voices of women and members of the LGBTQIA+ community, so much so that one might argue that these traditionally undervalued perspectives are foundational to the concept of

---

28 Miller-Wells, "Modern Pillow Book Lists" 2.
29 Miller-Wells, "Modern Pillow Book Lists," 4.
30 Clinton, Jenkins, and McWilliams, "New Literacies," 16.

fanfiction itself. In this way, fandoms have moved faster than the academy and provide a model for it. Now, it is true that fanfiction is not always progressive in every way; Lori Morimoto says flatly, "Media fandoms, and media fan studies, have a race problem,"[31] a sentiment echoed by Mel Stanfill.[32] However, as the culture at large grows painfully more aware of racial and other inequalities, fandom is sharing in that increasing awareness.[33]

One subgenre of fanfiction that is particularly amenable to a more inclusive approach, and is therefore the focus of this project, is so-called "fix-it lit." As described in chapter 1, fix-it lit "changes something about canon that the fan writing the fic wasn't happy with,"[34] often seeking to right what fans perceive as a wrong perpetrated against characters by their creator. Much professional canon fanfiction makes this same move, changing point-of-view character, setting, or plot to portray aspects of the human experience largely ignored by canon literature: the perspectives of women, LGBTQIA+ characters, people of color, and every variety of "Other." The novels discussed in chapter 2 all take an explicit or implicit "fix-it" approach to adapting literary history and so provide models for students who are likely to look at, say, *Chanson de Roland* and see nothing but the blatant vilifying of black skin and Muslim (if it can even be called Muslim) culture. Giving such students an opportunity to rewrite the story from, say, the perspective of the Saracen King Marsile or his captured wife Bramimonde, may not only free their faculties to see and respond to the other aspects of the poem (the issues, for instance, of hubris or kin betrayal), but it also gives them the only avenue available for seeking justice in a case that is not only almost a thousand years old, but fictional.

There are a number of hazards and potential pitfalls in this approach, which I will explore in the following section, but the last salient point in the argument for the pedagogical use of canon fanfiction is that the act of writing it—particularly when it is fix-it lit—is actually not entirely different from the act of doing literary scholarship. Although the product is different, the thought process is very similar, especially if we're talking about the kind of scholarship undergraduate non-majors are likely to do. A reader troubled by Prospero's takeover of Caliban's native land could write an article analyzing *The Tempest* from a postcolo-

31 Morimoto, "Ontological Security and the Politics of Transcultural Fandom," 268.

32 Stanfill, "The Unbearable Whiteness of Fandom and Fan Studies," 305.

33 See Morimoto, "Ontological Security and the Politics of Transcultural Fandom," Stanfill, "The Unbearable Whiteness of Fandom and Fan Studies," and Seymour, "Racebending and Prosumer Fanart Practices in *Harry Potter* Fandom," all in *A Companion to Media Fandom and Fan Studies*, edited by Paul Booth.

34 *Fanlore*.

nial perspective, or they could write a canon fanfiction focusing on Caliban's experience, as did Aimé Césaire in *Une Tempête*. A deconstructionist could write an article on the gaps and silences of *Beowulf*, or they could write a postmodernist canon fanfiction like John Gardner's *Grendel*. The fact that fanfiction is often motivated by emotional response does not, in fact, cut it off from scholarship, because scholarship, too, tends to come out of an emotional response to literature. The simple fact that most (though not all) scholarship strives to move beyond the emotional response to an analytical one does not mean canon fanfiction is remote from analysis: it represents that critique in the form of literature and actually invites further analysis of its own product. The sizable scholarship built up around seminal canon fanfictions like *Wide Sargasso Sea*, *Grendel*, and *A Thousand Acres* attests to the fact that fanfiction does not circumvent or stop short the analytical discussion but rather contributes to it in a unique way that is so engaging, scholars feel the need to respond to it in their own form.

Addressing Potential Drawbacks

I have already responded to the objection that writing canon fanfiction is not the same as writing literary criticism, an objection that is not unsurmountable on a pedagogical level especially when the population in question is undergraduate non-majors. But when working with that population or any other, there remain several potential drawbacks that teachers must decide how to address when using canon fanfiction as a teaching tool.

The first two questions relate to the teaching of published canon fanfiction. First, we must ask ourselves whether such novels produce a text that is too "easy," specifically because it "fixes" the problems of the original. Certainly this is a risk, and the reason that many canon fanfictions pale in comparison with the complexity of the originals: one might draw a parallel with the Disneyfying effect film adaptations have on deeply disturbing fairytales like *Snow White*. However, a well-written fanfiction simply asks different questions than the original story does. We might take as an example Geraldine Brooks's *March*, the Pulitzer Prize-winning canon fanfiction of Alcott's *Little Women*, which dismantles the all-too-perfect Marmie of *Little Women* by giving her and her husband a more checkered and realistic backstory. Instead of asking, "Why can't Alcott write Marmie as beloved *and* as a normal human being?" as we do when we read *Little Women*, *March* makes us ask, "Why wouldn't Marmie share her and her husband's past with their five girls?" The answer is historical, cultural, and personal, but the novel does not tell us any of that outright: it trusts us to "in-fill" for ourselves, to use David Black's term.[35] In other words, the act of reading canon fanfiction itself requires attention and careful analysis.

As a subset to the question of complexity, one might also ask whether canon fanfiction might age poorly because it is too topical, too tied to the concerns of the historical moment in which it is written; for instance, Karley Adney analyzes how Leon Garfield used his 1985 retold *Hamlet* "to create awareness of important social issues in 1980s Britain."[36] However, if this objection can be lodged against fanfiction, it can be lodged equally against any socially conscious literature and most forms of literary criticism. Besides that, the concerns of one historical moment (for Garfield, "the status of women, teen sex, and domestic abuse"[37]) tend to remain concerns, in one form or another, of every other.

The second, perhaps more important question, is whether published canon fanfictions are part of the problem of imposing an authoritarian system on the act of reading, or potentially the best solution. Unlike popular fanfic, published canon fanfictions participate in the traditional system of publishing and, as such, may perpetuate the distinction between "real literature," to which very few will ever have access as creators rather than as consumers, and "fan work," which anybody can create but which nobody but the members within the community give any heed to. This is a legitimate objection, and one that might lead an instructor to ask students to write their own canon fanfictions without being influenced by reading published examples at all. On the other hand, precisely because canon fanfictions work *within* the traditional system, they may be in a position to change it by questioning our long-established interpretations of frequently taught works. Most of our students will not go on to be published novelists of any sort, much less canon fanfiction writers, but the fact that professional authors are engaging in issues of race, gender, and identity as they rework well-known stories—and the fact that the publishing industry, slow to change though it is, is making progress in the representation of diversity among its authors as well—holds the potential, at the very least, to make those identities visible in works that have ignored or downplayed them.

The other questions have to do with the potential pitfalls of asking students to write canon fanfiction themselves. The first questions are practical. One is the concern that students will be "stealing" something from a respected author. For the works discussed in this book, copyright is not an issue, and indeed, a student "stealing" from Shakespeare is only doing what Shakespeare did to all of

---

35 Black, "Character; or, The Strange Case of Uma Peel," 102.

36 Adney, "Leon Garfield's *Hamlet*," 92.

37 Adney, "Leon Garfield's *Hamlet*," 92.

his sources. For classes focused on literature that is still in copyright, the activity admittedly resides in a legal gray area. However, instructors can find some security in the advocacy of Organization for Transformative Works (OTW), the body that operates the Archive of Our Own (AO3) fanfiction website, which continues to argue that such work is permissible primarily because it is not written for profit and because it is "transformative" and therefore does not violate copyright.[38] In addition, even published appropriations of copyrighted material have sometimes been successfully defended as legal transformations of the original work. When Margaret Mitchell's estate objected to Alice Randall's retelling of *Gone with the Wind*, titled *The Wind Done Gone*, Judge Stanley Francis Birch, Jr., found that the new novel "reflects transformative value because it 'can provide social benefit, by shedding light on an earlier work, and, in the process, creating a new one.'"[39] Perhaps not many of our students will strive to publish their schoolwork in a professional capacity (though I have had students who pursued it), but the important point is that there is legal precedent to justify their act of writing.

The next question, also practical, is whether, when students rewrite, say, Griselda from the *Clerk's Tale* so that she is less of a martyr (or doormat) and more of an empowered protector of herself and her children, students will come to think of their retellings as somehow representing "the truth" that misogynist storytellers like the Clerk have "obscured" by their bias. It seems, perhaps, a little frivolous to be concerned that students will not be able to keep fact from fiction (or even fiction from fiction) separate in their minds, but it is a question I have increasingly pondered as we see more and more historical fiction films and television series that represent women (or other subjugated groups) as empowered, independent, and, frankly, modern. That is not to deny that there were empowered, independent women in the Middle Ages or the Renaissance—Margery Kempe and Queen Elizabeth I leap to mind just as examples from England—but they operated within a context and culture that is difficult for students to reconstruct.

The question we are encountering then, is whether students writing canon fanfiction in the classroom can distinguish between their fictions and reality and—perhaps more importantly—whether those fictions can have an effect on reality as our students live it. Jeremy Rosen raises this issue in his discussion of canon fanfictions (though he does not use that term) that alter the point-of-

---

38 See "What We Believe," *Organization for Transformative Works*.
39 United States, Court of Appeals for the Eleventh Circuit, *Suntrust vs. Houghton Mifflin Co.*, citing *Campbell v. Acuff-Rose Music* (92–1292), 510 U.S. 569 (1994).

view character to "give voice" to previously silenced figures. He says, "A kind of reflectionism—the belief that literary images reflect a preexisting reality—underlies this imaginary politics [of reforming canon to reflect social diversity]. That female characters speak with authority or demonstrate radical agency in Shakespeare's plays does not mean that women of his period were emancipated."[40] He then points out that such canon fanfiction "does not remedy structural inequalities or obtain representation for those who lack it."[41] This is true, of course, and only the most naïve of readers would say that letting women speak their minds in literature means they can speak their minds in real life—in the past or the present. But to object to canon fanfiction on those grounds would be equivalent to saying that casting people of color in films doesn't change the prejudiced underpinnings of Western society. It doesn't, but as we have seen from the "Oscars-SoWhite" hashtag to the furor over the casting for Disney's live-action remake of *Aladdin*,[42] that doesn't mean such gestures are not meaningful.

Nor does it mean that such "gestures" in the artistic world will have no long-term effects in the real world. Fandom can lead and has led to direct real-world action, as demonstrated by the Harry Potter Alliance (HPA), which advocates for social justice across a number of issues largely unrelated to *Harry Potter*. Neta Kligler-Vilenchik explains the perhaps not immediately obvious connection between fandom and real-world action: "For the HPA, the Harry Potter universe is so rich and diverse that almost any real-world cause could be linked to it, allowing the organization to respond quickly to current events as well as to pressing issues raised by its members."[43] In a similar vein, Jenkins, with his research team, describes fan activists' use of Superman as a mascot for immigration reform,[44] and he discusses the efforts of the HPA to create guidelines for other fandoms, like the Marvelverse, to engage in activism.[45] Kligler-Vilenchik studies, among other examples, the Hunger Is Not a Game campaign, which "sought to connect the release of the [*Hunger Games*] movie to the cause of world hunger."[46] Writing about participatory culture, of which fan activism is one manifestation, Jenkins says that the current political moment is defined by "grassroots media being deployed as the tool by which to challenge the failed mechanisms of in-

---

40 Rosen, "Minor Characters Have Their Day," 142, and *Minor Characters Have Their Day*, 88.
41 Rosen, "Minor Characters Have Their Day," 143.
42 See Mancini, "The Big 'Aladdin' Casting Reveal Doesn't Get Disney off the Hook on Race."
43 Kligler-Vilenchik, "'Decreasing World Suck,'" n.p.
44 Jenkins et al., "Important Reminder: Superman Was an Undocumented Immigrant."
45 Jenkins, "How the Extended Marvel Universe (and Other Superhero Stories) Can Enable Political Debates."
46 Kligler-Vilenchik, "'Decreasing World Suck,'" n.p.

stitutional politics."[47] The fact that such fan activism can be simplistic and blinded by "incredible amounts of privilege"[48] does not erase the fact that caring about social justice within a fandom, counter to Rosen's objections, has in fact led to attempts to enact social justice in the real world. As we have seen happen in the history of charity and activism at large, the more advocates learn about the needs they are trying to address, the more sensitive and conscientious their actions can become. Yet as an educator, I would concur with the fandom members who told Abigail De Kosnik that "even if the majority of effects engendered by fanworks [...] transpire in the minds and memories of individual readers, just that change in people's private worldviews is a change in the world."[49]

And in fact, this is the problem we encounter any time we try to touch the past: in making human connections with real or fictional people from hundreds of years before our time, our instinct is always to project our own beliefs and values onto them; I often ask my advanced Chaucer students, "Do you ever get suspicious about the fact that Chaucer seems to think so much like we do?" It is a problem tackled, if not solved, by the theories of new historicism as well as deconstructionism. And it is a problem we must resign ourselves to facing however we interpret the past, whether through scholarship or through canon fanfiction. I would not claim to have solved the problem in my own classrooms, but the fact that we continue to teach the original literature alongside the fanfiction, whether it is written by professionals or by students, keeps the real past—at least, the past as represented in its own voice, however dramatized—constantly in front of their eyes. And if the risk is between students thinking that people of the past were just like us, and continuing to think that any woman who spoke her mind in medieval England would "immediately be punished," I think the former is preferable. At least it breaks down the prejudice they hold against people of the past, and if they can abandon one prejudice, the hope of education is always that they will be willing to abandon other, more pressing biases against people they encounter in their daily lives. Indeed, Jenkins cites one fanfiction writer, Sweeney Agonistes, who explained that "getting inside the head of a character who was very different from herself helped her make sense of the people she saw around her in school who were coming from very different backgrounds and acting on very different values."[50] This increased empathy is not a guaranteed result of writing fanfiction, but it is a possible one, made more possible by the informed guidance of an instructor.

---

47 Jenkins, "Youth Voice, Media, and Political Engagement," n.p.
48 Pande, "Who Do You Mean by 'Fan'?" 322.
49 De Kosnik, *Rogue Archives*, 181.
50 Jenkins, *Convergence Culture*, 183.

The Problem of Speaking for Others

In a fraught cultural moment, perhaps the most important potential objection to address has to do with representation: is it acceptable for students to speak for characters who do not share critical aspects of their identity? For example, is it all right for a white student to write a canon fanfiction from Othello's point of view? Or for a Christian student to write a canon fanfiction from the point of view of Shylock? Rosen expresses skepticism over the ethical advisability of speaking for the Other. In counter to Edward Said's urging of scholars to "draw out, extend, give emphasis and voice to what is silent or marginally present or ideologically represented" in canonical literature,[51] Rosen says, "The claim that characters are 'given a voice' effaces [...] how such texts reproduce the power dynamic of an elite speaking on behalf of a subaltern to which much anti-essentialist feminist and postcolonial criticism has drawn attention."[52] In other words, Rosen's concern is that speaking for the Other comes from a position of power and therefore simply reinforces the problematic dynamics such speech is meant to resist.

Rosen, of course, is speaking of professional, published novels, in which the authors do on some level hold a power that the subaltern does not. However, when the authors themselves are members of the subjugated identity group (say, Aimé Césaire writing *Une Tempête*, in which Shakespeare's Caliban becomes a black slave, in still-colonial Martinique), the objection loses some of its potency: it is not so much the voice of the character that is being raised against the tide of hegemony but the voice of the author. Questions of cultural appropriation and who has the right to speak in the voice of another are important and highly contentious in the publishing industry.[53] But when we are working in a pedagogical context, such "speaking for the Other" may in fact be the most educational activity a student can engage in. To step into the mind of Shylock or Jessica, to see the world through the eyes of Othello or Caliban, is an act of profound empathy, and if there is one thing my students take away from my class, I want it to be a greater ability to empathize.

Students may do it poorly, of course; I recently had several students who looked at Ibsen's *Doll House* from Torvald's perspective, describing the play as a tragedy because Nora took away from him everything that made him happy. This was not in a canon fanfiction assignment; it was ordinary class discussion,

---

51 Said, *Culture and Imperialism*, 66.
52 Rosen, "Minor Characters Have Their Day," 160.
53 See the provocatively titled but ultimately balanced discussion of the issue in Kit de Waal's "Don't Dip Your Pen in Someone Else's Blood."

but they undoubtedly would have done the same thing if I'd asked them to retell the play from a different point of view and given them free rein in which character to choose. This is not the kind of empathy that is particularly useful: male students taking a male perspective to highlight the "injustices" perpetrated against a character who in fact brings his own disaster upon himself. They don't learn anything from this sort of activity aside from reinforcing their sense of righteous indignation that Nora would ruin a "perfectly good relationship" just to try to find herself. But if it had been a canon fanfiction assignment, it would have been my job as a teacher with a particular goal in mind to encourage them to reach beyond their biases—to see what the world looks like to, say, Mrs. Linde, or the children's nanny, or even Krogstad. If students writing a canon fanfiction of *Doll House* wrote about the only character that shared their identity and social status, it would in fact represent a failure of the assignment.

Additionally, to restrict students to writing from the perspective of only those characters who share their main identity categories is to reduce identity *to* those categories and, frankly, to underestimate students' ability to reach across barriers. In a recent Young Adult Literature course, we were discussing Sherman Alexie's *Absolutely True Diary of a Part-Time Indian*, and I discovered that a majority of the students had a strong fellow-feeling for the narrator, Junior, even though no one in my class was of indigenous descent. Trying to pin down why they connected with him so strongly, I asked how many felt like they fit in, were "comfortable in their skin," in high school. Not a single hand went up. This is only an anecdotal example, of course, but the point is that everyone feels marginalized in some way (whether they actually are or not), and they can connect with other marginalized people, in literature as well as in real life, on the basis of that shared emotional experience, even if they don't share what we would think of as more central identity categories. As Francesca Coppa concludes, "[T]he suggestion that you would restrict your *identification* to those characters with whom you share an *identity* feels limiting."[54]

Students may need guidance in how to write the Other respectfully; it may involve research, further reading of other narratives, even collaboration with more knowledgeable students or professors, but all of those activities are part of their education: they are what we want our students do regardless of the assignment. They may need to be warned that the publishing industry might not be interested in their finalized masterpiece, but in my experience, the risk of students writing the Other in a classroom setting are far outweighed by the potential benefits.

---

54 Coppa, "Slash/Drag," 199.

And when we focus in on students coming from historically (or currently) marginalized groups, letting them take up the pen may be a transformative experience even more empowering than seeing "people like them" represented in the original literature. As discussed by Coppa, visibility, such as representation in the media, invites scrutiny, surveillance, and even control by official powers. Being the creator, on the other hand, rather than the subject, opens wider doors with fewer splinters: "to direct [...] is to be in the catbird seat; the subject of the gaze, not the object. Women know all too well that to be the object of the gaze is the opposite of empowerment."[55] When Chaucer and Shakespeare feature Jewish characters in their work, it doesn't go well for those characters. Letting a Jewish writer reinvent Shylock, as Howard Jacobson does in *My Name Is Shylock* (no one, to my knowledge, has yet tried to fix the *Prioress's Tale*), grants that author the freedom of all authors—which is not total freedom, of course, but is much greater than what is granted to, say, a Jewish actor playing Shylock, bound to Shakespeare's original words. And if it is a meaningful exercise for a professional, award-winning writer, one hopes it can be equally meaningful to a student in a literature classroom. In speaking of her own experience looking for female identity and fulfillment in a literary world dominated by male perspectives, Adrienne Rich argues, "Re-vision—the act of looking back, of seeing with fresh eyes, of entering an old text from a new critical direction—is for us more than a chapter in cultural history: it is an act of survival."[56] I would add that the survival is mutual: speaking into the void or the negative spaces that literature has bequeathed to us is an act of survival for people whose identities have been ignored or maligned, but it is also an act of survival for the literature itself.

How to Use This Book

This book is designed to serve a dual purpose, as a work of scholarship and as a teaching text. This introduction, the conclusion, and the appendix are aimed at the teacher looking to evaluate or use this approach as a pedagogical tool in the undergraduate classroom. The intervening chapters are aimed at the scholar engaging in adaptation studies or a related field, but in language and approach, they assume that that scholarly audience includes undergraduate students. As such, chapter 1 offers students a foothold in the scholarly underpinnings of

---

55 Coppa, "Slash/Drag," 200.
56 Rich, "When We Dead Awaken," 18.

canon fanfiction and the theoretical lenses through which we might look at it. Chapter 2 examines professional, published canon fanfiction, applying those theoretical lenses in order to discuss the workings of fix-it lit. This chapter can be used as a resource for students studying either the original literature involved (*Macbeth*, the *Iliad*, the *Canterbury Tales*, *Othello*, and *Beowulf*) or the canon fanfictions thereof. Likewise, for students assigned to analyze some other example of canon fanfiction unrelated to those in this chapter, the studies here can provide examples of how this can be done in a scholarly way. Chapter 3 can likewise be used in teaching *Laxdæla saga* or the "Story of Thorstein Ox-Foot," but more specifically, it is intended as a model students might refer to when assigned to write and then analyze their own canon fanfiction. The appendix offers resources and potential assignments teachers might use in various college-level courses.

It is my hope that this book will not only contribute to the ongoing conversation about how contemporary culture continues to reuse and respond to cultures of the past but that it will also offer a concise set of resources for engaging students in this conversation, even—perhaps especially—if they are not literature enthusiasts by nature.

Chapter 1
Canon Fanfiction: Theory and Practice

If presented with the generic descriptions of two books, one whose plot was a product of the author's own mind and another whose plot has been retold dozens of times and was not even original to the author of its most famous version, most learned audiences would likely say that the "original" book was preferable to the retold one. However, the instinct to prioritize invention and originality is, as Terri Windling says, "a relatively newfangled notion."[57] In fact, "original" once meant "[b]elonging to the beginning or earliest stage of something; existing at or from the first."[58] The sense of original as "produced first-hand; not imitated or copied from another"[59] did not become its primary meaning until the seventeenth century. Retelling was the normal mode of storytelling in western Europe until the Renaissance.

At the 2019 Association of Writing Programs conference in Portland, Oregon, one panel speaker defended retold stories by challenging the notion of originality. In a panel on "Teaching Genre as Workshop," Camacho Rourks asked the audience if we could predict the plot of a hypothetical literary realist novel whose protagonist was a white, middle-aged college professor whose relationship with his wife had gone stale.[60] She clearly had several more details she was going to add to this description, but before she could say any more, someone shouted out, "He leaves his wife for a grad student!" And of course that was the right answer. This "original" story, though no less "literary," was hardly "original" at all. On the other hand, returning to those two books in the hypothetical situation with which I opened, the retelling we might pass over as "unoriginal" happens to be the Pulitzer Prize-winning novel *A Thousand Acres* by Jane Smiley, an adaptation of *King Lear* set in the 1960s American Midwest. And in fact, even if the reader knows *King Lear*, the conclusion of Smiley's retelling is much less predictable than that novel of academic middle-age angst.

Nancy Barta-Smith and Danette DiMarco declare, "Perhaps the highest form of both praise and critique is a tale retold."[61] This book represents a study of literary works that take as their basis a preexisting work or works from the traditional literary canon (specifically Classical, medieval and early modern litera-

---

57 Windling, "White as Snow," 8.
58 "Original, adj. and n." 2a, *OED*.
59 "Original, adj. and n." 5a, *OED*.
60 Rourks, "No Fantasy or Sci-Fi."
61 Barta-Smith and DiMarco, "Introduction," 2.

https://doi.org/10.1515/9781501515972-003

ture), reinventing and responding to the source text in the newly made product. Such products I term **canon fanfiction: literature that uses and consciously responds to traditional or canonical sources as its foundational material or inspiration for a new production, which includes retellings, prequels, sequels, crossovers, and spinoffs.** Although all the examples studied in detail in chapter 2 are novels or plays, I should point out that I do not exclude film and other media from this umbrella term. Film does, of course, introduce elements that text-based media lack; in studying a film, one can comment on casting, direction, music, lighting, and other visual effects that have no parallel in written forms. However, film is still a storytelling medium, and my main focus in this book is on storytelling. Hence I will with some frequency invoke film examples in support of points in this chapter and elsewhere.

Throughout, I argue that canon fanfiction allows scholars and literature students alike to find renewed value in canon literature while at the same time confronting its gaps and problematic aspects, like homophobia, classism, and other forms of bigotry. Canon fanfiction revives old but still culturally influential stories and makes them touch the present world by confronting failures and injustices that we are still trying to address today.

It may be useful to begin by asking why we as human beings are so driven to rework older stories—to ask why adaptation rather than innovation was the norm for so many centuries and, in fact, remains the norm in some sub-cultures. Many theorists have commented on the phenomenon. Sara Gwenllian-Jones claims that "fictional worlds, of necessity, always exceed the texts that describe them, relying in large part on the reader who must import exterior information to and imaginatively engage with the text."[62] The well-built fictional world, called the "storyworld" by David Herman,[63] seems to spill over the borders of the story that takes place within it (a fact not limited to but often keenly felt in science fiction and fantasy). We have the inescapable sense that more is happening in this world than the story told by the novel or other medium that originates it. The reader's subsequent exploration beyond the story's narrow bounds is given many names by theorists: hyperdiegesis,[64] metalepsis,[65] and in-filling.[66] In a more literary vein, Deborah Cartmell says we are drawn to the potential for "a plurality of meanings" as stories pass from one teller to another.[67] Shee-

---

62 Gwenllian-Jones, "Virtual Reality," 92.
63 Herman, "Storyworlds," 569–70.
64 Hills, *Fan Culture* 143.
65 Turk, "Metalepsis," 83.
66 Black, "Character," 102.
67 Cartmell, "Introduction," 28.

nagh Pugh, speaking of the body of myth surrounding Robin Hood, puts it most directly: "[T]here are simply never enough stories and we [do] not want them to come to an end."[68]

But I am interested in another reason we retell stories, particularly the stories of the traditional Western canon: a reason that has to do not just with pleasure but with conflict. Henry Jenkins famously declares that our impulse to revisit stories stems from "a mixture of fascination and frustration"[69] or even "antagonism"[70] in response to a work that at once pleases us and leaves us dissatisfied for some reason. Building on Wolfgang Iser's theories of reading, Cornel Sandvoss explains, "[T]hose texts that profoundly contradict readers' experiences and thus challenge our expectations require a reflexive engagement."[71] In other words, when we as readers encounter some aspect that troubles us in what is otherwise a powerful or moving piece of our artistic history, we must either ignore it (which is difficult to do in a world in which canonical texts still hold a great deal of cultural capital) or find a way to make sense of it. For a substantial number of readers, particularly those of interest to us in this book, that "way" is to rewrite the story.

Canon Fanfiction: Definition and Distinctions

I have coined the term "canon fanfiction" to describe artistic productions that use and respond to traditional sources in the production of new stories. Eyebrows may naturally be raised by my decision to call the practice I describe in this book "fanfiction," since the examples discussed in chapter 2 are all novels published by professionals in the conventional manner (in print, by established publishing houses). Let us, then, explore the commonalities as well as distinctions between canon fanfiction and what we might call popular fanfiction.[72]

Throughout this book, I will favor definitions generated from within fan communities or by fan scholars, rather than definitions created by external commentators like the Oxford English Dictionary, whose definition of fanfiction is per-

---

68 Pugh, *The Democratic Genre*, 9.
69 Jenkins, "Afterword," 362.
70 Jenkins, *Textual Poachers*, 22.
71 Sandvoss, "Death of the Reader?," 29.
72 For an accessible introduction to the history of fanfiction and approaches to its study, see Hellekson and Busse, *Fan Fiction Studies Reader*.

haps overly simplistic.[73] More comprehensive are Francesca Coppa's definitions of fanfiction in her *Fanfiction Reader*, which afford us an opportunity to evaluate the features of canon fanfiction. She offers five genre-defining factors:

1. "Fanfiction is fiction created outside of the literary marketplace."
2. "Fanfiction is fiction that rewrites and transforms other stories."
3. "Fanfiction is fiction that rewrites and transforms stories currently owned by others."
4. "Fanfiction is fiction written within and to the standards of a particular fannish community."
5. "Fanfiction is speculative fiction about character rather than about the world."[74]

Canon fanfictions, even examples like the published novels in chapter 2, most certainly match the second definition: whatever else they may or may not be, they are certainly transformative. "Transformative" is, in fact, the preferred term among practitioners of the art. Coppa herself acknowledges this connection between published work like *Rosencrantz and Guildenstern Are Dead*, Tom Stoppard's famous postmodernist take on *Hamlet*, and popular fanfiction.[75] The other four features less obviously match the examples discussed in this book, but a more probing examination of the underlying realities reveals surprising and important connections.

The most obvious difference, of course, is that published novels by professional authors are decidedly not "created outside of the literary marketplace." Fandom has traditionally been marked by its underground and communal nature: current fanfic is shared online, circumventing the traditional publication process. This circumvention gives fanfic more freedom in some ways (for instance, the freedom to ignore traditional plot structures, as in the "snippet," which may be no more than a scene or vignette), while published retellings still have to navigate the process of pleasing agents, editors, publishers, and a paying readership. However, fandom is not as free as outsiders might assume. Bronwen Thomas describes the practice of "hunting down and exposing examples of 'badfic'" on fan sites,[76] meaning that even though fans can post whatever they like, the community has well-defined rules as to what makes for acceptable

---

73 "Fiction, usually fantasy or science fiction, written by a fan rather than a professional author, *esp.* that based on already-existing characters from a television series, book, film, etc.; (also) a piece of such writing."

74 Coppa, *Fanfiction Reader*, 2–12.

75 Coppa, *Fanfiction Reader*, 4–6.

76 Thomas, "What Is Fanfiction," 14.

fanfic. In fact, Judith Fathallah makes the argument that many of the most influential fandoms derive legitimacy through being acknowledged by the copyright holders themselves. This happens, for instance, when actual episodes of the *Supernatural* television show give nods to well-known fan theories, thus legitimating those theories and the fandom at large. Fathallah argues, "Derivative writing that changes popular culture is legitimated and empowered—*because and so far as the author says so.*"[77] We can see the parallel with literary publishing, which is itself a community with its own set of rules and restrictions, and its own methods of legitimating works by passing them through the publication process. Each genre has its own measuring stick for legitimacy.

In fact, where fan communities can be highly regulated from within, literary publishing may enjoy flexibility the fandoms do not. Paul Booth describes an "alarming [...] lack of authorial freedom" on policed fanfic sites like Amazon's now-defunct Kindle Worlds,[78] and even on non-policed sites, "fans seek out texts that give them the pleasure of familiarity and that fulfill rather than challenge their expectations."[79] On the other hand, because the strictures of the literary publishing community are more stylistic than content-related, and because many of the source texts they use are out of copyright, authors of canon fanfiction can enjoy a freedom of theme and subject matter greater than that of the online fan community. For instance, in contrast with fandoms like those of *Pride and Prejudice*, which tend to value loyalty to their author's tone, style, and ethos,[80] canon fanfictions like Maria Dahvana Headley's *Mere Wife* often deliberately undermine the ethos of the source text—in Headley's case, by turning the hero Beowulf into a cowardly villain.

The distinction between popular fanfiction's production outside of the marketplace and canon fanfiction's production inside of it is not insignificant. I should emphasize that I am not treating the published examples studied in this book as being exactly of the same nature as popular fanfiction. However, as I will argue, their *process* is very much the same, and both forms of fanfiction participate in a robust culture of legitimation and discourse-building. If we are willing to admit that being different does not entail being polar opposites, then, we can see how much the two types of transformative works share.

In terms of the fifth feature Coppa highlights, that fanfiction is by nature speculative fiction focused on character, it is true that published canon fanfic-

---

77 Fathallah, *Fanfiction and the Author*, 10.
78 Booth, "Fandom: The Classroom of the Future," 2.11.
79 Thomas, "What Is Fanfiction," 14.
80 See Thomas, "Canons and Fanons," 6.

tion tends to favor realism over the fantasy and sci-fi (i.e. speculative fiction) approaches common in popular fanfiction.[81] However, one of its most noticeable features is its focus on character, particularly in response to early works that are largely uninterested in the characters of women, servants, and background figures. Jean Rhys's famous *Wide Sargasso Sea* centers on Bertha Mason, Rochester's mad wife, who appears in *Jane Eyre* only a handful of times and never speaks. Hence, even though canon fanfiction actually tends to strip fantastical elements from a work in favor of realism, it remains speculative in the larger sense of asking the question, "What if?" It simply asks that question in a different way: not "what if Bertha Mason was a vampire?" but "what if Bertha Mason was the protagonist?"

Coppa's third and fourth features are the most important in terms of making the argument that canon fanfiction is a sibling and not a distant cousin of popular fanfiction. None of the source works studied in chapter 2, all of which are Classical, medieval, or early modern literature, is under copyright. And the copyright status of the works that inspire fanfiction is important: as Coppa observes, intellectual ownership of literary products "has marginalized a group of (mostly female) writers and their literary practices."[82] However, I would point out that in the rarified world of literary publishing, the authors of canon fanfiction are often themselves members of historically marginalized groups: women, writers identifying as LGBTQIA+, people of color, etc. They are perhaps uniquely privileged in having successfully navigated the brutal world of professional publishing, but they are raising their voices in a conversation dominated by the traditional "owners" of culture, usually white, cisgender, heterosexual, male authors. In a metaphorical sense, then, their professionally published responses to such powerful voices importantly coincides with popular fandom's responses to the holders of their fandom's copyright.

The copyright question broadens into the larger issue of choice of source text, and this subject is also worth addressing in the context of comparing canon fanfiction with popular. Henry Jenkins notes that even though fanfiction may result from a mixture of "fascination and frustration,"[83] "[f]ans have chosen these media products from the total range of available texts precisely because they seem to hold special potential as vehicles for expressing the fans' pre-existing social commitments and cultural interests."[84] The reason that most popular fanfiction is based on works still in copyright is that those works are closer to our

---

81 See Coppa, *Fanfiction Reader*, 12.

82 Coppa, *Fanfiction Reader*, 6.

83 Jenkins, "Afterword," 362.

84 Jenkins, *Textual Poachers*, 34.

own day and our own concerns. Works out of copyright tend to align themselves less with the values and beliefs of our current culture. Hence, it is not unusual to find a canon fanfiction written out of loathing rather than love (more of Jenkins's "frustration" than "fascination"), which is less common in popular fanfic. If one absolutely hates *Harry Potter*, it would presumably be more efficient to ignore the series than to spend time and effort writing fanfic about it. However, especially in school, canon literature can be hard to escape. Confronted with a canonical text we are told is "great literature" but which irritates or offends us, we might write a retelling in a completely oppositional mode as an act of protest against a canon that still shapes our educational experiences despite all that canon wars' claims to the contrary. Such a literary response, as Toby Zinman says, "acknowledges the power and persistent presence of those masterworks and a dwarfing of the contemporary playwright [or novelist] who often seems to feel overshadowed, even humiliated by the legacy; the defense is often mockery of the old. There is a kind of anti-nostalgia at work here, simultaneously depending on the old context to define the new context."[85] A good example would be Howard Jacobson's retelling of *The Merchant of Venice*, entitled *Shylock Is My Name*. Shakespeare's depiction of Shylock as embodying the stereotypical image of the greedy Jew seems to strike a particular chord with Jacobson, who is himself Jewish. Where many authors of canon fanfiction express their affection for the work and author they are drawing from, Jacobson says flatly in his acknowledgments section, "I won't thank the writer of the originating play," refusing even to invoke Shakespeare by name.[86]

This kind of resistance and sense of rebellion does occur in popular fanfiction, but it is often in response to a particular feature of a work that a fan otherwise admires.[87] In the above example, it seems to be the entirety of *Merchant of Venice* that comes under fire. The choice of source text and the motives for engaging in canon fanfiction may be the most important difference between canon and popular fanfiction. In fact, they are important to the definition of canon fanfiction as a distinct category from popular fanfiction.

Having acknowledged this distinction, though, the parallels remain an underlying and foundational connection between the two types of creative production. In fact, regarding Coppa's fourth defining feature, I would argue that canon fanfiction is every bit as shaped by its target community as popular fanfiction is. Coppa says, "[F]anfiction is shaped to the literary conventions, expectations, and

---

85 Zinman, *Replay*, 8.
86 Jacobson, *Shylock Is My Name*, 279.
87 See "Fix-It Lit," below.

desires of that community, and is written in genres developed by and in commu-nity."[88] This claim certainly holds true for canon fanfiction written for traditional publication: its target community is an (increasingly narrow) body of devotees who seek in their reading material certain aesthetics, certain standards of quality and expression, and certain types of storytelling, even if that type happens to be postmodern or experimental. While traditional publishing has for several centu-ries been a dominant force in culture, the pressures of film, television, and other forms of entertainment media have begun to force literary publishing into an in-creasingly more confined circle of influence. If it is possible for dominant culture to become a subculture, we may in fact be witnessing that movement in the realm of traditional literary arts.[89] Traditionally published canon fanfiction, then, is very much written for a niche audience; it is just a different (if overlap-ping) audience from popular fanfiction.

The overlap between audiences and authors of canon and popular fanfiction is a final and important connection: Sherlock Holmes and Jane Austen are two of the largest fandoms, and while much of the popular fanfiction written within those fandoms is based on film adaptations, there is a strong representation of fics identified by their authors as being based on the original novels and sto-ries.[90] Likewise, plenty of popular fanfiction writers are also professional au-thors: one might think of Rainbow Rowell (*Fangirl*, *Carry On*) and E. L. James (*Fifty Shades of Grey*), whose work began as fanfiction but was later revised and published as stand-alone novels. Fanfiction itself has a subgenre called "profic."[91] While some members of the fanfiction community would use the term "profic" as the opposite of "fanfic," seeing the lack of pay as the defining factor of fanfiction, another definition is simply transformative work written for pay. In this case the term would apply to "tie-ins," books written within a fan-dom like *Star Trek* or *Star Wars* that are endorsed by the fandom's copyright owners. Such professionally published works again forge ties between popular fanfiction and the examples featured in this book. In fact, applying the term "fanfiction" to such works as *Wide Sargasso Sea* and *Rosencrantz and Guilden-stern Are Dead* has been done by fanfiction writers themselves with some regu-larity, as we will see below.

---

88 Coppa, *Fanfiction Reader*, 9.
89 For a suggested reading list in the field of fanfiction studies, see Coppa, *Fanfiction Reader*, 16–17.
90 In the Sherlock Holmes fandom, 7,560 book-based fics posted in the Archive of Our Own fan-fiction archive as of April 4, 2022; in *Pride and Prejudice* alone, 2,127.
91 Definitions in this section are drawn from *Fanlore*, a wiki maintained by members of fan communities.

One final distinction that might be made between popular and canon fanfiction is simply the prestige of being involved in it, either as a writer or as a scholar. A graduate student could propose a dissertation on *A Thousand Acres* without a qualm, but studies on *Lord of the Rings*, *Harry Potter*, and even Sherlock Holmes fanfic have had to fight for a place in the academy. Matt Hills discusses how academics have repackaged aesthetic judgments of fan media as political or social analysis[92] and hide their own status as fans out of a "fear of a loss of respect."[93] And while it is true that popular fanfictions can be amateurish or lacking in depth, the key understanding is that they do not have to be and in fact often aren't. The mechanisms of fanfiction writing enable deep intellectual engagement with the most urgent concerns of the humanities. Coppa's *Fanfiction Reader*, in addition to offering the above definitions of fanfiction, provides a foundational example of the scholarly study of popular fanfiction and its engagement with those urgent concerns.

The body of such scholarship is growing, but academia is slow to change—much slower, in fact, than fandom, which reacts to developments in culture with the speed of the internet. Academics, in part because their work is subjected to the slow process of peer review and traditional publication, and partly because they themselves were successful in a system that rewards adherence to particular modes of discourse, tend to perpetuate a system of conservative approaches to literature and even to learning. Canon fanfiction stands in the gap between traditional literary criticism and popular forms of expression, and as such, it has great potential to contribute to the literary environment, particularly in the college classroom.

From Canon to Fandom: A Brief History

Although we have just examined a number of distinctions between popular and canon fanfiction, the broad parallels in process are evident. In fact, fanfiction writers themselves have steadily and determinedly defended their activity by citing just such parallels. Perhaps the best example is an impassioned response by Aja Romano to an anti-fanfiction diatribe by Diana Gabaldon.[94] The response

---

92 Hills, "Media," 39–40.

93 Hills, *Fan Cultures*, 28.

94 Gabaldon's original post was taken down, but it was largely recreated by Kate Nepveu on *Live Journal*. Among other things, Gabaldon says of fanfiction, "[I]t makes me want to barf whenever I've inadvertently encountered some of it involving my characters" (quoted in Nepveu, "Diana Gabaldon & Fanfic Followup").

was first posted in 2010 but continued to be updated for several years thereafter. Romano writes:

> Dear Author of the Week,
> You think fanfic is a personal affront to the many hours you've spent carefully crafting your characters. You think fanfic is "immoral and illegal." You think fanfiction is just plagiarism. You think fanfiction is cheating. You think fanfic is for people who are too stupid/lazy/unimaginative to write stories of their own. You think there are exceptions for people who write published derivative works as part of a brand or franchise, because they're clearly only doing it because they have to. You're personally traumatized by the idea that someone else could look at your characters and decide that you did it wrong and they need to fix it/add original characters to your universe/send your characters to the moon/Japan/their hometown. You think all fanfic is basically porn. You're revolted by the very idea that fic writers think what they do is legitimate.
> We get it.
> Congratulations! You've just summarily dismissed as criminal, immoral, and unimaginative each of the following Pulitzer Prize-winning writers and works.[95]

Romano then lists eleven award-winning works, mostly novels but also some plays, that take as their starting point a preexisting work of literature. Not content with that, they[96] add, "But those are just rare exceptions, you say. Have some more!" The list that follows, when printed, runs to ten pages in length. They conclude, "[I]n every single instance above, the action and the result, the practice of writing and the story produced are *both identical to the act of producing fanfic. There is no difference*" (italics in the original). Romano's point is not that *A Thousand Acres* is the same as a Harry-Draco slash fic in subject or theme but rather that the process that leads to the two products is ultimately the same: taking someone else's influential work and responding with a new creative piece.

Some scholars, of course, have resisted drawing parallels just as strongly as fans have insisted on defending them. In discussing retellings of the Homerian epics, Shannon Farley declares, "Fandom's desire to claim the *Aeneid* and other canonical works as fan fiction is an attempt to borrow prestige at a meta level."[97] It is interesting to note that this declaration implies the only reason to make a connection between the *Aeneid* and fanfiction is to elevate fanfiction to the level of canonical literature—an implication that only reinforces the "high" and "low" culture boundaries that cultural studies and postmodernist scholars have been trying to break down for the last forty years. What Farley does not

---

95 Romano, "I'm Done Explaining Why Fanfic Is Okay."
96 Romano's Tumblr page lists "they/them" as their primary pronouns.
97 Farley, "Versions of Homer," 6.4.

claim is that the activity itself, whether done by Virgil or by an online author writing under a pseudonym, is essentially different.

In fact, other scholars have made that argument directly. Sheenagh Pugh, for instance, claims that what published novelists like Jean Rhys do when they write novels like *Wide Sargasso Sea*, a prequel to *Jane Eyre*, does not "differ materially from what fan fiction writers all over the world do every day."[98] Karen Hellekson and Kristina Busse make the same point, also invoking *Wide Sargasso Sea*,[99] then further explain, "These texts resemble fan fiction in modus operandi. They use settings, characters, and scenes from well-known texts while telling a fundamentally different story, be it an expansion, subversion, or counternarrative."[100] While we have already noted the material differences,[101] the process itself is largely the same whether you are John Milton rewriting Genesis as *Paradise Lost* or surname-less Carol posting "Ae Fond Kiss," an alternate-universe retelling of *Pride and Prejudice*, to *Mrs. Darcy's Story Site*.[102]

Additionally, a number of scholars have sought to find the roots of modern fanfiction in the history of canon literature itself. First, fan theorists make the argument that fandom itself is not limited to pop culture phenomena, but that, in fact, one can be a "fan" of anything. Matt Hills sets a challenge for fan theorists by asking "why fan studies has largely failed to engage with 'high cultural fandom,' restricting its attention to pop-cultural objects and fan cultures."[103] Scholars are, in fact, making ground in bringing the study of so-called "high culture" fandoms under the purview of the field; Roberta Pearson draws parallels between the fans of Bach and Shakespeare and those of *Star Trek*,[104] and John Tulloch studies fan responses to Chekhov.[105] My hope is that this book will contribute to that ongoing conversation. But we should also remember that much of what we now think of as serious or traditionally canonical literature was once pop culture itself. In his study of Shakespeare in modern culture, Douglas Lanier points out that "Shakespeare's special status in the literary canon springs from a complex history of appropriation and reappropriation, through which his image and works have been repeatedly recast to speak to

---

98 Pugh, *The Democratic Genre*, 11.
99 Hellekson and Busse, *Fan Fiction Studies Reader*, 2–3.
100 Hellekson and Busse, *Fan Fiction Studies Reader*, 22.
101 See "Canon Fanfiction: Definition and Distinctions," above.
102 Described in Thomas, "What Is Fanfiction," 14.
103 Hills, "Implicit Fandom in the Fields of Theatre, Art, and Literature," 477.
104 Pearson, "Bachies, Bardies, Trekkies, and Sherlockians."
105 Tulloch, "Fans of Chekhov."

the purposes, fantasies, and anxieties of various historical moments."[106] In other words, Shakespeare would not be *Shakespeare* if he had not first been immensely popular, and if his fans (whether literary or academic) had not turned him into an icon of class and style. In fact, I will go so far as to ask a pointed question: what is academia if not a very large, very long-lived fandom with an enormous amount of influence?

That is not to say, of course, that popular fandom and the perpetuation of canon literature, or even the rewriting of older works by authors we now consider canonical, are all exactly the same thing. Anne Jamison admits that "our understanding of the key relationships—those that exist variously among writer, written, reader, publisher, object published, and source—changes over time."[107] In fact, if academia is a fandom, it may effectively be a negative-image fandom, because rather than giving ordinary people a continued stake in Shakespeare's work, as popular fandoms do for *Harry Potter* or *Star Trek*, academia has put Shakespeare on a pedestal few can reach—a process Lanier refers to as the "unpopularization" of Shakespeare.[108] If we take up the challenge of rewriting his material ourselves, then, not as academics but as ordinary citizens of the literary world, we are empowered to "[recognize] certain formal and ideological limits of its Shakespearian source (or the limits of how that source has been traditionally interpreted) and [seek] to push against those limits, in a spirit of critique, anarchy, pleasure, recuperation, participation."[109] That is, we play a role in "actively perpetuat[ing] and interven[ing] in the cultural afterlife of Shakespeare."[110]

Examples of what we might consider historical examples of canon fanfiction abound in works that study the deep roots of fanfiction. Lev Grossman notes that the modern resurgence of retold stories was unofficially launched in 1966 with the publication of Jean Rhys's *Wide Sargasso Sea* and the first performance of Tom Stoppard's *Rosencrantz and Guildenstern Are Dead*—a year that also happened to see the premier of *Star Trek*, the series that launched the most recognizable first wave of American fandom as we now understand it. Looking at this coincidence, he comments, "It's unlikely that Jean Rhys or Tom Stoppard would have been much tempted to contribute to the pages of *Spockanalia* [a fan zine about *Star Trek*], [...] but in a way they and the Spockanalians were engaged

---

106 Lanier, *Shakespeare in Modern Popular Culture*, 21.
107 Jamison, *Fic*, 35.
108 Lanier, *Shakespeare in Modern Popular Culture*, 22.
109 Lanier, *Shakespeare in Modern Popular Culture*, 85.
110 Lanier, *Shakespeare in Modern Popular Culture*, 21.

in very much the same project: the breaking down of a long-standing state of affairs that made stories and characters the exclusive province of their authors, and that locked readers and viewers into a state of mute passivity."[111] Reaching back before the twentieth century, Anne Jamison gives a "pre-history" of fanfiction, citing examples from Chretien de Troyes (twelfth century) and Miguel de Cervantes (seventeenth century) to the Marquis de Sade and Thackeray.[112] Lanier traces the history of Shakespeare fanfiction back as far as Shakespeare's own lifetime, when John Fletcher published *The Woman's Prize, or The Tamer Tamed* (1611), "in which Petruchio, now widowed from Katherine, is once again about to marry, this time to Maria who, determined to avoid his patriarchal domination, appeals to female solidarity for help."[113] Jamison even cites non-professionals who engaged in the activity of appropriating others' work, such as Lady Bradshaigh, who, after a lengthy correspondence with Richardson about the subject, rewrote *Clarissa* so that she liked the ending better.[114]

In other words, fanfiction has a long and varied history in which every generation recasts the important works of its predecessors in its own image, "forc[ing] cultural 'master-texts' to address the issues, needs, and pleasures they don't engage."[115] Students of literature are no doubt keenly aware of the stories literary culture can't let go of, the stories we return to across centuries and cultures because they still seem to contain something meaningful. Virgil rewrote Homer as a nationalist epic and dozens of Classical and medieval authors took on the story of Troy after him.[116] Lydgate wrote himself into the *Canterbury Tales* as an additional pilgrim narrating the *Siege of Thebes*, itself an adaptation of material from Classical myth. Chaucer, too, has refused to lie quiet; Andrew Higl dedicates an article to retellings of the *Wife of Bath's Tale* alone,[117] and *The Miller's Tale* gets a whole book.[118] King Arthur made his way around northern Europe in Celtic, English, and French forms (before going even farther abroad) and continues to be revisited in so many forms by so many artists that it seems foolish to list even a sampling of them, though one thinks of the influential twentieth-century examples of T. H. White's *The Once and Future King*, Marion Zimmer Bradley's *Mists of Avalon*, and Lerner and Lowe's musical *Camelot*. And of

---

111 Grossman, "Foreword," xi.
112 Jamison, *Fic*, 26–36.
113 Lanier, *Shakespeare in Modern Popular Culture*, 83.
114 Jamison, *Fic*, 31.
115 Lanier, *Shakespeare in Modern Popular Culture*, 82.
116 See Fantuzzi, *Achilles in Love*.
117 Higl, "Wife of Bath Retold."
118 Beidler, *The Lives of the* Miller's Tale.

course, though this book is focused on Western examples, the phenomenon is in every way a global one. *The Tale of Genji* in Japan, the legend of the Monkey King in Hinduism and Buddhism, and *Layla and Majnun* in the Arabic-speaking world are all examples of cultural monoliths that seized the imagination of their first audiences and continue to inspire adaptations, retellings, and reinventions not only in their culture of origin but worldwide.

Theoretical Foundations: From Narratology to Fan Theory

The subject of rewriting preexisting literature is not new; very few subjects of study are. In fact, from Classical and medieval rhetoric manuals to directors' commentaries in modern film, people have always been reusing others' material and talking about how and why they did so. Within the academic realm, various theories have arisen to define and categorize works of the type we are describing here, and to grapple with why they have the power that they do.

The first and most prestigious field is **cognitive narratology**, which is primarily interested in theorizing about how the process of reading works in the mind of a reader. This is how Gwenllian-Jones describes the act of reading: "The implicit aspects of the fictional world are, in imagination, rendered explicit; gaps are filled in; inconsistencies are smoothed out by means of plausible explanations that are in keeping with the interior logics of the fictional world; creative interventions are made."[119] This is how any reader makes sense of the facts presented in a text, and yet it looks remarkably like what writers do when they reinvent preexisting stories: they fill in gaps, make sense of contradiction, imagine what is left unspoken. In other words, what I am calling canon fanfiction is simply a written record of the act of interpretation that goes on in the process of reading. Student scholars new to narratology will undoubtedly notice its proclivity for fancy, often Greek-derived terms for very simple concepts: for instance, "diegesis"[120] is a dandified term for "plot" or "story," while "spatio-temporal immersion"[121] makes "sensory detail" sound more complicated than it is. However, once the hurdle of terminology is overcome, the interested student will find much to value in narratology's insights about reading and writing.

The second field of inquiry that touches on canon fanfiction is the study of **intertextuality.** The term was first popularized by theorist Julia Kristeva, and

---

119 Gwenllian-Jones, "Virtual Reality," 92.

120 Turk, "Metalepsis," 86.

121 Van Staanhuyse, "The Writing and Reading of Fanfiction," 3.

Mary Orr translates her definition from French: intertextuality is "a mosaic of quotations; any text is the absorption and transformation of another."[122] This notion has come to cover a broad range of meanings, all based on the idea that texts talk to one another. Sometimes this intertextuality is deliberately invoked by the author, and sometimes it is unconscious. A straightforward example would be Chaucer's deliberate use of multiple genres in *The Miller's Tale*. As discussed by Peter Beidler, the cuckolded husband John, who is duped into thinking he is the new Noah, invokes biblical narrative; the trickster/lover Nicholas comes from theatrical farce; the would-be lover Absolon is a pastiche of the conventions from courtly romance; and the lusty wife, Alison, is out of a fabliau.[123] Chaucer draws all these kinds of texts together in his multi-layered take on what had been a simple bawdy story when he first encountered it in the Low Countries.[124] In this mode, canon fanfiction engages in intertextuality by playing with the boundaries between authorial text and new material, and often between genres too, as when Christina Henry takes *Peter Pan* and turns it into a horror story in *Lost Boy*. But as we have already seen with the hypothetical novel about the college professor, even a text that does not consciously invoke other narratives actually does, simply by virtue of having to share literary culture with other books.

Intertextuality can also refer to texts brought together by the reader and not by the author. For instance, a reader of *Mansfield Park* who has also just read something like *The Life of Olaudah Equiano* may be sensitized to the fact that Sir Thomas Bertram is an enslaver, despite Austen's careful avoidance of the subject, and this reader's experience of *Mansfield Park* will be different because Equiano's narrative of enslavement casts its shadow over the story. Phyllis Frus and Christy Williams discuss intertextuality in this way,[125] and just as narratology shows canon fanfiction to be a formalization of the reading process, intertextuality shows us that it is likewise a formalization of the act of responding to a text based on our knowledge of things left unstated or unacknowledged in the story.

The third field that has offered a great deal of insight into retellings is **adaptation studies**, usually under the umbrella field of film studies. Film adaptations of novels have long been of interest to scholars, and despite the difference in medium, they are, in a very real way, close cousins of the works studied in this

---

122 Orr, *Intertextuality*, 21.
123 Beidler, *The Lives of the* Miller's Tale, 17–26.
124 Beidler, *The Lives of the* Miller's Tale, 12.
125 Frus and Williams, "Introduction," 10–11.

book. Julie Sanders provides a history of film studies drawing on the work of eminent theorists from Derrida to Barthes and Foucault,[126] but for the present discussion, Sara Gwenllian-Jones and Roberta Pearson are more useful in their argument for the value of studying popular media: "Cult television's imaginary universes support an inexhaustible range of narrative possibilities, inviting, supporting, and rewarding close textual analysis, interpretation, and inventive reformulations."[127] This same argument could be made for the value of studying canon fanfiction novels like those in this book, as they provide a record of reader response and reception. Nicholas Abercrombie and Brian Longhurst have studied how audiences (in our case, readers) fall onto a spectrum of involvement, from general consumer to fan to enthusiast and beyond.[128] In their formulation, the act of rewriting places readers on the high end of the spectrum as enthusiasts, who differ from fans and general consumers in their depth of immersion and expertise in the subject. This notion of the spectrum is a helpful reminder that the act of retelling stories is a continuation of rather than a departure from the activities we engage in in other aspects of our lives. When we talk about adapting stories, then, we are talking about an activity that is simply an extension of what we do when we consume any media.

Another insight offered by film studies is that the influence between source and adaptation does not move down a one-way street. While the adaptation could not exist without the source, the source is not independent of its adaptations. As Amanda Gilroy says of teaching Jane Austen, "It is a truth not always, or not easily, acknowledged that student engagement with Austen's novels today is always already mediated by film adaptations as well as the wealth of sequels, prequels, and rewrites."[129] In other words, once an adaptation is popularized, it affects the way readers respond to its source. A non-Austenian example would be Franco Zeffirelli's film version of *Hamlet*, which leans so heavily on Freud's diagnosis of Hamlet with an Oedipus Complex that, once one has seen the film, it becomes nearly impossible to see Hamlet and Gertrude's relationship in any other terms even in a different adaptation. (In fact, I occasionally receive papers in which students mention Gertrude kissing Hamlet because the scene in the film is so memorable they forget it is not in the original play.) Gwenllian-Jones borrows Pierre Lévy's term to describe this new, patchwork *Hamlet* as "deterritorialized fiction"—that is, removed from the sole influence of Shakespeare, whose ter-

---

126 Sanders, *Adaptation and Appropriation*, 1–5.
127 Gwenllian-Jones and Pearson, "Introduction," xii.
128 Abercrombie and Longhurst, *Audiences*, 140.
129 Gilroy, "Our Austen."

ritory the play originally was, and popularized as a new creation that he might not even recognize.[130] Another term for this phenomenon, drawn from fandom, is "head canon": a reader's idea of the "real story" based not only on the original but on retellings and any other influences they have encountered.

The reason I spend some time on this concept and this film example is that it makes a key connection between adaptations or retellings and literary criticism: as Imelda Whelehan says, adaptations "mimic the function of scholarly critics who always find more to add to their analyses of the text, until our academic understanding of a classic literary work becomes in more ways than one the sum of its commentaries."[131] In the above examples, just as Freud influenced literary scholars to the extent that professors can't seem to teach *Hamlet* without invoking the Oedipus Complex, so Zeffirelli took that psychoanalytic theory out of the classroom and moved it into the cinema, where it probably did more to influence the popular notion of *Hamlet* than any undergraduate survey ever could. Such is the power of adaptation.

The last and, for our purposes, most important field that offers a framework for discussing literary reworkings is **fan theory.** Fan studies originated as a subfield within media studies and so is a cousin to adaptation and film studies. Outsiders often denigrate fanfiction as trivial, narcissistic, and stylistically naïve; Sandvoss cites Terry Eagleton, the great advocate for traditionalism, as a scholar who dismisses fanfiction in this way.[132] Yet fan studies has a long and rather heady intellectual history. Most scholars in the field cite Roland Barthes's "Death of the Author" as the intellectual (if unknowing) grandfather of fan studies because of his famous notion that the act of publication removes a text from the power of the author and puts it into the hands of consumers to interpret, revise, and reimagine at will. I suspect that authors' (as opposed to scholars') common though not universal reaction against fanfiction may stem from the cult of authorial power, which has persisted in the field of writing even as it has dissipated, at least in theory, from the academic and popular worlds. Living authors, that is, are often reluctant to relinquish control of their creations. Matt Hills calls this cult of authorial power "auteurism,"[133] a notion that is directly challenged by fans' insistence on writing their own contributions to the worlds of previously published stories. Despite resistance to the notion of fan studies, though, I have

---

130 Gwenllian-Jones, "Virtual Reality," 84–85.
131 Whelehan, "Adaptations," 16.
132 Sandvoss, "Death of the Reader?," 19.
133 Hills, *Fan Cultures*, 138.

not found a framework that is better for discussing published retellings, rework-ings, and reinventions.

It is worth grounding our discussion with a brief history of fan theory in order to understand how this book relates to, or sometimes resists, the guiding principles of the field. Fan studies has gone through three waves of theory,[134] deeply indebted to Marxism and to Michel de Certeau's theories of popular read-ing. De Certeau claimed in 1985 that "readers are travelers; they move across lands belonging to someone else, like nomads poaching their way across fields they did not write, despoiling the wealth of Egypt to enjoy it themselves."[135] This idea of readers gleaning the best of what they consume and making it their own in various ways led Henry Jenkins to borrow a term from de Certeau and call fanf-ic writers "textual poachers." The publication of his book of the same name in 1992 marked the real beginning of the first wave of fan theory. Unlike de Certeau, who thought of writing as a medium inaccessible to the common person and that therefore aggregated no power to the reader-poacher, Jenkins claimed that fan media allowed readers to be "active producers and manipulators of mean-ings."[136] This heavily Marxist reading (the proletariat reader rebels against the controlling power of the media giant) was recognized by the second wave as being perhaps too idealistic in outlook: as Bronwen Thomas says, the second wave saw fans as "not so much operating outside of social hierarchies as them-selves participating in the construction and maintenance of the uneven distribu-tion of power."[137] In other words, not all fanfiction is progressive and self-aware; in fact, much of it is complicit in maintaining the status quo of the traditional canon. This is particularly true of Jane Austen fanfic, in which participants often share a nostalgia for "a more genteel past,"[138] ignoring its problematic as-pects.

The third wave of fan studies has primarily been interested in dealing with the ways in which globalization and almost constant internet access have affect-ed fandoms. Cross-cultural exchange is more accessible now than ever before, and we are constantly inundated with media. Thus, just as narratology and film studies show that rewriting stories is actually just an extension of reading and consumption, fan studies demonstrates that fandom is not a discrete aspect of our lives but a thread running through practically everything we do. Addition-

---

134 See Gray, Sandvoss, and Harrington, "Introduction," 1–10; and Thomas, "What Is Fanfic-tion," 3–5.
135 De Certeau, *The Practice of Everyday Life*, 174.
136 Jenkins, *Textual Poachers*, 23.
137 Thomas, "What Is Fanfiction," 4.
138 Thompson, "Trinkets and Treasures"; see also Gilroy, "Our Austen."

ally, the third wave has forged something of a middle ground between the first two, admitting that "audiences have agency, but they do not have autonomy; various forms of power shape what meanings they can assert."[139] Though this third wave is very important in how we think about fanfiction, for our purposes it is less central except for this acknowledgment of the middle ground between audience-as-rebel and audience-as-dupe. In fact, much of my analysis will look very much like first- and second-wave fan theory, discussing how canon fanfictions both critique and do homage to their source texts. The reason I seem to be taking a step backward in the progress of the field is that I am discussing the rarified world of traditionally published novels whose explicit purpose is to rebel against the shortcomings of past literatures, while at the same time honoring what they see as valuable in the canon. Such novels can often be discussed most productively in terms of their conscious resistance to particular aspects of the original (first wave) and yet, sometimes, their complacence in other realms of social justice (second wave).

It is important to point out the limitations in equating published literary output, especially output of the past, with fanfiction; for one thing, the term "fan" was not popularized until the 1880s, when it was used to describe baseball devotees.[140] What we think of now when we think of "fan" or "fandom" has been shaped by radio, film, television, and most importantly in recent decades, the internet. The Classical, medieval, and Renaissance cultures that provide the context for the works studied in this book did not see quite the same thing when artists rose to popularity. But in this study, we are not talking about fans themselves but rather about their output, and as we have seen, writing using other people's material has been a practice worldwide for millennia.

Still, of the four fields of theory that touch upon retellings, I see fan studies as the most useful. Its vocabulary is more developed, more flexible, more accessible, and more well-established than the vocabulary of narratology or adaptation studies; I have yet to encounter an idea I want to discuss that fanfiction does not have a term for, and the terms are widespread among ordinary, as opposed to scholarly, audiences. Any reader of fanfic knows the terms "head canon" (what a reader considers to be the "real story," influenced by both the original and its fics), "shipping" (putting characters in a non-canonical romantic relationship), "AU" (alternate universe), and "crossover" (combining two or more fandoms in one story). Pugh includes a useful dictionary of fanfic in her

---

139 Jenkins, "Fandom, Negotiations, and Participatory Culture," 15.
140 Edwards, "Literary Fandom and Literary Fans," 53. On the history of the term, see Cavicchi, "Foundational Discourses of Fandom."

appendix,[141] though the internet, being fandom's native environment so to speak, will probably always be the most up-to-date and authoritative source for such terms.

The Problem of Terminology

Scholars new to the field will soon realize that the study of what we might broadly call "derivative works" has no universal vocabulary, a fact often noted by commentators.[142] The most basic question that the field has yet to resolve—and probably never will—is simply what to call an artistic work that uses another artistic work as its basis.

Part of the problem stems from an anxiety that our analysis will be limited to examining whether the work in question is "faithful" to its source. In an effort to achieve a theoretical outlook that "adds depth to meaning rather than plunging us into questions of origin and influence,"[143] scholars of various approaches apply different terminology. Sandvoss calls the source text the "urtext" and the resulting works "fan objects."[144] Barta-Smith and DiMarco prefer "hypotext" and "hypertext."[145] The current study does not share the anxiety of influence that leads scholars to eschew the term "source" and rather *wants* to look at the newer text in light of the older and vice versa, so I will generally use the term "source" or "original" for the predecessor text.

There remains, however, the problem of what to call the text that results from a reworking of that source. *Derivative*, which I use above, is perhaps the most obvious term, but it carries negative connotations of the work being a knockoff and is therefore almost never used among scholars. Below are other terms that students may encounter, each attempting to capture some particular aspect of the broad concept:

Retelling applies to a specific band of works that revisit, with some identifiable closeness, the events narrated in the source. Although it is sometimes applied to them, such a term would properly exclude *Grendel* and *Wide Sargasso Sea*, which are primarily prequels to *Beowulf* and *Jane Eyre* (respectively), not retellings of them.

---

141 Pugh, *The Democratic Genre*, 242–44.
142 Sanders, *Adaptation and Appropriation*, 5; Frus and Williams, "Introduction," 5.
143 Barta-Smith and DiMarco, "Introduction," 2.
144 Sandvoss, "Death of the Reader?," 23.
145 Barta-Smith and DiMarco, "Introduction," 5.

Emulation is broader but implies a particular, generally positive attitude toward the originating work.[146] Virgil may be said to be emulating Homer in the *Aeneid*, but the same could not be said of works in the "fix-it" genre, discussed below, which resist rather than embrace the original.

Adaptation is perhaps the best general term for works that revisit other works. Although not technically limited to this definition, it is traditionally associated with changing medium, usually from text to film. It also covers a huge range of texts that would not necessarily qualify as more specific terms like "canon fanfiction." The Andrew Davies *Pride and Prejudice* miniseries is an adaptation because it takes Austen's novel and puts it on film; however, it is largely loyal to the original (and beloved because it is so). Specifically because it changes so little of its source text, I happily call it an adaptation but would hesitate to consider it "canon fanfiction."

Appropriation is likewise accurate and has been used by scholars,[147] but the term has accrued deeply negative connotations due to an increased awareness in popular culture of the harms and hazards of cultural appropriation.

Remix and *replay* are umbrella terms for works whose basic material comes from a preexisting work.[148] Although the former term is originally derived from the music industry and the latter from theater, both have been applied to various genres of artistic production. Students casting about for a simple word that describes the concept in question will certainly find these good options, though they may not be recognized by audiences outside the field.

Fanfiction has long been my favorite term for referring to works based on other works, though as discussed above, popular fanfiction arises out of a particular context and within a particular subculture. However, the term is particularly attractive because it has been associated with empowering readers to own the material they use as their source. Still, fanfiction is a very broad concept, deeply tied to its popular, as opposed to scholarly, origins.

Canon fanfiction, then, is the subgenre I propose to bridge the gap between popular and academic production: it embraces the broad spectrum of approaches and well-developed vocabulary of fanfiction but narrows the focus to works whose source text belongs to the traditional literary canon, however the author or scholar in question may choose to define it. What follows is a brief explanation of the scope that I have set for this particular project.

---

146 I am grateful to David Bradshaw for introducing me to this term.
147 Sanders, *Adaptation and Appropriation*.
148 On remixes, see for example Jenkins and Kelley, *Reading in a Participatory Culture*. On replays, see Zinman, *Replay*.

Canon Fanfiction: Features of the Genre

The term "canon fanfiction" is admittedly subjective: what I think of as a throw-away piece of fluff might strike another reader as a profound take-down of some hierarchy I do not know exists. Likewise, a work I have never heard of may, to another scholar, be an important member of what they consider the literary canon. I would consider the Icelandic sagas to be part of the medieval "canon," and yet the Norton anthology (long an arbiter of canonicity) never even acknowledges that medieval Iceland existed. I make no attempt here to close the borders on this intellectual territory; if there is one thing literary scholars have learned to embrace in the decades since the advent of poststructuralism, it is ambiguity and subjectivity. The fact that a new commentator might come along and argue that something I had dismissed is actually of value is the very essence of the field. We as scholars are continually realizing that writers who lived, for instance, in the shadow of Chaucer or Shakespeare have something to say that is worth hearing after all. Embracing subjectivity is one of the strengths of twenty-first-century scholarship: it is the feature of academia that opens the doors to new and unexplored perspectives.

A few specific genres of literature should be mentioned here because they could very reasonably fall under the umbrella concept of canon fanfiction, but I do not include them in this study. The idea of talking back to an "original" will explain why retold fairytales and myths are of less interest to this particular project than are other kinds of retelling. For those who are interested in fairytales, the *Snow White, Blood Red* series edited by Ellen Datlow and Terri Windling is a good place to start, and for those interested in myths, the Canongate Myth Series includes retellings of myths from a number of cultures including non-Western ones. While such retellings do the same work as the novels I will explore here, I focus more narrowly on fanfictions that respond to an identifiable original. As Phyllis Frus and Christy Williams explain,[149] fairy tales often appeal because there is no easily defined canon: they float free of a named author and belong equally to everyone. Does Cinderella have mice helpers, or birds? Does she have a fairy godmother or a magic tree? Do her stepsisters cut off toes and heels to fit in the shoe or don't they? The answer is yes and no, either/or: anything goes. If we see ourselves as taking back the narrative by writing our canon fanfictions, in the case of fairy tales there is no one to take it back *from*.

The Trojan War material that provides the foundation for several novels I discuss in this book walks the fine line between mythology and "belonging"

---

149 Frus and Williams, "Introduction," 6–7.

to someone. But since modern audiences generally think of Homer when we think of the Trojan War (even if Homer himself was a fantasy or composite figure), when we write canon fanfiction about Achilles or Aeneas, we, like Virgil, feel that we are "talking back" to Homer, and not to a set of amorphous myths. When there is a definite original, even if that original is anonymous or is itself a patchwork of sources as it often is, we as readers know who, or at least what, the canon fanfiction author is responding to. We can find a parallel in the way popular fanfiction writers talk back to the creators of their fandoms on sites like Archive of Our Own (AO3). For instance, 440 *Harry Potter* fics posted on AO3 in the first five months after J. K. Rowling's transphobic tweets went viral in June 2020 are tagged as having a "transgender character."[150] These 440 fics would seem to be an implicit or explicit response to those tweets: they represent the fandom's individual and collective "taking back" of the inclusive *Harry Potter* world from an author who would exclude some from it. In the same way, authors who reuse material by Shakespeare are talking back to Shakespeare as much as they are talking to their contemporary readers.

Likewise, I largely exclude from this book retellings or adaptations of historical events (or, at least, events that are primarily historical). While there is a subgenre of fanfiction called "real person fic" (RPF), the genre is controversial even within fan communities because it is seen as violating real, often still-living people.[151] Historical fiction proper, though it could be classed as RPF, is perhaps less uncomfortable because the people being reinvented are dead, but it carries with it a whole separate set of questions, not the least of which is how much artistic license an author is allowed to take with historical fact before it becomes just plain fiction.[152] As intriguing as it is to consider historical fiction as canon fanfiction—for the connections are not insignificant—historical fiction is its own field of study, and it would take a whole second book to treat its relation to fanfiction properly.

I should also note that translations, even loose translations, are not my particular interest here, though some undoubtedly qualify as canon fanfiction. The Icelandic "translation" of *Dracula*, *Makt Myrkranna*, for instance, has not only a fascinating textual history but also drastically reworks the source material.[153] Likewise, the Russian *Lord of the Rings*, both in its early censored form and in

---

150 Data from November 7, 2020.

151 See Moonbeam's Predilections' discussion of "RPF."

152 See, for instance, Torfi Tulinius's discussion of novelizations of historical figures in Iceland, "Re-writing the Contemporary Sagas."

153 See the English translation and notes by Hans de Roos (*Powers of Darkness*).

its later competing interpretations, has garnered measurable critical attention.[154] Translation study has its own branch of theory, often involving both broad ethical questions (what obligation does the translator have to the author?) and more minute comparisons (is this word an accurate representation of the idea in the original?). As should be clear from the preceding discussion, such questions are not usually asked in comparing canon fanfictions to their source texts. It is in part because of the additional considerations that I avoid using translations as examples in this book, but the questions listed below could often be applied as fruitfully to free translations as they can to the examples used here.

Fix-It Lit

One could write a book on any subgenre of fanfiction from ships to Mary Sues, but because of my interest in "talking back" to a canon full of unacknowledged injustices and aggressions both micro and macro, this book centers on "fix-it lit." In fandom, fix-it lit, as the name suggests, "changes something about canon that the fan writing the fic wasn't happy with,"[155] often responding to what fans perceive as injustices perpetrated by the author upon the characters. The outpouring of fanfiction repairing and re-pairing characters after the close of the *Harry Potter* series is a good example (9,977 fics tagged as "fix-it" on AO3 alone), as is the number of fics "fixing" issues like the widely disparaged ending to the television series *Game of Thrones* (2,363 "fix-it" tags on AO3).[156]

Some fix-it lit is aesthetic or emotive in nature (fans wanted Harry and Hermione to end up together, so they get rid of Ron and put them together), but it can equally be meaningful on a thematic and cultural level. In *Hornblower*, a high-seas adventure television series set during the Napoleonic Wars and based on the books by C. S. Forester, the much-loved character Archie Kennedy is killed in action in the sixth of eight TV films, and the fandom exploded with protest. The reason for killing off the character has never been made clear; Archie is not a lead in the book series, so either book fans or, perhaps more likely, the Forester estate seems to have pressured A&E/Meridian to remove him.[157]

---

154 Andrei A. Kistyakovsky's *Khraniteli*, the first book in the *Vlastelin Kolets* trilogy, was published in censored form in 1982. See commentary by Mark T. Hooker on the various Russian translations, *Tolkien through Russian Eyes*.

155 *Fanlore*.

156 Both statistics as of April 16, 2022.

157 The few commentaries available on the decision are archived on fan sites like *Archieology101* ("Who Killed Kennedy?").

Fans, however—even ones who did not write fanfiction—widely viewed Archie and the protagonist, Horatio Hornblower, as having an unspoken attraction for one another. Killing off this would-be love interest looks to fans very much like yet another example of mainstream entertainment's erasure of a gay character. Other examples of gay erasure that aroused fan ire include the death of Willow's lover Tara in *Buffy the Vampire Slayer* and, more recently, the death of Lexa in *The 100*.[158] Nearly one third of the total *Hornblower* fanfictions on the AO3 archive ship these characters, often bringing Archie back from the dead in defiance of canon to do so.[159]

"Fixing" the series by writing Archie back in also calls attention to the injustices of history, in which "those convicted of buggery [in the British navy ...] were far more likely to receive death sentences than men charged with mutiny or murder."[160] Other forms of sexual contact between men received lesser punishments, usually whipping, but the British navy continued hanging men for sodomy until 1829.[161] The disarming innocence of these two characters as portrayed in the series stands in stark contrast to the reality of the punishment they would have faced if they had been lovers in the real British navy in the early nineteenth century. By shipping them in defiance of both canon and history, fanfiction writers register their protest not only against the erasure of gay identity in media but also the denial and persecution of such identity in the past.

Systems of Categorization

Scholars of various theoretical backgrounds have made attempts to create classification systems for adaptations and retellings, and in finding ways to talk about canon fanfiction, these systems can provide a helpful framework. The two most useful systems of categorization come from adaptation and film studies and from fan studies.

Geoffrey Wagner, writing on cinematic adaptations of novels, uses three broad categories of classification:

---

158 On Tara, see Mangels, "Lesbian Sex = Death?"; on Lexa, see Stanhope, "Bury Your Gays."
159 Of the 1015 *Hornblower* fics, 271 are tagged with "Horatio Hornblower/Archie Kennedy" as of April 16, 2022.
160 Gilbert, "Buggery and the British Navy, 1700–1861," 81. The data for the above assertion is for the period 1756–1806.
161 Gilbert, "Buggery and the British Navy, 1700–1861," 85.

Transposition is a situation in which a story is moved from novel to film with as little difference as possible. None of the works discussed in this book fall into this category.

Commentary is an approach in which the film makes deliberate changes to deal with issues not sufficiently addressed in the novel, like racism or misogyny.

Analogy represents "a fairly considerable departure for the sake of making *another* work of art."[162] A classic example of analogy is Amy Heckerling's 1995 film *Clueless*, which moves Jane Austen's *Emma* into a 1990s Beverly Hills high school with a valley girl as the protagonist.

Broad categories like these are useful because they define the distance between the original and the adaptation. Most of the canon fanfictions discussed in detail in this book fall into the "commentary category," but some of them combine commentary with analogy; *Sometimes We Tell the Truth* is technically an analogy, moving Chaucer's pilgrims to twenty-first-century Washington, DC, but as we will see in the discussion of the novel, it is very much a commentary on the ethics of Chaucer's original.

The second system comes from the realm of fan studies. In his seminal work *Textual Poachers*, Henry Jenkins outlines ten different approaches to adapting an earlier story. He is specifically referring to fanfiction of television series, but the categories apply broadly to any sort of fanfiction:

Recontextualization refers to fanfictions that add missing scenes or fill in gaps in the storyline.[163]

Expanding the Series Timeline includes prequels and sequels.[164]

Refocalization changes the point-of-view character or protagonist.[165]

Moral Realignments "[i]nvert or question the moral universe of the primary text, taking the villains and transforming them into the protagonists of their own narratives."[166]

Genre Shifting refers to fanfictions that change the prevailing genre, changing sci-fi to romance, etc.[167]

Cross Overs combine two or more fandoms.[168]

Character Dislocation describes "[w]hen characters are removed from their original situations and given alternative names and identities. The program char-

---

162 Wagner, *The Novel and the Cinema*, 227.
163 Jenkins, *Textual Poachers*, 163.
164 Jenkins, *Textual Poachers*, 164.
165 Jenkins, *Textual Poachers*, 165.
166 Jenkins, *Textual Poachers*, 168.
167 Jenkins, *Textual Poachers*, 169.
168 Jenkins, *Textual Poachers*, 170.

acters provide a basis for these new protagonists, yet the fan-constructed figures differ dramatically from the broadcast counterparts."[169] A fanfiction might change characters' race or culture and put them in a different scenario or time.

Personalization is work in which the authors "efface the gap that separates the realm of their own experience and the fictional space of their favorite programs."[170] Writers of fanfiction know this sort of approach as a "Mary-Sue" narrative in which an idealized version of the narrator becomes a protagonist in the story.

Emotional Intensification is, as the name suggests, a reemphasis on pathos. Jenkins writes, "Because fan reading practices place such importance on issues of character motivation and psychology, fans often emphasize moments of narrative crisis."[171] One common feature of published canon fanfictions is an omniscient narration style, which intensifies the emotional life not just of a single protagonist but of a whole cast of characters.[172]

Eroticization is perhaps what non-fanfiction writers first think of when they hear the term "fanfiction": fics in which the characters are put in often non-canonical relationships that can be (but aren't always) graphic.[173]
Most of the canon fanfictions discussed in this book fall into one or more of Jenkins's categories, but the fact that a work can fall into more than one is a helpful reminder that categorization is not an end in itself; attaching labels to what we're studying is only useful insofar as it allows us to make comparisons or say something we couldn't say without the label. Our instinct to box literature in is always going to be foiled by literature's refusal to stay in the boxes to which we assign it.

That is why one of the other key systems for categorizations comes from fandom itself, not the scholars who study it. The terminology of fanfiction is both more expansive than the categorization systems discussed above and more familiar to readers; even college students who don't read or write fanfic are likely to know the term "ship" or "head canon." Below is a list of useful fanfiction terminology—a far smaller list than could be generated but one that strives to capture the most relevant terms for this study.[174] The terms are used by fans in tag-

---

169 Jenkins, *Textual Poachers*, 171.
170 Jenkins, *Textual Poachers*, 171.
171 Jenkins, *Textual Poachers*, 174.
172 A number of the novels in the Hogarth Shakespeare series, including *Macbeth* and *Dunbar*, demonstrate this trend.
173 Jenkins, *Textual Poachers*, 175.
174 Unless otherwise noted, all definitions in this list are drawn from Moonbeam's Predilections, "Fanfiction Terminology."

ging their work on fan sites so that other fans know what sort of story they are about to read. I will often use film or television as examples in the definitions below because they are more familiar to readers than published novels.

Angst: this term is used for fictions that emphasize the emotional suffering of a canon character. It is a relevant term in canon fanfiction because so much of the drive to rewrite canon literature seems to come from a desire to enter into the emotions of characters, especially villains, who seem underdeveloped in the original.

AU (alternate universe): while the name suggests science fiction, AU refers broadly to any fic set in a different time or place than the original. Setting Shakespeare in the twentieth or twenty-first century, as the novels in the Hogarth Shakespeare series do, would qualify as AUs under the fanfiction community's definition.

Backstory/Pre-series: these two terms essentially refer to prequels, imagining events before canon begins. They can be canon compliant (matching what we know about a character from the original) but do not have to be.

Crossover (sometimes tagged **X-over**): as in Jenkins, a crossover combines two or more fandoms. These fandoms can come from the same genre or may be wildly unrelated (*Buffy the Vampire Slayer* and *NCIS*, *Sherlock* and the Marvel universe).

Dark-fic: these fanfictions develop the darker side of a canon character. Robert Zemeckis's 2007 film of *Beowulf*, with its deconstruction of the hero, could qualify as a dark-fic.

Fix-it: "a specific type of alternate universe story in which the author attempts to correct or rewrite something that they feel the original canon should not have done or failed to do properly." All of the published works discussed in chapter 2 are fix-it lit.

Genderswap:[175] an umbrella term used variously to describe scenarios in which a character's gender is changed—either within the story through magic or alien intervention, or outside it, with the author casting a canon male character as "always" having been female or vice versa. A broader term, existing outside of fandom since the 1970s but being adopted by fan communities, is "genderfuck," which more generally disrupts gender norms and therefore might, for instance, include nonbinary characterization. "Genderbend" is a related term that could be either a synonym of "genderswap" or of "genderfuck." Although these fics are often written for humor (Captain Kirk suddenly becomes a

---

[175] This definition draws on the discussion in *Fanlore*, which is more expansive than that of Moonbeam's Predilections.

woman due to alien intervention), genderswap/genderbend fictions can also be done seriously; Prospero becoming Prospera in Julie Taymore's film of *The Tempest* is an example not of cross-casting but of genderbending because Helen Mirren does not play the role as male; Prospera is a woman who must deal with the gender conventions of her day.

Missing scene: as the term indicates, a "missing scene" fic adds an event mentioned but not depicted in the original. The battle of Dol Guldur in Peter Jackson's *The Hobbit* trilogy, which is only alluded to in the novel, could be viewed as an example of missing scene fic.

Outsider PoV (point of view): fanfics tagged "Outsider PoV" present events in the point of view of a non-major character; this character could be a secondary character in the canon or an original character (OC) invented by the author. J. M. Koetzee's *Foe* takes an Outsider PoV on the events of *Robinson Crusoe* by creating an OC, a shipwrecked woman named Susan Barton who shares the island with Crusoe and Friday.

Plot bunny: this charming term refers to something in the original narrative that simply begs to be explored in a fanfic. It is "the rampant and often uncontrollable story idea that smacks an author in the face [...] and demands to be written. Such fuzzy pests are generally wild and quick to breed subplots, but are also ridiculously irresistible." While fanfiction as a whole has been characterized as growing out of "what if" scenarios,[176] perhaps plot bunnies even more than other sub-genres often originate with that question (what if Voldemort had chosen Neville as his nemesis instead of Harry?).

Post-canon/Future-fic: two terms referring to fics set after the canon series of events concludes. Compare with "sequel," below.

Racebending: racebending does to race what genderbending does to gender, altering the race of one or more characters and exploring how that character's experiences would be affected as a result. An informative example comes from fan art commentor spritzeal: "if harry is dark-skinned well [that] kind of explains why the uber-white middle class world of privet drive so easily accepted that this scrawny child in too-big clothes was a 'criminal' and 'disturbed' and why nobody called the goddam police."[177]

Reboot: reboot takes canon material and starts again using a changed scenario. The genre is familiar to comic book fans as well as fans of films like *Star*

---

176 Coppa, *Fanfiction Reader*, 12.
177 Quoted in Seymour, "Racebending and Prosumer Fanart Practices in *Harry Potter* Fandom," 338.

Trek, which rebooted *The Original Series* with a new cast for its film franchise beginning in 2009.

Self-insert/Mary-Sue: broadly, self-insert fiction features an OC that represents the author. Some commentators have seen Aeneas as self-insert in which "Vergil elevates a minor character from Homer's *Iliad* to the level of protagonist in his own epic, and then puts him through all the trials of Odysseus only to have him breeze through them in less than half the time."[178] Although it is not a fanfiction, *The Tempest* could be viewed as self-insert fiction at its best because Prospero is a stand-in for Shakespeare. When self-insert fiction is done badly, the original character is often dismissed as a Mary-Sue (Marty-Stu or Gary-Stu for male characters), "annoying and completely unrealistic figures as they have not a single human flaw." Wesley Crusher has often been viewed by fans as a Gary-Stu character in *Star Trek: The Next Generation*.

Sequel: while post-canon and future-fics could be considered sequels by the general definition of the term, sequels in the fanfiction community generally refer to fics that take place after another fic, not after the canon events.

Ship: possibly the most familiar fanfiction term to those outside of the fanfiction community, a ship is a non-canonical relationship between characters (Harry/Hermione, Frodo/Sam). The creation of a ship is called shipping. The term "Pairing" is also used to tag such relationships.

Slash: a same-sex relationship between characters who are not so paired (and often are not explicitly gay) in the original. The name derives from the practice of labeling such relationships with a slash between the character names (Frodo/Sam). Jeanette Winterson creating an unfulfilled sexual relationship between Polixenes and Leontes of *A Winter's Tale* in her novelization, *A Gap of Time*, is an example of slash in the world of published canon fanfiction.

Additional terms from the world of fanfiction, which are not necessarily categories but are nevertheless useful in our current discussion, appear below:

Canon compliance: a fic whose details do not contradict those of the source text is deemed canon compliant. Such a fic may expand beyond the details of the source, but it does not undo the events in the source. For instance, a backstory fic exploring events that occur before those of the original storyline would have to account for any facts we know about the characters' history from the original. A profic example is Christopher L. Bennett's *Star Trek: The Buried Age*, which depicts the first mission Captain Picard and Data share together;

---

178 Farley, "Versions of Homer," 3.1. Farley goes on to point out that Aeneas is so close to perfect because his is a nationalist symbol, but that simply makes Aeneas a cultural rather than a personal Gary-Stu.

the novel goes well beyond what we learn about the characters' past from the television series, but it is canon compliant in that it does not contradict any detail mentioned in the series about that past.

Filing serial numbers off: this term refers to the action of making enough changes to characters and story that the author can claim the work as original and publish the work legally without violating copyright. The most famous example in recent times is *Fifty Shades of Grey*, which began life as a fanfiction of *Twilight*.

Head canon: a very useful term referring to what a fan personally believes is true within a fandom. Head canon generally does not actively go against official canon but goes beyond it. As mentioned above, the Freudian reading of *Hamlet* has been so ingrained in Shakespeare studies that it is effectively head canon: it is difficult to read the play without seeing the Oedipal overtones.

Meta: in one sense, "meta" refers to works that are self-consciously about fandom or fanfiction, such as "stories which break the 'fourth wall.'"[179] Such self-awareness does not have to be expressed within a fanfic, though. Used in its other sense, "meta" can refer to any commentary about fanfictions or fandom, even essays circulated separately from a fic.[180] A reader who posts comments about fandom or a particular fic within the community, or a fanfic author who writes an explanatory essay as an "Author's Note" are both writing "meta." Such author's notes are common in published canon fanfiction, especially in the Hogarth Shakespeare series.

Profic: fictions written and sold for publication. Although the fanfiction community is not completely decided on what qualifies as profic (does *Fifty Shades of Grey* count, or does the term only refer to works like the official *Star Trek* novels?), it serves as a reminder that popular fanfiction and published fiction stand on a spectrum and are not entirely independent endeavors.

For ease of comparison, the three above systems of categorization have been placed in Table 1, with equivalents appearing in the same row across the three systems.

---

179 Moonbeam's Predilections.
180 Booth describes Fan Meta Reader, a now-inactive website for hosting such essays and commentary, in "Fandom: The Classroom of the Future," 1.5–1.6.

Table 1: Systems of Categorization

Wagner (*Novel and the Cinema*, 222–30)	Jenkins (*Textual Poachers*, 163–75)	Fanfiction (Angelfire)
Transposition	n/a	n/a
n/a	Recontextualization	Missing scene Plot bunny
n/a	Expanding the Series Timeline	Backstory/Pre-series Post-canon/Future-fic Sequel
n/a	Refocalization	Outsider PoV
Commentary	Moral Realignment	Fix-It
n/a	Genre Shifting	some Crossovers some AUs
n/a	Cross Overs	Crossover (or X-over)
Analogy	Character Dislocation	AU (Alternate Universe) Reboot Genderswap (or Genderbend) Racebending
n/a	Personalization	Self-insert/Mary-Sue
n/a	Emotional Intensification	Angst Dark-fic
n/a	Eroticization	Ship/Pairing Slash

Approaches to Canon Fanfiction

When we engage with a piece of canon fanfiction, we can come at the subject from any number of angles, just as we can approach any piece of literature. However, studying a work that directly responds to another, preexisting work opens up particular avenues of investigation. Below are a number of questions we might ask about any given example of canon fanfiction:

Does the author expect us to know the source text? When the source is Shakespeare or some other member of the traditional canon, we might generally assume the answer would be yes: John Updike clearly assumes readers of *Gertrude and Claudius* have read *Hamlet*, and indeed, the novel would not make an enormous amount of sense if one had not. Updike expects us to know from the beginning that these seemingly innocuous characters will become the betrayers of the Old King, and that the headstrong teenager who enters the scene in the second half of the book will go on to be the most famous tragic hero of the English stage. He does not have to explain or even explicitly foreshadow what will happen in the characters' future because readers already know; the entire book, in a way, functions as implicit foreshadowing. Authors who can assume their readers' familiarity with the original operate very much like popular fanfiction writers in this regard: a fanfic about the school days of Harry Potter's parents gains a good deal of its interest and emotional impact from the foreknowledge fans bring to the text that Lily and James are doomed to die young, and that the sycophantic Peter Pettigrew will be the one to betray them while their roguish friend Sirius will take the fall for it. The source text provides the assumed background even when the author alters the canon of events. If the *Harry Potter* fanfic author decides to save Lily and James, they are responding explicitly to the fact that their death in the original is so unjust, and they expect their readers to feel the same way. If Updike had made Claudius innocent of his brother's murder, his innocence (and hence his undeserved persecution at the hands of Hamlet) would be meaningful specifically *because* in the original play he is guilty.

On the other hand, canon fanfiction authors might not be able to assume familiarity with their material. Straightforward retellings and many film adaptations, like Jonathan Myerson's award-winning animated series *The Canterbury Tales*, stand on their own and make no assumptions about their audience's background knowledge of the subject. Yet in almost every example that goes beyond a simple retelling to respond explicitly to the source text, knowledge of the original becomes essential to a full appreciation of the newer work. When this is the case, canon fanfiction authors usually find a way to ensure readers have that knowledge even if the source text is slightly obscure. Jeanette Winterson opens *A Gap of Time* with a summary of Shakespeare's *A Winter's Tale*, which is her source. Though Shakespeare is probably the most firmly rooted member of the English canon, *A Winter's Tale* is not one of his better-known works, and without the summary, Winterson could have expected many of her readers to take the novel as a stand-alone work and, as a result, they would have found its plot strange and perhaps a little forced. The power of the novel (and it does have power) stems from the very fact that it responds to one of Shakespeare's "problem plays," and the bizarre twists of plot stem from the novel's source in a stage tradition that was much less reluctant to suspend disbelief. Only by comparison with Shakespeare does Winterson's work seem remarkably naturalistic and believable.

Is the work canon compliant? This is a difficult question to ask as well as to answer, because if a work is fully canon compliant (that is, does not in any way contradict the events or characters of the original), it may be nothing more than a transposition, according to Wagner's categorization. But in practice, almost no retelling, adaptation, or other derivation is going to be one hundred percent canon compliant. Where the question becomes useful is in recognizing the shades and degrees of canon compliance in a reworking. Film and stage adaptations have been setting Shakespeare in the modern period and with modern costumes for so long that such a change feels hardly worth noticing anymore. Yet the point in making such a shift is to drive home the fact that Shakespeare is still relevant, and the concerns of his characters still touch our current world. AU canon fanfictions do the same thing; as discussed above, although "alternate universe" implies science fiction, it is in fact a broad concept applying to altering any aspect of the canon setting. The entire Hogarth Shakespeare series, of which Jeanette Winterson's *A Gap of Time* was the inaugural publication, is a collection of AU Shakespeare canon fanfictions whose purpose is to bring those concerns and themes into the contemporary world in a way that goes beyond what can be accomplished simply by staging the original play in modern costume.

Connected to the question of canon compliance is the issue of whether there is an identifiable path from the events of the fanfiction, which purports to be the "true story" we have not been told, and the original, which is the "corrupted story" we all know. *The True Story of the Three Little Pigs* by Jon Scieszka, because it is written for children, is probably the most familiar example of a work that provides such a path back to the original. The story, told from the perspective of the Big Bad Wolf, tells us "what really happened" while explaining how the nursery story we all know came about. The wolf wasn't out to eat the pigs; he came to ask for a cup of sugar. He wasn't trying to blow the house down; he had a cold that made him sneeze. We don't believe the unreliable narrator, of course, but the point is that he tells a story in which the events are given a completely different interpretation, yet nothing in those events significantly differs from the original tale. There is often a strong sense of irony, either humorous or biting, in telling a tale that claims to correct the inaccuracies of a story that has been a part of culture for decades or even hundreds of years.

Film provides a useful pair of examples that fall at opposite ends of the spectrum of canon compliance. In David Lowery's 2021 film, *The Green Knight*, audiences experience a version of *Sir Gawain and the Green Knight* that is almost unrecognizable as an adaptation of the fourteenth-century Middle English poem. On his journey to his rendezvous with the Green Knight, the Gawain of the film encounters headless saints, marauders, and a magic fox. All these adventures could conceivably have occurred to the Gawain of the original poem, which summarizes his journey by saying, "So many a marvel among the mountains the man found, it would be too difficult to tell a tenth part of them."[181] One might consider these additions to be "missing scenes" in fanfiction terms. However, Gawain's character bears no resemblance at all to the original, nor does the plot follow the same lines. Gawain turns from the pious and courteous "tulk" of the poem to a heedless, prideful, and promiscuous ne'er-do-well whose acceptance of the girdle against the agreement he had made with his host is not at all surprising. Nor is the ending of the film recognizable in relation to the original; whereas in the poem, Gawain has to be called out on the breaking of his word but then is spared by the mercy of the Green Knight, in the film Gawain gives up the girdle of his own accord, but we are left uncertain of what the Green Knight does with him afterward. There is no direct route by which the "true" story as retold by Lowery could have become the "corrupted" version we know from literature. That the film differs significantly from the original is not a mark against it; it is an artistic and meaningful production. But it is so far from canon compliance that it feels more properly like a reboot of the story with its own aims that are independent of the material that inspired it.

More interesting to me are the works that, like *The True Story of the Three Little Pigs*, offer an origin story not of their protagonist but of the original work itself. The 2007 film version of *Beowulf* is one such example. Although it suffers aesthetically from having been made during the short-lived craze for 3-D movies filmed using motion capture and CGI, the screenplay by Neil Gaiman and Roger Avery is as clever a piece of canon fanfiction as a *Beowulf* fan could wish for. One of those clever aspects is how the story told in the film "results" in the version we know from the epic poem. The film is a take-down of the heroic figure, depicting Beowulf as egotistical, lust-driven, and eager for violence. At first blush it is difficult to imagine this character turning into the politic, pious leader of men in the poem, but the film manages the transition by having Beowulf be the one who reports his adventures to his comrades. In the swimming match with Brecca, in which he does not kill all the sea monsters but makes love to one of them, Beowulf is alone; therefore, when he reports his deeds to Unferth (a canonical scene from the poem), his hearers have only his word on what happened. Likewise, in the underwater grotto, where he does not kill Grendel's mother but makes love with her too (he has a thing for aquatic creatures), he is alone again; therefore, when he reports the scene to Hrothgar (another canonical event), no one can second guess his depiction of himself

---

181 "So mony meruayl bi mount þer þe mon fyndez,/ Hit were to tore for to telle of þe tenþe dole" (ll. 718–19), author's translation.

as the slayer of monsters. This fact nicely accounts for why in the original poem, Beowulf brings Grendel's head back to Heorot rather than his mother's: in the film, she's not dead. The film drives home the hero-making business of storytelling by having an Anglo-Saxon *scop* (bard) performing *Beowulf* in Old English in the background of a feast scene. By making the connection between the "real" story and the "false" one we've all been told, the film both tips its hat to canon literature and deconstructs it, insisting with modernist cynicism that there are, in fact, no heroes, only fictions invented to make us hope there are.

What does the fanfic change, and what are the thematic effects of the change? One can ask questions about character and other features too, of course, but theme is often the most interesting subject of study. Students will immediately see in this question the setup for a classic compare-and-contrast essay: identify points of comparison and then analyze them. The analyses of selected canon fanfictions in chapter 2 go into this subject in some detail, so we will largely pass over this question here, but it is the question that lies at the heart of any source study.

This notion of comparison is also the question that sets the study of canon fanfiction apart from that of popular fanfiction. Fan studies often deal with fan behavior in the aggregate, while studies of fanfiction itself often focus on the fanfic text almost independent of the features of the source media it derives from. In other words, study of popular fanfiction tends to be forward-looking —what new thing is the author creating for what particular audience with what particular desires and needs?—whereas the study of canon fanfiction may be more backward-looking: how is this text responding to the specific concerns of the original in a new context? We have a cultural prejudice in favor of looking forward as opposed to looking backward, but if we are to be scholars of Classical, medieval, or Renaissance literature, we are destined to have the face of Janus, at once looking back toward the past and looking forward to where we want it to take us.

Are there risks involved in making the changes the canon fanfiction makes? Often addressing one problem in the original creates another in the fanfiction, like a battle against Hydra, or like a literary game of Whack-a-Mole. Jo Nesbø's retelling of *Macbeth*, for instance, explicitly addresses the issue of class in Shakespeare, pulling the lofty Thane of Glamis and Cawdor down off his usurped throne and casting him as an ambitious but corrupt police commissioner from the wrong side of the tracks. But, as we will see in section 2.1, because he is focused on class as a category in the novel, when he tries to figure out what to do with Shakespeare's gender-ambiguous Weird Sisters, Nesbø runs afoul of a different set of identities. This is not to say that a canon fanfiction that introduces one problem in solving another is without value, but this Hydra-like tendency of

literary problems does bear careful analysis just like any other aspect of literature.

What complexity of the original does the canon fanfic lose? Just as it is difficult to solve one problem without creating another, it is difficult to bring out one
under-noticed aspect of a piece of literature without sacrificing some other element of complexity. This is most evident in characters. Again film provides a
good example. In the *Beowulf* film discussed above, critiquing the nature of
heroism necessarily sacrifices some of the complexities of Beowulf in the original poem. In the poem, Beowulf is many things: a young man eager for fame, a
shrewd talker who takes care to protect the honor first of Hrothgar and then of
Hygelac and his son, and later on an old man who sacrifices himself for his people but who leaves them vulnerable because he did not take Hrothgar's advice to
learn the difference between a king and a hero. In the film, Beowulf is a sex-
driven brute. His complexity in the poem—and hence the many different themes
we can investigate in relation to that complexity—is sacrificed in the film in service of a single theme the filmmakers judged more important to its contemporary
audiences. Yet while we must admit that the canon fanfiction will often reduce
the original in focusing more sharply on one or two ideas, this is nothing
more than what literary criticism does: no one work of criticism can tackle
every aspect of *Beowulf*—historical, prosodical, religious, ethical, ecological,
etc.—nor would we want it to. Hence, just as there are always more works of criticism to be written in response to a single originating work, so there are always
more canon fanfictions that can be written about the same work by future authors.

What new complexity does the canon fanfic introduce? Although sacrifices are
often made for the sake of bringing out an underlying issue, equally often, canon
fanfiction introduces themes and concerns that are not present in the original
work. Only in the most oblique way could *King Lear* be called a work of ecocriticism, but much of the scholarship written in response to Jane Smiley's canon
fanfiction *A Thousand Acres* focuses on the environmental consciousness evident
in her retelling of *Lear*.[182] Likewise, while Margaret Atwood's *Hag-Seed*, a Hogarth Shakespeare retelling of *The Tempest*, shares many thematic concerns
with *The Tempest* (theater, retirement, revenge, love for a daughter), it is also
about education. Felix, Atwood's incarnation of Prospero, is a theater director
who ends up working with inmates in a Canadian prison. The attention paid
to how one might adapt Shakespeare for performance by minimally literate con-

---

182 See, among others, Hestetun, "Palimpsest of Subjugation"; Farris, "American Pastoral";
and Ozdek, "Coming out of the Amnesia."

victs, including the details drawn out for how student learning might be assessed and presented to policy-makers, goes well beyond the use of theater as a mirror for nature in Shakespeare. In fact, it looks more like the ruminations of a teacher (which, of course, Atwood is) than a response to Shakespeare's last play. In cases like these, the study of such canon fanfiction may grow into something that looks much more like the study of a stand-alone work.

Canon Fanfiction through the Lens of Identity Theory

The examples discussed in the preceding sections have implied the links between identity politics and the arts. In chapter 2, I explore examples of published canon fanfictions through the lenses of class politics and identity theory, ideas that the authors of those canon fanfictions have already consciously applied to their own work. The examples mentioned here, some of which I study in greater depth in chapter 2, demonstrate how canon fanfiction applies the cultural and theoretical movements of the second half of the twentieth century and beyond. Although any theory can be used as a lens through which canon fanfiction can look at canon literature, and through which scholars can look at canon fanfiction, the schools outlined below are the key lenses for fix-it lit in particular because they theorize the issues we most often find problematic in literature of the past.

Marxism: class politics is the grandfather of identity politics. Marxist theory is the school of thought that focuses on power structures as they relate to economics and labor. Turning the critical gaze from kings, queens, and nobility as the model protagonist, Marxism demands to see the proletariat, the worker, the lower classes. For example, Jane Smiley's novel *A Thousand Acres*, mentioned above, recasts King Lear as a despotic farmer in mid-century Iowa. Likewise, Jo Nesbø's *Macbeth*, in addition to turning Shakespeare's play of a royal usurper into a mid-century crime thriller, also makes the protagonist a working-class drug addict. The result is two novels that insist, like Arthur Miller's *Death of a Salesman*, that workers contain within them the same seeds of cosmic tragedy as kings and queens.

Feminism: the earliest school of identity theory, feminism, as its name suggests, focuses on the experiences of women in a patriarchal world. This is an exceedingly common approach in canon fanfiction. Madeline Miller's *Circe*, Pat Barker's *Silence of the Girls*, and Margaret Atwood's *Penelopiad* are just three instances of professional authors wrenching the androcentric world of the *Iliad* and the *Odyssey* out of the hands of male protagonists and seeing the former heroes through the eyes of the epics' women. The feminist drum has been beaten for so long that consumers of literature may grow weary of the sometimes-predictable exposé of patriarchal injustices, but as women in the real world still have not achieved parity in employment, pay, or human rights, there would seem to be some justification in continuing to beat the drum.

Queer Theory: building in part on the insights of feminism, queer theory destabilizes the heteronormative worldview and insists both on the existence and the importance of queerness in the arts as well as in human history. By queer, we often mean lesbian, gay, bisexual, transgender, intersex, or asexual (the terms that give us the acronym "LGBTQIA"), but the plus sign often added to the end of the list is a reminder that any number of other identities, including ones that do not fit easily into any category, can fall under the umbrella of "queer." Though the field itself is vast, canon fanfiction that deals with queerness often takes the most obvious form of reading canon characters as lesbian or gay. Madeline Miller reads Homer's Achilles and Patroclus as gay in *Song of Achilles,* and in a less obvious move, Jeanette Winterson's *A Gap of Time* interprets the emotional immaturity of Leontes in Shakespeare's *Winter's Tale* as stemming from his suppressed feelings for Polixenes. Kim Zarins, in *Sometimes We Tell the Truth*, retells Chaucer's sexually ambiguous Pardoner as a gay intersex teenager, recuperating his character for a generation more attuned to the importance of difference than Chaucer was.

Postcolonial and Critical Race Theory: if feminism opened the door to paying attention to women in literature and queer theory opened the door to paying attention to gay people, postcolonial and critical race theory opened the door to paying attention to people of color. The roots of postcolonial theory lie in the era when former French, British, and Spanish colonies gained their independence from their European occupiers and discovered that, despite their newfound freedom, their culture had been forever altered by being colonized. Postcolonial readings of literature, then, focus on how European powers affect—generally for the worse—the indigenous populations of occupied lands, both during and after the colonial period. Critical race theory is more American-focused, stemming from racial situations that are not unique to the United States but loom large in its history and current culture. Critical race theory, which has entered common parlance since the rise of the Black Lives Matter movement, developed in relation to the specific racial situation in the United States, but its insights have so far been applied primarily to historical, legal, and sociological subjects rather than literary ones, at least within the academy. Canon fanfiction that takes a race-focused approach is plentiful in response to later literature: Nancy Rawles's *My Jim* is a feminist, race-conscious response to *Huckleberry Finn*, Alice Randall's *The Wind Done Gone* is the same for *Gone with the Wind*; even *Pride and Prejudice* has been reimagined as a story of black American teenagers in

Ibi Zoboi's *Pride*. Perhaps because the audience for Classical, medieval, and Renaissance literature continues to be predominantly white, and perhaps because race tends to come less to the forefront of such works, examples are less plentiful in canon fanfiction of these earlier texts.

One example, however, would be Aimé Césaire's 1969 play *Une Tempête*, which established a postcolonial reading of Shakespeare's *Tempest* with Caliban as an indigenous person robbed of his land and oppressed by a colonizing Prospero. In Lanier's analysis, "With its references to the ghetto and Malcolm X, Césaire's adaptation resituates Shakespeare's play within the contemporary aftermath of the colonialism Shakespeare seems to endorse, and it provides a distinctively African voice and culture, a full-fledged cultural alternative to Prospero's European way of life, that Shakespeare's play denies Ariel and Caliban."[183] Césaire's reading has deeply influenced adaptations of the play, including Julie Taymor's 2010 film version, and further novelizations like Margaret Atwood's *Hag-Seed*. A more recent example would be Howard Jacobson's *Shylock Is My Name*, a postmodernist response to the antisemitism in *Merchant of Venice*. Although Jewishness is not a racial category by the usual definition, it was understood in what we would recognize as racial terms from the Middle Ages onward,[184] and Jewish identity is included among the subjects covered by critical race studies.[185] Novelists and playwrights alike have also tackled the race questions of *Othello*, as is done, for instance, in Toni Morrison and Rokia Traoré's *Desdemona* and Tracy Chevalier's *New Boy*.

Trauma Studies originates in the theories of psychoanalysis, though it has expanded to include a number of other approaches, psychological, sociological, and identity-based. Although psychological research into the connection between trauma and identity is limited,[186] it is difficult to deny that survival of trauma can become a central aspect of personal self-image, and so trauma is not without a place as an identity category. As the name suggests, it is concerned with the experience of and response to traumatic events, primarily individual but also collective, like colonization or genocide. Consciousness of individual trauma is a particular mark of the fanfiction community, and in this way, fandoms work in synch with or even in advance of academic discourse. Tumblr, AO3, fanfic.net, and other sites frequented by fans have a robust culture of trigger warnings, which, though they are still debated in academic settings, are intended within the fandom to enable consumers to avoid or at least be fore-

---

183 Lanier, *Shakespeare and Modern Popular Culture*, 47.
184 See Heng, *Invention of Race*, 55–109.
185 See Rubin, "Hebcrit."
186 See Truskauskaite-Kuneviciene et al., "Does Trauma Shape Identity?"

warned about content that may cue trauma responses like anxiety or panic attacks. While trauma is often implied in characters' backgrounds in canon fanfiction, however, not as many professional authors have engaged it head-on as a guiding principle for their work. Two who do are Kazuo Ishiguro, whose Arthurian spinoff, *The Buried Giant*, centers on collective repression and recovery of traumatic memory, and Maria Dahvana Headley, whose reimagining of *Beowulf* recasts Grendel's mother as a twenty-first-century war veteran with PTSD.

Disability Studies originates in sociology and is invested in understanding the concept of "disability" as a medical and/or social construct and in advocating, like the other fields of identity politics, for the rights and wellbeing of disabled people, however that term is understood. Although disability studies and trauma studies would seem to overlap, practitioners have not made a habit of combining them.[187] Very few canon fanfictions take disability studies as their foundational principle, though the source literature is rife with potential material. From blind gods and poets to amputees and madmen, the traditional Western canon is filled with bodies and minds marked with difference. Scholarship has made inroads in this direction, particularly as mental illness has gradually come to fall under the umbrella of disability. Paula Leverage interprets Chretien de Troyes's Perceval as autistic,[188] while Elizabeth J. Donaldson reads the madness of *Jane Eyre*'s Bertha Mason not as a symbol of feminine rebellion against oppression but rather—or also—as a disability independent of Bertha's own will.[189] But no one to my knowledge has yet attempted to engage deeply in disability theory through canon fanfiction. The best example of which I am aware is *Flint and Silver*, one of John Drake's three prequels to *Treasure Island*, in which he not only narrates the process by which Long John Silver loses his leg but explores to some extent how that loss affects his identity and his interactions with the nondisabled men he sails with. The subject of disability is, however, a minor subplot in a story invested in other things. This is why I use disability studies as the lens for my case study in chapter 3: to provide (for myself as well as for others) an experiment in engaging deliberately in the subject of physical difference.

Intersectionality is a simple concept with far-reaching implications. The term refers to the overlapping of identity categories either in life or in literature, and the theory seeks to explore the interaction between those categories: how is a woman's experience of the world different if she is also black? How is a gay

---

187 See Berger, "Trauma without Disability."
188 Leverage, "Is Perceval Autistic?," though also see Terje Falck-Ytter and Sofia Loden, "The Perils of Suggesting Famous Historical Figures Had Autism."
189 Donaldson, "The Corpus of the Madwoman."

man's experience made more complex if he also has a disability? As one might expect from these questions, the answers reveal that the result of combination is always greater than the sum of its parts. Although popular fanfiction furnishes occasional examples (there are, for instance, at least seventeen fics on AO3 in which Harry Potter is recast as both female and black),[190] professional canon fanfictions tackle the complex issue less often. This is not to say that they never depict characters who are more than one thing, but the tendency is to focus on one identity category as thematically central and treat the other(s) as background. Chapter 3 offers an example of intersectional canon fanfiction based on medieval Icelandic literature, although as the author I can say that I did not set out to write it that way; I meant initially only to deal with disability. Intersectionality found its way into my work simply through the inescapable circumstances of the source texts: the characters with disabilities whom I was rewriting also happened to be women.

Ecocriticism is not properly a subgenre of identity politics. It is, however, deeply political in addition to being philosophical and may therefore logically claim a place here. Ecocriticism has a long history in other forms before it finally takes on the name, but in essence it is the study of the natural world and human relationships with it, particularly in light of the threat the latter pose to the former. While the theory itself is a branch of posthumanism, ecological thinking is deeply felt in literature from the industrial era on—from Tolkien's Ents all the way back to the Romantic poets, mourning with Wordsworth that "little we see in nature that is ours." And, of course, ecocritical scholars have explored the subject in much older works—within my own period of study, the approach has been applied to everything from *Piers Plowman* to the *Canterbury Tales* to *Sir Gawain and the Green Knight*.[191] And although the ecologically conscious undertones of Jane Smiley's *A Thousand Acres* have often drawn critical commentary, ecocriticism is hardly Smiley's dominant focus in that novel, and few other examples of canon fanfiction that I am aware of pay more than lip service to ecology. Perhaps the human-centric approach to fiction writing is partly to blame (the main point of ecocriticism is to think about something other than the human as the center of the universe), but the potential to create canon fanfics with an ecological focus is certainly there. One advantage ecocriticism has over the other fields discussed above is that anyone can feel they have a right to speak on the subject: a white, cis, het male will not be told he has no business

---

190 Data based on "Female Harry Potter" and "Black Harry Potter" tags, from April 16, 2022.
191 Respectively (as a sampling): Johnson, "The Poetics of Waste"; Rudd, "Being Green"; and Ralph, "An Animal Studies and Ecocritical Reading."

expressing opinions on ecology as he might when speaking about feminism or race. Ecology is something everyone has an equal stake in.

For students who wish to know more or who wish to apply a certain theoretical lens to their own canon fanfiction or their analysis of published works, Peter Barry's *Beginning Theory* offers a thorough but accessible overview of most of the above theories. He does not include critical race theory, trauma studies, or disability studies; Bennett and Royle's *Introduction to Literature, Criticism and Theory* does cover trauma theory and, though it does not mention critical race theory by name, includes a more wide-ranging discussion of race in literary studies.

The above examples should make it evident that canon fanfiction can think and function in ways similar to those of traditional literary criticism. It is true that most literary scholarship now does not tie itself explicitly to a single theoretical school as did scholarship of the 1980s and '90s, but neither do the above novels. *A Thousand Acres* may be Marxist in its focus on the proletariat and its economic ambitions, but it is also invested in feminism, ecocriticism, and trauma theory. It is more the form—creative rather than academic—that divides canon fanfiction from literary criticism, and as a result, the novels above actually encourage *further* engagement than scholarly articles. While a scholarly article aims at clear and thorough explication of its subject, a novel that explicates its theme in an obvious way fails as a novel and becomes propaganda. Canon fanfiction must trust its readers to do the work of interpretation themselves, and as a result, it opens the doors to further conversations by asking rather than answering the most important questions faced by the human community.

Examples of Published Canon Fanfiction

The list that follows is just a small sampling of published canon fanfiction of the twentieth and twenty-first century. The list could extend back into the Classical period with examples like the *Aeneid*, a canon fanfiction of the *Iliad* and the *Odyssey*, but I focus here only on comparatively recent examples. Canon fanfictions whose sources are Classical, medieval, and Shakespearean works are predominant because that is the focus of this book, but I have included examples from other periods as well. Aficionados of this kind of writing will no doubt find this list grossly inadequate and full of gaps; for instance, I have made no attempt to list the published canon fanfictions of *Pride and Prejudice*, which run into the triple digits. Instead, I have sought to identify works that are particularly intriguing or under-studied, and although the list leans heavily toward novels, I have also included a number of plays, short stories, and poems.

The intention of this list is to give a taste of the vastness of this genre, and to provide potential projects for scholars or students interested in engaging in its study. For enthusiasts who find that I have not included their chosen fandom in my list of source materials, a good starting point for discovering if that source text has inspired canon fanfiction is, oddly enough, Wikipedia. At the end of the entry on a source text (for instance, a Shakespeare play), many Wikipedia pages include a section titled "Adaptations," which lists not only film versions but also novelizations, non-authorial sequels, and other such examples of canon fanfiction. Further resources include lists by Toby Zinman and Jeremy Rosen.[192] Thus, a literature fan has a number of ready resources for identifying fanfiction of their favorite work, and if they discover that none exists, I would suggest they take that as an invitation to write some themselves.

Table 2: Examples of Published Canon Fanfiction

Source	Canon Fanfiction	Author	Year	Form
1984	*1985*	György Dalos	1983	novel
Aeneid	*Lavinia*	Ursula Le Guin	2009	novel
Alice in Wonderland	*Alice*	Christina Henry	2015	novel
Alice in Wonderland	*After Alice*	Gregory Maguire	2016	novel
Beowulf	*Eaters of the Dead*	Michael Crichton	1976	novel
Beowulf	*Grendel*	John Gardner	1989	novel
Beowulf	*Mere Wife*	Maria Dehvana Headley	2018	novel
Beowulf	"Grendel's Mom"	Benjamin Cutler	2019	poem
Bible (Dinah)	*The Red Tent*	Anita Diamant	1997	novel
Bible (Gospels)	*The Last Temptation of Christ*	Nikos Kazantzakis	1955	novel
Bible (Noah's Ark)	"The Stowaway"	Julian Barnes	1989	short story
Canterbury Tales	"Wife of Bafa"	Patience Agbabi	2000	poem
Canterbury Tales	*Sometimes We Tell the Truth*	Kim Zarins	2016	novel

---

192 Zinman, *Replay*, 253–57; Rosen, *Minor Characters*, 187–90.

Table 2: Examples of Published Canon Fanfiction *(Continued)*

Source	Canon Fanfiction	Author	Year	Form
Christmas Carol	*Marley's Ghost*	Mark H. Osmun	2000	novel
Dr. Jekyll and Mr. Hyde	*Mary Reilly*	Valerie Martin	2001	novel
Great Expectations	*Jack Maggs*	Peter Carey	1997	novel
Hamlet	*Rosencrantz and Guildenstern Are Dead*	Tom Stoppard	1966	play
Hamlet	*Fortinbras*	Less Blessing	1991	play
Hamlet	"Gertrude Talks Back"	Margaret Atwood	1992	short story
Hamlet	*101 Reykjavik*	Hallgrímur Helgason	1996	novel
Hamlet	*The Prince of Denmark*	Graham Holderness	2002	novel
Hamlet	*The Story of Edgar Sawtelle*	David Wroblewski	2008	novel
Hamlet	*Gertrude and Claudius*	John Updike	2012	novel
Hedda Gabler	*The Further Adventures of Hedda Gabler*	Jeff Whitty	2008	play
Henriad	*Falstaff*	Robert Nye	2012	novel
Huckleberry Finn	*My Jim*	Nancy Rawles	2005	novel
Huckleberry Finn	*Finn*	Jon Clinch	2008	novel
Iliad	*Cassandra*	Christina Wolf	1983	novel
Iliad	*Ransom*	David Malouf	2011	novel
Iliad	*Song of Achilles*	Madeline Miller	2011	novel
Iliad	*Silence of the Girls*	Pat Barker	2018	novel
Isle of Dr. Moreau	*The Madman's Daughter*	Megan Shepherd	2013	novel
Jane Eyre	*Wide Sargasso Sea*	Jean Rhys	1966	novel
Jane Eyre	*The Wife Upstairs*	Rachel Hawkins	2021	novel
King Arthur	*Camelot*	Alan Jay Lerner and Frederick Loewe	1960	play
King Arthur	*The Once and Future King*	T. H. White	1965	novel
King Arthur	*Mists of Avalon*	Marion Zimmer Bradley	1983	novel

Table 2: Examples of Published Canon Fanfiction *(Continued)*

Source	Canon Fanfiction	Author	Year	Form
King Arthur	*Guinevere* trilogy	Rosalind Miles	1999– 2000	novel series
King Arthur	*Buried Giant*	Kazuo Ishiguro	2015	novel
King Lear	*A Thousand Acres*	Jane Smiley	1991	novel
King Lear	*Dunbar*	Edward St. Aubyn	2017	novel
"Lady with the Pet Dog" (Chekhov)	"Lady with the Pet Dog"	Joyce Carol Oates	1972	short story
Laxdæla saga	*Fire in the Ice*	Dorothy James Roberts	1961	novel
Laxdæla saga	*Hush: An Irish Princess' Tale*	Donna Jo Napoli	2002	novel
Little House on the Prairie	*Caroline: Little House, Revisited*	Sarah Miller	2017	novel
Little Women	*March*	Geraldine Brooks	2005	novel
Madama Butterfly	*M. Butterfly*	D. H. Hwang	1988	play
Medea	*Medea: A Modern Retelling*	Christina Wolf	1998	novel
Merchant of Venice	*Shylock Is My Name*	Howard Jacobson	2016	novel
Moby Dick	*Ahab's Wife: Or, the Stargazer*	Sena Jester Naslund	2005	novel
Nutcracker	*Hiddensee: A Tale of the Once and Future Nutcracker*	Gregory Maguire	2017	novel
Odyssey	*The Penelopiad*	Margaret Atwood	2005	novel
Odyssey	*The Lost Books of the Odyssey*	Zachary Mason	2011	novel
Odyssey	*Circe*	Madeline Miller	2018	novel
Othello	*Desdemona: A Play about a Handkerchief*	Paula Vogel	1987	play
Othello	*Goodnight Desdemona (Good Morning Juliet)*	Anne MacDonald	1990	play

Table 2: Examples of Published Canon Fanfiction *(Continued)*

Source	Canon Fanfiction	Author	Year	Form
Othello	*A Walking Fire*	Valerie Miner	1994	novel
Othello	*Desdemona*	Toni Morrison and Rokia Traore	2012	play
Othello	*I, Iago*	Nicole Galland	2012	novel
Othello	*New Boy*	Tracy Chevalier	2017	novel
Othello, among others	*Desdemona, If Only You Had Spoken*	Christine Brückner	2008	monologues
Peter Pan	*Lost Boy*	Christina Henry	2017	novel
Pygmalion	*My Fair Lady*	Alan Jay Lerner and Frederick Loewe	1956	play
Raven	"Small Blue Thing"	Madison Smartt Bell	2000	short story
Robinson Crusoe	"Crusoe in England"	Elizabeth Bishop	1971	poem
Robinson Crusoe	*Foe*	J. M. Coetzee	1986	novel
Romeo and Juliet	*West Side Story*	Arthur Laurents, Leonard Bernstein, Stephen Sondheim	1957	play
Room with a View	*Sex and Vanity*	Kevin Kwan	2020	novel
Taming of the Shrew	*Kiss Me, Kate*	Bella and Samuel Spewack, Cole Porter	1948	play
Taming of the Shrew	*Vinegar Girl*	Anne Tyler	2016	novel
Tempest	*Une Tempête (A Tempest)*	Aimé Césaire	1969	play
Tempest	*Indigo*	Marina Warner	1992	novel
Tempest	*Hag-Seed*	Margaret Atwood	2016	novel
Tempest	"By Inch-Meal, a Disease"	Nabila Lovelace	2020	poem
Treasure Island	*Silver: Return to Treasure Island*	Andrew Motion	2012	novel
Tristan and Isolde	*The Enchanted Cup*	Dorothy James Roberts	1953	novel
Tristan and Isolde	*Twilight of Avalon* trilogy	Anna Elliott	2009–2011	novel series

Table 2: Examples of Published Canon Fanfiction *(Continued)*

Source	Canon Fanfiction	Author	Year	Form
Völsunga saga/ Nibelungenlied	*Wodan's Children* series	Diana L. Paxson	1993– 1996	novel series
Völsunga saga/ Nibelungenlied	*Rhinegold*	Stephen Grundy	1994	novel
Völsunga saga/ Nibelungenlied	*Sigurd and Gudrun*	J. R. R. Tolkien	2009	poem
Winter's Tale	*The Gap of Time*	Jeanette Winterson	2015	novel
Wizard of Oz	*The Wiz*	Charlie Smalls	1974	play
Wizard of Oz	*Wicked*	Gregory Maguire	1995	novel
"Young Good-man Brown"	"The Man in the Black Suit"	Stephen King	1994	short story
Zorro	*Zorro*	Isabel Allende	2005	novel

Chapter 2
Fix-It Lit: Examples from Published Works

This chapter offers brief analyses of how a number of relatively recent works engage in the action of canon fanfiction—more specifically, of the "fix-it" genre, addressing problematic material in the original source text. Each is categorized under one of the theoretical schools discussed in chapter 1: Marxism, feminism, queer theory, postcolonial/critical race studies, and trauma studies. While none of these works can be reduced to being *simply* about any one of those theories, and indeed many of them touch on more than one, each offers a response to their source texts that can usefully be viewed through one of those critical lenses.

A word should be said about the selection of the below examples. Although fix-it texts abound in response to nineteenth- and twentieth-century literature, I limit my analyses to canon fanfictions that take Classical, medieval, or Shakespearean texts as their source, partly because I have training in premodern literature and partly because these are often the most remote-feeling texts to undergraduate readers. Most importantly, they are often the most likely to offend today's readers with their worldview, which is so different from our own. When professional writers respond to such works, they are at once keeping them alive by bringing them into the present day through modern language and characterization, and refusing to let the venerable authors of the past dictate our experience of their work. Each study provides an example of how professionals have done this work: earnestly, sometimes imperfectly, but always interestingly. Students of canon fanfiction can study these examples in their own right, as models of how we can talk about such work, or as inspiration for writing their own canon fanfictions.

With one exception, all of the texts in this study are novels. Toni Morrison and Rokia Traoré's *Desdemona* is a play, which I have specifically selected as a contrast to Tracy Chevalier's novel *New Boy*, which also takes *Othello* as its source. I have also limited my selection to works that have been published since the year 2000. There is no presentist prejudice underlying this choice; rather, canon fanfictions of the twentieth century (like *Rosencrantz and Guildenstern Are Dead*) have been studied rather extensively, and there is no need for me to duplicate the efforts of other scholars. The newer works have yet to garner such a large body of scholarship, and indeed, many of them will be unfamiliar to students, so that offering these brief studies may bring a younger body of work before the eyes of tomorrow's readers.

https://doi.org/10.1515/9781501515972-004

2.1 Marxism. The Double Tragedy of the Working Class: Nesbø's *Macbeth*

It is perhaps fitting to begin with Jo Nesbø's Hogarth Shakespeare retelling of *Macbeth* as a gritty crime novel because, like popular fanfiction, this example of canon fanfiction has been largely passed over by scholarship; although Nesbø's other work has drawn some critical interest, this novel has yet to be considered in a scholarly fashion. We will look at it here through a Marxist lens, highlighting the ways in which Nesbø "fixes" the ruling-class bias in Shakespeare by making the now-classic argument that tragedy is not the exclusive purview of "pompous plays, [with] incomprehensible dialogue and megalomaniac kings who die in the last act."[193] Indeed, Nesbø's work argues that the concerns of ordinary, working-class people draw the attention of the powers of chaos just as surely as rulers do, and the effects of their tragedies can be as communally devastating as those of Shakespeare's kings and usurpers. However, this novel also participates in the great paradox of Marxism: it at once demonstrates an optimism about the power of the proletariat and, in complete opposition to that ideal, expresses a sense of inevitability about class struggle. Ambition and the thirst for power just keep winning, both in individuals and in systems.

In Nesbø's *Macbeth*, the setting is an industrial city of uncertain geographical location in the late 1960s. The city's law enforcement is locked in a battle with two rival drug gangs: the Norse Riders, led by Sweno (who in the original is the king of Norway, Scotland's enemy), and a cartel run by Hecate (the goddess of witchcraft in the original, who in Nesbø's version has perhaps oddly been transposed as a man). Macbeth and Banquo are SWAT team leaders, while Duff (Shakespeare's Macduff) is the inspector leading the Narcotics Unit. Duncan is the chief commissioner and Lady Macbeth ("Lady" being her given name) is the owner of the Inverness Casino. As in Shakespeare's original, Hecate is really the prime mover of the conflict, but in the play, Hecate's three Weird Sisters approach Macbeth perhaps for no other reason than creating chaos. In Nesbø, however, Hecate maneuvers Macbeth first to take out his rivals, the Norse Riders, then to take out the greatest threat to his cartel, Duncan, with the intention of making a puppet of Macbeth as the new chief commissioner so that the cartel can carry on its business uninterrupted.

Although the supernatural elements have not been entirely stripped from the story, the main concerns of the novel are steeped in a gritty realism. This is a novel about working-class concerns: drugs, industrial pollution, ambition, and

---

193 Nesbø, *Macbeth*, 320.

corruption. Hecate's primary product is called "brew," a nod, of course, to the witches' brew in Act 4, scene 1 of the play. We discover that Macbeth is himself a recovering addict, having fallen into substance abuse after suffering sexual abuse and poverty as an orphan. In fact, Macbeth falls victim to Hecate's manipulation in part (though not wholly) because Hecate gets him to begin using again. Then, to strengthen his hold over him, Hecate offers Macbeth a new, more potent narcotic called "power"—a deliberately obvious allegory for what really drives Macbeth. For Marx, religion was the opiate of the masses, but for Nesbø, ambition is their drug of choice.

Industrial pollution plays a background role in this novel, but it is another aspect of poor and working-class experience whose double-sidedness is acknowledged by the narrative. On the one hand, Banquo's wife Vera dies of a lung complaint she first picked up working as a teenager in the city factory, which was then aggravated by the polluted air that the factory continued to pour over the town even after she stopped working there. On her death, Banquo recognizes that her death was a matter of economics: "[h]e hadn't been able to scrape enough money together to move the family [...] to somewhere with a bit of sunshine and fresh air you could breathe."[194] On the other hand, cracking down on industrial pollution proves to be almost equally devastating: Duncan closes the very factory that cost Vera her life, and it costs the city five thousand jobs. After Duncan's death and Macbeth's rise to power, a taxi driver comments, "Only some upper-class twit from Capitol could be so snobbish. Macbeth, on the other hand, is one of us. [...] Let Macbeth take charge for a bit and maybe people will be able to afford a taxi again in this town."[195] From an ecocritical point of view, the closing of the factory was an undoubtable victory for the environment; but from the Marxist perspective, it is not so simple, nor does the novel propose any solution to this impasse of priorities.

The taxi driver voices the very argument that convinces Macbeth, an idealistic reformer, that the murder of Duncan is in fact best for the city. He reasons to himself, "[W]hatever dreams Duncan had, the common people of the town wouldn't follow an upper-class stranger from Capitol, would they? No, they needed one of their own."[196] In many ways, Macbeth resembles Nesbø's most famous creation, Detective Harry Hole, who, like so many detectives of the gritty crime drama, is "the driven avenger out to right the wrongs of aggrieved communities at no matter what cost to themselves, and in so doing, re-weave the fractured so-

---

194 Nesbø, *Macbeth*, 79.
195 Nesbø, *Macbeth*, 303.
196 Nesbø, *Macbeth*, 106.

cial fabric."[197] Yet while Hole manages to carry on in his quest, whatever his failings and whatever damage he suffers personally, Macbeth almost immediately loses himself in the quest to move up the ladder. In the great irony of the novel, Macbeth realizes even in this moment before he kills Duncan that "power corrupts and poisons,"[198] yet he does not realize it will do to him exactly what it does to everyone else.

A thin ray of Macbeth's initial idealism shines at intervals in the narrative, illuminating that foundational Marxist dream of the proletariat rising up to overthrow the bourgeoisie. In place of the parade of Banquo's descendants in the play, representing the line of kings "stretch[ing] out to the crack of doom,"[199] in the novel Macbeth is confronted with a painting in Duncan's old office:

> It was big and showed a man and a woman, both dressed as workers, walking hand in hand. Behind them came a procession of children and behind that the sun was high in the sky. The bigger picture.[200]

Macbeth, though not yet far removed from his murder of Duncan, cannot "work out what it [means]."[201] Already he has lost touch with the worker in his quest to be the chief. And when he turns his back on the people, it is they, as much as Malcolm and his allies, who rise up against him in the end:

> [T]he crowd was made up of people with ordinary jobs in accounting offices and fire stations, who had never fired a shot in anger. Or been shot at. And yet they had come here. They were willing, despite their inadequacy, to sacrifice everything.[202]

In fact it is the people, not primarily Malcolm or Duff, who are responsible for fulfilling the prophecy that heralds the fall of Macbeth. The city has no wood, of course, so in this urban *Macbeth*, Birnum is an antique steam engine nicknamed Bertha, set up at the foot of Inverness Casino as a monument to industrialization. Hecate offhandedly tells Macbeth, "[O]ld Bertha will roll again before anyone can push you out of office."[203] And in the siege of Inverness Casino, the laborer and office workers who have come to fight destroy Bertha's concrete

---

197 Pratt, "Detective Harry Hole," 91.

198 Nesbø, *Macbeth*, 106.

199 Shakespeare, *Macbeth*, 4.1.117.

200 Nesbø, *Macbeth*, 284.

201 Nesbø, *Macbeth*, 284.

202 Nesbø, *Macbeth*, 425.

203 Nesbø, *Macbeth*, 207.

plinth and send the symbol of the Industrial Revolution smashing into the steps of Macbeth's stronghold.

Yet Nesbø, who, in addition to writing gritty crime dramas, trained as a financial analyst and lives in a Social Democratic nation,[204] cannot be rosy about the prospects of the proletariat in the face of unrestrained capitalism. For one thing, every attempt to displace the ruling class seems only to recreate it. Macbeth, the idealist, dreams of making things right, defeating the drug lords and corrupt officials, and making the city a place where people can live safely. Yet the minute he puts himself in a position to take action on behalf of others, he becomes capable of acting only for his own advantage. As in the play, he almost immediately begins ordering the assassinations of his former friends and allies, descending even to murdering Duff's wife and children in their home—a crime more heinous in the novel because the wife, Meredith, was once Macbeth's own sweetheart. In the end, he comes to argue for a sort of self-interested moral relativism, suggesting only half-jokingly that "corruption" be relabeled "pragmatic politics."[205]

Other characters also demonstrate the precarious nature of ethics when ambition is in play. Lennox, who in this version is the head of the Anti-Corruption Unit, is himself in the pocket of Hecate. He justifies his actions because they have given his family a house in a "safe neighborhood, where the kids hadn't got involved in any nastiness."[206] Yet it is a betrayal of duty that only encourages corruption to continue eating away at the social fabric of the city. Even ordinary middle-class aspirations like Lennox's lead to someone—in this case as in many others, the most vulnerable—being thrown under the bus. The proletariat doesn't rise; individuals rise on the proles' backs.

In fact, a general air of cynicism pervades the novel, from the unbending and merciless individuals to the broken and apparently unfixable larger system. Macbeth we have already seen in his moral decay; Lady accompanies him, as she does in the play, but on a different trajectory. From the beginning, she sees avarice as the primary human motivator, and the thing that allows her, the owner of a casino, to rule over her customers:

> [P]eople were like wet clay: they were shaped by opportunity, motive and what you told them today, and they could blithely do what had been inconceivable the day before. Yes,

204 "Biography," *Jo Nesbø*.
205 Nesbø, *Macbeth*, 333.
206 Nesbø, *Macbeth*, 310.

that was the only thing that was fixed, the only thing you could count on: the heart was greedy. Lady knew that. She had that kind of heart herself.[207]

As is typical of canon fanfiction, this novel delves more into the backgrounds of characters than is usual for the canon literature that inspires it, and Nesbø gives Lady a double-edged background that elicits sympathy for her and robs us of the ability to sympathize all at once. In the play, Lady Macbeth makes a mysterious reference to her child (who presumably has not survived into adulthood), and she taunts a waffling Macbeth by saying, "I would, while it was smiling in my face,/ Have pluck'd my nipple from his boneless gums,/ And dash'd the brains out" if she had sworn to do so.[208] Nesbø develops this hypothetical situation into actual backstory, in which a thirteen-year-old Lady is raped by her father and gives birth to a daughter, Lily, whom at first she defends from her violent parents but later decides to kill. In an inversion of the play, in which Lady Macbeth cannot murder Duncan because he looks like her father in his sleep, Lady dashes her baby's head against a wall when its face suddenly resembles her father's. The scenario, gruesome though it is, does elicit a certain amount of understanding for Lady's actions, but then the narrative immediately whisks it away again. Asked by her psychiatrist why she killed her child, she replies, "If you want to achieve your aims you have to be able to renounce what you love. If the person you climb with to reach the peak weakens, you have to either encourage him or cut the rope."[209] Infanticide is, in Lady's mind, a necessary step on the path out of poverty, the path to having "what everyone else has."[210] Even the discovery that Lady has worked lilies into the carpet patterns for Inverness Casino, essentially dedicating her achievements to the daughter whose death made them possible, is not enough to blunt the hard edge of her calculating character. Nesbø seems to see her as more emblematic of the novel's tragic story arc than Macbeth himself, because he gives the iconic "tomorrow" speech to her. Whereas Lady Macbeth dies offstage and without a last word in the play, in the novel her suicide note says, "Tomorrow, tomorrow and tomorrow. The days crawl in the mud, and in the end all they have accomplished is to kill the sun again and bring all men closer to death."[211]

The Macbeths, then, are simply intensified as the fallen figures that they are in the play, but Nesbø goes a step further to sully even the play's heroic figures.

---

207 Nesbø, *Macbeth*, 69.
208 Shakespeare, *Macbeth*, 1.7.57–59.
209 Nesbø, *Macbeth*, 280.
210 Nesbø, *Macbeth*, 279.
211 Nesbø, *Macbeth*, 409.

Duff has a much larger role in the novel than Macduff does in the play, but he comes off as no better than Macbeth in many ways. Aside from having an ongoing affair with his coworker Caithness (recast as a woman in the novel), he repeatedly tosses off one-liners that color his character as something of a psychopath. While torturing a Norse Rider into giving the police information, he observes mentally, "[E]ternal loyalty is inhuman and betrayal is human."[212] While debating Malcolm's apparent suicide with his coworkers, he claims that all people will ultimately pursue a logical course of action and that "[r]emorse is a sign of illness."[213] He seems to want to be better; before Macbeth murders Duncan, Duff is presented with a mission to eliminate Hecate, and he sees the charge as "slaying the dragon," an opportunity to begin "[l]ife as a different, better man."[214] He even admits that (at least as far as he knows) Macbeth is a better man than he is, for all his lawlessness and violence. As he observes to Caithness toward the end of the novel, "Macbeth's driven by love [for Lady] while I'm driven by envy and hatred."[215] But this judgment of Macbeth is not entirely accurate; as we have seen, Macbeth is driven as much by his own ambitions as by his love for his wife, and we can perhaps draw a conclusion about the usefulness of good intentions when we note that, although Duff does at one point talk himself into breaking with Caithness and renewing his commitment to his wife and children, his family is killed by Macbeth's forces before he can put those good intentions into action. In short, the world of ambition and corruption is a world in which there are no heroes.

Indeed, the odds seem stacked against equity or positive change as envisioned by Marxism or any of the social justice movements. Pratt's comment on corruption in the Harry Hole novels can as aptly be applied to this geographically ambiguous city as it can to Norway:

> [T]he scale and severity of the disorder that risks the Social Democratic dream [is ...] all-pervasive and unpredictable. Always already at its core, Oslo is a city, as are all our cities, poised on the edges of the corruption and capitalism that corrode our social heart, and the terrors that rip apart our dreams.[216]

---

212 Nesbø, *Macbeth*, 46.
213 Nesbø, *Macbeth*, 153.
214 Nesbø, *Macbeth*, 55.
215 Nesbø, *Macbeth*, 371.
216 Pratt, "Detective Harry Hole," 98.

Macbeth's city, not being a Social Democracy, is even worse off than Oslo; it is fully in the grips of an industrial capitalist system that sees people as tradable, disposable goods.

Nesbø demonstrates the bleak outlook of such a situation in his only use of the supernatural in the book. Whereas the play is steeped in spirits and hauntings, only one character in the novel is actually more than human, and that is Seyton, originally a member of the Narco Unit, later promoted as the head of SWAT, which becomes Macbeth's personal armed force. In the play, Seyton appears only near the end, bringing Macbeth the news of his wife's death and arming him for his final battle. Nesbø, however, playing on the fact that "Seyton" is a homophone of "Satan," makes him a constant presence throughout the novel. There are early hints that Seyton is preternatural: he heals almost immediately upon being shot in the arm, and when he goes sniffing after Duff "like an animal," Lennox gets the feeling he can "assume the shape of [...] [s]omething that wasn't human."[217] But it is only at the end of the novel that he reveals himself to be a demonic power. Macbeth, in one of his nobler moments, forbids him to shoot a young hostage, and in response Seyton turns on him. Macbeth invokes his famous prophecy in a unique way: "You're not born of a woman, you were made. Made of bad dreams, evil and whatever it is that wants to break and destroy."[218] In the end, Macbeth kills him with a dagger made of silver—the metal that traditionally slays werewolves and vampires.

While the slaying of demonic Seyton is a moral victory for Macbeth, it is a short-lived one: minutes later, Macbeth himself is killed by Duff, and although the story purports to end with the balance restored—the police back in order, Hecate and the Norse Riders destroyed, Duff determined to be a decent man professionally and personally—the final dialogue takes place between Jack Bonus, Lady's erstwhile croupier who fed Hecate information on the Macbeths, and an unnamed man we glean is Sweno, the leader of the Norse Riders. Bonus tells him,

> The town council and the chief commissioner have finally begun to lower their guard. Downsizing. The timing's perfect. The potential for new, young customers is unlimited, and I've also found the sister who survived when Hecate's drug factory exploded. And she still has the recipe. Customers won't have alternatives to what we can offer them, sir.[219]

---

217 Nesbø, *Macbeth*, 254.
218 Nesbø, *Macbeth*, 433.
219 Nesbø, *Macbeth*, 446.

In other words, the whole cycle is about to start again. The fact that Sweno wears a horned biker's helmet makes the allegorical nature of his character clear: the devil cannot be destroyed, and it will arise wherever there is opportunity. Even Duff, in his triumph, seems to realize this. In his moment of victory after killing Macbeth, he idly spins the wheel on a roulette table. When the ball stops rolling, it lands "[i]n the one green slot, which means the house takes all. None of the players wins."[220] Nesbø, then, reclaims the world of tragedy for ordinary people, but he does little—indeed, does less than Shakespeare—to assure his readers that there are bright spots to be had in the tragedy's aftermath.

A word should be said, however, about one way in which Nesbø's cynical and gritty approach to "fix-it lit" may in fact cause an additional set of problems. Nesbø's work has been accused of problematic content, particularly in relation to women; in the case of *The Son*, whose plot shares many elements with *Macbeth*, one review comments that the backstories of his female characters are "vestigial" and that the plot is "larded with violence."[221] Such socially uncomfortable material appears in his approach to adapting Shakespeare as well. First of all, the supposed hero, Duff, speaks in stereotypes about femininity and male-female relations: "[T]he heart is the woman in us. Even if the brain is bigger, talks more and believes that the husband rules the house, it's the heart that silently makes the decisions."[222] Caithness, the only female character besides Lady with a major role, comes off frequently as a vapid stereotype as well: when Duff refuses to leave his wife for her, citing the happiness of his children, she crumples into his arms, saying, "I'm crying because of my own hard heart. While you, you're a man with a real heart, darling. [...] Forgive me. And if I can't have everything, give me what you can of your pure heart."[223] Such hero worship and feminine self-loathing is very nearly cringeworthy.

Moreover, other characters' sexuality and race come into play in troubling ways. In the original play, the Weird Sisters are gender-ambiguous: Banquo observes of them, "You should be women,/ And yet your beards forbid me to interpret/ That you are so."[224] Nesbø's modernization of this motif turns Strega, Hecate's main enforcer, into a character coded as transgender, consistently referred to as a "man-woman." Jack Bonus, Hecate's informant, shows hints near the end of the novel of being gay: "Jack smiled and knew he held the newly employed

220 Nesbø, *Macbeth*, 440.
221 McDermid, "Review."
222 Nesbø, *Macbeth*, 146.
223 Nesbø, *Macbeth*, 191.
224 Shakespeare, *Macbeth*, 1.3.45 – 47.

boy's eyes a moment too long."[225] And the other two Weird Sisters, though not gender-ambiguous, are described as "Asiatic-looking,"[226] and it later comes to light that they are the originators of the recipe for brew. They are largely silent, taking orders from Hecate after having surrendered their recipe to him. Nesbø's sidekick villains, then, are coded trans, gay, and foreign in a stereotypically orientalist fashion (pliant, exotic, and linked inextricably to the opium trade).

Surely Nesbø would respond to objections to such depictions in the same way Murray Pratt does in response to Val McDermid's criticism of *The Son:* that "extreme violence, together with misogyny and other forms of discrimination and hatred, while featured within detective stories, do so, in exaggerated forms, as part of the plot's bid to represent the social disorder that must be eliminated."[227] But the problem is, as we have seen, that this novel does not make an argument for the elimination of injustice in society. If anything, it insists that injustice will inevitably continue. And if the novel takes tragedy out of the exclusive purview of the ruling classes and redistributes it among everyday citizens, it could be argued that by reinforcing these stereotypes and negative images, it, like Macbeth himself, is only perpetuating the very system it acknowledges to be flawed.

2.2 Feminism. How to "Fix-It" When It Can't Be Fixed: Miller's *Song of Achilles* and Barker's *Silence of the Girls*

In the original *Iliad*, Achilles is unambiguously the central figure. He is *Aristos Achaion*, "Best of the Greeks," the man on whom they place all their hopes of conquering Troy, yet at the same time he is a brooding, temperamental time bomb. First, he sulks in his tent over Agamemnon's confiscation of his war prize, Briseis, while the Greeks die in droves all around him. Then, when he launches back into action over the death of his companion Patroclus, he takes his revenge too far, not only killing Hector, the admirable prince of Troy, but dragging his body around the city behind his chariot and denying him proper burial for days on end. Ambiguous though he is, he remains the unquestioned center of the epic. However, the narrative attaches two slightly mysterious secondary characters to him who have drawn the interest of canon fanfiction authors: his best friend Patroclus and his concubine Briseis. Although Homer ex-

---

225 Nesbø, *Macbeth*, 398.
226 Nesbø, *Macbeth*, 64.
227 Pratt, "Detective Harry Hole," 98.

presses sympathy for each of them, they are never more than vague outlines standing in Achilles's shadow. Canon fanfiction writers from the Classical period right up to our present day have been compelled to revisit the Trojan War over and over again, and particularly in recent years, those shadowy secondary figures have taken central stage.

This present discussion will focus on the feminist approaches taken by two different novelists. I will begin with a discussion of Madeline Miller's 2012 *Song of Achilles*, whose primary point-of-view character is Patroclus, the young man who in Miller's retelling (and in many others) becomes Achilles's lover. Although the novel centers on male relationships, Miller does a great deal of narrative bending to make the characters and their experiences gentler than they are in the original; this includes Briseis and her life as a prisoner of war given to Achilles as a concubine in reward for his service to Agamemnon. On the other hand, Pat Barker tells her 2018 canon fanfiction, *The Silence of the Girls*, primarily from the point of view of Briseis herself, with full recognition of the brutality of her existence. Both are engaging in "fix-it lit" of different sorts: Miller's is more traditional in altering the facts of the original to show a little mercy toward Homer's suffering characters; Barker takes a different approach, emphasizing the suffering that Homer only acknowledges as a rhetorical device. But both of these novels, in their own and really quite opposite ways, acknowledge the one hard truth about canon fanfiction: we can retell Homer all we want, but in the end, he still exists, indelible no matter how we layer our own interpretations on top of his.

We know very little about Briseis from the *Iliad* itself. Although her name appears with some regularity throughout the work, it is almost always in the mouths of others, as Achilles and Agamemnon argue over who has the right to her. Achilles complains of the theft of "the prize the armies gave [him],"[228] and even when he claims her as his beloved wife, his possessiveness and self-centeredness suggest his protestations of love are nothing more than rhetorical posturing to justify his grudge against Agamemnon:

> Any decent man,
> a man with sense, loves his own, cares for his own
> as deeply as I, I loved that woman with all my heart,
> though I won her like a trophy with my spear ...
> But now that he's torn my honor from my hands,
> robbed me, lied to me—don't let him try me now.[229]

---

228 *Iliad* 1.466.
229 *Iliad* 9.413 – 18.

In fact, at this point Agamemnon has agreed to return Briseis, and if Achilles really loved her and not just his honor, he would not refuse her return as he does in this scene.

All we know of Briseis herself is that she is described as leaving Achilles's camp "reluctant, every step,"[230] and then she does not appear in person again until she sees Patroclus's body, his death completely overshadowing her return to Achilles in the care of Nestor and Odysseus. Here Briseis finally speaks in her own voice, calling Patroclus "dearest joy of my heart, my harrowed broken heart."[231] Now we rather belatedly learn her background: that she was married to a man Achilles killed in the sack of Lyrnessus, a battle that also took her three brothers. We also learn that, despite Achilles's protests to the contrary in Book 9, she is not in fact his wife. She says to Patroclus,

> [A]gain and again you vowed
> you'd make me godlike Achilles's lawful, wedded wife,
> you would sail me west in your warships, home to Phthia
> and there with the Myrmidons hold my marriage feast.
> So now I mourn your death—I will never stop.[232]

Given that they never sailed to Phthia and the Myrmidons never held a marriage feast—and given that she mourns Patroclus's death as the end of these hopes she had had for her future—we can reasonably deduce that she has never been anything more to Achilles than his sex slave. And so she remains; the last time her name appears is when, having finally granted Priam permission to retrieve and bury Hector's body, Achilles rests "with Briseis in all her beauty sleeping by his side."[233] He may have lost Patroclus, but he has regained his war prize.

Song of Achilles

Both Madeline Miller and Pat Barker gravitate toward the two satellites that orbit Achilles's star: Miller toward Patroclus and Barker toward Briseis. The first act of Miller's *Song of Achilles* is a Bildungsroman; the second and third acts are much closer to the events of the *Iliad* in terms of large-scale events, though as we will see, she deviates significantly from her sources in the causes of, motives for, and responses to those events. In other words, Miller purports to tell the "true story"

---

230 *Iliad* 1.412.
231 *Iliad* 19.339.
232 *Iliad* 19.351–55.
233 *Iliad* 24.794.

whose events have been misinterpreted by the canon version recorded by Homer. Unlike Barker, Miller's aim is not so much to oppose Homer as to bring him closer to readers, only in a more emotionally and ethically conscientious way. Asked in an interview why she wanted to retell the *Iliad*, she says, "I think right now a lot of people are weary of war, so it speaks to what is going on in the world. *The Iliad* is always waiting in the wings, ready for a new generation to discover it."[234] Her affection for the source text is clear. Changing the point of view from the epic narrator to that of Patroclus allows Miller to tell a story whose heart is personal relationships—and, as a result, she grants Achilles the air of a tragic hero, justifying or even altering his more problematic actions in favor of validating love in a world whose every circumstance mitigates against it.

On the surface, Miller's approach is more aligned with queer theory than it is with feminism. The greatest plot difference between Miller's version and Homer's is that she openly acknowledges the sexual relationship between Patroclus and Achilles, a subject on which, as Marco Fantuzzi explains in his analysis of Classical versions of the Achilles myth, Homer is either silent or just ignorant.[235] Although the erotic element in their relationship enters the poetic record in the Classical period, Aeschylus's fragmentary *Myrmidons* from the fifth century B.C.E. being the earliest surviving witness,[236] Homer gives no direct admission that the two characters are lovers. Nevertheless, once one becomes aware of the possibility of a relationship between Achilles and Patroclus, the notion almost inevitably enters a reader's "head canon" and influences their interpretation of the text from that moment on. In other words, as Fathallah points out, "Fanfic inflects and alters statements from the source text through reiteration with variation, using hints, lines and references to create alternative explanations and expansions, which are then read back onto the source text."[237] That is, even though Miller is following Aeschylus rather than Homer by engaging in the popular fanfic practice of m/m (male/male) shipping, we cannot help but layer that relationship back over Homer's text, like a palimpsest.

However, Miller's aim is not titillation or the pleasure of transgressing authorial taboos but rather to examine what a committed gay relationship might look like in a militarized society in which sex between males was permitted but the relationship treated as completely transitory. Fantuzzi makes the point that Aeschylus's depiction of the Patroclus/Achilles relationship may not so

---

234 Goldenberg, "*PW* Talks with Madeline Miller," 56.
235 Fantuzzi, *Achilles in Love*, 3.
236 Fantuzzi, *Achilles in Love*, 16.
237 Fathallah, *Fanfiction and the Author*, 31.

much have been a story about personal emotions but a depiction of a cultural practice which encouraged "[sexual] relationships among soldiers in order to stimulate reciprocal emulation" for the purpose of raising up better warriors.[238] For Miller, that is not enough: she resists this utilitarian element in her sources by envisioning the kind of committed relationship that we would recognize today.

She achieves this depiction by making the first act of the novel effectively a prequel to the *Iliad*. Still using references by Homer and stories from other Classical sources for events—like the fact that Achilles is trained by Chiron the centaur, or that he is forced to cross-dress by his mother Thetis in an attempt to hide him from Odysseus, who has been sent to recruit him for Agamemnon's army— she freely "in-fills" scenes from Patroclus's childhood and teenage years. She takes one detail from Homer, when a wounded Eurypylus begs Patroclus to heal him using "the powerful drugs they say you learned from Achilles/ and Chiron the most humane of Centaurs taught your friend,"[239] and adjusts the scenario just slightly so that Patroclus is schooled by Chiron directly, alongside Achilles. These teenage years provide both boys an education not just in weaponry and medicine but in sexuality.

The male sexuality in the novel, however, is in constant contact—and constant contrast—with the women in the narrative. In Miller's version, Patroclus's sexual expression stems partly from his natural proclivities, of course, but also partly from his observation of heterosexual relationships. Before he and Achilles ever admit their love for one another, Patroclus says, "I watched a boy fumbling at a girl's dress, the dull look on her face as she poured his wine. I did not wish for such a thing."[240] On the other hand, his first kiss with Achilles is narrated with the immediacy of present tense: "[m]y stomach trembles, and a warm drop of pleasure spreads beneath my skin."[241] In Miller's telling, both men are expected, even obliged to engage in sexual relationships with women, yet those relationships are always tainted by a culture that treats women as objects even when they are not slaves as Briseis is. In such a world, Miller implies, the only true human connection they can rely on is a homosexual one.

As a result, Miller's Achilles becomes a deeply sympathetic character, though not a flawless one. She turns his pride and his stubborn streak to positive effect when Odysseus reveals that he knows about the relationship between him

---

238 Fantuzzi, *Achilles in Love*, 222.
239 *Iliad* 11.993 – 94.
240 Miller, *Song of Achilles*, 59.
241 Miller, *Song of Achilles*, 63.

and Patroclus. Patroclus's instinctual reaction is shame and a desire to protect Achilles's reputation, observing, "Our men like conquest; they did not trust a man who was conquered himself."[242] However, when Patroclus suggests hiding their intimacy, Achilles scoffs, "The Phthians will not care. And the others can talk all they like. I will still be *Aristos Achaion* [Best of the Greeks]."[243] Achilles, in fact, is a sensitive man at heart, traumatized by the bloody sacrifice of Iphigenia,[244] and only his destiny and the martial talent he never asked for force him into the role of warrior. After his first battle, he tells Patroclus that fighting came naturally to him once he started, and he resigns himself to his role saying, "This is what I was born for."[245] Ultimately war itself proves to be the real enemy in this novel, robbing young lovers of the life they should have had together. When Ajax and Hector engage in single combat during Achilles's absence from the front, Achilles gets caught up in the news of their fight—and in excitement over the fact that the troops were whispering, "[I]t would not have ended so if Achilles were here."[246] At this point, when Achilles first "dreams of killing," Patroclus observes, "I cannot escape the feeling that, below the surface, something is breaking."[247] For their innocence and for their relationship, this is the beginning of the end.

Yet for all that male love resides at the center of the story, Miller is just as interested as Barker in feminist concerns. Miller, in fact, published another canon fanfiction of Homer six years after *Song of Achilles*, this one from the point of view of Circe, the enchantress who bewitches Odysseus's crew until she is cowed by Odysseus. In Miller's *Circe*, when she gets to tell her own story, the enchantress has a very different perspective on their interactions. Briseis is an important character in *Song of Achilles*, receiving more attention as a human being than Homer ever grants her. But because of her love of Homer and her abiding sympathy for Achilles, Miller cannot bear allowing Briseis to suffer as Homer does. Thus, her approach to "fixing" it is to portray Briseis's relationship with Achilles and Patroclus in largely—though not wholly—positive terms.

Achilles's claiming of her as a war prize is framed as a rescue: the captives are placed on a dais for distribution, and Patroclus sees Agamemnon eyeing Briseis. Patroclus says, "He was known—all the house of Atreus was—for his appetites. I do not know what came over me then. But I seized Achilles's arm and

---

242 Miller, *Song of Achilles*, 176.
243 Miller, *Song of Achilles*, 176.
244 Miller, *Song of Achilles*, 210.
245 Miller, *Song of Achilles*, 220.
246 Miller, *Song of Achilles*, 303.
247 Miller, *Song of Achilles*, 304.

spoke into his ear. 'Take her.'"[248] Agamemnon clearly resents Achilles claiming the girl he'd been interested in, giving him a motive for confiscating Briseis from Achilles later in the narrative. And despite the fact that it is difficult to imagine such a scenario historically, Achilles does not rape Briseis in this version; when she does not at first understand their language, Patroclus reassures her that she will not be raped by kissing Achilles in front of her.[249] This gesture seems to win her trust, though eventually Briseis confesses that she has fallen in love with Patroclus. If this moment were told from Briseis's perspective, it could potentially sharpen her role as a tragic character. Told, as it is, in Patroclus's voice, it instead serves to reinforce his unswerving devotion to Achilles and his certainty of his sexuality. When Briseis observes, "[Y]ou do not wish to take a wife," he simply replies, "No."[250]

In the epic, Briseis is the source of conflict between Achilles and Agamemnon; in Miller's novel, she is both that and the source of the greatest conflict between Achilles and Patroclus. Possibly because he has no intimate connection with her, when Achilles breaks with Agamemnon and the king demands Briseis in order to humiliate him, Achilles actually rejoices in the theft, telling Patroclus, "He will pay, now. [...] Let him come for her. He has doomed himself."[251] Patroclus, much the tenderer of the two men, is horrified at Achilles's betrayal of someone he has befriended, and his mind becomes "filled with cataclysm and apocalypse."[252] He immediately intervenes, following Briseis to Agamemnon's tent without Achilles's knowledge and warning Agamemnon that if he rapes Briseis, "the men will turn on [him ...], and the gods as well."[253] Agamemnon points out that Patroclus is betraying Achilles by interfering with their dispute, and Patroclus privately agrees: "Achilles has given Agamemnon a sword to fall upon, and I have stayed his hand."[254] Patroclus succeeds in preserving Briseis from rape, but again, what might in a different sort of narrative highlight Briseis's fear, relief, and continued suspense as to her safety, in Patroclus's point of view becomes another moment focused on his relationship with Achilles. Achilles's sense of betrayal is exactly as painful as Patroclus expects, but it has an unexpected ending, in that Patroclus takes the opportunity to argue that Achilles's reputation depends more on goodness than on violent acts like killing Aga-

---

248 Miller, *Song of Achilles*, 226.
249 Miller, *Song of Achilles*, 228.
250 Miller, *Song of Achilles*, 267.
251 Miller, *Song of Achilles*, 284.
252 Miller, *Song of Achilles*, 286.
253 Miller, *Song of Achilles*, 292.
254 Miller, *Song of Achilles*, 293.

memnon, which is what he'd been hoping to do. In the end, Achilles admits, "You are a better man than I."[255] It is a moment of anagnorisis that has everything to do with the hero and nothing to do with the woman; Briseis is only a means by which that anagnorisis can be brought about.

Despite the backbends Miller works into her narrative to save Briseis from the fate of a woman captured in war, the novel does not end with a blithe or rosy resolution for her character. Independent of any source I have been able to identify, Miller adds a scene in which Pyrrhus, Achilles's son, claims Briseis after his father's death. In the course of trying to explain to him that Achilles never slept with her, Briseis outs Achilles's relationship with Patroclus. Pyrrhus responds as many hypermasculine men have responded upon hearing such a thing said of a relative. He tells Briseis, "I will teach you what it means to lie to *Aristos Achaion*."[256] The fact that he applies his father's title to himself indicates how strongly he identifies with Achilles and, hence, how threatening he finds Briseis's assertions. When he threatens to reestablish his masculinity by raping her, Briseis takes a stab at him with a knife in self-defense and then runs into the sea to escape him. But Pyrrhus, with supremely cold calculation, fells her with a spear to the back, just seconds before she is beyond his reach. Miller, then, actually goes beyond what Homer tells us to give Briseis the same tragic end as Achilles (shot in the back by an enemy's weapon). Although she preserves Briseis from rape, she acknowledges by her death the inability to "fix" the epic by giving her character a happy ending; such a thing is unimaginable and unrealistic for a woman prisoner of war in the Classical period. However, the enemy in her adaptation is not Achilles, and even the death of the main female character comes about not as a result of anything inherent to Briseis but rather stems from the relationship between Patroclus and Achilles: Pyrrhus kills Briseis simply because he does not want to hear that his father was gay.

Silence of the Girls

Where Miller's humanizing of Homer's characters leads her to treat them more gently than the epic does, even if they nonetheless end as tragically, Pat Barker does nothing to soften the edges of her retelling of the events through the eyes of Briseis. Her "fixing" of Homer doesn't involve making the situation less painful for the characters; it involves acknowledging the characters' pain to its fullest

---

255 Miller, *Song of Achilles*, 296.
256 Miller, *Song of Achilles*, 359.

extent. When Briseis is given to Achilles, she is most definitely raped, saying, "He fucked as quickly as he killed, and for me it was the same thing. Something in me died that night."[257] She is simultaneously very aware of her status as an object in the eyes of those around her: "[H]e wasn't doing anything he didn't have a perfect right to do. If his prize of honour had been the armour of a great lord he wouldn't have rested till he'd tried it out [...]. That's what he did to me. *He tried me out.*"[258]

Yet she has to relearn that status repeatedly, thinking at first that "it made no sense [...] that the two most powerful men in the Greek army should fall out over a girl."[259] In her first observations of the conflict between Agamemnon and Achilles, she thinks she is the center of the dispute. Only when the men come to fetch her does she overhear Achilles complaining to Nestor that Agamemnon has claimed something to which he has no right. His statements echo in Briseis's head: "Honour, courage, loyalty, reputation—all those big words being bandied about—but for me there was only one word, one very small word: *it. It* doesn't belong to him; he hasn't earnt *it.*"[260] After the first night with Agamemnon, during which he both rapes and further humiliates her by spitting a wad of phlegm into her mouth, the king's only interaction with Briseis is to make her pour wine for his guests every night. Here, too, Briseis recognizes her status as an object: "Men carve meaning into women's faces; messages addressed to other men. [...] Here, in Agamemnon's compound, it was: *Look at her, Achilles's prize. I took her away from him just as I can take your prize away from you.*"[261] The situation is unchanged from Homer, except that in the *Iliad*, it is left to us to decide whether or not we believe Agamemnon when he swears to Achilles that he has not touched Briseis. But giving Briseis the ability to narrate the events drives home the humanity of these "objects" traded back and forth between the "heroes" of the epic.

Agamemnon is more or less an irredeemable character in Barker, but Achilles, though much darker and less sympathetic than Miller's version, is nevertheless a complex figure, whose dehumanizing behavior toward Briseis is perhaps all the more chilling because he is not wholly a monster but someone who looks like a real person. Barker has Briseis demur about the nature of his relationship with Patroclus, saying,

---

257 Barker, *The Silence of the Girls*, 24.
258 Barker, *The Silence of the Girls*, 24.
259 Barker, *The Silence of the Girls*, 95.
260 Barker, *The Silence of the Girls*, 97.
261 Barker, *The Silence of the Girls*, 107.

[P]erhaps they were lovers, or had been at some stage, but what I saw [...] went beyond sex, and perhaps even beyond love. I didn't understand it then—and I'm not sure I do now—but I recognized its power.[262]

In a move that is "exemplary of Barker's narrative method,"[263] the novel also shifts perspective at several key moments, into Patroclus's point of view, though Briseis remains the only first-person narrator. This shift confirms that our view of Achilles is not entirely biased by being filtered through the eyes of one of his victims. Patroclus, his best friend, compares Achilles in one of his famous paroxysms of wrath to "a toddler, purple with rage, screaming till he gasps for breath."[264] And when we shift into Achilles's own point of view, it is pointedly too late for us to care about his lingering pain over the loss of Patroclus, which comes off as self-centered and almost as immature as his rages: "Surely he ought to be better than this by now? He's done everything he promised, killed Hector, cut the throats of twelve Trojan youths and used their bodies as kindling for Patroclus's funeral pyre."[265] Yet Barker makes it impossible to dismiss him entirely. When he finally releases Hector's body to Priam, Briseis stows away on the cart bearing the body back to Troy, but then at the last moment, she decides to return to Achilles's camp. When she encounters Achilles, he reveals that he knew all along that she had stowed away. Rather than punishing her, as she expects, he shares a meal with her, and Briseis is left trying to parse what it all means:

> We ate and drank in silence, but I sense the atmosphere had changed. I'd tried to escape, but then—*for whatever reason*—I'd come back. He'd known I was in the cart and—again, *for whatever reason*—had been prepared to let me go. So this was no longer, straightforwardly, a meeting of owner and slave. There was an element of choice. Or was there? I don't know, probably a lot of it was wishful thinking—and I don't suppose for a second any of this crossed his mind.[266]

This odd interaction grants nuance to Achilles's otherwise rather blunt and blustering character, but more than that, it raises difficult questions about the mentality of a captive. Barker makes no effort to clarify for her readers what Briseis does not understand about herself: is she somehow content living with Achilles? Has she developed Stockholm Syndrome? Have she and Achilles reached some

---

262 Barker, *The Silence of the Girls*, 66.
263 Ward, "Erotohistoriography," 333.
264 Barker, *The Silence of the Girls*, 80.
265 Barker, *The Silence of the Girls*, 216.
266 Barker, *The Silence of the Girls*, 262.

kind of truce after he had blamed her for Patroclus's death? Is it even possible for a war captive to find contentment in her captivity, and if so, is it all right for us (who have never been war captives) to suggest such a thing? Barker is perhaps most famous for her World War I trilogy, *Regeneration*, in which she explores the alternate histories of countercultural groups whose stories "are at odds with narratives of national totality, now as well as then."[267] Her works of fiction reside in the space between the narratives we want to tell ourselves about the past and the narratives that can never be told because they are lost to time. As such, imagining the experience of a sex slave in the Trojan War is not a matter of describing certitudes; Barker gives Briseis words, but she does not speak for her. In war, as in life, motives are mixed and rarely are we certain why one thing happens instead of another. We can rejoice that Briseis has found a way to persevere in adversity, or we can be disappointed at her lack of gumption in the critical moment when she could have escaped; either way, Barker seems to insist, her actions are her own and she owes us no explanation.

It may feel unsatisfactory to leave Briseis in this limbo, not to see her give Achilles one good dressing down for his inhumanity toward her. In fact, Ovid does just that in his *Heroides*, when he allows Briseis to complain that Achilles fails to ransom her back when Agamemnon first offers her: she demands, "For what fault have I deserved to become worthless to you, Achilles?"[268] Ovid has her say some disturbingly servile things as well (begging him to take her back as a slave and defend her to his future wife by saying, "This, too, was mine"[269]), but Ovid was thinking of her as a spurned lover who could not overcome her passion, and he was nevertheless following the instinct we still have to give the wronged woman the opportunity to remind her oppressor of his crimes. Barker gives us no such cathartic moment. Instead, her version of Briseis ends by being married unceremoniously, a few hours before Achilles's death, to a minor Greek warrior named Alcimus, whom Achilles selects for a now pregnant Briseis because "he'll take care of the child."[270] Troy falls, we witness along with Briseis the horrible grief of Hecuba and the other royal women now enslaved by their conquerors, and in the end, Briseis sails away with Alcimus and the rest of the Greek fleet. If she feels "coarse, lumpen and degraded"[271] in comparison with Polyxena, who preferred to die as a human sacrifice than to live as a

---

267 Ward, "Erotohistoriography," 322.
268 "[Q]ua merui culpa fieri tibi vilis, Achille?" (Ovid, *Heroides*, 3.41, author's translation).
269 "[H]aec quoque nostra fuit" (Ovid, *Heroides*, 3.80, author's translation).
270 Barker, *The Silence of the Girls*, 277.
271 Barker, *The Silence of the Girls*, 290.

slave, she nevertheless professes, "I was glad I'd chosen life."[272] Once again, we are asked to confront the difficulty of what choice means to a slave, and if we think Polyxena made the nobler choice, still Briseis does not apologize for her own. Unlike Miller, whose Briseis ends with a spear between her shoulder blades, Barker lets her Briseis claim a happy ending. She declares as she leaves that "[o]nce, not so long ago, I tried to walk out of Achilles's story—and failed. Now, my own story can begin."[273] Barker's implied question for us as readers is whether we believe her.

The question is very much a real one: the narrative of the novel (at least the parts in Briseis's voice) is formulated as direct address to an unnamed audience, and on occasion, that audience intrudes into the narrative with the kinds of questions we, as twenty-first-century readers, would ask. When Patroclus tells Briseis, as he does in the epic, that he will get Achilles to marry her, the audience asks Briseis if she would really marry her brothers' killer. She answers, "Yes. I was a slave, and a slave will do anything, anything at all, to stop being a thing and become a person again." When the audience says, "I just don't know how you could do that," Briseis responds, "Well, no, of course you don't. You've never been a slave."[274] Such moments at once collapse the distance between readers and Briseis, by making us interlocutors with her, and throw into stark relief the gulf between us: we have never been slaves, nor lived in a world in which that was a commonly accepted state of being. The power of this literary device is in its ability to let Briseis speak across the distance of centuries, not to an anonymous listener but to "us."

The limitation of this approach—and it is surely a limitation Barker recognizes—is its patent artifice. When Briseis is first captured in Lyrnessus, Nestor tells the women to forget their past identities. Briseis's unspoken response is, "So there was my duty laid out in front of me, as simple and clear as a bowl of water: *Remember*."[275] The novel, then, purports to record the memory of this war captive, yet as we have seen, the point of view shifts to other perspectives because Briseis's voice alone is not sufficient to encompass the complexity of the narrative. The trick about retellings is that the audience will almost always know more about the story than the narrator can, putting us in a superior position to the one supposedly telling us the "true story." One of the refrains of the novel is "Silence becomes a woman," invoked for the last time in the final scene,

---

272 Barker, *The Silence of the Girls*, 291.
273 Barker, *The Silence of the Girls*, 291.
274 Barker, *The Silence of the Girls*, 83.
275 Barker, *The Silence of the Girls*, 18.

when Briseis resolves to let her own story begin.[276] Only that is where the story ends: if we are to imagine Briseis's life after she leaves the shores of Troy, we must invent it ourselves, because she has fallen silent.

In discussing *Double Vision*, another novel by Barker, Ashlee Joyce points out the potential ethical pitfall of presenting readers with a narrative of trauma, as indeed we are in *Silence of the Girls*, with the aim of fostering empathy with the victim: a side effect may in fact be a certain kind of voyeurism, or even the appropriation of another's pain, flattering our image of ourselves as more sensitive than other people.[277] In another vein, discussing the *Regeneration* trilogy, Ward says that "writing about or commemorating the war, and thus choosing what and whom to remember and how to remember it, replays the war's primary political maneuver [...]. To put it another way, the trilogy displays the discursive protraction of the war's enmity."[278] In other words, both of these commentators point to the double-edged sword that is writing about the past, even a fictional one. To write about a rape survivor is to risk losing sight of the survivor and instead flatter the audience with its own sensitivity; to write about war is to keep that war from dying, even to dredge back up its causes and animosities.

No one is going to suggest a sack of Greece in revenge for fallen Troy, but Ward does remind us what this current book set out to do: to preserve the old canon by giving it life in new forms. We must ask ourselves whether that goal is one we should be pursuing. The answer of Miller and Barker is clearly yes: Barker is willing to risk the voyeurism of depicting trauma, and both she and Miller see something in Homer that is worth keeping—or at least, worth talking back to. Rewriting Achilles through the eyes of his satellites, Patroclus and Briseis, indeed keeps him alive, but he is not the same demigod presented to us by Homer, and once we see him as Miller and Barker depict him, he will exist in our minds as a complex layer of differences, perhaps unresolvable into a single whole. But the murder of Briseis in Miller and her lapsing into silence in Barker remind us of the limitations of the canon fanfiction project: we can rewrite our literary past in any number of ways, but in the end, we cannot change what it already is.

In fact, both of these novels would present themselves as targets for Jeremy Rosen's objection, discussed in the introduction, that retellings that take an oppressed character's point of view "perpetuate the epistemological problem they endeavor to solve, contesting previous fictional narratives while posing accounts

---

276 Barker, *The Silence of the Girls*, 290.
277 Joyce, "Gothic Misdirections," 461–62.
278 Ward, "Erotohistoriography," 323.

that are equally subjective and open to contestation from another side."[279] Yet one might argue, as Miller and Barker undoubtedly would, that that is the very essence of retelling: to make us see, to acknowledge the subjective nature of human perception, even if doing so perpetuates that subjectivity rather than subverting it. And perhaps we should not want to change what it already is; to do so would be to erase the faults of the past and create a revisionist history that perpetrates its own injustices against the victims, real and fictive, of historical wrongs. Acknowledging the tragedy of Briseis is a way of "fixing" the original by honoring the suffering it mostly ignores, but it does not make Homer more aware of that suffering: it can only change us.

2.3 Queer Theory. The Pardoner Doesn't Need Pardoning: Zarins's *Sometimes We Tell the Truth*

Kim Zarins's little-known novel *Sometimes We Tell the Truth* is different from the other novels selected for study in this project for a number of reasons. First, it is written for and marketed specifically to teenagers rather than adult readers, and second, Kim Zarins is an academic by trade and has published an article analyzing her own work and placing it in the context of scholarly discussions of Chaucer. As such, the novel presents a unique opportunity to see canon fanfiction through the author's own eyes and analyzed in her own voice.

Most young people are introduced to the *Canterbury Tales* at some point during their high school years, and often they come away with a deeply negative impression, seeing Chaucer as outdated, dusty, and having nothing to do with them. Zarins's explicit purpose in retelling the *Canterbury Tales* is to revitalize a great classic of her field for a new generation, and she does this primarily by hitching Chaucer's wagon to the train of fanfiction. Although each tale could be usefully studied individually, I will mention just a few tales as examples of her approach. Then we will look at how Zarins "fixes" two of the most memorable characters in Chaucer's frame story: the Wife of Bath and the Pardoner. While her approach to the Wife is a "fix-it" in the vein of Pat Barker's *Silence of the Girls*, her approach to the Pardoner not only embraces a queering of the character but also talks back both to Chaucer and to the academics who have commented upon the Pardoner for the past fifty years. Zarins refuses to fall in line with theoretical academic discourse and instead insists on seeing the Pardoner as a fully embodied, and fully bodied, human being.

---

279 Rosen, *Minor Characters Have Their Day*, 107.

In Geoffrey Wagner's classification system, *Sometimes We Tell the Truth* is properly an analogy to Chaucer's *Canterbury Tales* because Zarins transports the collection to modern-day America, turning the pilgrims into a busload of high schoolers going to Washington, DC, for a field trip. A few of the characters retain their original names (the Franklin is called Franklin and the Wife of Bath keeps the name Alison), but most are renamed, often with a nod to their original persona. Hence, Geoffrey Chaucer becomes Jeff, the Cook becomes Cookie, and the Pardoner becomes Pard. One thing Zarins does is diversify the cast, turning some of Chaucer's male pilgrims into young women (the Man of Law becomes Sophie, for instance) and implying through names that a number of them are people of color (the Physician becomes Reiko, the Manciple becomes Lupe, and Alison's surname is changed to Chavez). Yet despite the dramatically altered setting, Zarins tackles the project with remarkable attention to the details of her source text, retelling or reinventing every single tale in Chaucer's collection, including the three unfinished tales. The *Cook's Tale* becomes a story told by Cookie the stoner, who falls asleep partway through; the *Tale of Sir Thopas* becomes a Mary-Sue (or rather Gary-Stu) story about a surfer dude that the listeners impatiently interrupt; the *Squire's Tale* becomes a wild Narnia spinoff whose teller so exhausts herself that she cannot continue.

Zarins does, however, allow herself very free rein with the stories themselves. While a few are clear retellings, many of them are only vaguely recognizable; she has to include a list of "dramatis personae" at the end of the book to make connections for baffled readers.[280] Sometimes these alterations are related to her project of plugging Chaucer into the world of fandom, but in one very noticeable instance, the alteration of a tale is certainly an act of protest. The *Prioress's Tale* is a disturbing story of a Christian child martyred by Jews incited by Satan, who "hath in Jues herte his waspes nest."[281] It is difficult to imagine how one could "fix" this blatantly antisemitic story while still retaining any recognizable element of the original. So Zarins does not try to: she swaps it out for an obviously unrelated story about a boy finding the twin he never knew he had. In this case, Zarins's silence on Chaucer's tale is a speaking silence: it says that there are some things better left in the past.

The rest of the novel, however, makes the opposite argument, seeking to recapture the fascination the *Canterbury Tales* had for its early audiences. Zarins's academic training is in medieval studies, and her explicit aim in writing her novel is to bring Chaucer closer to her target audience of young adults who

---

280 Zarins, *Sometimes We Tell the Truth*, 431–32.
281 Chaucer, *Canterbury Tales*, *Prioress's Tale*, l. 559.

might encounter him in school but probably won't like him. She doesn't mention Chaucer in the title, and that is probably because, unlike Mr. Darcy or Sherlock Holmes, the subjects of much popular as well as canon fanfiction, Chaucer's name is more likely to drive young readers away than to draw them in. Instead, she signals her investment in Chaucer by giving a lengthy and interesting afterword about how her work connects with Chaucer's.

In this afterword, she points out that she chose the style of her tales with a purpose. Several of the stories are explicitly fanfiction: the *Franklin's Tale*, about a rash promise and a tricky but ultimately honorable magician, becomes a *Harry Potter* fanfic, in which the protagonist is a Hogwarts student and the magician is none other than Severus Snape. The *Nun's Priest's Tale*, the familiar beast fable of the rooster and the fox, is set in the barnyard of *Charlotte's Web*, so that Wilbur the pig and Templeton the rat become commentators on the action. Zarins's afterword makes a pointed connection between premodern storytelling and fanfiction: "like a proto-fanfiction culture, [medieval readers] had something like a passion for retellings."[282] As noted in chapter 1, Chaucer himself has been retold many times; yet Zarins notes that Chaucer's own sources (Boccaccio, Aesop, Ovid) don't have the cultural capital that they once did. While it is true that Boccaccio and *Harry Potter* are not in all ways parallel—for instance, Boccaccio wrote for an adult, educated, and comparatively elite audience—Zarins argues that, foundationally, both Chaucer and popular fanfiction writers retell and refer to stories that are familiar to their readers; she says, "If Chaucer were a teenager writing today, he'd likely pull from culturally known material to make his own stories."[283] Taking Chaucer's liberty with his sources as permission to deviate from her own, she nevertheless insists, "Chaucer's version and its borrowings are right there underneath, to give modern readers this same layered encounter of a tale retold."[284] Indeed, this approach is a better way to replicate a premodern reading experience than if she had simply transposed the stories into modern prose because, unlike Aeschylus and Statius, the pop culture referents in Zarins are familiar (at least for now) to her target audience. It is true that the ephemeral nature of pop culture may give her work a shorter shelf life than less topical works, but that would, presumably, simply invite future readers to update Chaucer again with their own works of canon fanfiction.

---

282 Zarins, *Sometimes We Tell the Truth*, 426.
283 Zarins, *Sometimes We Tell the Truth*, 426.
284 Zarins, *Sometimes We Tell the Truth*, 427.

Alison's Prologue and Tale

Aside from her treatment of the *Prioress's Tale*, we have so far only seen how Zarins pays homage to Chaucer's landmark story collection. But she is also invested in talking back to Chaucer, "fixing" problems he either does not realize exist or, like Homer and the abuse of Briseis, does not sufficiently address. Zarins's retelling of the *Wife of Bath's Prologue* and *Tale* serves as an example of how she uses the modernized setting to shed light on the most troubling aspects of Chaucer's original. Zarins's Alison is instantly recognizable as Chaucer's Alisoun, or the Wife of Bath: gap-toothed, confident, and hypersexual, she is a commanding presence throughout the novel. Jeff, the narrator, says in introducing her, "[S]he's the only girl who has ever grabbed my ass."[285] In Chaucer's original, her prologue provides her autobiography, focusing on the marriages she has been in "sith [she] twelve yeer was of age."[286] This was a fairly young age for a merchant-class girl to be married even in Chaucer's day, but when Zarins's Alison describes the loss of her virginity at the age of twelve, tempted by an eighteen-year-old boy named Pete, her autobiography highlights the sadness of a child brought into the adult world too young. Interestingly, all the other students on the bus recognize immediately how wrong the situation was: Jeff says the story "makes [him] want to rush in a time capsule and beat the crap out of Pete."[287] Yet Alison herself seems unaware of how she was wronged; she treats the entire episode as a story of liberation, comparing herself to the Liberty Bell: "[c]racked, but still the icon of freedom."[288] She accepts her childish eagerness as an indication that it was all right for adult Pete to behave as he did. In this blithe unawareness, she resembles Chaucer's Wife of Bath, who is more interested in justifying her marriage to five men in sequence than she is in confronting the injuries she has suffered at the hands of a husband like Jenkin. However, just as the *Wife of Bath's Tale* hints that perhaps Alisoun is more sensitive than she consciously realizes, in the tale Alison tells, both she and then her fellow students get to talk about what has gone wrong.

Zarins's version of the *Wife of Bath's Tale* is not dramatically different from Chaucer's: it follows a nameless Arthurian knight who rapes a peasant girl and then, as penance, is obliged by Queen Guinevere to find out "what women most desire" or lose his head.[289] But when Zarins's Alison admits that she doesn't have

---

285 Zarins, *Sometimes We Tell the Truth*, 9.
286 Chaucer, *Canterbury Tales, Wife of Bath's Prologue*, 1. 4.
287 Zarins, *Sometimes We Tell the Truth*, 160.
288 Zarins, *Sometimes We Tell the Truth*, 159.
289 Zarins, *Sometimes We Tell the Truth*, 163.

a name for the knight, one of the other students suggests "Sir Peter,"[290] casting her statutory rapist as the main character. Zarins even acknowledges one of the problems with the tale that Chaucer himself seems not to notice: that declaring that all women want the exact same thing is both reductivist and, frankly, insulting. No one would suggest that the Miller and the Parson want the same thing just because they are men. Chaucer's tale implies a pro-woman stance, in teaching the rapist knight who robbed a young woman of her right to say no that what women want is "sovereynetee,"[291] but it descends back into misogyny when it explains that "sovereignty" means power "[a]s wel over hir housbond as hir love,/ And for to been in maistrie hym above."[292] So not only do all women want the same thing, but what they want is to lord it over their husbands and lovers. In response to this underlying and unacknowledged misogyny, Zarins gives both Jeff and Pard better answers to "what women most desire" than the actual answer, which in the retelling as in the original is "sovereignty over her man."[293] Jeff says, "You can't boil down desire to one thing," while Pard suggests, "Love."[294] Likewise, even though Alison insists that the story "is about the knight,"[295] not his victim, Jeff voices to himself the objection that many readers have had to the *Wife of Bath's Tale:* "It's like Alison knew the real story was about that unnamed girl raped in the woods, but she chose to tell the knight's story."[296] As Jeff and Pard discuss her tale, Jeff concludes that Alison may secretly know how she has been abused, but she doesn't know what a good relationship looks like, and so she will likely go looking for another knight who makes her feel wanted, but not loved.

Zarins tries, though, to offer hope for Alison's character in the end; her last appearance in the novel is when she stands in the Reflecting Pool with her red stockings (a Chaucerian detail) in her hand like a banner, "both flesh and monument, [...] confronting things head-on."[297] The gesture is still sexualized, still full of the bravado she has shown throughout the novel, but the image is a tribute to her strength as a character. An objection to Zarins's approach might of course be that she is treating Alison like a real person and not the literary pastiche Chaucer intended her to be. He did create the Wife of Bath out of a patchwork of misog-

---

290 Zarins, *Sometimes We Tell the Truth*, 162.
291 Chaucer, *Canterbury Tales, Wife of Bath's Tale*, l. 1038.
292 Chaucer, *Canterbury Tales, Wife of Bath's Tale*, ll. 1039 – 40.
293 Zarins, *Sometimes We Tell the Truth*, 168.
294 Zarins, *Sometimes We Tell the Truth*, 165.
295 Zarins, *Sometimes We Tell the Truth*, 162.
296 Zarins, *Sometimes We Tell the Truth*, 172.
297 Zarins, *Sometimes We Tell the Truth*, 406.

ynist stereotypes, but at the same time he imbued her with such a compelling voice that the other pilgrims in *Canterbury Tales*, like the Clerk, refer to her in their own introductions and epilogues, and even one of the characters within a tale itself (Justinus in the *Merchant's Tale*) defers to her as an authority on marriage.[298] Zarins confronts the dehumanization of misogyny by reclaiming Alison as a person—a character we perceive as damaged and perhaps not entirely self-aware but who is also indomitable and even, in her own way, admirable.

Pard: Neither Gelding nor Mare

This insistence on the human reality of Chaucer's characters carries over into Zarins's treatment of the other most controversial pilgrim on the trip to Canterbury. In *Canterbury Tales*, the Pardoner is a silver-tongued devil who sells false relics and cheats old ladies out of their last pennies. Reflecting a medieval tradition in which the physical body manifests the evils of the soul, Chaucer describes the Pardoner as lank-haired, bug-eyed, and beardless. The narrator famously says of the Pardoner, "I trowe he were a geldyng or a mare."[299] Probably more academic ink has been spilled over how to interpret this line than any other in the work: is the Pardoner a eunuch or a woman posing as a man? Is he transgender or gay? Chaucer seems to have little interest in answering these questions, assuming he would even understand them. But as Zarins makes clear, there is deep inhumanity in treating the Pardoner as evil because his gender is ambiguous. This is, of course, how we read it now even if Chaucer meant it the other way around: to treat his gender as ambiguous because he is evil. There is a tradition of medieval homoerotic poetry, from fourth-century Ausonius to twelfth-century Occitan Bieris de Romans and Andalusian Hamda bin Zayid (both women); one can likewise trace depictions of trans and nonbinary figures throughout the period.[300] However, although there are some interestingly sympathetic cases in early modern law,[301] the default position in medieval literature tends to be that any deviation from standard and easily identifiable sex and sexuality is treated as a sign of wickedness. So Zarins, who "wanted to write with

---

298 Chaucer, *Canterbury Tales, Merchant's Tale*, l. 1685.

299 Chaucer, *Canterbury Tales, General Prologue*, l. 691.

300 On homoerotic poetry, see Battis's introduction in *Thinking Queerly*. On trans and nonbinary characters, see the "My So-Called Merlin" chapter in the same book.

301 See Greenblatt, *Shakespearean Negotiations*, 73–75; though also see a counterargument against considering the case "sympathetic" toward sexual ambiguity in Gilbert, "'Strange Notions,'" 152.

inclusion and affirmation about a LGBTQIA+ teen,"[302] decided to write her version of the Pardoner, Pard, as intersex.[303]

Intersexual individuals, when they were known as hermaphrodites, have historically been eroticized and Othered in grotesque and dehumanizing ways.[304] They are still rare in literature. Zarins is not the first young adult author to include or even focus on an intersex character portrayed in a positive way (*Pantomime* by Laura Lam and *Golden Boy* by Abigail Tarttelin are examples that precede *Sometimes We Tell the Truth*), but such novels are not nearly as common as, for instance, traditional coming-out narratives. Zarins's decision to make Pard intersex achieves several effects. First, she moves Pard out of the realm of stereotyped sinner and trickster and into the realm of realism, in which he is a socially marginalized teenager who must overcome the fear of being rejected by his best friend, who is naïve enough to hear "intosex" instead of "intersex" when Pard tells him the truth.[305] Although Pard is not the point-of-view character for the novel, we learn something of how his life has been shaped by his physical difference. His father, we discover, cut ties with him because "Pard wasn't manly enough."[306] Perhaps as a result, Pard has become aggressively sexualized, making out with Alison as a public show of his virility even though his audience knows he is gay.[307] This aggressive sexuality is a defensive front. We later learn that he has spent time working out his own sense of self, at one point posing for a photograph in a bikini and presenting as a girl.[308] And although he has now settled into his self-presentation as a gay male, there remains the ever-present problem of how to accept his own ambiguous body when the rest of the world wants to see things in binary terms: "[G]ay or straight aside," he says, "people expect you to be male or female. Less is more, they say. Which I guess implies that more is less."[309] The novel does not attempt to solve this problem for Pard because it is a problem that intersex people in reality must still encounter. But Pard does get some important affirmation in the end of the novel when his best friend accepts him for who and what he is.

---

302 Zarins, "Intersex," 3.
303 For a study of similar projects that merge medievalism and writing for young adults, see Battis, *Thinking Queerly*.
304 See, for instance, Gilbert, "'Strange Notions.'"
305 Zarins, *Sometimes We Tell the Truth*, 297.
306 Zarins, *Sometimes We Tell the Truth*, 191.
307 Zarins, *Sometimes We Tell the Truth*, 46.
308 Zarins, *Sometimes We Tell the Truth*, 293–94.
309 Zarins, *Sometimes We Tell the Truth*, 299.

This brings us to the second thing Zarins gains by portraying the Pardoner in this way: she gets a little *ad hominem* revenge on Chaucer by making that best friend the narrator himself, Chaucer's stand-in. From the beginning, Jeff struggles with his feelings for Pard because he considers himself straight, insisting, "[T]his feeling ... it's not attraction. Not a lot of attraction anyhow."[310] Eventually we discover that Pard's self-protective, sexualized persona developed in large part because Jeff rejected him when Pard came out three years ago. When Pard commented in ninth grade that Jeff was "a preeminently kissable boy," Jeff ghosted him, saying in retrospect, "I never explained, but I'm sure he figured it out."[311] If Pard's vulnerability makes him aggressively sexual, Jeff's self-doubt makes him simply aggressive. He describes Pard's make-out session with Alison as "two girls kissing"[312] and proceeds to call Pard a "flaming extrovert skank."[313] Despite the fact that such homophobic language should forfeit all right to charity, Pard accepts Jeff's apology when the latter comes to his senses almost a hundred pages later, and Jeff reluctantly admits to himself that he may be "bi."[314]

But that progress in Jeff's self-knowledge is thrown backward again when Pard confesses that he is in fact intersex. Jeff, having only just resigned himself to being attracted to a boy, now reacts in anger and confusion over discovering that that boy is not physically what Jeff thought. He begins by putting his foot in it and asking Pard, "You have both kinds of parts?"[315]—a question Pard declines to answer. Having defined himself as a gay intersex man, Pard, like the Pardoner, refuses to reveal what he has under his clothes, knowing, as perhaps the Pardoner does not, that he is not obliged to give those around him anything more than his word on who he is. Jeff quickly makes the leap from fretting over Pard's body to panicking about what it means to be attracted to him. He asks himself, "If someone liked Pard, would he be gay, bi, or straight? Or would it even matter, because what does sex even mean for someone like him?"[316]

Jeff does not find an answer to those questions, but the implication is that he doesn't have to. After realizing a few things about other people in his life, and breaking with a bad influence or two, he apologizes a second time to Pard and admits that, ambivalent as he is about defining himself in broad terms,

---

310 Zarins, *Sometimes We Tell the Truth*, 128.
311 Zarins, *Sometimes We Tell the Truth*, 204.
312 Zarins, *Sometimes We Tell the Truth*, 50.
313 Zarins, *Sometimes We Tell the Truth*, 197.
314 Zarins, *Sometimes We Tell the Truth*, 291.
315 Zarins, *Sometimes We Tell the Truth*, 298.
316 Zarins, *Sometimes We Tell the Truth*, 299.

there is one boy he likes, and that is Pard.[317] He also recognizes that he has no right to a relationship with him after what he has done and said. Pard, however, claims his own right to happiness by declaring, *"But I do!"*[318] Thus, the reconciliation is saved from being a story about Jeff's redemption to being a story that affirms Pard and his right to be loved. Jeff even comes to recognize Pard's different body, with its inability to grow a beard, as a beautiful one, saying, "I touch his neck, his face, and then I bend down and kiss that softest peach fuzz corner of his mouth, and it's the most beautiful part on any human body ever born."[319] Only then does Jeff, who has suffered from paralyzing writer's block for 420 pages, unlock his creative faculties. When they have sealed their budding relationship with a kiss described in great detail, he tells Pard, "The words I couldn't use, I can use them now. [...] *Love, lovely, lover, beloved, boyfriend.*"[320] This ending is an additional dig at Chaucer, hinting that perhaps the reason he couldn't find a proper designation for the Pardoner's body in the *General Prologue*—indeed, perhaps the reason the entire *Canterbury Tales* is unfinished—is that his own sexuality was too repressed for him to write down the words.

Zarins's decision to portray Pard as intersex also reminds us that canon fanfiction, on many levels, does the same kind of work as literary criticism. In fact, Pard's character seems to have grown almost entirely out of Zarins's response to the history of academic work on the Pardoner. In a lengthy and clearly impassioned article on the subject, Zarins explains that "[t]he scholarly community has mostly moved away from an *either / or* approach to the Pardoner's body—either he is this or that—and more toward a *both / and* limitlessness, characteristic of queer readings."[321] This movement, though it stems from queer theory, which is generally supportive of LGBTQIA+ realities, nevertheless represents "a retreat from the body."[322] That is, in an effort to stop trying to pin down the features of the Pardoner's body, scholars have denied him a body at all; it is an ironic if inverted return to Chaucer's own implied formulation. Where for Chaucer, the Pardoner's physical traits were mere symbols for his moral failings, for scholars those traits are mere symbols for his liminal and uncontainable nature. In other words, to scholars, the Pardoner is a metaphor, not a person, and although being a metaphor for something positive is better than being a metaphor for

---

317 Zarins, *Sometimes We Tell the Truth*, 410.
318 Zarins, *Sometimes We Tell the Truth*, 420, emphasis in original.
319 Zarins, *Sometimes We Tell the Truth*, 420.
320 Zarins, *Sometimes We Tell the Truth*, 421.
321 Zarins, "Intersex," 3.
322 Zarins, "Intersex," 3.

something negative, it does nothing to validate, represent, or take seriously the real intersex people in the world.

Zarins highlights the hypocrisy of recent scholarly treatment of the Pardoner as a mere tool for theory, saying, "[w]ithout a body, he must do our bidding."[323] It is perhaps ironic that, in making the authorial decision to portray Pard as intersex, Zarins runs the risk of appropriating the perspective of a community of which she is not a part and likewise making her character "do her bidding." However, it was clearly a risk she was willing to take. In fact, she was rewarded for her intrepidity by having a trans, gay college-age reader tell her that "Pard seemed to be written just for him."[324]

Zarins's novel is many canon fanfiction approaches rolled into one: AU, shipping, spinoff, crossover. Her overarching purpose is to remind us of what made Chaucer's original audience fall in love with his work to begin with: its vitality, its creativity, and its range of emotion and technique. But *Sometimes We Tell the Truth* also proves that admiration does not preclude disagreement; loving Chaucer does not mean swallowing his antisemitism or misogyny whole. So Zarins at once sets out to demonstrate that Chaucer remains meaningful in the current world and registers her protest at his inevitable shortcomings of worldview and social values. Perhaps most importantly, though, in portraying Pard as intersex and as worthy and capable of a loving relationship, Zarins not only talks back to Chaucer but also works to correct the assumptions and deficiencies of the current academic community of which she is herself a member.

2.4 Postcolonial/Critical Race Theory. Is the Past Really Past? Chevalier's *New Boy* and Morrison's *Desdemona*

Theater and opera innovator Peter Sellars says in his foreword to Toni Morrison and Rokia Traoré's *Desdemona* that Shakespeare's *Othello* was "for four centuries the most visible portrayal of a black man in Western art."[325] As such, the play has been burdened with the unasked-for responsibility of representing blackness to white audiences, almost in an artistic vacuum, for hundreds of years, and that representation of blackness is troubling: Othello may be a great general, but he is insecure, easily swayed, violent, and lacking in self-awareness. Even in his final speech, he characterizes himself as "one not easily

---

323 Zarins, "Intersex," 3.
324 Zarins, "Intersex," 56.
325 Sellars, "Foreword," 7.

jealous" and employs a racial slur not unlike the ones directed at him earlier in the play, calling a Turkish enemy a "circumcisèd dog."[326] Othello is a blunt instrument, lacking in the intellectual and emotional nuance of Shakespeare's other tragic heroes. In the wake of the Civil Rights Movement and the growing cultural awareness that followed it, audiences have tended to find the play unsatisfying; remarkable as it once was for its choice of protagonist, it nevertheless fails to fully realize the dynamics of race in that protagonist's tragedy.

Othello has been reimagined and rewritten a number of times, but two recent examples provide a useful contrast in their approach to "fixing" the lack of awareness in the original. In 2012, Toni Morrison wrote a play with Malian singer/songwriter Rokia Traoré entitled *Desdemona*; five years later, Tracy Chevalier published the novel *New Boy* as part of the Hogarth Shakespeare series. While theatrical productions have dimensions that novels do not, and therefore in a sense we are comparing apples to oranges in putting these two works side by side, nevertheless they offer an opportunity to ask how we are to come to grips with the power of race and racism in Shakespeare's play, and indeed, to ask who is in the best position to do so. Both works grapple with this issue by delving into the inner lives of the characters, as we have come to expect in modern adaptations of canon literature. But both also make the decision to change the setting: Morrison to a timeless afterlife and Chevalier to the 1970s in Washington, DC. These settings are significant in the question of race because setting the story in the 1970s implies a historical dimension to racism, while setting it outside of time both insists that the problem still exists and simultaneously implies that it will always continue to do so.

New Boy

Tracy Chevalier departs from her more usual mode of historical romance (*Girl with the Pearl Earring, The Lady and the Unicorn*) to recast *Othello* as essentially a playground war fought by sixth-graders in a DC suburb in 1974. Her novel has all the breathless haste of the original play, condensing Shakespeare's three days to a single school day, morning to afternoon. In that span of time, Dee (Desdemona) falls in love with Osei (Othello), the titular "new boy," a diplomat's son from Ghana, and their budding romance is sabotaged by Ian (Iago) with the unwilling help of his reluctant girlfriend Mimi (Emilia). The choice to make her reenvisioned characters schoolchildren gives the novel heavy shades of Robert

---

326 Shakespeare, *Othello*, 5.2.363, 365.

Cormier's *Chocolate War* and implies that the taint of racism, which is much more of a constant presence in the novel than in the original play, poisons even the supposed innocence of childhood.

The most consistent expression of racism in the novel is the casual, unexamined prejudice expressed by the teachers as well as the other students. The principle, Mrs. Duke (Shakespeare's Duke of Venice), tells Osei's mother over the phone that she suspects Osei "may not be used to behaving in the ways we expect of our children" and then, in response to Mrs. Kokote's anger at the implication, tells the school secretary she is "uppity."[327] Mr. Brabant (Brabantio) is the worst offender, bitter at losing a job (as he sees it) to affirmative action[328] and having, we suspect, an inappropriate interest in his beautiful student Dee. His first acknowledgment of Osei is to say, "I think I hear drums."[329] When Dee and Osei touch each other's hair, his reaction is far too extreme for the circumstances of breaking up an innocent sixth-grade flirtation: "You are *not* to touch other students inappropriately," he tells Osei, though Dee was the one to initiate the contact. "Maybe things are different where you come from and you don't know any better, [...] but at this school boys and girls don't touch each other like that."[330] When Ian pulls Mimi out of the jungle gym and throws her onto the concrete, Mr. Brabant assumes Osei is the culprit (despite the fact that he surely knows Ian's reputation), and in his anger uses the novel's only instance of the N-word.[331]

Mr. Brabant is an unredeemed and unredeemable character in the novel, but the students are no less prejudiced than he is. In the play, Iago famously has insufficient motive for the chaos he inflicts on those around him; losing a promotion just doesn't seem a dire enough offense to warrant destroying everyone in the play. In the novel, Ian is no different. Chevalier gives him very little backstory, instead depicting him as an ambitious and acquisitive social climber who sucks up to the teachers and intimidates his peers. Ian targets Osei at least ostensibly because he upsets the order in the kingdom Ian has built for himself: watching Osei, Ian can "see the rearrangement going on to include this new leader—the shifts as other students subtly [turn] toward him, as if he were a light they followed, like plants seeking the sun."[332] And in the end, when Osei asks Ian why he has hurt everyone he has touched, his only response

---

327 Chevalier, *New Boy*, 179–80.
328 Chevalier, *New Boy*, 162.
329 Chevalier, *New Boy*, 10.
330 Chevalier, *New Boy*, 84.
331 Chevalier, *New Boy*, 202.
332 Chevalier, *New Boy*, 88–89.

is, "Because I can."[333] This is slightly more communicative than Iago's "What you know, you know,"[334] but it does nothing to justify his actions. However, the novel subtly acknowledges a racial motivation that Iago never admits to: throughout the story, Ian repeatedly has to stop himself from calling Osei "black boy," instead always shifting the designation to "new boy." The implication, then, is that Ian's particularly strong reaction to Osei may be as much a result of Osei's race as it is a result of Ian's psychopathic tendencies.

Even Dee is guilty of judging Osei by his skin, though her judgment is one of fascination rather than repulsion. Having heard the teachers talking about him, in her first interaction with Osei she is "eager to show off her prior knowledge of him," making the assumption that he is easily knowable and that she has mastery of the facts that make him so.[335] As it turns out, she is wrong about his background and, in fact, is wrong every time she makes a guess about him (she thinks he is from Nigeria when he is from Ghana; she thinks Ghana is the same as Papua New Guinea). But because she is friendly—and, one suspects, because she is pretty—Osei is patient with her ignorance, and toward the end of the story, Dee does come to a certain kind of revelation about her own shortcomings. When their short-lived romance has already begun to crumble, Dee realizes that there was already a barrier of difference between them, and it was one she had helped construct: "He was black, and all day they had treated him that way [...]. Dee knew she herself found him interesting because he was black, and that was not necessarily a good reason—to like someone for their skin color."[336] This revelation does not save her, though in Chevalier's version Dee survives; instead, she suffers the public disgrace of Osei calling her a whore, which to a sixth-grade girl in 1974 probably felt very much like death. But what is striking is that, while Dee learns something about herself from this disastrous school day, Osei himself, the titular character, seems never to reach that level of clarity.

In commenting on Morrison's *Desdemona*, Peter Erickson observes that "Othello's capacity for a new understanding beyond Shakespeare cannot keep up with Desdemona's development"[337] and wonders whether "there is an authorial imprint inherited from Shakespeare that makes Othello's character an impervious structure and limits its depth."[338] He could have said the same thing about Tracy Chevalier's version, in which Osei is constantly meditating upon his older

---

333 Chevalier, *New Boy*, 201.
334 Shakespeare, *Othello*, 5.2.311.
335 Chevalier, *New Boy*, 18.
336 Chevalier, *New Boy*, 175.
337 Erickson, "Late," 12.
338 Erickson, "Late," 13.

sister's growing interest in Black Power and his ambivalence toward the movement because it draws his sister's attentions away from him. When he falls for Ian's convoluted deceptions (the strawberry-embroidered handkerchief of the play becomes a strawberry-embossed pencil case here), the vengeance he visits upon Dee reeks of a racially based self-loathing he never seems to recognize. When he humiliates her in front of their classmates, he plays into the stereotype of the hypersexual black male, saying to his audience, "She has even touched my dick, that is how much she wants it. How much all white girls want it."[339] He may see this as an empowering statement; in fact, he follows it up, just before he throws himself from the top of the jungle gym, with the Black Power slogan, "Black *is* beautiful" (emphasizing "*is*" because he has not been certain about it, all through the book).[340] This claim is framed as a defiant self-declaration, the revelation for which we have waited. But it is profoundly unsatisfactory as such. Osei's claim that black is beautiful comes in the wake of doing something genuinely ugly to an innocent person, and besides that, it is simply a non-sequitur: Osei's race did not make him more vulnerable to Ian's lies; if it did, it would only reinforce the stereotype, which we see in *Othello*, of a black man who is not clever enough to make it in a world of Iagos. Osei's actions had everything to do with a mistrust of females and female sexuality and a prioritizing of male bonds. He trusted Ian not because he was black and Ian was white but because he and Ian were both boys. This is, in fact, the conclusion Desdemona comes to in Morrison's version as well.

Chevalier's decision to set this canon fanfiction AU in the 1970s elicits different responses from different readers, based largely on their age. Anecdotally, all the readers I have spoken with who lived through the 1970s interpret the setting as a reminder that, despite the gains of the Civil Rights Movement a decade before, very little had actually changed. Probably this was Chevalier's intension: the Black Lives Matter movement, which was ramping up as Chevalier wrote and published her book, was reminding us forcibly that racism was every bit a part of the American landscape in the twenty-first century as it was in 1974. However, for readers who were born after the 1970s, the usual impression is that setting the novel almost fifty years ago implies that racism is a problem of the past. We have a strong tendency when looking backward to see ourselves as more advanced, more aware, more civilized than people who lived in the world before we entered it, and we perhaps naturally feel that anything that occurred before our birth is ancient history. Unlike most of the other Hogarth Shakespeare novels,

---

339 Chevalier, *New Boy*, 194.
340 Chevalier, *New Boy*, 203.

New Boy is not accompanied by an author's note, so we have no explicit explanation for her authorial choices. And it would be unfair to blame Chevalier for younger readers taking away an impression she never intended to give them. But no element in this story necessitates its being set in the 1970s; it could have just as easily been set in 2017, when it was published, and its treatment of American racism would have been all the more meaningful for acknowledging that it is not at all a problem of "the past" but one we are still living through now.

One can imagine that a black author might have made a different choice. In the introduction, I acknowledge the potential pitfalls of canon fanfiction whose authors seek to write a perspective they don't share, and while I argued there that the benefits can be worth the risk, *New Boy* offers an occasion to examine how not sharing a key identity category with one's protagonists can lead to unintended consequences. I credit Chevalier with deliberately giving Osei a false sense of what the end of his own story meant; it is a technique she shares with Morrison. However, there are other details that seem less intentional, particularly in the physical descriptions of characters. Osei's dark skin is described using the old trope of comparing non-white skin color to food—in this case, black coffee.[341] It is true that this observation comes through Dee's perspective, so that one could argue it is Dee using the trope and not Chevalier, but another, similar trope occurs too often to feel that Chevalier was conscious of it. Osei is repeatedly compared to animals and natural elements. When Dee first sees him, she compares him to a black bear at the zoo;[342] she then decides he is more like a panther[343] and characterizes his short hair as being "like a forest of trees dotted in tight clumps over the curves of a mountain."[344] When the perspective shifts to Ian, he imagines Osei as a bear again, this time one "puzzled by a wounded paw."[345] Even from his own perspective, Osei describes himself as "a wolf growling."[346] Dee is admittedly compared twice to a cat,[347] but the weight of evidence suggests that Chevalier may have been subconsciously employing a trope in a way that a black writer is unlikely to have done without actively deciding to do so. More than that, though, the very story arc, in which Osei comes to see all of his troubles literally in black and white, plays into yet another stereo-

---

341 Chevalier, *New Boy*, 175.
342 Chevalier, *New Boy*, 8.
343 Chevalier, *New Boy*, 10.
344 Chevalier, *New Boy*, 14.
345 Chevalier, *New Boy*, 121.
346 Chevalier, *New Boy*, 194.
347 Chevalier, *New Boy*, 38, 82.

type: if white people complain that black people "make everything about race," Chevalier has given us a narrative in which the protagonist does exactly that. Osei's failure to realize all the other things the story is about (misogyny, objectification, abuse, violence) may be deliberate, but it nevertheless gives uncharitable readers another excuse to shrug and say, "Well, of course he'd think it was all about race. He's black."

Desdemona

Desdemona operates in a very different vein. With the dialogue written by Toni Morrison and the song lyrics written by Rokia Traoré, a Malian celebrity famous for her hybridized music that combines traditional African griot styles with international forms of jazz and blues, *Desdemona* works at "undoing the authenticity-as-primitivism trope associated with African peoples and cultures."[348] It insists, unlike *New Boy*, that we need not speak of Africa (or indeed of racism) "in the past tense."[349] If *New Boy* is breathless in its pace, *Desdemona* is even more so, spanning less than sixty pages of text. In that brief span, though, it covers a great deal of territory. Desdemona speaks from the other side of death, meeting the other dead characters including Othello, Emilia, and her mother's nurse, Barbary. In staging, the actress who plays Desdemona voices all the other parts (in English) except for Barbary, who is played by Rokia Traoré (in Bambara).[350] Iago is deliberately absent, allowing Desdemona and Othello to be the ones "responsible for coming to terms with their own actions."[351] The lyrics of the songs Traoré wrote and performs are translated into English and projected onto a scrim above the actors, as is common in opera productions. In his foreword, Sellars explains that Barbary was in fact the genesis of Morrison's play: mentioned only once, as the originator of the famous "Willow Song,"[352] her name "meant Africa" to Shakespeare's first audience, and hence, "there is another African character in his play."[353] *Desdemona* came about, then, to explore the silenced voices in the original—not just Desdemona's but Barbary's and Emilia's and others'. Sellars calls the work "a dialogue between Toni in New York,

---

348 Guarracino, "Africa as Voices," 68.
349 Guarracino, "Africa as Voices," 68.
350 Guarracino, "Africa as Voices," 67.
351 Erickson, "Late," 4.
352 Shakespeare, *Othello*, 4.3.28 – 35.
353 Sellars, "Foreword," 8.

Rokia in Bamako ... and Shakespeare, wherever he is."[354] Morrison and Traoré are talking back to Shakespeare, and they do it through Desdemona.

In fact, the play is framed not primarily as a meditation on race but as a meditation on womanhood. Letting Desdemona speak, as Jo Eldridge Carney points out, fills a gap in critical discourse, in which (until fairly recently) the women of the play have been seen as unimportant and largely ornamental to the story of the men.[355] Desdemona opens the play by explaining that her name means "misery," and that her parents gave her the name because "being born a girl gave them all they needed to know of what [her] life would be like."[356] When she then declares, "I am not the meaning of a name I did not choose,"[357] she makes a claim for independence and even redemption of her own identity as a woman. But while she begins the play with a strong sense of her own womanhood, what she learns over the course of the play is that she must also come to grips with her privilege as an upper-class white woman.

First she encounters Emilia, whom she rebukes for selling her out to Iago. Emilia flares up, saying, "I exposed his lies, you ingrate! That is your appreciation for my devotion to you?"[358] When Desdemona discovers that Emilia's scrappiness comes from her having grown up an orphan, she immediately reaches out for a connection: "I wish I had known you when we were children. [...] You had no mother. I had no mother's love."[359] The impulse is charitable: Desdemona wants to forge a bond of sympathy and shared suffering between them, but Emilia reminds her that being a valued (if not beloved) child in a wealthy household is "not the same" as being a starving orphan.[360] Desdemona has to check her privilege, admitting, "You were right to correct me."[361] Such a sudden shift does not happen often or easily in reality, but this is the afterlife, where "[t]he apologies that we have waited four hundred years to hear are finally spoken."[362]

---

354 Quoted in Fricker, "Creating the Space," 219.
355 Carney, "'Being Born a Girl,'" 4.
356 Morrison, *Desdemona*, 13. Note: for clarity of citation, Morrison will be identified as the author of quotations from the play; however, all lyrics except the "Willow Song" and "Someone Leans Near" are written by Rokia Traoré.
357 Morrison, *Desdemona*, 13.
358 Morrison, *Desdemona*, 43.
359 Morrison, *Desdemona*, 44.
360 Morrison, *Desdemona*, 44.
361 Morrison, *Desdemona*, 44.
362 Sellars, "Foreword," 11.

The reconciliation is harder with Barbary because Desdemona has so far to go in understanding the true nature of their relationship. When Desdemona first introduces us to her memory of Barbary when the latter was her childhood nurse, she idealizes her, saying, "Unlike the staid, unbending women of my country, she moved with the fluid grace I saw only in swans and the fronds of willow trees. [...] She was more alive than anyone I knew and more loving."[363] Commenting on this description, so similar to the descriptions of Osei in *New Boy*, Serena Guarracino points out, "This portrait of Barbary/Africa as a woman/land of communion with nature and 'primitive' freedom from social customs could not be more exoticizing."[364] Immediately upon her reconciliation with Emilia, Desdemona meets Barbary in person and greets her with all the warmth of remembered affection. Barbary throws cold water on that warmth when she says, "[Y]ou don't even know my name. Barbary? Barbary is what you call Africa. Barbary is the geography of the foreigner, the savage."[365] Her real name is Sa'ran, which, in contrast to Desdemona's name, means "joy."[366] The printed text affirms her identity, changing the speech tags from "Barbary" to "Sa'ran" from this point on. Desdemona is less definitive, saying, "Well, Sa'ran, whatever your name, you were my best friend," to which Sa'ran replies, "I was your slave."[367] An argument ensues in which Desdemona persists in trying to affirm some connection with her former nurse while Sa'ran keeps reiterating the impossibility of such a thing across the boundaries of race and class. Finally, Desdemona asks, "Was I ever cruel to you? Ever?" and Sa'ran admits that she was not.[368] The lack of outright cruelty seems a very low bar to set for a positive human interaction, but Morrison herself sees this moment as pivotal: referring to these lines in an interview, she says, "Well that's it. It's just me and you. It's not about class anymore, it's not about race anymore. [...] This is what can happen when it's just the two of us."[369] The idea that something is possible "when it's just the two of us," without the interference of external forces, is central to the play's treatment of race and reconciliation.

Desdemona makes her peace with Barbary, but even when she and Othello interact, "just the two of them," their resolution is much less certain. In fact, it is so ambivalent that commentators have disagreed profoundly over how it turns

363 Morrison, *Desdemona*, 18.
364 Guarracino, "Africa as Voices," 65.
365 Morrison, *Desdemona*, 45.
366 Cucarella-Ramon, "Decolonizing *Othello*," 92.
367 Morrison, *Desdemona*, 45.
368 Morrison, *Desdemona*, 48.
369 Sellars, Morrison, and Traoré, "*Desdemona:* Dialogues," 19:00.

out. Othello rebukes Desdemona for exoticizing him even more profoundly than she exoticized Barbary:

> You never loved me. You fancied the idea of me, the exotic foreigner who kills for the State, who will die for the state. Everyone I slaughtered was someone who wanted your head on a pike. How comforting it must have been—protected by a loyal black warrior. What excited you was my strange story [...]. And you thought that was all there was to me—a useful myth, a fairy's tale cut to suit a princess' hunger for real life, not the dull existence of her home.[370]

Just as we saw with Dee and her feelings for the exotic Osei, there is something to Othello's rebuke. However, Erickson considers the complaint "flat and unconvincing" because Othello himself played up the black knight angle in wooing her.[371] Shakespeare's Othello tells the duke, "She loved me for the dangers I had passed,/ And I loved her that she did pity them."[372] In Morrison's version, we even get to hear a number of these stories in full, so that we see firsthand how he plays to her tastes in describing his suffering as an orphan adopted by a "root woman" and then kidnapped into the Syrian army.[373] Even his most horrifying confession—Morrison's own invention—is calculated to earn Desdemona's trust through a shared secret: he confesses that he and Iago raped a pair of old women after a battle, then left a boy alive to be witness to their cruelty. Erickson says this about the incident:

> From Othello's point of view, the secret should function as a bond of trust with Desdemona, though at its core this secret negates the marriage. Othello's secret with Desdemona can never equal Othello's prior secret with Iago.[374]

And although Carney seems to take Othello at his word when he claims to be offended by Desdemona's impulse to exoticize him, she nevertheless observes, "Homosocial bonding [among men] is destructive in that it results in violence against women and turns on itself."[375] Both these commentators, in other words, agree that despite Desdemona's claims that she can still "love [Othello] and remain committed to [him],"[376] the real bonds of healing in this play happen between the women, specifically because they are not the perpetrators of violence but rather its victims.

---

370 Morrison, *Desdemona*, 50–51.
371 Erickson, "Late," 12.
372 Shakespeare, *Othello*, 1.3.169–70.
373 Morrison, *Desdemona*, 31.
374 Erickson, "Late," 6.
375 Carney, "'Being Born a Girl,'" 16.
376 Morrison, *Desdemona*, 39.

The fact that Barbary is the only other character physically present on the stage besides Desdemona is evidence for the central importance of their coming to terms with one another. The staging of the play has other implications for the overarching treatment of character and race as well. Because the actress who plays Desdemona ventriloquizes the other characters, everyone who is not Desdemona or Barbary fades into the background—even Othello himself. Carney argues that through this ventriloquizing effect, "Desdemona fully internalizes their experiences, signifying her developing empathy and understanding."[377] This is true of her conversation with Emilia, for instance, in which she gets to step into her attendant's perspective and voice the anger of someone who has been ordered around like an inferior, the pain of someone who has grown up unloved and alone. But it also means that the other characters become less important: we are less invested in Othello coming to grips with what he has done (in fact, it is not clear he ever manages to) than we are in watching Desdemona work her way toward letting go of the fact that he murdered her. It also means that when she voices characters like Cassio, who is still alive and now effectively the governor of Venice, she takes part in their faults as well. Cassio, through Desdemona, describes Othello as "swanning about above his station and way above his geography and his history. A dangerous godless mix, unable to govern, to know with certainty what is best for the State. I am compelled now to repeal and replace whatever they have initiated into law."[378] When these arrogant, prejudiced words come through Desdemona's mouth (even though Desdemona herself immediately abjures them, saying, "To think I tried to save him"[379]), we are reminded that she has been complicit in the system that favors men like Cassio and is always eager to see the demise of an "upstart" like Othello.

Yet there is a tenderness, too, in the ventriloquizing of voices, and it gives the play some of its cautious hope. When Desdemona tells an anxious Othello that she cannot forgive him for raping those old women but can nevertheless still love him, the scene is followed by a song whose voice is ambiguous. When Rokia Traoré sings, "Do you know what torments me?/ Do you want to know my anguish?/ I fear the ultimate betrayal,"[380] it is not clear whether the song is supposed to come from Othello or Desdemona. Both are afraid of losing what they value, which is each other, and that shared vulnerability is one of the play's notes of optimism. Another comes early on, in the unexpected reconcilia-

377 Carney, "'Being Born a Girl,'" 10.
378 Morrison, *Desdemona*, 52.
379 Morrison, *Desdemona*, 53.
380 Morrison, *Desdemona*, 40.

tion between the now-dead mothers of Othello and Desdemona. Once they recognize each other, Soun, Othello's mother, asks, "Are we enemies, then?" Madame Brabantio replies, "Of course. Our vengeance is more molten than our sorrow."[381] And yet they show no open hostility, and within a few lines, they have agreed to engage in a mourning ritual of Soun's people (pointedly, not a ritual of Madame Brabantio's people), in which they will "build an altar to the spirits who are waiting to console [them]."[382] Likewise, Desdemona and Barbary bond over their shared exultation that, having once been destroyed by men, they cannot be victims a second time: Sa'ran sings, "I will never die again," and Desdemona echoes, "We will never die again."[383] When Othello asks Desdemona if it is too late for them to reconcile, she tells him, "'Late' has no meaning here."[384] Vicent Cucarella-Ramon describes this "here" as "the ethnoscape where Morrison's characters are ready to forgive each other, make amends and speak the lines that the Shakespearean characters could not utter."[385] This claim seems supported by Sellars's own statement that "[i]n a time outside of time that illuminates and infuses the present, Des-demon-a confronts her 'demons,' reconciling the past, and now, no longer alone, prepares a future."[386]

But if all of these reconciliations happen in the afterlife, does the play perhaps imply that they can't happen before that? Such is the implication, indeed, if we return to Morrison's idea that interacting "just the two of us" is the central requirement for good relations. In the final scene, Desdemona observes to Othello, "Alone together we could have been invincible."[387] Her claim begs two questions: if they were alone together, whom would they have had to defeat to be invincible, and, because being "just the two of us" is impossible in the flesh and blood world, is countercultural love bound to fail? The answer to the first question is, of course, that the only threat to their love would have been themselves, and without an Iago to plant the seeds of doubt, the hope is that Othello would have never talked himself into mistrusting his wife—though, knowing Othello, one rather doubts even that. An answer to the second question is harder to find. Desdemona's last line is, "We will be judged by how well we love," and critics are divided over whether this claim is optimistic or the opposite. Cucarella-Ramon calls it "a transcultural and yet beautiful mode of social

---

381 Morrison, *Desdemona*, 26.

382 Morrison, *Desdemona*, 27.

383 Morrison, *Desdemona*, 49.

384 Morrison, *Desdemona*, 55.

385 Cucarella-Ramon, "Decolonizing *Othello*," 91.

386 Sellars, "Foreword," 11.

387 Morrison, *Desdemona*, 54.

atonement,"[388] whereas Erickson calls it "far more provisional" than her procla-mation with Sa'ran that "we will never die again."[389] In fact, for all Sellars's in-sistence on the effectiveness of the reconciliations at the end, Erickson declares that "*Desdemona* deliberately withholds a happy ending."[390] And indeed Traoré's concluding song, which is the play's last word, is deeply ambivalent. Its last verses are,

> I have no ambition to exist
> in this world
> except as an impermanent
> element
> facing eternity
> with no choice
> but to burn
> then finish
> one way
> or another.[391]

In this final moment, we withdraw from the eternity of the dead and return to the finite world of the living, where every action is bracketed by the knowledge that nothing is permanent. The song does affirm that eternity is waiting on the other side of death, but for those of us still in life, we are faced "with no choice but to burn." In this way, Desdemona's statement that "we will be judged by how well we love" becomes a challenge, not an accomplishment. It is an action that must be taken day to day as we continue to burn, and given the pressures and influ-ences of the world that will never leave us "alone together," we are as likely to love poorly as we are to love well.

These two works address *Othello*'s nagging lack of insight into the influence of race in the protagonist's downfall, and yet their approaches are almost exactly opposite. Tracy Chevalier makes *New Boy* a tragedy in an Aristotelian sense: a good character overwhelmed by forces that are too big for him to resist. In her hands, the story becomes a reminder that even the innocence of children is pois-oned by hatred. But just as Shakespeare wrote his tragedies about the kings whose actions stood at a safe distance in the chronicles of history, Chevalier sets her tragedy in a recent but not so very recent past where its issues may not directly challenge us. Toni Morrison and Rokia Traoré, on the other hand,

---

388 Cucarella-Ramon, "Decolonizing *Othello*," 93.
389 Erickson, "Late," 11.
390 Erickson, "Late," 13.
391 Morrison, *Desdemona*, 57.

create a sequel in which tragedy has no permanent hold on the characters, but we are given no assurance that the privileges they enjoy in death to reconcile and come to terms are things we can expect to see in life. *Desdemona* is, as Cucarella-Ramon says, a "counter-narrative to the long-dominant white-supremacist patriarchal metanarrative of the Western canon,"[392] but it is not one that fixes the issue by erasing it from the picture of the present.

2.5 Trauma Studies. Questioning Trauma: Headley's *Mere Wife*

In many ways, Maria Dahvana Headley's *Mere Wife* is an amalgamation of all the identity-based approaches in one: although its most evident approach is feminist, it also incorporates Marxist, postcolonial, queer, disability, and to a certain extent even ecocritical theories in its densely psychological plot. In Jeremy Rosen's formulation, this novel is a minor character elaboration,[393] taking the two minor female roles of *Beowulf*—Hrothgar's queen, Wealhtheow (here, Willa), and Grendel's nameless dam (now Dana)—and making them the leads of the reinvented story. It is also, in Henry Jenkins's categorization,[394] an example of moral realignment, explicitly demanding that we ask ourselves, "Who are the monsters?"[395] It is a "fix-it" in that it leads us to quite the opposite conclusion than we do when reading *Beowulf*. Despite this almost overwhelming mix of approaches and potential lenses through which we might examine this novel, perhaps the most useful is the least obvious: trauma theory. Since the oppression of the Other (in whatever form that Other takes) is frequently experienced as trauma, looking at the novel in this light allows us to gain something like a holistic reading that any of the other lenses would narrow to one or two aspects. Headley's two leading ladies, Willa and Dana, model opposing types of trauma and responses thereto, highlighting the fact that stock literary treatments of trauma sidestep the complexity of human response; in *Mere Wife*, trauma is not always what it seems, and victims can be perpetrators themselves.

Although the novel is laced with constant references to *Beowulf* (the cup that raises the dragon's wrath, for instance, becomes an heirloom plundered by Willa from Dana's own family), only a reader who knows the epic poem well will see much of the original in this free-styling canon fanfiction. In *Mere Wife*, Grendel's

---

392 Cucarella-Ramon, "Decolonizing *Othello*," 94.
393 See Rosen, "Minor Characters Have Their Day."
394 See Jenkins, *Textual Poachers*, 168.
395 Headley, *Mere Wife*, 36.

dam becomes Dana Mills (a name that suggests that she could represent the Danes, not the spawn of Cain), an American woman of color who joins the Marines after 9/11, is captured in an unnamed Middle Eastern country, and is impregnated by an unknown man before being released. Once back on American soil, she escapes the military hospital and returns to the land of her ancestors (probably the Catskills, based on the proximity to New York City) to live in a cave at the bank of a mere with her newborn son, Gren. Wealhtheow becomes Willa Herot, a frustrated housewife in a suburb called Herot Hall; she is married to Roger Herot (Hrothgar) and is the mother of Dylan, nicknamed Dil. Later, after Dana kills Roger, Willa marries Ben Woolf (Beowulf), a veteran and local police officer in charge of the search for the murderess. It seems that even in a loose adaptation, modern audiences cannot resist shipping Wealhtheow and Beowulf any more than the makers of Zemeckis's 2007 film could.

Gren and Dil and the Return of the Repressed

The action of the novel is precipitated by Gren falling in love with Dil as a child. The two function as a complementary pair throughout the novel: Gren + Dil = Grendel. While the shared mother/son relationship could potentially unite Dana and Willa as women living in a man's world—a direction we would probably expect the novel to take—instead, the unity of Gren and Dil highlights the chasm between the two women, who take each other—and each other's child —as their mortal enemy. In Willa's quest to destroy Dana and Gren, she initiates the renovation of an old train line that used to terminate in the mountain cave and, in a drugged stupor, kills her own son, Dil. In Dana's quest to isolate her son from any outside influence, she loses her own arm to gangrene and drives Gren further into the outside world, where he is killed by Ben Woolf. Ultimately she hijacks the renovated train (i.e. the dragon) on its maiden voyage and runs over Ben, derailing the train and falling to her death in the mere. It is a novel without soft edges, in which there are no heroes, least of all Beowulf/Ben Woolf. They are, instead, characters made up of various kinds of emotional damage.

Cathy Caruth, one of the founding figures of trauma theory, builds on Freud's *Beyond the Pleasure Principle* to define trauma in this way:

> [T]he wound of the mind—the breach in the mind's experience of time, self, and the world—
> is not, like the wound of the body, a simple and healable event, but rather an event that [...]
> is experienced too soon, too unexpectedly, to be fully known and is therefore not available

to consciousness until it imposes itself again, repeatedly, in the nightmares and repetitive actions of the survivor.[396]

Throughout the novel, Willa, Ben, and Dana forget, refuse to remember, and flash back to experiences and emotions they cannot master. The world of the novel becomes a nightmarish dreamscape, functioning—as so often happens in horror—as an externalization of internal turmoil. The most obvious instance is in the doppelgangers, Gren and Dil, who are as much projections of their mothers as they are actual people. For Willa, the unwanted and unloved Dil is a projection of everything negative in her frustrated world, whereas for Dana, Gren, the product of her captivity, ironically becomes the projection of everything worth living for.

Constantly, the characters and even the narrative itself blend and confuse the two boys until they become almost indistinguishable. For instance, when Willa finds a claw sheath in her carpet, she along with the reader assumes it came from Gren, who has begun visiting Dil. However, much later in the novel, at the moment a drugged Willa murders her own son thinking he is Gren, she sees "claws protruding from the fingertips [of his hand], long pearlescent claws, like the sheathings found in the hallway carpet, so long ago that she hardly remembers what they looked like."[397] The sleeping pills she has taken allow her to act on her impulse, but the impulse of seeing her son as a monster, expressed throughout the novel, comes to a head when she conflates him with the wild child, Gren. In contrast to Willa's failure to recognize, Gren provides Dana with one of her moments of anagnorisis, when she follows Gren to New York City and, watching him navigate the crowded world without incident, realizes, "Maybe I've been hiding for myself, not him."[398] The realization comes too late to prevent the oncoming disaster, but nevertheless, Dana comes to recognize her Freudian act of projection when Willa never does.

As in many horror stories, the Freudian return of the repressed plays an essential role in the emotional response not only of the characters but of the audience. Dominick LaCapra, another founding figure in trauma studies, explains, "Something of the past always remains, if only as a haunting presence or revenant."[399] As projections of their mothers, Gren and Dil frequently play the role of the revenant that refuses to stay repressed. On a literal level, Dil will never stay in his room, appearing always at Willa's elbow when she least wants him there;

---

396 Caruth, *Unclaimed Experience*, 3–4.
397 Headley, *Mere Wife*, 261–62.
398 Headley, *Mere Wife*, 232.
399 LaCapra, "Trauma, Absence, Loss," 700.

Gren moves so silently that he constantly sneaks up on Dana without even meaning to. And it is Gren and Dil who dig out the antique train in the mountain cave, the metal dragon that comes to symbolize the relentless march of "progress" over the bones of the past. In this Freudian sense, the train is the repressed traumatic memory of the entire, fractured community. But it is a community that remains fractured until its members are thrown together in death. Caruth argues that trauma has the potential to connect people in mutual sympathy: "one's own trauma is tied up with the trauma of another, [...] trauma may lead, therefore, to the encounter with another, through the very possibility and surprise of listening to another's wound."[400] *Mere Wife*, however, is a story about the failure of such potential connections.

Willa and Structural Trauma

If we take a trauma theory lens to *Mere Wife*, we can view Willa and the other suburban mothers as representatives of what LaCapra calls structural trauma —that is, a kind of generalized, "transhistorical" trauma that has to do with the inevitable disappointment of being human, of being unable to attain the perfection and happiness we can conceive of but not realize.[401] LaCapra associates structural trauma with absence rather than loss: we may yearn for utopia, but we have never lived in one and never will. As he says, "[O]ne cannot lose what one never had."[402] Historical trauma, on the other hand, has to do with loss: specific events from the individual (the death of a loved one) to the societal (the Holocaust), in which what once existed has now ceased to be.[403] Willa might be seen as having experienced genuine loss: as a young woman, she was briefly married to a musician before her mother, deeming the match unworthy, severed the relationship and forced Willa to have an abortion. This could be the stuff of historical trauma, and yet Willa does not seem to have been traumatized by it. We discover at the funeral of her second husband that Willa did not love the first either; she "digs a pit for her marriages and kicks sand over the faces of her former men."[404] And if her relationship to Dil is any indication, she is untouched by the loss of her first pregnancy as well: when Dil chokes on a Lego

---

400 Caruth, *Unclaimed Experience*, 8.
401 LaCapra, "Trauma, Absence, Loss," 700.
402 LaCapra, "Trauma, Absence, Loss," 701.
403 LaCapra, "Trauma, Absence, Loss," 700.
404 Headley, *Mere Wife*, 175.

king's head, Willa reaches into his throat and, instead of trying to fish the object out, pushes it farther in, thinking of herself as "a princess," "a queen," "a heroine."[405] In fact, her pain and grief are public performances, self-aggrandizing and manipulative. When Roger is killed and Dil temporarily kidnapped, she pictures herself as "a marble statue, Mary in a cathedral, her dear one draped across her lap, her face a mask of tragedy."[406] Her campaign to renovate the train and underground train station are likewise a bid at her own immortality. She uses her status as grieving widow to steamroll problems with the construction, including the desecration of a graveyard. Then she imagines the completed train as a symbol of her triumph: "[s]he'll drink champagne in the dining car, sit against the window and look down on everything that's tried to keep her from getting what she deserves."[407] Only when she sees Gren's severed head in Ben Woolf's hands does she realize that she has been the monster all along, with "talons long and curved, pearlescent."[408] Even then, one wonders whether it was really the sight of the boy's head or the fact that she is being arrested for the murder of her own son that sparks this moment of recognition.

The question, then, is what exactly has precipitated the trauma response that Willa has—the moments of hallucination, blackouts, nightmares. One answer may come from the "mothers" of the novel: Willa's mother, Roger's mother, and the other women of the older generation in Herot. These women, too, have been the victims of genuine historical trauma: they deny having experienced abuse but have certainly suffered it;[409] they deny having contemplated suicide but have certainly considered it.[410] But, like Willa, they have weaponized their suffering and used it to browbeat those they can control. A telling moment occurs when Dil has been kidnapped and Willa is waiting for Ben Woolf to find him; the mothers console Willa for her loss by listing for her "all the awful things that have happened since the beginning of time."[411] What they are referring to are historical traumas, genuine losses, but they are not *their* traumas or losses. The mothers are engaging in what LaCapra calls "vicarious victimhood,"[412] "intrusively arrogating to oneself the victim's experience or undergoing (whether consciously or unconsciously) surrogate victimage" that rightly is the experience

---

405 Headley, *Mere Wife*, 114.
406 Headley, *Mere Wife*, 124.
407 Headley, *Mere Wife*, 224.
408 Headley, *Mere Wife*, 295.
409 Headley, *Mere Wife*, 268.
410 Headley, *Mere Wife*, 204.
411 Headley, *Mere Wife*, 193.
412 LaCapra, "Trauma, Absence, Loss," 699.

of another.[413] What has really made them unhappy is not loss but absence: they, like Willa, dream of unassailable power, perfection, invulnerability, but these things are fantasies. Appropriating the role of victim is an act of narcissism,[414] and as a result they have become threats to those around them, buying into "the dubious ideas that everyone (including perpetrators or collaborators) is a victim, that all history is trauma, or that we all share a pathological public sphere or a 'wound culture.'"[415] They are indeed victims—victims of misogyny and middle-class snobbery and even violence—but they see themselves as victims on a cosmic scale, as vessels for all the crimes that have ever been perpetrated against women, and as a result, they do exactly what LaCapra claims such people do when they conflate absence with loss:

> [They assume] that there was (or at least could be) some original unity, wholeness, security, or identity which others have ruined, polluted, or contaminated and thus made 'us' lose. Therefore, to regain it [they] must somehow get rid of or eliminate those others.[416]

In this way, the Othering of Dana and Gren echoes the Othering that Grendel and his dam experience in *Beowulf*. The difference is that in *Mere Wife*, we cannot see that Othering as justified. Similarly, Wealhtheow, the good queen, "mindful of propriety"[417] and seemingly without purpose or ambition beyond her concern for her children, exists in the background of this story as the fantasy of the "perfect" woman who cannot exist.

Ben Woolf and the Trauma of the Guilty

Ben Woolf, like Dana, has experienced historical trauma as a veteran of the wars after 9/11. However, his trauma is not that of a victim. He has a taste for violence and is nostalgic for the war: he numbers the dead in his mind, recalling that "[s]ome were killed by bombs, some by drones, some by Ben's gun. He did okay. Better than here," in the Herot Police Department, where he asks himself, "What kind of heroics are possible?"[418] His own repressed memories of the war violence are forcibly kept at bay so that "[a]ll he knows is that he's one of

---

413 LaCapra, *History and Memory*, 182.
414 LaCapra, *History and Memory*, 183.
415 LaCapra, "Trauma, Absence, Loss," 712.
416 LaCapra, "Trauma, Absence, Loss," 707. See also LaCapra, *History and Memory*, 187.
417 "[C]ynna gemyndig," *Beowulf*, l. 613, author's translation.
418 Headley, *Mere Wife*, 63–64.

the few good men. He is the front line against the nightmare."[419] We never discover what exactly he did during the war, but we know as well as Willa does
that his stories of saving children from burning buildings[420] are fantasies of a
man who, like the original Beowulf, is "most eager for fame,"[421] but who, unlike
the original, is not worthy of it. Even though he recognizes a fellow Marine in
Dana when he first encounters her, he sees the fact that she bests him in combat
as "unnatural" and decides that "[s]he needs to be burned, staked, any of those
options."[422] Like Willa and the mothers, then, he identifies Dana as the Other
who must be eliminated for him to remain a hero, and we are not surprised
when Dana recognizes him as a coward. Ben Woolf has suffered historical trauma, but as LaCapra points out, "[N]ot everyone traumatized by events is a victim."[423] In the case of Ben, he is the perpetrator.

Dana and Historical Trauma

Dana is the character who best represents the victim of historical trauma, but it
turns out not to be the trauma we expect. When we first meet her, stumbling out
of the desert six months pregnant by an unknown man, we assume her paranoia,
memory gaps, and flashbacks are a result of having been captured and raped.
She diagnoses herself with PTSD[424] and describes her sense of uncertainty
about reality as her brain "trying to make sense out of smoke."[425] But from the
very beginning, details make us doubt that the story we impose upon her is
what really happened. We discover, for instance, that her first trauma was not
the war but the loss of her mother while she was deployed. Likewise, when
she charges into Willa's kitchen in search of Gren, who has snuck in to visit
Dil, the white tiles make her flash back, not to her captivity in the desert, but
to the military hospital; she has to remind herself, "No one's taken us back to
the police, or to the military prison."[426] In fact, whenever she remembers a snippet of her time in the desert, she sees it in the most positive terms:

---

419 Headley, *Mere Wife*, 67.
420 Headley, *Mere Wife*, 151.
421 "[L]ofgeornost," *Beowulf*, l. 3182, author's translation.
422 Headley, *Mere Wife*, 162.
423 LaCapra, "Trauma, Absence, Loss," 723.
424 Headley, *Mere Wife*, 31.
425 Headley, *Mere Wife*, 10.
426 Headley, *Mere Wife*, 103.

I run up a flight of stairs to get out of the way of the storm, and there's someone in the upper room of the house I've tried to hide in. [...]

Am I dead? I ask.

Maybe, he says.

[...]

Are you some kind of god?

He turns around and I see his face. I don't know if he's a man or a monster, or something made of fire. I don't know about me either. I could be all of that too, a woman, a monster, someone made of flames.

[...]

Now it's later and I'm wearing a ring on my finger, and the ring is wrapped in thread from my uniform to make it fit. He's smiling at me, my hands in his hands, my body against his body, and my heart is pounding with joy. There's a room with a bed, curtained, lanterns, and he is waiting for me in it and I'm home.[427]

These memories, so redolent with Christian imagery (the upper room, the question about the man's divinity, the marriage to a more-than-human like a nun's marriage to Christ), are probably a further symptom of her trauma. The one thing we know for certain about her captivity is that her captors made her participate in the filming of her own staged beheading, so they were hardly benevolent figures. But the fact that she has filled in the gaps in her memory with a narrative in which she is chosen, and in which her child is a miraculous demigod, contrasts sharply not only with *Beowulf*'s claim that Grendel and his dam are the "kin of Cain,"[428] but also with what she suddenly remembers of her experience after being "rescued":

"Nothing happened to you," said the men when I woke up in the hospital.

"Nothing happened to you that didn't happen to a hundred men. They were kidnapped, but they kept their mouths shut. You were a soldier. You were approached."

"I was taken."

"You sympathized with the enemy."

"Who are you, if you don't?"

They poured water into my face. They drowned me, baptized me in ice, resurrected me, drowned me again.[429]

Dana may have been raped by her captors, but maybe she wasn't. The trauma that comes back to her most powerfully in moments of high pressure is the trauma caused by being betrayed and tortured by the people who were supposed to be "the good guys."

---

427 Headley, *Mere Wife*, 186–87.

428 "Cāines cynne," *Beowulf*, l. 107, author's translation.

429 Headley, *Mere Wife*, 237–38.

But this individual trauma is not what ultimately precipitates the climax of the novel. That is caused by communal trauma: historical trauma that involved the losses on a scale much larger than the individual. Dana is either black or Native or some combination of both, and she feels the communal suffering of centuries of oppression—not because she is appropriating the pain of people she never met but because it still plays out in her daily existence. She knows that the color of Gren's skin puts him at risk: "My son shouting would be my son attacking. My son sleeping would be my son addicted. My son in love with the boy from down there would be my son hanging from a tree."[430] And she recognizes that the desecration of the graveyards, first to build Herot and then to expand the rail station, is a crime against those, like her, who still have loved ones buried there. Her mother's grave has been obliterated to build Willa's neighborhood, and Dana reflects, "The whole planet is paved in the dead, who are ignored so the living can dig their foundations."[431]

But it is not until the trauma of her mother's death is made visible by Willa creating a museum in the renovated train station to display the bones of Dana's mother and the silver cup that she buried with her that Dana is galvanized by the pain of that communal loss:

> I'm seeing everyone from Herot Hall and everyone they came from. Thousands of them, stealing and stealing. Thousands of them breaking open graves and taking our bodies out of them. Thousands of them marching over land that should belong to us.[432]

In the novel's emotional climax, Dana's individual traumas, whatever they are, become swept up and magnified by being combined with the traumas of her lost community. When she attacks Ben Woolf in a final, futile attempt to save Gren, she says, "I let all the blood of centuries of murders pour out of my hands, all the agony of childbirth and all the panic of waiting for someone to find us on that mountain, all the fury of keeping someone safe in the dark when you should be bringing him out into the sun."[433] But even the force of collective trauma is not enough to save the Others of this novel. Ben Woolf beheads Gren, and Dana's last act of hijacking and crashing the train is not an act of defiance but an act of hopeless revenge.

---

430 Headley, *Mere Wife*, 238.
431 Headley, *Mere Wife*, 33.
432 Headley, *Mere Wife*, 236.
433 Headley, *Mere Wife*, 287.

Ecocriticism and the End of Trauma

What, then, is the end of trauma? Caruth outlines an "ethical imperative" in being witnesses, a responsibility of the observer watching another person working through their trauma. The "awakening" of the trauma victim, she says, "consists not in seeing but in handing over the seeing it does not and cannot contain to another."[434] If literature hands over to us a trauma its characters do not understand, what are we to do with it? Dana is a fiction, but the communal trauma she experiences is not, and so Caruth's ethical imperative still applies. The solution in *Mere Wife*—if it can be called a solution—invokes another theoretical lens: ecocriticism. Throughout the novel, the natural world is placed in opposition to the urban and suburban ones, with the more sympathetic Dana being associated with the natural world and the antagonists being associated with the urban. Dana's lullaby to Gren is a song of comfort in nature: "All is well and will be well. [...] And the squirrels will be fed and the trees will grow taller. [...] The snows will come and pile up, but we'll be warm."[435] On the other hand, suburban Ben sees trees falling on houses as "nature committing crimes against property,"[436] and he sees his duty as holding back that tide of natural chaos.

The natural world speaks at intervals in the first-person plural, "protect[ing] those who live inside them,"[437] and more than once it claims Dana and Gren, who have grown up on the mountain and whose family line is buried in its soil, as two of their own: "We are a white deer and we are a black raven and we are blood in the snow. [...] [A]nd we are a woman standing before her mother's bones, holding her family treasure, broken."[438] Nature seems to sympathize with historical loss, especially communal, as is appropriate to the "we" of its voice. But at the same time, and what is important from an ecocritical perspective, nature refuses to be chained to the will of or even affection for human beings, claiming, "We love what we love and we kill what we kill."[439] This independence is what makes it capable of absorbing the losses of human beings into something akin to healing. The mere itself is a space of memory, and everyone immersed in it—both Dana and Ben—are washed with their own remembrances. When Dana derails the train and it plunges into that mere, Dana experiences a flash of eternity:

---

434 Caruth, *Unclaimed Experience*, 111.
435 Headley, *Mere Wife*, 28.
436 Headley, *Mere Wife*, 61.
437 Headley, *Mere Wife*, 143.
438 Headley, *Mere Wife*, 243.
439 Headley, *Mere Wife*, 209.

I'm in a crowd and we are all walking together, my mother and my grandmother, my husband and my heart, my son and his beloved, my ghosts, the soldiers I fought beside, the people we killed, and the people who killed us.[440]

Like Toni Morrison's *Desdemona*, the afterlife is a place where the traumas of life are rendered painless, where barriers are no longer insuperable. But unlike *Desdemona*, that healing is not achieved by human effort but rather by being absorbed into a natural state.

Headley does not portray the natural world as an alternative to a traumatized human one but rather as its inevitable end. LaCapra resists such resolution, aligning himself with Freud's atheistic skepticism and insisting that the redemption that trauma narratives hope for is "not there."[441] He hopes for a partial healing, not a mastery over the trauma but rather a sense that the trauma is no longer the master of the traumatized. Headley, for all the bitterness of the novel, offers greater hope in the end, perhaps consciously refuting the bleak end of *Beowulf* with its keening Geatish woman and the oncoming "humiliation and captivity" of her unprotected people.[442]

Ultimately, while the novel's overt purpose is to "fix" the original by looking at heroism and monstrosity through the eyes of women and monsters, it also makes a broader statement, not just about literature but about history. *Mere Wife* asks us to see both history and literature as a tradition of trauma, not in the negative mode of a "wound culture" as LaCapra describes it but as a series of takings and overpowerings that echo through time in which the truth is as inaccessible to us as it is to the traumatized characters. The opening word of each chapter is one of the many possible translations of the Old English word "hwæt": "so, hark, behold, now," etc.[443] The first and most powerful translation is "listen," which forms a refrain for Part I. If literature is a record, however morphed, of historical traumas, the novel reinforces Caruth's ethical imperative that listeners take heed of what it has to say, but it is also a warning against doing what Willa does and taking that trauma as our own.

---

440 Headley, *Mere Wife*, 305.
441 LaCapra, "Trauma, Absence, Loss," 706.
442 "[H]ȳnðo ond hæftnȳd," *Beowulf*, l. 3155, author's translation.
443 Headley, *Mere Wife*, "Selected Translations."

Chapter 3
A Case Study: Writing Disability and
Intersectionality in Medieval Literature

Despite the fact that disability was probably more the norm than non-disability in the Classical, medieval, and early modern periods, very few canon fanfictions take on disability as a focal point. Some imply it (intersexuality falls under the umbrella of disability studies,[444] but Pard's character in *Sometimes We Tell the Truth* is treated more in terms of gender than disability), and others include it obliquely (Dana's lost eye and amputated arm in *Mere Wife* qualify her as a person with disabilities, but neither physical feature seems much to affect her day-to-day existence). But it remains a largely underexplored realm in the creative world. Indeed, even in the critical world, disability studies have been slow to make inroads into premodern scholarship because of the difficulty of reconstructing what disability would have meant to cultures of the past.[445] Yet that does not mean there is nothing to be said about it.

In the following case study, I have undertaken to write canon fanfictions of two episodes from medieval Icelandic literature: the story of Melkorka, the Irish slave in *Laxdæla saga*, and that of Oddny Geitisdottir in "Þorsteins þáttr uxafóts" ("The Story of Thorstein Ox-Foot"), a short story preserved in the Flateyjarbók manuscript (GkS 1005 fol.). Both of these women do not speak: Melkorka by choice, Oddny by nature. Their stories are remarkably similar, and my purpose in retelling both is to explore two different sides of disability (or perceived disability): one that is empowering and one that is limiting. Although there are many disabled men in the sagas—and, indeed, disabled gods[446]—the fact that both of these disabled characters are women allows us additionally to explore intersectionality, the interaction of multiple "Othering" factors in their lives.

In the following pages, I present a text of each episode translated from the Icelandic, with my own fic following each original text. Because translations of *Laxdæla saga* are readily available online and in book form, I have summarized, for matters of efficiency, parts of the Melkorka episode that do not concern her directly. "Þorsteins þáttr uxafóts" is not so easily found in translation, and so I

---

444 See Garland-Thomson, "Feminist Disability Studies," 1558.
445 For a brief overview of disability studies on the subject of the Icelandic sagas, the genre of interest in this chapter, see Ármann Jakobsson et al., "Disability before Disability," 440–42.
446 On disabled men and disabled gods, see Bragg, "Impaired and Inspired."

https://doi.org/10.1515/9781501515972-005

have included the entire story, even though Oddny is absent from the second half. In these translations, I have striven for more or less idiomatic language, regularizing verb tenses and anglicizing names as far as seemed reasonable, and I have minimized explanatory footnotes; more detailed studies of the original texts exist elsewhere.[447] These translations are included to provide a context for and contrast with the canon fanfics that follow them.

The chapter concludes with an analysis of the fics in the vein of Kim Zarins's self-analysis of her *Canterbury Tales* retelling. It should be noted that one remarkable advantage canon fanfiction has over straight analysis is that retelling a piece of literature allows the author to "comment" upon dozens of details in the original that could never be included in a coherent scholarly analysis. In this way, canon fanfiction can function almost like a line-by-line commentary. This is an advantage to the genre that I myself did not discover until I wrote this case study. Nevertheless, the analysis I include not only completes the case study as such, but it also provides an example of the kind of self-analysis that students may aim to write if assigned a similar project, as discussed in the appendix.

Content warning: both *Laxdæla saga* and "The Story of Thorstein Ox-Foot" imply rape; both canon fanfictions depict or discuss it. *Laxdæla saga* and its fanfiction depict slavery, sex trafficking, and kidnapping. "Thorstein Ox-Foot" depicts graphic violence.

3.1 *Laxdæla saga* (Melkorka Episode)

Chapter 12

It happened at the beginning of summer that the king[448] went east on an expedition to the Brännö Islands to keep peace over his land, as the law decreed for every third summer.[449] A meeting of the chieftains was arranged to decide the cases the king was to judge. It was considered an entertaining trip to attend that meeting because men came there from nearly every land we have heard

---

447 A starting point for the study of *Laxdæla saga* would be Bergljót Kristjánsdóttir, "Introduction"; for "Þorsteins þáttr uxafóts," Ármann Jakobsson et al., "Disability before Disability," and Binns, "The Story of Þorsteinn Uxafót."
448 Haakon I Haraldsson, king of Norway.
449 The chapter numbers within section 3.1 are those of *Laxdæla saga* itself, included for ease of cross-reference with the full work.

of. Hoskuld[450] launched his ship. He also wished to attend the meeting because he had not met the king over the winter. There was also a market to attend. This meeting was attended in great numbers. There was much entertainment, drinking, and games and all kinds of merriment. Not much of note happened. Hoskuld met many of his friends there who were in Denmark.

And one day when Hoskuld went to enjoy himself with some men, he saw a splendid tent, far from the other booths. Hoskuld went into the tent and there sat a man in fancy clothing, and he had a Russian hat on his head. Hoskuld asked him his name.

He was called Gilli. "But many know me better if they hear my nickname. I am called Gilli the Russian."

Hoskuld said he had often heard him mentioned and called the richest of the men in the merchants' league.

Then Hoskuld said, "You must have things to sell that I would like to buy."

Gilli asked what his fellow travelers would like to buy.

Hoskuld said he wanted to buy a maidservant, "If you have one to sell."

Gilli answered, "You intend to embarrass me by asking for something which you expect me not to have. But we'll see whether that's the case."

Hoskuld saw that there was a curtain across the width of the booth. Gilli lifted the curtain and Hoskuld saw twelve women sitting in the inner part of the tent. Then Gilli said that Hoskuld should go in and see if he wanted to buy any of these women. Hoskuld did so.

The women sat all together across the length of the booth. Hoskuld looked closely at them. He saw one woman sitting at the edge of the tent. She was poorly clothed, but to Hoskuld she seemed beautiful, as far as he could see.

Hoskuld said, "How much would that woman cost if I wanted to buy her?"

Gilli answered, "You'll have to pay three silver marks for her."

"I think," said Hoskuld, "you value this slave rather highly: that is the worth of three."

Gilli answered, "You speak true. I do rate her more highly than the others. Choose any one of the eleven and pay one mark of silver for her, but this one will be mine."

Hoskuld said, "Let me first see how much silver is in the purse I have on my belt," and asked Gilli to take out his scale while he examined its contents.

Then Gilli said, "I will not deal deceitfully: there is something very wrong with the woman. I want you to know it, Hoskuld, before we close the bargain."

---

450 Hoskuld Dala-Kollsson is the saga's protagonist at this point in the story, an Icelander traveling in Norway and Denmark. He is the grandfather of Kjartan, the saga's great tragic hero.

Hoskuld asked what it was.

Gilli answered, "This woman doesn't speak. I have tried many times to speak with her and I have never gotten a word out of her. It is my opinion that this woman doesn't know how."

Then Hoskuld said, "Get out the scale and see how much this purse of mine weighs."

Gilli did so. They weighed out the silver and it came to three marks.

Hoskuld said, "So now that's done, and we can strike our bargain. Take the money and I will take this woman. I must say you have behaved generously in this matter because you didn't try to deceive me."

Afterwards, Hoskuld went home to his booth. That same evening, he slept with her.

The next morning when everyone had gotten dressed, Hoskuld said, "There's not much to say for the clothing that wealthy Gilli has given you. It is true that it takes more for him to clothe twelve than for me to clothe one."

Then Hoskuld opened a chest and took out a good dress and gave it to her. Everyone said the fine clothes suited her well.

And when the chieftains had dealt with their cases according to the law, the meeting was dissolved. Afterward Hoskuld went to meet King Haakon and greeted him worthily, as was fitting.

The king looked at him and said, "We would have received your greeting, Hoskuld, if you had greeted us a bit earlier, but we will do so even now."

Chapter 13

After this the king welcomed Hoskuld with good cheer and invited him aboard his ship. "And stay with us as long as you want to stay in Norway."

Hoskuld answered, "Thank you for your invitation, but I have much to do this summer. The reason I have so long delayed seeking an audience with you is that I intended to acquire timber for housing."

The king invited him to sail to Vik. Hoskuld stayed there with the king for a while. The king procured house timber for him and had it loaded onto his ship.

Then the king said to Hoskuld, "I will not keep you with us longer than you wish, though I think it will be difficult to replace you."

He led Hoskuld to his ship and said, "I have proven you to be a worthy man, but I think you're now sailing from Norway for the last time while I am its ruler."

The king drew a gold ring from his arm, which weighed a full mark, and gave it to Hoskuld, as well as a sword and other treasure, which came to half a mark of gold. Hoskuld thanked the king for his gifts and for all the honor he had shown him.

Then Hoskuld boarded his ship and sailed out to sea. They made good progress and came around the southern coast, then sailed west for Reykjanes and from there around Snaefellsnes and into Breidafjord. Hoskuld landed at the mouth of the Lax, had the cargo unloaded, drew the ship up on the inner shore of the Lax, and built a boatshed over it; the foundations are still visible where they built that boatshed. There he set up booths, and so it is called Budar-dal.[451]

After that, Hoskuld had the timber carried home, and it was easy because it was not a long way. Hoskuld rode home after it with some of his men and received a warm welcome, as was to be expected. His property there had been well cared for. Jorunn[452] asked who this woman was who came on the journey with him.

Hoskuld answered, "You will think I'm taunting you, but I don't know her name."

Jorunn said, "Either the rumors that have reached me are lies or you must have talked with her at least enough to have asked her name."

Hoskuld said he couldn't deny it and told her the truth, then committed the woman to her special care and said he very much wanted her to be at home at their homestead.

Jorunn said, "I will not pick fights with your concubine that you have brought from Norway, even though she hasn't got the manners of decent people. It seems to me perfectly fitting if she is both deaf and dumb."

Hoskuld slept with his wife every night after he came home and was not often with his concubine. To everyone it was obvious that she had a noble bearing and that she was no fool.

And in the late winter, the woman bore Hoskuld a baby boy. Hoskuld was summoned and shown the child, and he and the others thought they had never seen a more beautiful or noble infant. Hoskuld was asked what the boy should be called, and he said the boy should be called Olaf because Olaf Feilan, his uncle, had died a little before that. Olaf surpassed most children, and Hoskuld loved him dearly.

The summer after that, Jorunn said that the concubine should take on some work or else be sent away. Hoskuld told her to work in the house and look after

---

451 That is, Booth Dale.
452 Hoskuld's wife.

his child. By the time the boy was two years old, he was well-spoken and ran about on his own like a child of four.

It happened one morning that Hoskuld had gone out to see about his farm. The weather was good: the sun shone but was not yet high in the sky. He heard people talking and went over to where a stream fell over the edge of the home meadow. There he saw two people he recognized. It was Olaf, his son, and Olaf's mother. Then he realized she was not mute at all, because she was talking fluently with the boy. Hoskuld went to them and asked her her name and said there was no point in concealing it any longer. She said that was true. They sat down at the edge of the meadow.

Then she said, "If you want to know my name, I am called Melkorka."

Hoskuld asked her to tell him more about her family.

She answered, "Myrkjartan is the name of my father. He is a king in Ireland. I was abducted from there at the age of fifteen."

Hoskuld said she had been silent rather too long about such a good heritage.

Afterwards, Hoskuld went in and told Jorunn what a strange thing had happened on his walk. Jorunn said she wasn't convinced the woman was speaking the truth and wanted nothing to do with foreign folk, and that was the end of their discussion. Jorunn was hardly better to her than before, but Hoskuld was rather more so.

A little while later, as Jorunn was getting ready for bed, Melkorka was drawing off her shoes and laying them on the floor. Jorunn took her socks and hit Melkorka in the head with them. Melkorka grew angry and drove her fist into Jorunn's nose so that it bled. Hoskuld came and parted them.

After that he let Melkorka leave the household and put her in a homestead farther up in Laxardal. That place has been known since as Melkorkustadir.[453] It is now deserted. It is south of the Lax. There Melkorka set up a home, and Hoskuld provided her with everything she needed for a household; their son Olaf went with her. It was quickly evident as Olaf grew that he would surpass other men for beauty and courtesy.

Chapters 14 – 16 deal with a separate family feud that leads to a divorce. Thord Goddi, a rather spineless man, seeks Hoskuld's support when his ex-wife's family lays claim to half his estate. In exchange for Hoskuld's help, Thord offers to foster his son Olaf, now seven years old, and to make Olaf his sole heir after his death. All that is said of Melkorka's response to the arrangement that takes her child from her is this:

---

453 Melkorka's Homestead.

It weighed heavily on Melkorka, who thought the fostering arrangement too lowly.

Hoskuld told her she did not know how to look at the situation rightly: "Thord is an old man and childless and intends to leave Olaf all his goods when he dies, and you can see him whenever you want."

Olaf, raised by a rich man, grows into a strapping youth with a penchant for finery, so that Hoskuld nicknames him "Peacock."

The following chapters describe another inheritance dispute between Hoskuld and his brother Hrut, which threatens to turn into an all-out feud until Jorunn intervenes and talks Hoskuld into making an equitable settlement. A number of years pass in relative peace.

Chapter 20

Hoskuld now stayed at his homestead and began to decline into advanced age, but his sons were now grown men. Thorleik[454] set up house at the farm that is called Kambsnes and Hoskuld provided for him out of his property. After that, he married a woman called Gjaflaug, daughter of Arnbjorn Sleitu-Bjarnarson and Thorlaug Thordardottir from Hofdi. It was a noble match. Gjaflaug was a beautiful woman and very vain. Thorleik was not easygoing but was the boldest of men. Things were not amicable between the kinsmen Thorleik and Hrut.[455] Bard, Hoskuld's other son, was still at home with his father. He had no less responsibility over the farm than Hoskuld did. Hoskuld's daughters are not much mentioned here, though there are men descended from them.

Olaf Hoskuldsson was now grown and was the best-looking man anyone had ever seen. He arrayed himself well in weapons and in clothing. Melkorka, Olaf's mother, lived at Melkorkustadir, as was written before. Hoskuld cared less about overseeing Melkorka's upkeep than he once had and said it now seemed as much Olaf's responsibility as his. Olaf said he would offer her his assistance as best he could. Melkorka thought Hoskuld was behaving dishonorably toward her, so she decided to do something that he would not like. Thorbjorn the Frail had primary charge of Melkorka's farm. He had asked her to marry him when she had lived there only a short time, but Melkorka had refused.

---

454 Thorleik and Bard (mentioned later in this paragraph) are Hoskuld's sons by Jorunn.
455 Thorleik's uncle, Hoskuld's brother.

There was a ship docked at Bordeyri in Hrutafjord. The captain's name was Orn. He was a king's man to Harald, son of Gunnhild.[456]

Melkorka told her son Olaf when they next met that she had discovered he wanted to go abroad to meet his noble kinsmen. "Because I told you true when I said that Myrkjartan was really my father and that he is a king among the Irish. It would be possible for you to sail with the ship at Bordeyri."

Olaf said, "I have talked about that with my father, and he was not much in favor of it. Regarding the situation with my foster-father's money, it is more in land and livestock than in tradable goods."

Melkorka answered, "I do not wish you to be called the son of a slave any longer. And if the concern is that you think you have too little money, I will get it for you by marrying Thorbjorn if you will then make the journey that you couldn't before. I think he will supply the goods you need if he gets to marry me. And the other consequence is that Hoskuld will be displeased by two things when he finds out: that you have gone abroad and that I am married to another man."

Olaf told his mother to do as she decided, then asked Thorbjorn if he could take his goods on loan, and a large quantity at that.

Thorbjorn answered, "That will only happen if I can marry Melkorka. Then I expect you will have as equal right to my goods as you have to anything else in your keeping."

Olaf said that's what they would do; they talked about what each wanted and decided it should be done quietly.

Hoskuld asked Olaf to ride to the Thing[457] with him. Olaf said he couldn't because of farm business, saying he wanted to have a pasture built for the lambs on the Lax. Hoskuld was pleased that he wanted to be a capable farmer. So Hoskuld rode to the Thing, but while he was gone, the bridal feast occurred at Lambastadi and Olaf arranged the marriage contract. Olaf took thirty hundreds of goods before they were divided between husband and wife, and he was to make no payment for them. Bard Hoskuldsson was at the wedding feast and witnessed the transaction between them. When the feast was ended, Olaf rode to his ship and met Captain Orn and arranged his passage.

---

456 King Harald II Ericsson, named instead in the narrative by his matronym, Harald Gunnhildarson.
457 A legal assembly.

But before they parted from each other, Melkorka put in Olaf's hand a large gold finger ring and said, "My father gave this treasure to me as a teething gift, and I expect he will recognize it if he sees it."

Then she put into his hand a knife and belt and bade him give them to her foster mother.[458] "I don't think she will deny these tokens."

Then Melkorka said, "At home I have prepared you as best I can, and taught you to speak Irish, which will serve you well wherever you land in Ireland."

They parted after that. A fair wind arose when Olaf came to the ship and they sailed off to sea.

Chapter 21

As predicted, Hoskuld is none too pleased to discover what happened while he was at the Thing, but since his sons were involved, he takes no action.

Olaf, now eighteen years old, spends the winter in Norway, well received by King Harald and even better received by the queen mother, Gunnlaug, who had a great affection for Olaf's uncle Hrut. Come summer, though, Olaf wants to sail to Ireland to meet his grandfather. When Orn refuses to take his own ship in that direction, Gunnlaug steps in and outfits a ship and sixty companions for him.

The ship struggles with contrary winds and fog, and when they finally reach Ireland, they are far from any trading settlement and surrounded by skerries and shallow water. They put in at a river mouth and, as they expect, the local Irish claim their ship and cargo as stranded goods.

The Irish, however, are not prepared for a trading ship to be manned by warriors, and when their attempts to take the ship are rebuffed, they back off until news of the arrival reaches King Myrkjartan, who happens to be in the vicinity. He rides down to the shore with his armed retinue, making Olaf's companions fearful of a harder fight than they had with the locals.

But when Olaf heard the murmur among his men, he told them to take heart. "Our business has taken a good turn. The Irish are now greeting Myrkjartan, their king."

---

458 Throughout the saga, Melkorka's childhood caretaker is referred to as her "fóstra," her foster mother. Given her clear dependency on Myrkjartan (he has the power to prevent her leaving with Olaf later in the saga), many translations refer to her rather as Melkorka's "nurse."

The retinue rode near enough to the ship that each side could hear what the other said. The king asked who was captaining the ship. Olaf gave him his name and asked the identity of the valiant rider he was addressing.

He answered, "I am Myrkjartan."

Olaf said, "And are you the king of the Irish?"[459]

He said he was. Then the king asked after the common news. Olaf answered well to everything he was asked about. Then the king asked where they had come from or what sort of men they were. And he inquired more closely about Olaf's family than before because the king discovered that this man was proud and would not volunteer more than he was asked.

Olaf said, "I shall tell you that we sailed from Norway and those who are aboard here are the men of King Harald Gunnhildarson. And regarding my own family, it is to be said that my father lives in Iceland and is called Hoskuld. He is a man from an important family. But I think you will have seen more of my mother's kinsmen than I, because Melkorka is my mother's name and I am told faithfully that she is your daughter, King, and that is what has driven me on this long journey. Much rests for me on what answer you will now give to my speech."

The king fell silent and spoke to his men. His advisers asked him what this man's words meant.

The king answered, "It is obvious that this Olaf is a man of an important family, whether he is my kinsman or not, and he speaks the best Irish I've ever heard."

After that the king stood up and said, "We shall now answer your speech: I will offer safe passage to you and your shipmates, but regarding our relation that you speak of, we will discuss it further before I offer you a response."

Then they extended the gangway and Olaf and his companions went ashore. Now the Irish were struck by how splendid and warlike this man was. Olaf greeted the king well and took off his helm to bow to him, and the king welcomed him very warmly. They then entered into talk. Olaf laid forth his claims anew and spoke of his business both at length and wisely. He finished by saying he had on his hand the gold ring Melkorka had given him at their parting in Iceland. "And she said that you, King, had given it to her as a teething gift."

The king took the ring and looked at it and his face turned very red.

Then he said, "Your tokens are true, and on top of anything else, it is clear you have so inherited the traits of your mother that you can be recognized by

---

459 The original does not make a distinction between "the king" and "a king." There were as many as nine kings in Ireland at any one time in this period, but Norway, the Icelanders' context for monarchy, as a rule had only one. Hence, the narrative never designates what part of Ireland Myrkjartan is king of, implying instead that he rules the whole island.

them. And because of this, I wish to acknowledge our kinship, Olaf, in the witness of these men who are present and hear my words. It follows that I should invite you into my court with all your company. Your honor there will depend on what kind of man I find you to be when I have tried you further."

Then the king had horses fetched for them to ride, and he set men to look after their ship, and he had their cargo guarded.

The king rode to Dublin and people thought it marvelous news that his daughter's son traveled with him, the daughter who long ago had been captured at the age of fifteen. But the one most moved by this news was Melkorka's foster-mother, who now lay bedridden both with affliction and with old age. But even so, she got up and went without her crutch to meet Olaf.

The king said to Olaf, "Here comes Melkorka's foster-mother, and she will want to have news from you about her situation."

Olaf received her with both hands, set the old woman on his knee, and said that her foster-daughter was living in good condition in Iceland. Then Olaf gave her the knife and belt, and the old lady recognized the treasures and was taken with weeping, saying it was true that the son of Melkorka was splendid, "Just as he ought to be."

The old woman was well and in good spirits all winter long.

The king was not often at rest because there was constant fighting around Ireland and Britain. The king drove the Vikings and raiders away that winter. Olaf and his company were on the king's ship and those who encountered them in battle thought them rather vicious. The king began to consult with Olaf and his fellows about all his decisions, because Olaf proved himself both wise and eager in every peril.

And at the end of the winter, the king called an assembly, which was attended in large numbers. The king stood up and spoke.

He opened his speech thus: "It is known to you all that this man who came here last autumn is the son of my daughter and of an important family on his father's side. Olaf has proven himself a man of accomplishment and a great leader, so much so that we have no other such man in these parts. Now I wish to offer him my kingdom after my day, because Olaf is better suited as a ruler than my own sons."

Olaf thanked him for this offer with great eloquence and fair words but said he would not risk the murmuring of his sons after Myrkjartan's death; he said it would be better to have a short-lived honor than a long shame and said he wished to go to Norway once it was possible for ships to travel between the two lands. He said his mother would be little pleased if he did not come back. The king told Olaf to decide for himself. Then the assembly was dissolved.

And when Olaf's ship was prepared, the king followed Olaf to it and gave him a gilded spear and well-appointed sword and many other riches. Olaf asked to take Melkorka's foster-mother away with him, but the king said there would not be any need for that, and she didn't go. Olaf and his men boarded their ship and took their leave of the king in great friendship.

After that, Olaf and his company sailed out to sea. They had a good passage and reached Norway, and Olaf's journey became very famous. They beached their ship. Olaf got them horses and went to meet King Harald with his companions.

Chapter 22

Olaf spends the following winter in the Norwegian court, now a celebrity and officially a king's man. The following summer, at his request, Harald reluctantly parts with him, giving him a ship to send him off in style.

Arriving back in Bordeyri, Olaf is immediately welcomed by his father and spends the winter with Hoskuld and his half-brothers. Olaf's fame spreads far and wide in Iceland, partly because he is now known to be the son of the Irish king and a favorite of King Harald, and partly because he has brought great wealth back from his travels.

Melkorka came swiftly to meet her son Olaf. Olaf greeted her very warmly. She asked him a great many things about Ireland, first about her father and other kinsmen. Olaf answered everything she asked. Then she asked if her foster-mother was alive. Olaf said she certainly was. Melkorka asked why he had not done her the kindness of bringing her to Iceland.

Olaf answered, "It didn't please people, Mother, that I should take her from Ireland."

"So it is," she said.

It was clear that it was much against her liking.

Melkorka and Thorbjorn had a son who was named Lambi. He was a large man and strong, and like his father in looks and disposition.

Hereafter, Melkorka disappears from the narrative of Olaf Peacock and his descendants. The last mention of the Irish captive occurs in chapter 38:

Thorbjorn the Frail by then had died, and so had Melkorka. They lay together in a cairn in Laxardal, and Lambi their son lived there afterwards. He was a very bold man and had great wealth. Lambi was more honored than his father because of his mother's kin. He had a good relationship with Olaf.

3.2 Melkorka (A Piece of Canon Fanfiction)

By the time they discovered the Vikings, it was already too late. They came, as they always did, on a night of deep fog, and they wrapped their sword hilts in wool so they did not rattle when drawn at the foot of the wall.

When the alarm was raised, Melkorka was asleep beside her old nurse, the two women curled together against the chill and the damp of the Irish spring. Myrkjartan was on his feet and armed before even his readiest followers had pulled on their boots. Theirs was not the first cashel to be attacked this season.

"Stay here," he told Melkorka and Siobhan. "If they make it over the wall, keep perfectly silent. They may miss you in the looting."

"Be careful, Father," Melkorka whispered, and he kissed her copper hair before shutting them into the sleeping compartment.

In the pitch dark, the two women crouched, listening, and hardly had Myrkjartan left them when they heard the shouts and cries of fighting at the outer wall.

"We'll drive them off," Melkorka said to her nurse. "Don't be afraid, Siobhan. I won't let them hurt you."

The old woman laughed at that, her voice choked.

"Hang *me*, dear one," she said. "They have no use for an old woman. No one does. It's you they'll want."

Melkorka tossed her head. "Because I'm the king's daughter?" But Siobhan's answer was so low she could barely hear it.

"Because you're fifteen years old and beautiful."

Melkorka's confidence dissipated like smoke. Surely the Vikings would value a princess for something more than that. Surely?

The shouts were growing louder, and now they could hear the clash of metal on wood, blade on blade. Someone was screaming in Irish, then he stopped abruptly.

"There are too many of them," Siobhan said.

"Will they kill Father?" Melkorka asked.

"If he survives the fighting, they'll probably let him buy his life. It's gold they want: blood isn't worth anything."

Someone shouted in Norse, not far away.

Melkorka was surprised to hear herself whisper, "I don't want to be a slave."

"No one does."

There was more screaming, then the crash of a door being hammered in.

"Father will have left his dagger on the wall when he took his sword," Melkorka said. "I'm going to slip out and get it."

"No!" cried the old nurse. "If you fight them they will kill you. They don't want slaves who make trouble. If they find us, you must go with them quietly." When Melkorka tried to tug her arm from Siobhan's grip, the old woman only pulled her closer. "You're all I love in this world, child. I live only as you do."

Melkorka looked at Siobhan in the dark, though she could not see her. In her mind the old woman's creased face and sweat-stained kerchief were as clear as at noon. But then she saw the face again, as if for the first time, in the stark light of impending capture.

Myrkjartan had taken Siobhan in a raid long ago and given Melkorka to her to nurse when his wife died of a fever. She had never wondered why Siobhan had milk to give her. What had happened to Siobhan's own baby? With the confidence of a cosseted child, she had always taken for granted that Siobhan loved her. How could Melkorka fail to capture the heart of anyone who saw her, the copper-haired child of the king? But now, with the Vikings at the gates, she imagined what the world must have looked like through Siobhan's eyes when the raider at the gates was her father.

"How can you love me?" Melkorka asked.

Siobhan stroked her curly hair. "Because it was my right to, my only right." Again she caressed her hair. "I have cared for you since you were two weeks old. Long before you cut your first tooth, you were more mine than you were your mother's."

"You should hate me," Melkorka said, because all she could feel just now was hatred for the Vikings and for what they would do to her. She would never forgive them, and they had not even breached the hall yet.

"I chose to live," Siobhan said. "You must choose to live too, Melkorka. Every day. If you don't, that is when they defeat you."

The outer door of the hall burst open. Ten paces away from where the women lay hidden, the Vikings threw down the benches, looking for hidden coffers. Both women knew there was no way the raiders could miss them.

Siobhan clutched Melkorka's fingers. "Choose to live!" she pleaded. "Promise, Melkorka!"

Melkorka kissed the old nurse's mouth. "I promise," she said.

They heard a pair of hands fumbling at the latched door of the compartment, and Melkorka whispered a desperate "Slán" in farewell.

Then the door slid away, and they were blinded by a torch thrust in their faces.

"Ha!" barked the Viking. He said something to his companions in Norse, and they laughed. He seized Melkorka's arm and dragged her into the hall. She could hear Siobhan weeping from the bed.

Stumbling after the big man in her bare feet and light woolen shift, Melkorka searched the hall and then the yard for her father. If only he and Siobhan survived, Melkorka thought she might be able to bear whatever awaited her at the hands of the Vikings.

Finally she saw him, bleeding from a sword cut to his upper arm but standing on his feet, negotiating with the Viking captain through a translator, an Irish captive with the remains of a tonsure. When Myrkjartan spotted her, he took an impulsive step in her direction. Hope flared in Melkorka's heart. Would he be able to ransom her?

But Myrkjartan had little gold in the cashel, having sent most of it inland where it was safer from raids. What he had on hand would buy one life, not two, and the clan needed a king more than they needed a princess. Myrkjartan stepped back again and closed his eyes. Melkorka could not look at him as she was led away.

She was bound at the wrists and brought down to the edge of the water, where the big Viking tossed her over his shoulder like a sack of grain and waded out to where the three longships swayed in the tide. He threw her aboard the nearest and clambered in after her. There were no benches, just the sea chests of each sailor, so Melkorka was pushed down onto the bare boards of the deck, looking up at her captors from below.

As the other raiders returned, Melkorka was joined by several other girls from the cashel, all wearing just their sleeping shifts with their heads uncovered. They huddled together in the stern and some of them wept, but none of them cried out. This was the way of things.

The big Viking took the rudder, and the others pushed the shallow-drafted ship off the sand bar and leapt in, taking stations at the oars.

Not having much to do but keep the ship pointed straight down the river mouth until they raised their sails in the open water, the big Viking poked Melkorka's back.

"What is name?" he asked. He had to ask twice before she understood him. Some of the Vikings who had taken up residence in the newly founded towns to the east were learning to speak passable Irish, but these raiders were surely from abroad. This one had produced from his sea chest a hat like those sometimes worn by the Rus traders.

When Melkorka did not immediately answer his question, the Viking reverted to Norse, grumbling to himself as the captain shouted directions to the crew from the ship just behind them. Now that they were on the water, they had no reason to hide: the Irish boats were no match for a longship.

When the captain fell quiet, the big Viking tried again. "What is name?"

Melkorka hesitated, wondering if she should tell him she was a princess, wondering if that would save her. In the few heartbeats between his question and her decision, the Viking clucked his tongue impatiently and asked her yet again. His frustration sent a surge of satisfaction through Melkorka's shivering body, and this time she chose not to answer. Let him threaten, let him beat her: he would not have her name. She would not give him her words, even if they took everything else. She could thwart them in this one small thing, and she would.

No one touched the girls that night on the ship, much to their surprise, and the next day the captive monk explained to one of them in Melkorka's hearing, "Don't worry. Gilli has told the men not to spoil you for sale." He pointed at the big Viking, still wearing his showy fur hat. "You're safe until we reach Norway."

"Why are you helping them?" the girl asked.

He shrugged and ran a hand resignedly over the stubble that was growing on his shaven crown. "This seemed better than dying."

From Ireland, the ships brought their cargo east to Brännö Island, where the king of Norway was holding an assembly. Traders had gathered from all over to hold a market, and the big Viking Gilli set up a booth of goods for sale. He had a dozen slave girls in total, assembled from various raids, whom he seated at the back of the tent behind a curtain where casual onlookers could not cheapen them with their stares. However, when a well-dressed man came in with a pair of comrades and bought several yards of good scarlet, Gilli beckoned him behind the curtain to view his most valuable cargo.

Only much later, after she had learned Norse, did Melkorka piece together from fragments and reminiscences what the two men said.

"This one is very pretty," the newcomer observed, passing his eye up and down Melkorka's body.

"She is," Gilli agreed, "so pretty she'll cost you three marks. But I mustn't sell you anything under false pretenses. She's lovely and untouched, but she does have one defect: she can't speak."

The newcomer stroked his short blond beard. "Some might say that's not a defect at all." And so she was sold.

She knew he would violate her. In the hours between her purchase and the late-coming northern dark, she contemplated slipping his knife from his belt and driving it into his throat. She imagined gouging his eyes with her fingernails. But then what? She herself had seen what happened to slaves who made trouble. She had promised to live.

So when he came to her that night, she offered no resistance. But she watched him so unblinkingly as he pushed up her smock that he had to extinguish the torches before he could proceed.

In the dark, she set her jaw and suffered his touch in relentless silence, and when he rolled off her with a contented sigh, he fell asleep at her side. She lay awake, thinking of Siobhan as she must have been when she was young.

The next morning, he was up early, boiling porridge over the fire. When he saw her rise, he pointed to the barrel in the corner and said, "Öl." He pantomimed bringing a mug to his lips.

Melkorka poured him his ale and brought it over.

"It's a rare thing," he said, "to find a pretty girl who knows her business and doesn't grumble doing it."

Melkorka learned these words by heart, because later on he was fond of repeating them to his neighbors.

He patted the bench beside him and she sat down, steeling herself not to pull away when he tousled her hair and ran its curls between his fingers. After breakfast, he dressed her in a fine blue dress with silver brooches and gave her a matching kerchief for her head, inviting his companions to come in and admire her.

On the third or fourth night, he thought to tell her his name was Hoskuld Dala-Kollsson.

Late that summer, Hoskuld sailed back to Iceland, taking his silent slave girl to warm him on chilly nights at sea in the open ship. Sailing into Breidafjord, they beached on the gently sloping shore and unloaded their cargo. Hoskuld's farmstead lay not far off, on the lowland between the water and the treeless mountains. Small stands of birch and evergreen huddled here and there like miserable animals in the cold. There were many stumps where others had been cut down. Melkorka felt the bleak land leeching the strength out of her. The rich groves of Ireland were no longer sacred, but they were part of her soul. How did people live in this waste?

When they arrived at the farmstead, Hoskuld presented Melkorka to his wife, Jorunn. "I bought her for you," he insisted cheerfully, "to serve you."

Jorunn looked the girl over, her eyes lingering on the dress that was already growing tight around the middle. "I think she's served quite well enough already," she observed.

Hoskuld laughed at his wife, but all the same, he took to her bed and abandoned Melkorka's. Melkorka, for her part, slept peacefully for the first time since her capture.

The first morning, Jorunn watched her folding her blanket from the far side of the hearth that ran down the middle of the hall and called to her through the smoke of last night's fire, "What is your name, girl?"

Melkorka paused and turned to face Jorunn, but she didn't say anything.

"Oh, she's mute," Hoskuld said over his ale mug. "Didn't I tell you? I don't know her name, actually."

He always called her "stúlka." Melkorka had thought it was a nickname until she realized that all girls were called "stúlka."

Jorunn folded her arms, still watching Melkorka. "I don't suppose I want to know what you paid for this deaf-mute."

"She's not deaf," Hoskuld said. "Watch. Come here, girl. Refill my cup."

Melkorka considered ignoring him. It would be so satisfying to watch them all shouting and gesticulating, trying to force her to understand. They were pagans; probably they would think she had been struck deaf upon setting foot on this island as a Christian—that she had offended Thor or Odin or whoever they worshiped here.

But a mute servant could be useful; a deaf one might be seen as more of a burden than she was worth—she wasn't sure what these people did to those they didn't think were useful. She came around the hearth and refilled Hoskuld's mug.

"Well," Jorunn said, "at least she can't talk back."

Jorunn set her to spinning yarn and tending the fire, tedious tasks but not physically demanding. At first Melkorka was surprised not to be confined to the house: there was no wall around the farmstead as there had been around her father's stronghold. But one morning, walking out to the privy, she looked around at the high fells above the farm and the gray fjord below it, and she realized there was nowhere to go.

When she felt her time come upon her, she slipped away into the hills. There she could endure her ordeal with no one to hear if she cried out. It was barely early spring, and the days were still short and cold, the rain coming in fits from a sunless sky. As she labored in the wet, she thought how easy it would be to die here, simply to let go and melt away into the bare earth along with the disappearing snow. But she had promised to live.

She had made no such promises for the child of Hoskuld, and she thought, if it came alive, she might just leave it on the hillside and pray to God for forgiveness. But when she heard the first strangled cry of the baby, a fierce feeling stabbed through her. If it was not love, it was something older and more tenacious, something she had no words for. She cut the cord and wrapped the boy in a length of linen. She thought of what Siobhan had said and finally understood, in a way. The baby was not Hoskuld's: he was hers.

When she had recovered the strength to stand, she made her way slowly back to the farmstead, where the old women of the household greeted her with astonishment. She knew enough Norse now to understand that they had given her up for dead. She thought one of them said something like, "You're luckier than you have any right to be."

Once the women had washed the infant, they presented him to his father, informing him, as men had no discernment in these matters, that he was a fine and likely looking boy.

"You've given me a good return on my investment, my girl," Hoskuld said, glancing at the baby and touching Melkorka's cheek.

"Return," said Jorunn, "or added expense?"

The boy was called Olaf after his great-uncle, because even if they had cared to ask Melkorka what she wanted to call him, they couldn't. This was the first time she regretted her decision to silence herself. She did not want him called by the name of Hoskuld's dead uncle. He was worthy of an Irish name. But to speak then would be to relinquish the one thin thread that still made her a princess, set apart from those around her, and so she remained silent. Olaf proved to be a precocious and active child, stronger than his half-brothers even though they were older.

Now that she was unburdened, Melkorka was set to work mostly out of doors, helping to oversee the sheering of the sheep in the spring and the slaughter of the yearlings in autumn; in the summer she managed the hay production. She had had no experience in any of these things in Ireland, but not speaking seemed to give her more time to listen and to watch, and she had learned most of what she needed to know even before she was put to work at it. Hoskuld said he trusted her with such work because she was competent and reliable—and she was, for she had no more desire to starve than the Icelanders did—but Melkorka guessed that Jorunn wanted her as far away from Hoskuld as she could keep her. Though he had not invaded her bed since their return, his hands still wandered like snakes under her skirts whenever Jorunn wasn't looking.

Only in the long, almost dayless winters when the whole household, slaves and freemen alike, huddled together in the hall did Melkorka spend long stretches of time with Hoskuld and his wife. And at those times, she was usually in whatever corner of the house the two of them were not.

Olaf was the only person she kept company with, bringing the boy with her to the haymaking or to the highland shieling to work with the sheep, letting him observe the running of the farm from his earliest age. When she looked at him, that fierce, ancient feeling overcame her, and sometimes she found herself smiling at the little tricks of his babyish nature: the way he worked his mouth in his sleep, his helpless surprise whenever he sneezed. His wonder at everything—the lambs and the bright green moss and the first snows of the season—made her see the world through less jaded eyes, and once, staring up at the northern lights in a deep winter, she found herself thinking that this land was beautiful.

But when, in Olaf's third year, she glanced down at him as he watched the hay rakers and saw the expression of Hoskuld playing across his pudgy face, that fierceness she felt for him spilled over into panic. She would not let him belong to his father.

She took him with her to the river to do the washing; it was a fine day, and the banks were dotted with nodding buttercups. Crouching down to look her son in the eye, and gripping his shoulders to hold his attention, she said to him in Irish, "You are no slave's son. Prince I call you. Kjartan I name you, after the king, your grandfather. You will be a great man and your greatness shall redeem the shaming of your mother."

This she repeated to him every day thereafter, and many other things too, pouring four years of pent-up words into his patient ear, making him hers. Eventually, he could repeat what she said and answer in the same language.

One day in the next spring, Hoskuld came wandering down by the riverbank and heard Melkorka say, "Prince I call you. Kjartan I name you."

And a child's voice said, "And I shall be a great man and avenge my mother."

But of course the words were in a language unknown to Hoskuld.

"What's this? You can speak after all!" he cried.

Melkorka's mouth snapped shut and she looked up at Hoskuld with wide eyes. Would he beat her for lying to him? Would he take her son away?

But Hoskuld seemed more curious than angry. "Come now, no use denying it anymore, you sly vixen." He put his arm around her shoulder and slipped his hand down the embroidered neckline of her dress. "What a trick you've played. But you've got to tell me the whole story now—starting with your name."

When she did not answer right away, her son tugged at her skirt. "Tell him, Mamaí. Tell him I'm a prince."

Melkorka looked into his proud, earnest little face. Perhaps he was right. Perhaps this was the moment to speak, when it could raise her son in the world. She was loath to give her captor this one last part of her, but it wasn't about her anymore. She looked at her son again. It had not been about her for a long time now.

So she told Hoskuld her name and her parentage, sparing no detail that would convince him that she spoke the truth.

"A prince, is he?" Hoskuld repeated, looking at the boy as though for the first time. "And I a father to a prince." He laughed. "How many Icelanders can say that, eh, my girl?"

Still she was "stúlka" to him. He said nothing more about her four years of silence; her power slipped from her like a veil blown away in the wind. Instead, he went and brought Jorunn to tell her the news about his son.

"I knew she was hiding something," Jorunn said.

Hoskuld declared that she should no longer be given the rough outdoor work of an overseer but should be assigned the easier tasks of a lady's maid, as—he was quick to point out to her—he had always intended her to be. He took much more interest in his son now that he was a prince than he had when he was the child of a nameless concubine, but no one suggested changing his name from Olaf to Kjartan.

Melkorka felt no gratitude at being put back within reach of Hoskuld's hands and Jorunn's tongue, but the words of a slave woman were not much louder than her silence, and she knew it would be useless to protest.

One evening, a few months into the new arrangement, she was helping Jorunn off with her woolen stockings, which were wet from the rain. Jorunn took one in her hand and said, "There's a hole in the heel." And she hit Melkorka across the face with the wet sock, which slapped loudly against her cheek.

Melkorka thoughtfully wiped her face with her sleeve, then leapt up and struck Jorunn so hard that her nose bled. The women stared at each other, perhaps equally shocked at what had just happened.

"You shall be out of my house by first light," Jorunn said from behind her hand, "and you will take your prince with you."

Hoskuld offered his wife a cloth to hold to her nose and looked long at Melkorka in the firelight.

"I'll set her up on the farmstead up the valley," he said. "She can help Thorbjorn manage it for me. It will be a good place for Olaf to learn the running of a farm."

Melkorka nearly wept. Perhaps she should have struck Jorunn a long time ago.

The next morning, long before it was light, she was woken by a hand drawing the blanket off her shoulder. Hoskuld slipped underneath it and put his hand over her mouth. "One last time, my girl," he whispered, his breath hot on her ear. Jorunn lay asleep in the bed chamber at the other end of the room.

When he had finished with her, he made a reluctant move to rise, but she put her hand on his wrist. "I have never asked you for anything, in all these years," she whispered. "I ask you this now: is it fitting for your acknowledged son to be the child of a slave?"

"People rarely care who a man's mother is," Hoskuld said, watching his fingers comb through her hair in the dying firelight.

"They do when he is a prince."

Hoskuld stroked his beard, which was beginning to show a little white among the yellow wires. She watched the sated haze in his eyes give way to keen calculation.

"I liked you better when you didn't talk," he said at last.

But he freed her nonetheless.

People in the district said it was a fall for Melkorka to go from the hands of Hoskuld Dala-Hollsson to those of Thorbjorn the Frail even though she was free, and at first Melkorka agreed. The hall at Melkorkustadir was small and drafty, the walls tarred with old smoke. And she was only really as free as a fish in a weir. She wore no chain, but there was still nowhere for her to go. But not being a slave gave her one thing she had not had before. The word "no" was more powerful than her silence, and she used it freely on Thorbjorn, who from the beginning expressed a clumsy, flat-footed infatuation with her.

For a few years Melkorka was content, if not happy, keeping Thorbjorn at arm's length and her son much closer. But then Hoskuld rode up the valley and let himself into the hall.

"Pack your things, Olaf," he said by way of greeting. "You're going to live with Thord Goddi."

Olafur, now eight, looked up in alarm from his game of stick-figure warriors. "Who's that?" he asked.

Melkorka leapt up from her spinning. "You can't take him," she said.

Hoskuld looked at her blankly. "Why not?"

She collected herself. "He's my son" would mean nothing now; only reason would sway Hoskuld. "Thord is a spineless little man," she said evenly. "He's no worthy foster-father for your son."

But Hoskuld waved off her words with a meaty hand. "He's struck a very good bargain with me," he explained. "He may be spineless, but he's rich as an earl and has no sons of his own. He's agreed to make Olaf his heir when he dies." He slapped his son on the shoulder. "Then *you'll* be as rich as an earl, my boy. How would you like that?"

Olaf looked to his mother uncertainly and she thought she would break in half. She knelt in front of him, looking up into his face in the firelight. "You are going to be a great man," she said in Irish. "Great men need wealth as well as courage."

He was starting to sniffle, though he tried to turn away so his father wouldn't see it. "Do I have courage, Mamaí?"

"You are my son," she said.

And then he was gone.

Melkorka visited Thord's farmstead as often as the weather and the business of the farm permitted, and she continued to pour Irish into Olaf's ears, pulling him word by word back from the Vikings' world and into her own. But as the years mounted up, she could feel the power of his father drawing him away, and she had no answering power to draw him back.

At seventeen, he was a ready youth, inquisitive and restless, but Hoskuld seemed content to keep him working the Thord's little farm, training him to be the heir of a bleak little outpost at the edge of the world.

So one day during a feast, when all the inhabitants around Breidafjord had gathered to enjoy Hoskuld's rich hospitality, Melkorka approached the dais where Hoskuld and Jorunn were sitting with their sons, Olaf sitting to his father's left. She said loudly in Norse, "It's time you began doing a man's work, Olaf. Your ancestors were not farmers but warriors. I want you to take a ship and sail for Ireland. Declare yourself to my father, or my brothers if he has died, and claim your birthright among my kinsmen."

Olaf jumped up from the bench. "May I, Father?"

"And who's going to pay for it?" Jorunn asked.

Hoskuld did not offer to finance the venture. So for a time, that was the end of the matter: even Melkorka could not fault Jorunn for wanting to protect her own sons' inheritance.

She did have another solution, though it took her a long time to decide to act on it. But by the next summer, Thord had died, and Olaf returned to his father's farm a wealthy heir. When Hoskuld went to the Thing to observe the lawsuits, she came to the farm to speak to her son.

"Will you go abroad now that Thord is dead?" she asked.

"You don't understand how it is, Mother," he said. "Thord's wealth is in sheep and hayfields. I'd need ready coin to go abroad, or at least tradable goods. They have sheep and hay in Ireland already."

Melkorka understood exactly how it was, but she also understood that sons liked to be smarter than their mothers. However, mothers were still smarter than their sons.

"I'm going to marry Thorbjorn," she told him.

"Mother, don't joke about that," Olaf said. "It's cruel to taunt him when he's been pining for you all these years."

"His patience is about to be rewarded."

Olaf laughed incredulously. "But he's ugly, and he's a dolt. Whyever would you want to marry him?"

"You let me worry about the reasons," she said.

And when Hoskuld returned to the north, he found Melkorka married to his tenant. The neighbors wondered at her rash decision, until it was discovered that Thorbjorn had bought Olaf a share in a ship sailing east.

"Mamaí, you shouldn't have," Olaf said, once again her little boy, if only for a moment. "It's too great a sacrifice."

She laid her hand on his head. "I've sacrificed more for less. Iceland is no place for you: go and be a great man."

"And avenge the shaming of my mother," he murmured by rote. His eyes were already set on the mouth of the fjord, where the narrow water poured into the endless sea.

The day he was to sail, Melkorka came down to the shore, her hair bound tight against the wind in a married woman's kerchief. She gave him a gold ring off her finger and an embroidered, gold-buckled belt from her waist. "Give the ring to my father," she said. "He gave it to me as a teething gift when I was young, so then he'll know you belong to me. Use the belt to buy Siobhan's freedom, if she's still alive. Tell her I chose to live. Do you hear me? Tell her I understand now."

"I'll tell her, Mamaí," he promised, a little baffled, and he kissed the top of her head, for he was by now much taller than she was.

Melkorka stood on the shore until the ship dropped over the horizon, filling the hollow left by her son with the feeling that she had achieved her purpose.

Then, in the springtime two years later, Olaf returned, windburned and hearty and bearing stories from abroad and rich gifts for his father. He cut a splendid figure now, wearing such fine clothes that almost immediately everyone began to call him Olaf Peacock. It was an affectionate nickname, perhaps a little tainted with the mild disdain of ambitious people who had never had his opportunities.

Most people in the dales praised Olaf's loyalty to Hoskuld in returning home when he could have been a prince among the Irish, but as the news spread up the valley, no one asked whether Melkorka had expected him to return.

When she heard of her son's arrival, she galloped all the way to Hoskuld's farm, arriving as breathless as her horse. But even as she embraced Olaf fiercely and desperately, her eyes were already roving over the crowd that had gathered to welcome him home.

"Is Siobhan still alive?" she asked.

"Yes," he said in Norse for the benefit of the others, "and Myrkjartan too. He was glad to hear you were well."

"Did you not bring her with you?"

"Siobhan? I did try, Mamaí. You should have seen us. I picked her up and sat her right down on my lap—like this!" He demonstrated with Melkorka and the crowd laughed.

"I liked the old woman very much," he went on, "and I offered my Seanat-hair Myrkjartan the belt in exchange for her. But he said there was no point in taking her away when she was already so old."

Olaf went on with his report to the others gathered around him, and he seemed not to notice when Melkorka left his lap and said nothing in reply.

3.3 The Story of Thorstein Ox-Foot

Chapter 1

There was a man named Thord Skeggi.[460] He settled all the land in Lon to the north of the Jokul River up to Lonsheidi, and he lived at Baer for two years. But when he found his high-seat pillars[461] in Leiruvogur below the heath, he handed over his lands to Ulfljot the lawyer, who came out to Lon. Ulfljot was the son of Thora, the daughter of Ketil Horda-Kari, who was the son of Aslak Bifru-Kari, the son of Unn Arnarhyrna. When Ulfljot was nearly sixty years of age, he went to Norway and stayed there three winters. Then he and Thorleif Spaki, his maternal uncle, set up the laws that were afterward called Ulfljot's Laws. But when he returned to Iceland the Althing[462] was established and all men had one law after that throughout Iceland.

It was a precept of the pagan law that men should not have figureheads on their ships at sea, or if they did, they should take them down before they came in sight of land and not sail in with gaping or grinning faces on poles that would frighten the guardian spirits of the land. A ring, worth two ounces of silver or more, should be left on the alter at each chief temple. Each godi[463] should have that ring on his arm at every Thing that he conducted and would redden the ring in the blood of the sacrificial cattle that he sacrificed himself. For

---

460 The chapter numbers within section 3.3 are those of "Þorsteins þáttr uxafóts."

461 A common practice of the early settlers as depicted in the sagas: upon sighting Iceland, the new arrivals would cast their high-seat pillars overboard and settle somewhere temporarily until the pillars were found washed up in the location the gods had selected for their permanent set-tlement.

462 The nationwide legal assembly, or parliament, held annually in southwest Iceland. Things, mentioned below, were local assemblies held multiple times a year, rather like district courts.

463 A goði (pl. goðar) was a political and, in the pre-Christian era, religious leader in Iceland.

every man who required legal proceedings conducted and judged, he must first take an oath on that ring and name two or more witnesses.

"I name you as witness," he should say, "that I am taking an oath on this ring, a legal oath. So help me Frey and Njord and the almighty god, I will conduct this case, or defend it, or bear witness, or hear the narrative, or pass judgment in the best and truest way I know and in accordance with the law, and I shall do everything prescribed by the law regarding those matters that come under my jurisdiction while I am at this Thing."

At that time the land was divided into quarters and there were to be three Things in each quarter and three main temples in each district. There, men were carefully selected to preserve the temple in wisdom and justice. They were to hold the nomination of judges at the Things and conduct lawsuits. For that reason they were called godar. Each person must also pay a tax to the temple, just as we now have the church tithe.

Bodvar the White from Voss in Norway was the first to build at Hof; he raised up a temple there and became the temple godi. He was the father of Thorstein, who was the father of Hall of Sida.

Thorir Havi settled in Krossavik to the north of Reydarfjord. That is where the Kross-Vikings come from.

Chapter 2

There was a man named Thorkel who lived in Krossavik. He was the son of Geitir. He was an excellent man and valiant, considered fearless. He was unmarried at the time this story happens. His sister grew up with him and was called Oddny, the most beautiful of women and more skillful than any other. However, she had a great defect in her speaking ability. She could not speak at all and had been born that way. The brother and sister loved each other a great deal.

Thorkel had a slave, of foreign extraction, who was called Freystein. He was neither ugly nor difficult to deal with like other slaves; rather he was meek and compliant and more handsome than almost every other man. For that reason he was called Freystein the Fair.

There was a man named Krum who lived at Krumsholt. That farm is now deserted. He was the son of Vemund, son of Asbjorn, son of Krum the Old. Krum the Old moved house from Voss to Iceland. He settled the land on Hafranes and all the outskirts, both Skrud and the other outlying islands, and the mainland to Thernunes. Krum the Younger was then married to a woman who was called Thorgunna, daughter of Thorstein, son of Veturlidi, son of Asbjorn (a noble man from Beitsstadir), son of Olaf Long-Neck, son of Bjorn Whale-Side. Thorgunna was a wise woman but not overly popular, very knowledgeable, not beautiful and rather old, quite hard-tempered even overbearing. Krum was not a rich man. There was a great disparity in age in the marriage. Thorgunna was a mature woman when this adventure happened. They had no children, according to the story.

Chapter 3

There was a man named Styrkar, son of Eindridi, son of Hreid. Hreid was the brother of Asbjorn, father of Jarnskeggi of Yrja, and their sister was Olof, who was married to Klypp the Norwegian chieftain who killed King Sigurd Sleva.[464] Their brother was Erling, a powerful chieftain of Hordaland, Norway.

Erling had a son called Ivar, the handsomest of the men who grew up at Hordaland. For that reason he was called Ivar the Radiant. He excelled every man in accomplishments and was so overly prideful that almost no one could equal him in speech or deed. He was unmarried for a long time because it seemed to him that there was practically no woman who was his match. He stayed a long time with Styrkar, his kinsman, at Gimsar in Trondheim. This Styrkar was the father of Einar Paunch-Shaker. Some say Eindridi, the father of Styrkar, and Asbjorn, the father of Eindridi Ilbreid, were brothers. The kinsmen Styrkar and Ivar were dear to each other for a long time. Ivar spent much of his time on trading voyages, both in England and in Denmark.

One summer he captained a trading voyage to Iceland. He brought his ship in to Gautavik in the Eastfjords. Thorkel Geitisson rode to the ship and invited the captain to come to his home with as many men as he wished to bring. Ivar thanked him and said he would accept. Ivar went with Thorkel to Krossavik with four other men and stayed there over the winter. Ivar was a cheerful man and open-handed with his money.

One day, Thorkel went to talk with Oddny, his sister, and told her that the captain had come to his home.

"I would like," he said, "for you to wait on him this winter, sister, because most of the other people around here are working."

Oddny carved runes on a stick because she couldn't talk, and Thorkel took it and looked at it.

The stick read, "I am not inclined to put myself into the service of the captain, because my heart tells me if I do serve Ivar, much evil will come of it."

---

464 A prince rather than a king of Norway, son of Eric Bloodaxe and Gunnhild.

Thorkel grew very angry when Oddny refused, and when she saw that, she stood up and went inside and began to serve Ivar, and she kept to it all winter. And eventually, people saw that Oddny was pregnant, and when Thorkel found out, he asked Oddny what her situation was—whether she was with child and who had fathered it.

Oddny carved runes again and they said, "Ivar could find no better repayment for your winter hospitality than to father the child I carry."

Then Oddny burst into violent tears and Thorkel went away.

The winter passed and when spring arrived, Ivar readied his ship in Gautavik and, when it was ready, prepared to leave Krossavik with his men.

Thorkel rode along the way with Ivar and when they had ridden for a while, he addressed the captain: "What would you like to do about the child that you had with my sister Oddny? Will you do the right thing and marry her? I will give her a dowry befitting you."

Ivar reacted with great anger and answered, "I will have been poorly paid for my trip to Iceland if I must marry your mute sister. I have had the choice of higher-born and nobler women, at home in Hordaland and even other parts of Norway. You don't need to assign to me this child that your sister might have had with your slave. You have spoken a great dishonor against me."

Thorkel answered, "If you do not wish to acknowledge Oddny's child but slight both me and her in your words, you will feel it yourself. I have not before suffered men to shame me so."

Then Ivar struck at Thorkel. The blow came down on his foot and caused a great wound. Thorkel drew his sword and struck at Ivar, but he rode underneath it and the blow hit the foot of his horse and struck it off. Ivar leaped from its back and ran after his companions, but Thorkel rode home to Krossavik.

The day after that, Thorkel gathered his men and rode to Gautavik with a company of thirty. But when he arrived, Ivar had drawn up the gangplank; the wind was driving away from the land and so they sailed out to sea and did not stop before they came to Norway. Ivar went home to Hordaland and stayed put there.

Thorkel rode home to Krossavik and was little pleased with the business because he had never been more slighted in his life.

Chapter 4

At midsummer or a little after, Oddny gave birth to a child. It was a boy, so large that people thought it did not look like a newborn. Thorkel was told that his sister had been delivered of the child she had with Ivar the Radiant. But when Thorkel heard this he became terrifically angry and said that the child should be exposed. It was the law at that time that poor men's children could be exposed if people wanted, though it was not considered a good thing to do. Thorkel called his slave Freystein and ordered him to destroy the boy, but he refused until Thorkel loosed his anger on him.

At that time, Geitir, Thorkel's father, was visiting Thorkel. He argued that the boy should not be exposed, declaring he was of a mind to say that the boy would not be of little worth if he managed to stay alive.

Thorkel was so furious that he did not want to listen and said the only thing that would happen was that the boy would be exposed.

Now Freystein, being forced to it, went to Oddny and took up the boy and went out with him to the wood. He wrapped the child in a cloth and laid a slice of bacon in his mouth. He made a shelter under some tree roots and put the child in it, settled him well, and then went away. He went home and told his master that he had seen the child off. His master praised him, and then all was quiet for a while.

Chapter 5

It must be said that immediately after this, Krum the farmer went into his forest to fetch wood. He heard the crying of a child and went toward it and found a boy both large and handsome. A piece of bacon lay next to him so that Krum thought it must have fallen out of the child's mouth, and it must have been the child that cried out. Krum had heard that a child had been exposed in Krossavik and how hard Thorkel had been in speaking about it, so he thought this must be the same child. And although he and Thorkel were great friends, he saw it was both a crime and a shame that a child so manly and likely to have a great destiny should die there, so Krum picked him up and took him home with him and said not a word about it. The child was found on the fourth day after he was exposed.

Krum named the boy Thorstein and said he was his son. He and Thorgunna came to an agreement about this. Thorstein grew up there and Thorgunna gave him affectionate care and taught him a great deal. Thorstein became both large and strong, eager in all endeavors. He was so strong that when he was seven years old he equaled grown men in strength, though they were very able themselves.

One day, as happened often, Thorstein came to Krossavik. He went to Thorkel's sitting room. There on the dais sat Geitir, father of the master of the house, murmuring into his cloak.[465] But as the youth came into the room, he moved very hastily as children are wont to do. He fell onto the floor and when Geitir saw that, he burst out laughing. But when Oddny saw the boy, she set up a great weeping.

The youth came farther in to Geitir and said, "Did you think it that funny when I fell just now?"

Geitir answered, "I did, because I saw what you did not see."

"What was that?" asked Thorstein.

"I will tell you. When you came into the room a polar bear cub followed you and ran in front across the floor. But when he saw me he stopped, but you kept on, hasty, and you fell over the cub; and it is my belief that you are not the son of Krum nor of Thorgunna but rather must be higher born."

The youth sat down with Geitir and they chatted, but when evening drew on, Thorstein said he had to go home.

Geitir invited him to come there often. "Because it seems to me that you must have kin here."

But when Thorstein made to leave, Oddny came to him and gave him new-cut clothes. Then he went home. Now he made a habit of coming to Krossavik. Thorkel paid little attention to the youth but nevertheless thought him a remarkable person in size and strength. Geitir told Thorkel that he thought this Thorstein was the son of Oddny and Ivar the Radiant and that he would be a great man.

Thorkel said he couldn't deny it. "Let us get the true tidings about him."

And in the morning Thorkel sent for Krum, Thorgunna, and Thorstein and when they came, Thorkel asked them outright how Thorstein came to them. And the couple told him everything. Freystein also told his story and it agreed with theirs. Thorkel now thought it had turned out well and thanked Freystein for his actions.

Thorstein now knew about his family and went to stay at Krossavik, and Thorkel treated him very well indeed.

---

465 This ritualistic activity foreshadows his abilities as a seer, which he is about to demonstrate.

Chapter 6

It is said that one autumn, when men were to go to the mountain to round up the sheep, Thorkel asked his nephew Thorstein to go with them. He agreed. He was ten years old then, and Freystein invited him to travel with him. They went along as they pleased and found many sheep, and on the way home, they came to a deep valley. It was just the two of them, Thorstein and Freystein, and it was late evening. They saw a large burial mound.

"I think we'll spend the night here," said Thorstein, "and you, Freystein, will take the night watch and not wake me no matter how I'm sleeping, because I intend to lie down there."

Freystein agreed to that. Thorstein went to sleep and as the night passed, he behaved wildly in his sleep, fighting against his saddle and their shelter. So it went right up until day. Freystein doubted whether he should wake Thorstein or not. The shouting was very difficult to bear.

But when day came, Thorstein woke up and was very sweaty and said, "You have faithfully kept the watch, Freystein. You have now done two things, either one of which would be worth repayment: the first time when you took me out to the wood, and now. I shall now repay you by getting my uncle Thorkel to free you—and here are twelve marks of silver that I wish to give you. But now I will tell you my dream. I thought I saw the cairn open and out of it came a man dressed in red. He was a large man and not entirely evil-looking ...."

The man went up to Thorstein and greeted him. Thorstein greeted him well and asked him his name and where he lived.

He said he was called Brynjar and lived in the mound, "which you see standing here in the valley. But I know your name and also of what family you come, and also that you will become a great man. Will you go with me and see my home?"

Thorstein agreed and stood up and took his axe, which Thorkel had given him, and went into the mound. When Thorstein entered it seemed very well appointed. He saw on the right-hand side eleven men sitting on a bench. They were all clad in red and rather reserved. On the other side of the mound he saw another twelve men sitting. They were all clad in black. One was the greatest of them all and very evil-looking.

Brynjar looked at Thorstein and said, "That is my brother, the large man, though we are not alike in character. He is called Odd and wishes ill to everyone. He is a troublesome neighbor, but he is entirely stronger than I am because he is larger, and I have been forced to agree that my men must give him a mark of gold every night, or two marks of silver, or some treasure of equal value. This has been going on for two months and we are reduced to using movable goods. Odd has in his keeping a piece of gold whose nature is that any man who is mute and who lays it under the root of his tongue will get from it his speech. From that gold your mother may get speech, but Odd keeps it so close that it never leaves him night or day."

Now Brynjar sat down with his companions, and Thorstein sat at the far end of them. When they had sat a while, Brynjar stood up and went over to his brother Odd and took off a heavy ring. Odd received it and Brynjar returned to his seat. Likewise, each of the others stood up and gave Odd some treasure, but he gave them no thanks in return.

When all of them had done this, Brynjar said, "You may want to do as the others, Thorstein, and give Odd some payment. Nothing less will do while you sit at our bench."

Odd frowned fiercely and sat up, towering over them and rather unpleasant looking. Thorstein stood up and took hold of his axe.

He went over to Odd and said, "I don't have a lot of luggage, Odd, to make this payment to you. You must not be exacting with me because I am not rich."

Odd answered rather shortly, "Your arrival is nothing to me, but won't you offer whatever you like?"

"I have nothing but my axe, if you want to take that."

Odd stretched out his hand, but Thorstein struck at him. The blow fell above the elbow and took his arm off. Odd sprang up and so did everyone else in the mound. Their weapons were hung up above them. They seized them, and a battle began. Thorstein saw that there was not so much difference between him and Odd now that Odd was one-handed. All the black-clad men seemed to him the hardier. He saw that, though they lost hands or feet or were wounded with other great wounds, the next moment they were whole again. But the injuries Thorstein inflicted behaved according to nature. Thorstein and the brothers did not cease before Odd was killed along with all his company. Thorstein by then was very weary but not wounded, because Brynjar and his fellows had defended him against all blows. Brynjar now took the piece of gold from the dead Odd and gave it to Thorstein and told him to take it to his mother.

He gave him twelve marks of silver and said, "You have won me great freedom, Thorstein, because now I rule here over this cairn and its goods. This is the beginning of the daring deeds that you will accomplish abroad. You will also make a change of faith and that faith is much better for those who can accept it, but harder for those who are not made for it—men such as I, because my brother and I were earth dwellers. Now it would mean a great deal to me if you would bring my name to baptism if it falls to you to have a son ...."

"After that," Thorstein said, "he led me out of the mound and before we parted he said, 'If my words have any power, then all your works will turn to honor and happiness.' After that, Brynjar turned back into the mound, but I woke up. And here is proof, for I have here both the money and the gold."

Afterwards, they drove home the sheep that they had found and the roundup went well. Thorstein reported all the events and gave his mother the gold, and she received her speech when it was placed under the root of her tongue. This burial mound stands in Jokulsdal and is called Brynjar's Mound; even today one can see the remains of it.

Chapter 7

Freystein got his freedom quickly according to Thorstein's word, and Thorkel did it well and willingly; he was well disposed toward Freystein because he knew that he was well born and of noble kin. Grimkel, the father of Freystein, lived at Voss, Norway, and was married to Olof Brunnolfsdottir; Brunnolf was the son of Thorgeir, son of Vestar. But Sokki the Viking had burned Freystein's father in his house and took his son and sold him into slavery. Geitir had brought him to Iceland from Norway.

Some say that Thorstein gave Oddny his mother to Freystein in marriage. Freystein the Fair lived in Sandvik on Bardsnes and owned Vidfjord and Hellisfjord and he was called one of the settlers. From him are descended the people of Sandvik and Vidfjord and Hellisfjord.

Chapter 8

Asbjorn Kastanrassi had a ship waiting aground in Gautavik. Thorstein set sail from there with him. He was then twelve years old. Thorkel gave him supplies sufficient for the voyage, and before Thorstein rode to the ship, he spoke with his mother.

She said, "Now you must make a kinsman of your father, Ivar the Radiant, and if he is reluctant to acknowledge himself your father, then here is a ring which you shall give him. Tell him that this ring he first gave to me; then he will not be able to deny it."

After that, the mother and son parted and Thorstein rode to the ship and went abroad over the summer. They came by the northern route to Norway in the autumn. Thorstein went to visit Styrkar at Gimsar and stayed there over the winter. Things went well with Styrkar because he saw that Thorstein was a man of great accomplishments; he equaled the strongest men in all their games.

During the winter a little before Yule, messengers came from Ivar the Radiant with the message that Ivar had invited Styrkar's household to a Yule feast. The man who had come to them was named Bjorn. Styrkar ordered preparations for the trip and went with thirty men. Thorstein was there on the journey. They came to the feast, and Styrkar was well received. He sat next to Ivar during the festivities.

The feast proceeded well and the last day, before men were to leave, Thorstein went before Ivar and said, "I have business with you, Ivar: to know whether you will behave at all as a father toward me."

Ivar answered, "What is your name and where have you come from?"

"Thorstein is my name. Oddny is my mother, daughter of Geitir in Iceland. And here is a ring which she bade me give you as evidence, and she said you would recognize that you gave it to her."

Ivar grew very red and said, "You have a much lower parentage than that. There are enough slaves in Iceland that your mother can introduce you to. Would it really be sound counsel for me to consent to being responsible for vagabonds' children and wretches, so that every whore's son should call me father?"

Thorstein grew vehemently angry, but he controlled his words well and said, "You have answered poorly and ungenerously, but I will come a second time so that you can behave better toward me; otherwise it will be your doom."

Then Thorstein turned away.

Ivar said to Styrkar, "I wish you would kill this fool, kinsman, because anything might be expected from him."

"I don't want to do that," said Styrkar, "because I think he has the right of it more than you do: I think he is of the noblest extraction."

Ivar and Styrkar parted coldly. Styrkar went home to Gimsar and Thorstein went with him. Styrkar had a sister named Herdis, the most beautiful of women. There was a great liking between her and Thorstein. He was there two winters. Then Thorstein went out to Iceland and came home to Krossavik, and he had greatly distinguished himself in his travels abroad. When he had been in Iceland for three winters, he went abroad with Kolbjorn Sneypi to Norway. Then he went again to Styrkar at Gimsar and Styrkar received him with open arms.

Chapter 9

It is well known that that summer there was a change of rulers in Norway; Haakon the idolatrous earl[466] fell from power and in his place came Olaf Tryggvason. He proclaimed the true faith to all men.

News came to King Olaf that ogresses had infested Heidarskog and were killing everyone there. The king called a meeting and asked who would go to free Heidarskog.

A man stood up, large and stately, who was called Brynjulf, a man who held lands from the king in Trondheim, and said, "I will go, my lord, if you wish it."

The king said that pleased him well.

So Brynjulf readied himself with sixty men. There was a man named Thorkel, and Brynjulf's company rode to stay with him. Thorkel received them

---

466 Haakon Sigurdsson.

well. They stayed there overnight and in the morning he followed them on their way and said it would be a great shame when the king no longer enjoyed the services of such men.

After that they rode on the way until they saw a great hall. From it they saw three she-trolls run out, two young and one who was the largest. She was shaggy all over like a gray bear. They all had swords in their hands. Brynjulf's company also saw a large man come out, if he should be called a man, and two boys with him. He had a drawn sword in his hand. It was so bright it seemed to throw off sparks. All the trolls were evil-looking to see. A battle began. The large man was a great striker of blows, and so was the shaggy she-giant. It ended with the death of Brynjulf and all his company except for four men, who got into the woods and went afterward to meet the king and tell him the news, which was reported widely.

Chapter 10

It is to be said that Styrkar spoke with Thorstein and asked whether he wanted to go with him to Heidarskog. Thorstein declared himself ready for that journey. They prepared early one morning and went on snowshoes up onto the mountain and did not stop until they came in the evening to a refuge hut and intended to stay the night there. They divided up the work; Thorstein was to find water and Styrkar to light a fire.

Thorstein then went out and took up a spear that Styrkar had given him and a bucket in his other hand, and when he came right up to the water, he saw a girl walking with a bucket. She was not especially tall but was awfully stout, and when she saw Thorstein, she started and threw down her bucket and ran back down the path. Thorstein also left his bucket and ran after her. When the girl saw that, she ran all the faster. Both ran as fast as they could, and neither gained nor pulled away. This went on until Thorstein saw a hall, very large and strongly built. The girl ran inside and slammed the door behind her. But when Thorstein saw that, he threw the spear after her and it reached the hall door and flew through it.

Thorstein then approached the hall and went in; he found his spear on the floor but could not see his girl. He proceeded through the hall until he came to a closed bed closet. Inside, a light was burning on a candlestick. Thorstein saw a woman lying in the bed, if it could be called a woman. She was both tall and stout and entirely troll-like. She was very big-boned in the face and her countenance both swarthy and dark. She lay in a silk shirt, which was very likely to have been washed in human blood. The ogress was then asleep and snored awfully loudly. A shield and sword hung up over her. Thorstein stepped up to the edge of the bed and took down the sword and drew it. He stripped the clothing off the ogress. He saw then that she was entirely shaggy all over except for a spot under her left arm, which he saw was short-haired. He thought that the iron would bite her there or it wouldn't bite anywhere. He laid the sword on this same spot and struck in up to the hilt. The sword pierced so deeply that the point stuck in the pillow. The hag woke then—and not from a good dream—and groped about with her hands and sprung upright. Thorstein in one quick movement put out the light and sprang up over the ogress in the bed, but she ran out across the floor, knowing that her killer would seek the doors,[467] but just as she got there, the sword did its work and she died.

Thorstein went up to her and drew out the sword and kept it with him. Then he went on outside until he came around to the hall door. It was set into the wall and not shut all the way. He saw a large man sitting on the dais, very big-boned, and armor hung all over him. On his other side sat a large she-troll, evil-looking but not very aged. Two boys played on the floor. Hair sprung from their heads.[468]

The she-troll began to speak: "Are you asleep, Father Iron-Shield?"

"No, Daughter Shield-Spirit. Thoughts of great men oppress me."

Then he called the names of the boys, one Hook and the other Crook, and told them to go to Shield-Edge, their mother, and find out whether she was awake or sleeping.

Shield-Spirit answered, "It is not a good idea, Father, to send young ones into the dark, because I will tell you that this evening I saw two men running down from the mountain. They were so swift-footed that I thought there must be few of our men who could match them."

"I do not think it is a problem," said Iron-Shield, "because all the men the king sends here I do not fear; there is only one man I fear, and he is named Thorstein, the son of Oddny from Iceland. But it is as though a veil hangs before my eyes regarding all my destiny, whatever may be the cause."

"It is unlikely, Father," she said, "that this Thorstein should ever come to Heidarskog."

The boys now went forth, but Thorstein turned away from them. They ran on and went out.

---

467 The geography of the hall is not entirely clear; it seems that the bed chamber has a door to the outside as well as a door into the hall, and it is the former that the ogress runs to.

468 The hall was unoccupied when Thorstein passed through it moments before; if it is not a narratorial mistake, the sudden appearance of the family is due to their troll magic. Their magic does not, apparently, extend to realizing that the mother they speak of was in the bed chamber inside the hall.

Then after a while, Shield-Spirit said, "I'm ready to go."

Now she ran to the door fast and foolishly. Thorstein drew back, but when she came out the door, she fell over her dead mother. She grew cold and fey at that. She charged out of the hall. Thorstein came at her and struck off her arm with the sword, Shield-Edge's Gift. She then wanted to go back into the hall, but Thorstein defended the doors from her. She had a short-sword in her hand. They fought for a while, but in the end, Shield-Spirit fell dead. At that, Iron-Shield came out. He had his drawn sword in his hand, both bright and sharp, so that Thorstein thought he had never seen its like. Iron-Shield struck out with it at Thorstein. Thorstein warded off the blow but was wounded on the thigh. The sword stabbed down into the ground up to the hilt. Iron-Shield gave way then, but Thorstein raised up the sword Shield-Edge's Gift, hard and ready, and struck at Iron-Shield. The blow landed on the shoulder, taking off both arm and leg. Iron-Shield fell. Thorstein quickly struck a great blow and cut off his head.

After that, Thorstein went into the hall, but when he went in, before he knew it he was grabbed and thrown down. Thorstein found that the hag Shield-Edge had revived, and now the encounter was clearly worse than before.[469] She bent down to Thorstein and intended to bite his windpipe asunder. It then occurred to Thorstein that he who had made heaven and earth must be very great. He had also heard many remarkable stories from King Olaf about the faith that he preached; he now promised with a clean heart and his whole mind to accept that faith and serve Olaf while he lived, if he could get away whole and alive with all his wits.

And when she brought her teeth to Thorstein's windpipe and he had steadfastly promised this, a sunbeam broke into the hall, terribly bright, and shone directly into the hag's eyes. It so damaged her sight that it drew from her all her power and strength. She began to gape helplessly. Then vomit burst out of her into Thorstein's face so that he barely withstood death from its evil effects and the terrible smell which came from it. It seemed to people that it was not impossible that some part of it must have gotten into Thorstein's breast, because to people it seemed that afterward he became not entirely single-shaped,[470] whether that was more because of Shield-Edge's vomit or because he had been exposed as an infant.

Both were now poised between life and death so that neither could stand.

---

469 Either because Thorstein is now wounded or because Shield-Edge is stronger as a revenant.
470 That is, he may have been "hamrammr," able to change his skin. No further mention is made of this hint that Thorstein may have become a shape-shifter as a result of his encounter with the ogress.

Chapter 11

It is to be said that Styrkar was now in the refuge hut and thought Thorstein was taking a long time. He cast himself onto the side-bench and when he had lain there a while, in ran two evil-looking boys, and each had a seax-sword in their hand; they attacked Styrkar, but he grabbed the stock of the bench and struck blows with it until he killed them both.

After that, he went out of the shelter, wondering what could be delaying Thorstein; he walked until he came to the hall and saw that two ogresses were lying slain on the threshold, but he did not see Thorstein. He feared that he must have landed in some distress; he now promised to the maker of heaven and earth to accept the faith that King Olaf preached if that night he could find his friend Thorstein alive and well. Then he went into the hall and came to where Shield-Edge and Thorstein lay. He asked whether Thorstein could speak. He said his speech hadn't failed, but he asked for help. Styrkar got hold of Shield-Edge and dragged her off him. Thorstein stood up immediately and was very stiff all over from the struggle he had had with the ogress and the embrace of Shield-Edge. Then they broke Shield-Edge's neck—with the greatest difficulty because she was extremely thick-necked. Thorstein told Styrkar all about his journey.

Styrkar answered, "You are a great hero, and it is most likely that this, your valiant deed, will be known as long as the northern lands are settled with people."

They now dragged all the ogresses and kindled a pyre and burned them down to cold charcoal. After that they explored the hall and found there nothing valuable; they left and went home to Gimsar. The news spread and was thought an important event.

Chapter 12

King Olaf was sitting at feast in Hordaland. Styrkar and Thorstein traveled there and went before the king and greeted him. Ivar the Radiant was there with the king in such high honor that only two men sat between him and the king.

Thorstein turned to Ivar with his sword Shield-Edge's Gift drawn. He stuck Ivar's breast with its point and said, "Choose one of these two things: either I thrust in the point of my sword—and not just a little—or you take up your role as my father."

Ivar answered, "It seems honorable to me to have you as my son. You also have so good a mother that I know that she has not spoken anything but the truth. I will certainly behave to you as a father."

The king explained the faith to them as he did to all others who came to meet him. They accepted it humbly and told the king clearly all the events of their coming and about the things that happened at Heidarskog. The king gave manifold praise to God for the miracles that he worked for sinful men here on earth. Afterwards, both of them were baptized. Styrkar went home to Gimsar and held all the feasts that he had held before, but Thorstein and his father Ivar became king's men to Olaf and followed him until their dying day, and they were thought to be the most valiant men.

Chapter 13

There was a man named Harek. He lived at Reina in Trondheim, holding land from the king, but he was not very popular. He had converted to Christianity, but the king was told that afterwards, there was still something of witchcraft in his behavior. So the king held a feast there, wishing to find out how much truth there was in this. It was a fair feast, but Harek was envious and ill-natured. He was jealous of the honor Thorstein received.

One day Harek talked with Thorstein and asked him about his great exploits, and Thorstein answered what he asked.

"Do you think there's a stronger man in Norway than you?" asked Harek.

"I don't know for sure," said Thorstein.

"Do you think the king may be stronger?" asked Harek.

"I am inferior to the king in everything other than strength," said Thorstein, "and yet I will not equal him even in that."

Then they broke off their conversation.

The day after, Harek said to the king that Thorstein had set himself up as a match with him in all feats. The king did not much care for that.

Some time later, the king talked to them about their decision to set up Thorstein as his equal in their endeavors. "Or is it true, Thorstein, that you have said that you are my equal or my better in such feats?"

"I have not said so, my lord," said Thorstein. "Who told you that?"

"Harek," said the king.

"Why didn't he tell you about the sacrificial oxen which he sacrifices in secret, since there is more truth in that? What I said, my lord, is that I fell short of you in all things but strength and yet I would not equal you even in that."

"Is there any truth in that, Harek?" asked the king.

"Little enough, my lord," said Harek.

"Let us see these cattle that you value so highly," said the king.

"This is your right, my lord," said Harek. "We must go out into the woods."

They did so and when they arrived they saw a great herd of cattle. It contained a terribly big, evil-looking ox so that the king thought its like had never been seen. He bellowed terribly and behaved very evilly.

Harek said, "Here are the cattle, my lord, and I value this ox so highly that he is very dear to me."

"I certainly see that," said the king, "and I don't like it. But what do you think, Thorstein? Will you try your strength and take on this ox? Because it seems to me that it would not be advantageous for him to live any longer."

So Thorstein ran forward into the herd to where the ox was. The ox retreated, but Thorstein grabbed its hind leg so hard that both hide and flesh tore, and the leg came off with the whole meat of the thigh. He held onto it and went to the king, but the sacrificial ox fell down dead. The ox had dug in so powerfully that its front feet were sunken into the earth up to the knee.

The king said, "You are a strong man, Thorstein, and you will never be short of strength if you deal with human beings. I will now add to your name and call you Thorstein Ox-Foot. Here is a ring that I wish to give you as a naming gift."

Thorstein accepted the ring and thanked the king because it was a great treasure. The king now went back to the town, laid claim to everything, and drove Harek out of the country for his disobedience and idolatry.

Chapter 14

Within a little while, it was heard again from Heidarskog that ogresses were oppressing the area so that men could not get out. Styrkar sent word to Thorstein that they should again go to Heidarskog. Thorstein reacted quickly and went with the king's blessing to meet Styrkar; the two of them went together and came to the refuge hut where they had been before and stayed there overnight.

The next day, when they were standing outside, they saw thirteen men in the woods, and one woman was with them. They turned toward the place. Thorstein recognized his girl there, and she had grown quite a bit, because she was now the largest ogress.

She called out to Thorstein and said, "You have come, Thorstein Ox-Foot, and you are here to remind me that you killed my father, mother, and sister, and Styrkar killed my two brothers, but now you are pursuing me. I was very afraid then, as was not unlikely for a girl of nine years, but now I am twelve. I went into a cellar when we parted, and while you were fighting with my father, I gathered together all the costly things that were in the hall and hid them down in the cellar under my mother's bed. A little later, I married this man, Skelking, and I agreed with him that he should kill both you and Styrkar. Now he has come here with his eleven brothers, and you will need to put up a manly defense, if even that will be enough."

So they struck up a battle. Shield-Guard went to where Thorstein was in front, attacking so hard that Thorstein thought he had hardly ever been in greater danger, but it ended in Thorstein striking a blow at Shield-Guard from above her hip with the sword Shield-Edge's Gift and cutting her in half. By then Styrkar had killed Skelking. They now went to work quickly with the eleven and killed them all. After that they went into the hall, broke open the cellar, and bore out of it many costly things; afterwards they went home to Gimsar and divided up the valuables between them.

Then Thorstein asked for the hand of Herdis, Styrkar's sister, and he married her. Men say that they had a son who was called Brynjar.[471] Thorstein then went to King Olaf and stayed with him from then on, and he died on Ormrinn Langi.[472]

3.4 Oddny (A Piece of Canon Fanfiction)

It was impossible not to be a little dazzled by Ivar. Thorkel brought him home to Krossavik with a four-man retinue, smelling of the sea and beaming at the farmsteaders who gathered to watch him pass. Beside the windburned, broken-toothed farmers, Ivar looked like Thor himself, his hair and beard the color of honey and his eyes as gray and changeable as the sea. Oddny was not given to girlish fancy, but she could not look away from him as he rode up on one of Thorkel's horses. She heard one of the servants calling him Ivar the Radiant.

"Oddny!" Thorkel hailed her, swinging down from his mare. "This is Captain Ivar Erlingsson, fresh from Norway. I've prevailed on him to stay the winter with us. Captain Ivar, this is my sister, Oddny."

Ivar crossed his hands over the pommel of his saddle and leaned over them, passing his eyes from Oddny's fine, dark hair and down her body all the way to her shoes, just visible under the hem of her dress. He grinned at her, flashing a row of fine, even teeth.

"You have a beautiful sister, Thorkel." And though the words were a compliment, the tone was like oil on water. Oddny found she liked him less than she had moments ago.

---

471 Thus, Thorstein honors the request of Brynjar the earth-dweller to Christianize his name.
472 Ormrinn Langi (Long Worm or Long Dragon), was King Olaf's ship, on which he died at the battle of Svolder. Ármann Jakobsson et al. identify the battle in discussing Thorstein Ox-Foot in "Disability before Disability," 454.

A feast was thrown together to welcome the new arrivals, and Ivar handed out gold finger-rings, of which he seemed to have an endless supply, endearing himself to all the company. All the company except for Oddny, who felt his eyes on her all through the meal. When she reached across the board to refill his cup, he caught her wrist.

"Would you like a finger ring, my pretty?" he asked, flashing his teeth at her again. "I have a special one for you."

"Oh," Thorkel said, "Oddny can't speak. Kicked in the head by a horse when she was a wee thing. But don't worry, she can understand you, and the scar is hidden under her hair."

Oddny's hand rose self-consciously to the little hollow in her skull behind her temple. It wasn't true that she couldn't speak. She practiced often when she was out on the farm, alone, forcing words piecemeal out of her stubborn mouth. They fell from her lips like spitting fish bones, one at a time, slowly. She knew perfectly well what she wished to say, but words fell out of the sentence as it passed from her heart to her tongue; only one out of every three or four made it out. She had long since stopped speaking in front of people. Even Thorkel laughed at her when she tried. He was her brother; she had other ways of communicating with him.

But she hated it when he spilled out her story to strangers. Unlike the warriors with missing limbs, the lisping children with hare lips, Oddny could pass unnoticed in the world unless Thorkel drew attention to her. It made them look at her differently, sometimes with pity (the singers usually looked at her with pity), sometimes with anticipation, thinking no doubt of the one-eyed god who could see things no one else could see, the one-handed god who bound the great wolf until Ragnarök: they seemed to expect that one who could not speak may have something important to say. How they expected her to say it, though, she never knew, and all she ever wanted to say were ordinary things anyway: be careful on the ice; thank you for the bread; my tooth aches; I love you. She was not a subject of interest to the neighbors. It was the interest of newcomers she had to contend with—newcomers like Ivar, who was regarding her now with a look that was neither pity nor anticipation but something she liked even less.

"Can't speak, eh?" he mused. "Well, as you say, it's no mark against her beauty."

There was a skald in the company tonight, a rare entertainment more often reserved for royal courts. He must have been in between kings at the moment. He struck up a recitation at the top of his voice and the conversation in the hall dropped to a background murmur. Oddny did not enjoy skaldic poetry, for the others would catch bits of it in their memories and recite it incessantly for weeks—an activity she could not take part in. She set down the jug from which she had been refilling the cups and went to the stable to check the horses.

There was water in their trough and hay in the manger, so she only leaned against the half-door, her back to the chill autumn air, and stroked their noses as they milled sleepily around in the light of the lamp she had brought with her. When she heard a step behind her, she turned in alarm, but it was only Thorkel.

"How do you like our guests?" he asked casually.

She gave him a look.

"Don't be impossible," he laughed. "Ivar is a great man in Hordaland."

She gestured at the dark landscape around them, but she wasn't sure he understood that she meant, "This isn't Hordaland."

"Listen," Thorkel said, picking a piece of hay from the forelock of his mare, who had come over to greet him, "I want you to take care of Ivar this winter."

She looked at him in surprise, and he would not meet her gaze.

"It's only good hospitality," he said. "We wouldn't want to insult him."

When she continued to stare at him, he sighed and finally turned toward her. "Look, Oddny, he's a wealthy man. If he should ask for your hand, it would be a lucky thing. You don't want to turn into some wrinkled old kerling and never marry, do you?" He tried to laugh, but Oddny wasn't laughing.

She dug in the pouch she kept knotted on her belt and drew out her knife and a flat stick of scrap wood. She and Thorkel had worked out this system when they were young: a horizontal score across the surface meant yes, a slanted one meant no. The answer was more emphatic the more scores she made. She could manage a halting spoken word, but normally she didn't have to; in fact a look was generally enough to communicate such simple things. But on important occasions, she registered her words with a knife's point. She braced the stick on her thigh and scored it three times on the slant: no, no, no.

Thorkel took the stick but barely looked at it. "Be reasonable, Oddny. He's handsome as well as wealthy. What more could you possibly want?"

She jabbed her finger at the stick, reiterating her statement. Thorkel threw it down, his temper flaring as it always did when he was crossed. "Do what you want," he said, "but do it under your own roof. If you don't like the way I run my own household, go find your own."

He turned on his heel and stomped off, not back to the hall but out into the home meadow, where Oddny knew he intended to recover his good humor before returning to his guests. She watched his back disappearing into the dark. She had nowhere to go if Thorkel cast her out. Taking a deep breath and smoothing the front of her dress like a fighter checking his byrnie before battle, she went back into the hall and refilled Ivar's cup.

It took Ivar precisely three days to help himself to more than ale from Oddny. Knowing it was going to happen made it no less painful when it did. And knowing it would happen repeatedly made it worse. When she began to be sick every morning, she tried to hide it from her brother, but he was so occupied in securing the comfort of his guests as the deep cold set in that she needn't have feared him. In the end it was the servants who found out first, noticing they didn't have extra scrubbing to do with her wool shift once a month, noticing that while her eyes went hollow with the lean time of year, her dress grew tighter and tighter around her waist. She never discovered who said something to Thorkel, but he came bursting into the hall one morning when the men were playing ball on the frozen pond and Oddny was alone, mending a shirt by the fire.

"Is it true?" he demanded, tearing his mittens off and throwing them into a corner. He looked her up and down, confirming. "Whose is it?"

She gave him an incredulous look. Whose did he think it was?

"You're sure?"

She glared at him.

He ruffled his dark hair, brushing ice from the tips. "Well, he'll have to marry you now. I'll talk to him." He raised a hand as if to silence her when she made a move toward him. "Just let me pick my own time for it."

That was not what she had wanted to say.

But both he and Ivar were silent on the matter as the long winter months passed slowly in the dark. Oddny thought she would hate this thing that grew inside of her, this reminder of her violation, but she discovered that, as soon as she began to show under her winter layers, Ivar lost all interest in her. Gone were his wandering fingers, his beery breath; even his eyes slid over her as though she was a trestle table, roving instead over the maidservants as they bent to collect the empty flagons or lay more wood on the fire. Not once from Yule to the first thaw did he flash his sharp teeth in her direction. At night, she curled protectively around her belly, thanking her child without words for rescuing her from Ivar the Radiant.

For she knew now that he would not marry her. If he could not stomach her now, while her body bloomed, how would he feel about her when the child was born and her flesh hung loose where once it had been firm and tender as a cut of meat? She did not intend to eavesdrop when Thorkel confronted Ivar about the marriage, but on the day when Ivar and his companions were taking their leave to return to their ship at Gautavik, Oddny was fetching in the water and heard the men talking as they saddled their horses. She stopped around the corner of the stable to listen.

"I hope you've found the hospitality at Krossavik to be up to your standards," Thorkel began politely.

"The best," replied Ivar, his saddle jingling as he tightened the girth.

"Good enough to repay?" Thorkel asked.

"Is this something you Icelanders have invented? I've never been asked to pay for hospitality before."

"I think you have never enjoyed quite so good hospitality before," Thorkel said, "nor of quite this kind."

Ivar did not reply and Thorkel, as he always did, lost patience. "Look, will you do right by marrying Oddny or not?"

Ivar scoffed. "A fine reward I'd have for coming to Iceland if I left married to your mute sister. Women throw themselves at me everywhere I go, nobler women than her. Don't go trying to foist off your sister on me just because she's gone and had a bastard with some slave of yours."

Oddny hardly heard the rest of his venomous speech. Mute sister. Mállauss systr. No one had ever made those words sound like a curse before.

Thorkel's voice was heavy with anger. "I have never before suffered a man to insult my family, and I don't intend to begin now."

She heard the hiss of swords sliding from their sheaths, and she dropped the bucket and ran around the stable as the blows fell. By the time she reached the scene, Thorkel lay on the ground next to a wounded horse, and Ivar was galloping away after his companions on Thorkel's mare. Thorkel's foot was bleeding into the mud.

"Help me up," he demanded through gritted teeth. "I'm going after him."

But slowed by his wound, he had no hope of catching up before the Norwegians had drawn the gangplank aboard and shoved off. Oddny, for her part, was not sorry to see her brother fail to secure Ivar for her husband.

Just after midsummer, Oddny gave birth. The baby was enormous and purple, his face squashed and his head a little conical, and at first he did not breathe. Oddny clutched him to her heart, promising the gods anything they wanted if only he would live. Then one of the maidservants took him from her and blew across his belly, and at the cold air against his hot, wet skin, he gasped and let out an outraged cry. Oddny wept at his beauty.

Someone must have gone to tell Thorkel the news, because he threw back the door to the bed chamber where Oddny lay and said, "Give him to me."

Oddny did not.

Thorkel stretched out his hand and opened and closed it a few times, as if demanding a knife or a cup that she was withholding. "Give him to me," he repeated. "No bastard of Ivar is going to live in this house. If he doesn't want a son by our family, then, by all the gods, he won't have one."

Oddny clutched the baby more tightly to her chest, shaking her head fiercely, but she knew he didn't understand that she meant, "He's my son too."

Thorkel grew impatient with waiting. "Keep him overnight if you insist," he said, storming out again, "but Freystein is taking him to the woods in the morning."

Freystein. Thorkel's favorite slave, but a man who had always been kind to Oddny. He was her baby's only hope. When he came to her the next morning, pale and grim with disapproval at what he was being ordered to do, her heart leapt. She had a chance.

"I'm sorry, Oddny," he murmured, reaching for the baby. "I tried to refuse." In the rushlight, she could see his left eye was already beginning to blacken.

Oddny did not prevent him from lifting the swaddled child from her arms, but she held onto Freystein's wrist, drawing him down to kneel next to the bed. She pulled the blanket away from the baby's sleeping face, which was now a ruddy pink, the head having mostly lost its conical shape and even showing a feathery tuft of reddish hair right at the crown. She looked at Freystein and then at the child, her eyebrows raised, demanding a response.

"He's a bonny lad," Freystein said. "Finest child I've ever seen."

Oddny knew people said this about babies, but she also knew that in this case, it was true. She fixed him with her eyes, demanding again.

"I can't, Oddny," he said. "It's worth more than my life to defy Thorkel when he's in this mood. You know what he's like."

Her expression did not change.

Freystein looked down at the sleeping boy again. "Perhaps ..."

Oddny's heart thudded.

"Perhaps ... I could leave him near Krum's farm. Krum and Thorgunna are good people. They wouldn't leave a baby out in the woods, not when they could take him in."

Oddny's grip tightened on Freystein's wrist, and when he looked up at her, doubt and fear mixing in his face, she nodded hard. That seemed to decide him, and he nodded back before standing up.

"Give him a kiss, Oddny," he said, bending down again, "to send him on his way."

Oddny pressed her lips to her baby's soft crown, imprinting a mother's desperate promise that she would see him again. When Freystein took him away, she covered her face and wept, as much from fear as from the loss. How close they had come to the precipice. She had convinced Freystein to save her child, but he only understood her because he wanted to. If he had been of Thorkel's mind, she shivered at the cold knowledge that all the looks, all the nods in the world would not have made him hear her.

For seven years, Oddny waited. For seven years, they heard stories of Krum's remarkable young son, born unexpectedly in Thorgunna's advanced age, for she was years older than Krum and he himself was not a young man. But Krumsholt was on the other side of the fell, and the families were not frequenters of the same feasts or sacrifices. Then one day, Oddny was spinning next to her father, Geitir, who had tottered over from Geitisstadir to sit at Thorkel's hearth and mutter to himself in between the hearty meals he no longer got at home. From outside, they heard the shouting of children engaged in some raucous game, and suddenly one of them burst through the door, laughing and looking back over his shoulder as he outran his pursuers. He wasn't watching where he was going, so he tripped over the raised threshold and sprawled out flat on the straw-covered floor. Oddny put down her distaff.

The boy got up, unperturbed by his tumble, and dusted himself off impassively. Geitir laughed long and loud. At the sound, the boy looked up at them, and Oddny knew. She meant to go to him, to take his hand or touch his head, but instead, she burst into tears and fled into the bed chamber until she could breathe again.

When she came back out, the boy was sitting on her stool, listening wide-eyed as Geitir talked nonsense about magic bears and portents in the sky. He had come to fancy himself a seer in his old age. Oddny approached and crouched down so that she could look the boy in the face. He looked back at her with the frank, mild curiosity of a child.

"Who are you?" he asked.

Oddny opened her mouth, but she made no attempt to speak.

"That's Oddny, my daughter," Geitir said. To Oddny, he added, "Oddny, this is Thorstein Krumsson. I've just invited him to come round more often. He's found the route over the fell and likes a good walk. Isn't that so, my lad?"

Thorstein nodded and Oddny reached out a trembling hand, which he took. His fingers were warm and his nails dirty, just as they should be in a boy his age. But his clothes were humble, and he had almost outgrown them. She held up a hand to make him wait and ducked back into the bed chamber. When she returned, she held out a tunic she had embroidered herself: the latest in a long line of gifts she had made and never been able to give him. The tiny stockings, the child's cap, these would be of no use to him now that he was so grown, but the tunic he could still have. She put it into his hands, and he took it uncertainly.

"Thank you?" he said, but when she smiled at him, he returned the smile. Geitir watched them keenly.

Thorstein didn't stay long. The pull of his new friends—or rivals—in the yard outside was too strong for him to keep indoors. He said the hasty farewell of a little boy and headed for the door. "But when I come back," he said, "will you finish telling me about the polar bear?"

"I will, my boy, I will," Geitir promised, though Oddny knew by the time Thorstein returned he would probably have forgotten the story and would have to make up a new one. It didn't matter. Her son was coming back.

"Who's that big lad I saw trouncing the other children in the yard today?" Thorkel asked over the evening meal. "He looked a promising fellow."

"Liked him, did you?" Geitir said.

"Hard not to like a boy who can take on three at a time. But I didn't recognize him."

"Didn't you?" Geitir said through a mouthful of lamb. "You ought to. He's your nephew."

Oddny dropped a tray of cups.

"How would you know that?" Thorkel asked skeptically, but he was watching Oddny with suspecting eyes.

Geitir tapped his temple. "I'm a seer, remember?"

"Well, we'll get to the bottom of it anyway." Thorkel rubbed his dark beard and called for a messenger to summon Krum and his family.

It all came out when they arrived; they had no good reason to hide what they'd done, and Thorkel was not a man to be refused. Freystein, when he saw that Thorkel was not inclined to fly into a rage over it, corroborated their story. Oddny held her breath, watching as her son listened to it all with an uncomprehending expression.

"Well," Thorkel said after a long silence, "I suppose there's nothing to be done for it now, and he seems a likely enough child despite everything. He'd better come and live with us."

Oddny clasped her hands to her mouth to keep the joy from escaping.

Thorgunna smoothed her dress in a gesture Oddny recognized. Then she stood up and steered the boy toward Oddny. "Thorstein," she said, her voice trembling, "this is your mother. Go and kiss her."

For just a few heartbeats, Oddny tore her hungry eyes away from her son and looked up at Thorgunna. She and her husband had to have known this was coming; they could not have been surprised. But all the same, Oddny recognized in that instant that regaining her son meant Thorgunna was losing hers.

But then he was in her arms, and even though his cheeks were wet with tears of confusion and fear, she kissed them away frantically, vowing that he would never want for anything. She looked through her tears at Thorgunna and formed her mouth into the silent shape of "thank you." She hoped Thorgunna understood.

For three years, Oddny lived a life she thought only existed in stories. Her son was hers, and he was strong and clever and loving. The only cloud in her sky was that Thorstein, having lived for seven years with a constant stream of talk from his foster mother, could never resign himself to his own mother's silence. She could teach him by example, and thus she picked up his education in farm husbandry just where Thorgunna had left off, but whenever she showed him how to use a new tool and he opened his mouth to ask, "But what's it *called?*" she flinched to see him close it again with the question still puckering his forehead. She once tried to answer, but her voice was hoarse with disuse and Thorstein asked her twice to repeat herself before he gave up. She didn't try again. He didn't need to know what an aul or an adze was called to know how to use it, but no matter how many times it happened, he never seemed to realize that.

One autumn, Thorkel set his cup down on the board with finality and said, "Thorstein should come to round up the sheep this year."

Oddny looked at him in alarm. The mountains were dangerous places, full of sudden gorges and rotten ice from last year's snows. Grown men died in the mountains.

Thorstein leapt from his seat, as he always did, all eagerness. "Thank you, Uncle! I'll find twice as many sheep as anybody else!"

Thorkel chuckled indulgently. He seemed to have completely forgotten that he tried to kill his nephew only a decade ago. Oddny would never forget.

She drew out her scrap of wood and scored it twice on the slant. She jabbed Thorkel's elbow with it.

He didn't need to look at it to know what she was saying. "Don't coddle the boy, Oddny. It's time for him to become a man."

She held out her five fingers, closed them, then opened them again. He's ten. But Thorkel was already talking with one of his men and didn't see her.

Freystein, who had been sitting at the far end of the hall, made his way quietly up to the dais. "Don't worry, Oddny," he said softly. "I'll make sure he's with me. I'll look out for him."

She gave him a weary smile of gratitude.

They were gone for nine days, every hour of which Oddny felt in her bones. Every mealtime, she went to the hall door to check the road, and every mealtime, it was empty. Until finally, on the tenth morning, it wasn't.

"You should have seen me, Mother!" Thorstein shouted, hopping down from his round-bellied gelding and bouncing around her like a farm dog. "I found thirty sheep! Maybe even forty!"

Oddny smiled, as proud as she was relieved, even though she suspected he was exaggerating.

"Freystein helped some," he admitted judiciously. "But guess what happened last night, Mother!"

Oddny raised her eyebrows, inviting him to tell on.

"We made camp by a grave mound!" Thorstein shouted. "And at night, it opened up. Freystein didn't see, but I went in. And there were men in red and men in black, and the men in black tried to make me pay tribute, so I cut off their arms with my axe!" He pulled from his belt the little wood-chopping axe Thorkel had given him for the trip. "And we had a great battle, me and the men in red against the men in black, and we won, but only because I was there. Otherwise the men in red would have lost. And to thank me, the chief of the men in red—his name was Brynjar—he gave me this!"

He brandished an ancient gold coin and held it, as children do, too close to her face for her to see it properly. She closed her hand around it and around his fingers, looking her question at Freystein.

Freystein shrugged helplessly. "We did camp by a cairn," he said, and let the sentence trail off into uncertainty.

"But here's the best part, Mother," Thorstein went on. "Brynjar told me that if someone can't speak, if they put this gold under their tongue, they'll be able to talk again. Try it, Mother, try it!"

The men were all looking at her now, and she was surprised to see they were waiting for her to do as he said. She looked back down at her son, eager to fix her, eager to give her what she did not have.

She sighed and put the coin in her mouth. It tasted of old earth and children's sweat, of the despair of the dead and the hope of the young who know only life.

"Well?" Thorstein asked breathlessly. "Do you feel any different?"

How she wanted to lie to him and say everything had changed. How she wished he didn't think she was broken. She thought for a long moment, tasting the metal on her tongue, before she very carefully framed her mouth to form the word, "No."

The sound was rough and low, but it was unmistakably a word. It was a word she had said hundreds of times, in dozens of ways, with mouth, face, eyes, and hands, and never been heard. She wondered if they would hear her now.

The men set up a cheer and Thorkel clapped Thorstein on the back as though he had indeed worked magic. They led him away to toast his exploits with ale and fresh lamb, and Oddny was left in the yard, watching her son's back as she quietly spit the coin into her hand.

She could see his life stretching out in front of him. Perhaps, with age, she was becoming a seer like her mad old father. But she could see it quite clearly: he would go abroad, as Thorkel intended for him. He would be a great man among great men. He would even cow his braggart of a father—she was sure of that, though she did not know why. He would be everything he was supposed to be. And he would hardly notice that she never spoke another word.

3.5 Case Study Analysis: Disability and Intersectionality in Medieval Iceland

In a very basic way, this case study of Melkorka and Oddny is a "fix-it" project because there are simply not enough narratives whose protagonists are people with disabilities. Even in contemporary literature, where one might expect representation to be broader, Lennard Davis says, "When characters have disabilities, the novel is usually exclusively about those qualities. Yet the disabled character is never of importance to himself or herself. Rather, the character is placed in the narrative 'for' the nondisabled characters—to help them develop sympathy, empathy, or as a counterbalance to some issue in the life of the 'normal' character."[473] In my reading of medieval Icelandic literature, I was struck first by Melkorka and then later by Oddny as bit-part characters (their narrative function is to give birth to the boy who becomes a protagonist later) who very much deserved their own stories. And even though Melkorka's mutism is feigned, the fact that others believe she cannot speak means she is socially in the same situation as Oddny: a woman with a disability in Viking Age Iceland.

Scholars have often pointed out that studying disability in a historical setting is a challenge. If we accept the foundational principle of disability studies that the concept of disability is importantly if not solely socially constructed, it follows that each culture will construct that concept differently. This is true even in the fairly recent past. Davis says, "Before the nineteenth century in Western culture the concept of the 'ideal' in relation to bodies was the regnant paradigm, and so all bodies were less than ideal."[474] The concept of normalcy as the opposite to disability, then, is a very recent one in human history; Ármann Jakobsson

---

473 Davis, "Crips Strike Back," 510.
474 Davis, "Crips Strike Back," 504.

goes so far as to say, "[T]he very notion of disability is modern."[475] Nevertheless, the wealth of material left behind by medieval Icelandic writers can give us a foothold in what physical and mental difference meant in that time and place. Lois Bragg, reflecting on the sagas with their Önund Wooden-Legs and Thorolf Crook-Foots, observes that what we understand as disability was almost "the rule rather than the exception" in medieval Scandinavia.[476] Yet while we tend to assume that premodern cultures were harder and less accepting than our own, Icelandic scholars often point to the following stanza of the eddic poem *Hávamál* as evidence for a surprisingly nonjudgmental attitude toward physical difference in the Viking era:

> A lame man can ride a horse,
> A handless man can drive a herd,
> A deaf man can fight and succeed;
> Being blind is better
> Than being burned:
> A corpse is no use to anyone.[477]

Although Ármann Jakobsson reminds us that "there is no single, coherent 'Viking attitude' toward persons with various impairments"[478] any more than there is a single, coherent "modern attitude," the eddic poem nonetheless expresses a clear notion that "flawlessness" was not a standard by which Viking bodies were judged for their ability to contribute to society. But the masculine grammatical endings on each of the descriptors also reminds us that the bodies being discussed so inclusively were male. The situation, we sense, may be different when that body is female.

In many ways, the stories of Melkorka and Oddny are doppelgangers: both narratives are about women who do not speak, and whose sons are the product of rape but who, as far as we can tell, are nonetheless beloved children who grow to be great men. Perhaps the key difference is that Oddny cannot speak, while Melkorka chooses not to. In modern terms, we could accuse Melkorka of faking membership in an identity community, but in her story, there is no community for her to join; her decision to refuse speech is an act of resistant isolation, not belonging.

---

475 Ármann Jakobsson et al., "Disability before Disability," 441.
476 Bragg, "Impaired and Inspired," 129.
477 "Haltr ríðr hrossi,/ hjörð rekr handar vanr,/ daufr vegr ok dugir,/ blindr er betri/ en brenndr séi,/ nýtr manngi nás," *Hávamál*, stanza 71, author's translation.
478 Ármann Jakobsson et al., "Disability before Disability," 456.

Scholars of Icelandic history will no doubt find a great many inconsistencies in my fics, just as creative writers will no doubt find many artistic faults. I make no claim to be a historian (though I aimed at avoiding obvious anachronisms) or a great artistic talent (though I attempted to make my fics ring true emotionally and aesthetically). Rather, my aims were intellectual and investigatory, the same as they would be if I were writing an academic paper on mutism among women in the sagas. I simply wanted to explore this subject with imagination and empathy rather than the cold eye of scholarship. Yet I believe the approach results in insight on a scholarly level too. Melkorka allows us to explore disability (in her case, perceived disability) as a route to empowerment, whereas Oddny's experience of disability centers on how the way others perceive her becomes a limiting factor in her life. Both stories unite, however, in demonstrating the workings of intersectionality, the overlap of identity categories. Specifically, these two stories make clear the interactions between a lack of speech and the status of women in a pre-feminist world.

Melkorka

I encountered Melkorka long before I discovered Oddny; *Laxdæla saga* is one of the most significant and widely studied of the Íslendingasögur (sagas of the Icelanders), whereas there is no complete translation of the texts of the Flateyjarbók manuscript, which contains "Þorsteins þáttr uxa-fóts," available in English. What always disturbed me about the Melkorka episode of *Laxdæla saga* is that her rape is not even registered as a rape by the narrative. My first interest in writing a fix-it fic for Melkorka, then, was to acknowledge what was done to her. Her decision not to speak to her captor and rapist is an act of rebellion, a way for her to hold onto a thread of the power she had when she was a clan king's daughter in Ireland. That power would have been limited in itself, of course, but a princess is not answerable to everyone who speaks to her; a slave is. The idea that Melkorka could use a disability (feigned though it is) as a route to power validates the theory promoted by a subset of disability studies called strong constructionism, which holds that disability, like any other form of difference, can be cast in a positive light and seen as a strength rather than a weakness, a feature to celebrate rather than overcome. It is a mode of thought not unlike the "Black is Beautiful" movement of the 1960s. In body theory, which incorporates strong constructionism, Tobin Seibers says,

> Pain [caused by disability] is most often soothed by the joy of conceiving the body differently from the norm. Frequently, the objects that people with disabilities are forced to live

with—prostheses, wheelchairs, braces, and other devices—are viewed not as potential sources of pain but as marvelous examples of the plasticity of the human form or as devices of
empowerment.[479]

Melkorka's performance in mutism is just such a reimagining of disability. However, in context, Seibers is critiquing body theory's blithe attitude toward the
physical realities of disability, and, as we will see, Melkorka experiences a
rude intrusion of those hard realities herself.

There is, in fact, another published canon fanfiction about Melkorka, which I
encountered long after I began my own work on *Laxdæla saga*, called *Hush: An
Irish Princess' Tale*, by Donna Jo Napoli. This novel, written for young adults and
covering only the period from just before Melkorka's capture to her arrival in Iceland, has an interesting take on Melkorka's story. I will not engage in an analysis
of it except to acknowledge that Napoli reaches this same conclusion about Melkorka's choice to pretend to be mute: that the refusal to speak grants her power
by making her unreachable in a way that speaking slaves are not. In the novel,
when Melkorka first refuses to speak to her captor, a longtime slave tells her,
"You're the one who started this silence—you have to keep it up. Or you lose
yourself. He'll just snuff you out. [...] A slave life counts for nothing unless the
slave finds a trick. You've found yours. Hush."[480] In Napoli's novel, Melkorka's
silence makes Gilli think she is an enchantress whom he must avoid offending,
a figure at once alluring and threatening. In my version, there is no such mispri-
sion: Melkorka interests Hoskuld because she is beautiful and unable to defend
her body from him. Her mind, though, he cannot reach, because she denies him
the access that he would gain if she conversed with him. Her mind is the one
thing she can keep for herself.

However, even if Melkorka's perceived disability is something she chooses,
something she sees as powerful, the saga narrative makes it impossible to see
her mutism as an unalloyed good, as perhaps body theory would like to see
it, unless we outright alter the events—something I did not wish to do. When
Olaf is born, Melkorka learns the consequences of silence: she cannot argue
against Hoskuld's naming the boy after his recently deceased uncle, and she
cannot advocate for his advancement in Hoskuld's family. It is not until she is
caught speaking to him, and hence "cured" of her mutism, that she can begin
to be the advocate he needs. Melkorka must give up the one source of her
own power in order to advance her son's.

---

479 Siebers, "Disability in Theory," 745.
480 Napoli, *Hush*, 134–35.

Oddny

The case of Oddny Geitisdottir is perhaps a more realistic portrayal of disability (despite the story's penchant for revenants and ogresses). Unlike Melkorka, Oddny does not choose to be perceived as mute, and as a result, her experience of actually being mute in a world full of speakers is much less about empowerment and much more about being faced with the limitations that society imposes upon her. Lois Bragg points out that Scandinavian society seemed to associate disability in the gods with some other compensatory power: "Of the thirteen male gods listed in Snorri's *Edda*, Odin is one-eyed [...], Tyr one-handed, Höd blind, Vidar mute [...], and Heimdall deaf."[481] She goes on to suggest that disability "may even have had some kind of social cachet, marking and thus identifying the great man as different from his normative but lesser peers"[482]—the operative word in this sentence being "man." I included this intriguing context in my own version of Oddny's story, in part to counter Melkorka's understandable sense that the Vikings were little more than animals, and in part to highlight the fact that even in a society where people (or gods) with disabilities are somehow magical, those people may very much have preferred just to be normative. Oddny has no ambitions to be special; in her own mind, she is ordinary and wants to be nothing more.

And, in fact, the original narrative treats Oddny as perfectly capable, in addition to being (as most saga heroines are) extremely beautiful. I did not have to intervene greatly to emphasize that Oddny can communicate with perfect clarity, if only in non-verbal ways. It is only when Ivar spurns her that her inability to speak becomes a serious detriment. Observing that Ivar's scorn for Thorkel's "mute sister" highlights her one non-normative feature, Ármann Jakobsson says, "One might argue that difference becomes disability precisely at this moment in the narrative."[483] Further exploring this notion, my fic draws out the fact that Oddny is perfectly capable of communication—but only if those around her choose to heed her. Unlike a person who can speak fluently, Oddny cannot raise her voice to get attention when she is being ignored, nor can she elaborate her points to make them more emphatic when what she communicates is dismissed. Ignoring Oddny is as easy as turning away or closing one's eyes. In this way, I wished to acknowledge that Oddny's mutism functions as disabilities often function: the behavior of the people around her is what causes her greatest

---

481 Bragg, "Impaired and Inspired," 130.
482 Bragg, "Impaired and Inspired," 131.
483 Ármann Jakobsson et al., "Disability before Disability," 454.

limitations. To use a parallel from Davis, "a person using a wheelchair [though they may never be able to walk] is only disabled if there are no ramps."[484] Just so, Oddny, though she will never be able to speak fluently, is only disabled when those around her choose not to understand her.

As part of affirming the value of ordinary people, I drained the magic out of my retelling of Oddny's story (which was possible only because I did not continue with Thorstein's adventures with the vomiting ogress in the second half of the *þáttur*). The move toward realism is a common approach in canon fanfiction, something that bothers Douglas Lanier in his commentary on the Hogarth Shakespeare series: "Elements of magic or intrusions of the divine," he complains, "are naturalized [...], quietly edited out, or treated as instances of the uncanny."[485] I believe the gravitational pull of realism works powerfully on authors of canon fanfiction specifically because we are trying to make connections between the past and our own world—a world more or less without fairies, magic gold, and hairy she-trolls. In the post-Enlightenment world, fantasy fills many literary roles, but making us feel closer to the past is not one of them. I also got rid of the elaborate inscriptions on Oddny's rune-stick, which would have taken hours to carve, though I kept the stick itself—unnecessary as it is in the strictest sense—as a nod to that detail in the original. In another move toward realism, I decided that Oddny specifically had Broca's aphasia (also known as expressive aphasia), which is caused by damage to the Broca's area of the frontal lobe.[486] None of the characters knows this about her, of course, but since there are not in fact a great many conditions that would render a person speechless without also seriously damaging their language comprehension or cognitive skills, I felt it was important for me to know what exactly was affecting Oddny in order to write her accurately.

Broca's aphasia is not a total inability to produce sound or even speech, but it is a limitation in the ability to construct fluent sentences; a sentence spoken by someone with Broca's aphasia is often "telegraphic," containing only a few key words and losing the rest. Because Oddny can, in fact, produce speech with an effort, I was able to reimagine the "healing" of Oddny's "defect" by her son's magic piece of gold in a way that upholds the events as narrated in the original but also maintains a sense of realism and the important elements of Oddny's character.

---

484 Davis, "Crips Strike Back," 507.
485 Lanier, "The Hogarth Shakespeare Series," 234–35.
486 For medical insights on aphasia, I am most grateful to Dr. Leah Acosta Tenney.

Narratives written by nondisabled people often portray disabled ones as being compensated with some other ability (Professor X may not be able to walk, but he is the most powerful telepath in the Marvel universe) or as being remarkable in "overcoming" their disabilities (Colin Craven in *Secret Garden* and Clara Sesemann in *Heidi* both leave their wheelchairs behind and learn to walk). As Simi Linton points out, "The idea that someone can *overcome* a disability has not been generated within the community; it is a wish fulfillment generated from the outside."[487] Just so, Oddny's son, Thorstein, feels the need to "fix" his mother by giving her the ability to speak, even though nothing in Oddny's behavior to him has ever indicated that she desires this. Because Oddny's gaining of speech is treated by the narrative as her ultimate happy ending, Ármann Jakobsson points out that this fact "may also seem to suggest that her mállaki [lack of speech] should have been understood as a kind of undesirable deficit or a crisis requiring remedy all along."[488] In other words, "curing" her in the end undoes the moral neutrality of her condition in the preceding narrative, recasting it as a "handicap" from which she must be rescued after all.

In the original, Thorstein's magic piece of cairn-gold is an actual remedy in typical wonder- or miracle-story style. In my fic, I used the fact that a person with Broca's aphasia would be able to produce a single word like "no" to let Oddny make a decision in this moment to placate her son, as many parents do, and give him what he wants instead of what she knows to be true. The fact that no one in the scene, not even her brother, seems to notice that Oddny has always been capable of producing such a word—or, for that matter, as she observes, that she does not take to speaking fluently thereafter—underscores how badly they all want to believe that Thorstein's cure has worked. And looking at the narrative arc of the whole, this desire seems to have more to do with their liking for the precocious Thorstein than it does for the welfare of Oddny.

Intersectionality

The reason no one is likely to care that Oddny doesn't speak again after her "cure" by the magic gold is that she is a woman, and we have been so long accustomed to the metaphor that powerlessness is voicelessness that we often forget it is a metaphor. Melkorka and Oddny draw attention to that metaphor by lit-

---

487 Linton, "Reassigning Meaning," 18, emphasis original.
488 Ármann Jakobsson et al., "Disability before Disability," 455.

eralizing it. Hence, Oddny's disability is not the only identity category that disadvantages her in her society; her status as a woman does the same thing. These women's positions as "multiply-disadvantaged"[489] persons give us the opportunity to consider the question of intersectionality.

Intersectionality was first formalized as a concept by Kimberle Crenshaw in the late 1980s in her study of the "intersection" of racism and sexism in the lived experiences of black women in the United States. The simple idea, which for some reason, as she demonstrates, neither culture nor the law was eager to acknowledge, is that the more non-default identity categories a person falls into (non-white, non-male, etc.), the more bias that person encounters in society, and those non-default identity categories interact and overlap in complex ways. Crenshaw's argument was that, "[b]ecause the intersectional experience is greater than the sum of racism and sexism, any analysis that does not take intersectionality into account cannot sufficiently address the particular manner in which Black women are subordinated."[490] While Crenshaw was specifically interested in the intersection of race and gender, the concept has since been expanded to include other identity categories like disability. In short, intersectionality reminds us that if Melkorka and Oddny had been non-speaking males, their experiences would potentially have been very different.

Scholars have often made the controversial claim that (non-white) race is "like a disability,"[491] and the same can be said—perhaps even more appropriately—about being a woman. In her discussion of feminist disability studies, Rosemarie Garland-Thomson sums up the argument thus: "[D]isability—similar to race and gender—is a system of representation that marks bodies as subordinate, rather than an essential property of bodies that supposedly have something wrong with them."[492] It is an expansion of constructivism (the concept that disability is socially constructed rather than inherent in bodily states) to include femaleness as a similarly constructed category: there is nothing impairing about being a woman unless one lives in a society that makes it so. Historically, as Garland-Thomson reminds us, "[f]emale biology and feminine ideology have both traditionally been interpreted as forms of disability in Western culture. Aristotle, after all, pronounced women to be 'mutilated males.'"[493] She calls this

---

489 Crenshaw, "Demarginalizing," 145.
490 Crenshaw, "Demarginalizing," 140.
491 See overview in Everelles, "Race," 145.
492 Garland-Thomson, "Feminist Disability Studies," 1557–58.
493 Garland-Thomson, "Feminist Disability Studies," 1563.

intersection of identity categories the "gendering of disability" and the "disabling of gender."[494]

As women in Viking society, even several generations apart, Melkorka's and Oddny's agency is limited by men's willingness to accommodate it. It should be noted that Oddny, as a freewoman, enjoyed more rights than many of her contemporaries in other cultures. She could, for instance, divorce a husband if she so desired, and women repeatedly play important roles as catalysts and even agents of action in the Íslendingasögur, though, admittedly, that action is not always portrayed in a positive light; women tend to be fomenters of blood feud and therefore bear the blame for the men getting themselves killed. Melkorka, as a slave, had no such rights, though the social line between slave and freeperson in Iceland seems never to have been as hard or uncrossable as it was in, say, the American South. It is true that the general assumption seems to have been that slaves deserved to be slaves (one thinks of the way in which Freystein is described as being "neither ugly nor difficult to deal with like other slaves" and therefore deserving of the freedom Thorstein eventually negotiates for him). However, because race as we understand it did not play a role in maintaining the gap between slave and free, when slaves are freed in Iceland, they more or less meld into the rest of the community, their status being determined by their wealth rather than their history. But nothing can change Melkorka's status as a woman, even when it is discovered that she is a princess; Hoskuld is said to treat her better at first, but as she ages, he completely loses interest in her welfare, foisting it off on their son instead.

Ármann Jakobsson makes the observation that when Thorkel overrides Oddny's refusal to attach herself socially to Ivar, "her experience parallels that of many other women in the sagas, who find their prudent, spoken words disregarded by their male relatives."[495] That is, Oddny's difficulty in making herself "heard" has nothing to do with the fact that she cannot speak and has everything to do with the fact that Thorkel sees her as a tradable good that he wishes to use to increase his status with a visiting Norwegian landowner. Simi Linton makes a claim about the depiction of disability in media that is useful in this regard:

> [D]isabled people are rarely depicted on television, in films, or in fiction as being in control of their own lives—in charge or actively seeking out and obtaining what they want and need. More often, disabled people are depicted as pained by their fate or, if happy, it is through personal triumph over their adversity. The adversity is not depicted as lack of op-

---

494 Garland-Thomson, "Feminist Disability Studies," 1564.
495 Ármann Jakobsson et al., "Disability before Disability," 455.

portunity, discrimination, institutionalization, and ostracism; it is the personal burden of their own body or means of functioning.[496]

If we are talking about premodern literature (indeed, if we are talking about many genres of modern literature, like the romance), we could just as easily swap out the phrase "disabled people" with the word "women" and the first sentence would be just as true; women in literature are often passive receptors of action rather than agents. What is interesting is that we cannot do the same for the second sentence: there is no "personal triumph" over the "adversity" of being a woman. When women act like men (if that's what it would mean to overcome one's impairment as a female), they become viragos doomed to punishment: one need only think of the "unsexed" Lady Macbeth. But swapping out the terms works again in the last sentence: a patriarchal world makes being a woman a disability, and then it blames women for their "inherent" feminine failings; think of the saga women blamed for encouraging the blood feuds that the men were undoubtedly perfectly willing to conduct on their own. Blaming rape victims is another example, as Thorkel implicitly does in his anger upon the discovery of Oddny's pregnancy, though in the end he redirects that anger at Ivar instead of his sister. Again, though, it doesn't occur to him that she might not want to marry her rapist.

Femaleness, then, has functioned for much of Western history as the ultimate bodily disability. In this light, Melkorka's adoption of a feigned mutism is less an appropriation of an identity category that doesn't belong to her than it is a way of expressing the identity category that does. Melkorka, though she doesn't realize it, is only literalizing what is metaphorically true: for both of these women, it doesn't really matter to those around them whether they speak or not.

Conclusion

It is possible, perhaps likely, that in my fics, I have imposed upon the past a set of attitudes that the characters, if they were real people, would not have recognized. Would it have occurred to Oddny to be embarrassed when her brother felt the need to explain her condition to a perfect stranger? Would she really have been saddened by her son's desire to "cure" her? I do not take lightly the med-

---

496 Linton, "Reassigning Meaning," 25.

dling that I have done in literary history. Torfi Tulinius, in discussing fiction about historical people, argues,

> We owe it to them to give them as much space to exist outside of our definitions, our pre-conceptions, our clichés, as we can. [...] At the same time—and this is the paradox in which we live, novelists, historians and readers—these long dead people can only exist through the fictions we create.[497]

Canon fanfiction will always exist inside that paradox: by seeking to address issues now that were not issues (at least, not consciously acknowledged ones) "back then," we are imposing upon the past our own values, views, and standards. However, unless we are content to sit on the far side of the gulf between us and our literary history and never seek to cross it, I believe that imposition is a sin we have to commit, though we must commit it knowingly. This is the value of the analysis of canon fanfiction: to bring to light those points upon which we disagree with the past, where we have cast our shadows back upon it and seen it in our own image.

It should also be acknowledged that in writing these two pieces, I have engaged in appropriation that some would, perhaps justifiably, find inappropriate or insulting. I am not a person with a disability (yet: age, as disability scholars often point out, is bound to disable us all eventually), nor have I experienced the level of violence and dehumanization imposed upon Melkorka and Oddny as women. I readily acknowledge that I have put words into their mouths and thoughts into their heads without having any right to do so. But that was part of the point: these fics were an exercise in empathy, in imaginatively inhabiting the radically Other and living in the world in a different body, just for a moment. It is the kind of exercise that I hope students will be willing to engage in as a way of both knowing the literary past and registering our protest against it. Students, with their myriad experiences and myriad voices of their own, will undoubtedly find ways of inhabiting those past bodies that are far beyond my own reach.

---

497 Torfi Tulinius, "Re-writing the Contemporary Sagas," 195–96.

Conclusion: Inhabiting the Past

Fanfiction, canon or otherwise, is part of an ancient tradition of refashioning stories to suit the needs and tastes of a particular audience. As narratology reminds us, retelling is really just an extension of the meaning-making process we engage in when we read anything. And reading—both what we read and how we read it —is an important part of how we shape culture. Abigail De Kosnik argues that "a culture's canon is defined by a culture's repertoire. That is, whatever texts a culture continually reperforms, restages, comments upon, rereads, and so on [...] comprises that culture's canon."[498] In other words, we will never really be without a canon: we only change what works that canon is made of, as we incorporate new ones and set others aside.

I hope I have made the case in this book that canon fanfiction is a useful method for maintaining those works of the traditional canon that we, as scholars and readers ourselves, do not want to see entirely set aside. Those who see no value in such works have no doubt stopped reading long before reaching this point in the book. It is true that the literature of the past shares all the failings of the past itself—indeed, all the failings of human beings, who seem doomed always to fall short of perfect justice, perfect equity, and perfect empathy. But just as the continuing fight for social justice is eloquent proof that we have not given up striving for better justice, equity, and empathy, the fact that we have the power to rewrite past literature is similar proof that what has gone before is not, necessarily, without its value for the current moment.

The case for finding better ways to empower contemporary readers, students, and professionals alike, is, I think, a rather urgent one. The study of the literary tradition is being relegated to the ivory tower, where dusty scholars debate how many angels can dance on the head of a pin. So goes the popular imagination of what we do. But what scholars really do is grapple with the most urgent and longstanding questions of the human community. Our problem, for many decades now, is that we have been having those conversations behind the closed doors of academic discourse, and the very people who should be most invested in the discussion—people whose identities have been marginalized by the hegemons of history, young people who care about the questions but who have no desire to climb into the tower—have not been invited to speak.

In a world often called post-literary, if we want to see literature survive its own predicted demise, sticking to exclusionary attitudes about what we're al-

---

498 De Kosnik, *Rogue Archives*, 66.

https://doi.org/10.1515/9781501515972-006

lowed to say about literature and how we're allowed to say it will not prove sustainable. Terri Windling offers an apt metaphor with which to conclude:

> There are two ways a lovely old house can be saved from the developer's wrecking ball. One is to declare it historic and inviolate, to set it carefully aside from life and preserve its rooms as a museum to the past. The other is to adapt it to modern use: to encourage new generations to live within its walls, look out its diamond windows, climb its crooked staircase, and light new fires in its hearth.[499]

If we want to be participants in a living tradition and not curators of a museum in which only a narrow population has any sense of investment, we might do well to meet the next generation of readers where they are and, in doing so, invite them to participate in that living tradition alongside us.

---

499 Windling, "White as Snow," 5.

Appendix: Teaching Resources

In the following pages, I list three different assignments I have developed for use in my own college classrooms. These resources are intended to make it easier for an instructor who would like to incorporate canon fanfiction into a course to do so without having to start from scratch. All are intended for use in a course that does not focus specifically on canon fanfiction, adaptation, or retellings, but rather is a general literature course in which this assignment would be one of a number of other teaching methodologies.

I have used these assignments in my own classroom in two ways. In classes populated with English majors, I have assigned the third topic (canon fanfiction through a theoretical lens) as a regular paper, treated as equivalent to a traditional academic paper both in terms of grade weighting and in terms of how much preparation time was expected to be given to it. In general education classes, I have more often assigned the first or second topics (general canon fanfiction and fix-it lit) as optional bonus papers. Students not used to the rigors of a college-level literature class are often dismayed at the low score they receive on their first or second paper, and writing canon fanfiction as a bonus activity gives them a meaningful way to process the material and salvage their course grade at the same time. I should point out that I have assigned these topics as bonus papers classes not because I believe them to be less rigorous or less educational than traditional academic papers but because there is an expectation at my institution for equivalency in major writing assignments among all the literature courses offered in the core curriculum.

Each assignment is accompanied by a list of goals and student learning outcomes. Although these terms are sometimes used interchangeably, I use "goal" to refer to broad concepts that I want students to encounter in the assignment, whereas "student learning outcome" refers to measurable benchmarks by which students prove that they are learning skills. A simple scoring rubric, applicable to all the included assignments, appears at the end of the appendix. While many universities will dictate the use of a department-wide rubric, an assignment-specific scoring sheet like this can be an additional tool for the student in interpreting the instructor's assessment of their performance.

https://doi.org/10.1515/9781501515972-007

General Canon Fanfiction

The following assignment is used in a medieval literature class; the "Suggestions to get you thinking" section can be adapted to reflect the material of any given course.

People have been retelling stories for millennia; retelling is one of the ways we make old stories remain relevant to our current interests and beliefs. For this assignment, **rewrite one of our readings** from a different point of view, or set it in a different time and place, or make some other alteration that allows the work to address issues current to our own interests.

Examples from history:
- In *Paradise Lost*, John Milton rewrote the Fall of Man in greater detail than appears in the Bible, infusing it with new views of why the first sin was committed and what it really meant.
- In *Grendel*, John Gardner rewrote *Beowulf* from Grendel's perspective, forcing us to question how monstrous the "monster" really is.
- In *Wide Sargasso Sea*, Jean Rhys wrote a prequel to *Jane Eyre* from the perspective of the "mad woman in the attic," revealing the deeply problematic attitude of English men toward Caribbean women.
- Disney's *The Lion King* turned *Hamlet* into a beast fable, expressing a desire to find hope and redemption in a situation which, in Shakespeare, ends in tragedy.

Suggestions to get you thinking:
- How would *Morte D'Arthur* be a different kind of story if told from the perspective of Mordred?
- Could *Sir Gawain and the Green Knight* be transferred to a modern American setting? What form would the temptation of Gawain take and what would he learn from it?
- What unexplored backstory can you imagine for Guinevere or Lancelot in *The Knight of the Cart* that explains their behavior?
- What kind of sonnet might Laura write Petrarch in response to the sonnets he wrote about her?

If the work you are rewriting is too long to do the whole thing, rewrite just one key scene.

Include an **analysis of your work.** Consider questions like the following (you do not necessarily have to address each one):

- What concern does your version address and why did you choose the changes you made?
- How does your new version affect our reading of the original?
- Does your version update, alter, or give a new angle on key themes in the original?

You will be assessed based on the evidence of critical thought, creative effort, and cogent analysis of your own work, particularly in relation to how your work reflects on the original text.

Goals

- Students will engage on an emotional and personal level with a piece of literature from the syllabus.
- Students will find a new way to value literature of the past by updating it to address aspects of contemporary interest to them.

Student Learning Outcomes (SLOs)

- Students will demonstrate creative thinking by producing a piece of fiction or poetry based on but differing from a piece of literature from the syllabus.
- Students will be able to analyze their own work and cogently explain its relation to the piece of literature they have chosen to retell.

Fix-It Lit

The following assignment specifically asks students to address what they see as a problem or objectionable element in the literature from the syllabus. This assignment is adapted for medieval/Renaissance content from an assignment originally given in a course on contemporary popular literature; as above, the specifics can be altered to reflect any given course content.

Fanfiction is a huge part of contemporary literature. But in fact, people have been writing fanfic for millennia: reimagining literature is one of the ways we make it meaningful. Particularly when there is something in literature that bothers us, we often want to "fix" what has gone wrong. **"Fix-it lit"** is a genre of fan-fiction that identifies a problem with the original story and rewrites it to address that problem. For this assignment, identify an injustice that bothers you about one of the works on our syllabus, either something we brought up in class or something we have not discussed, and **write a piece of fix-it fanfiction** that addresses it in some way.

One of the most productive approaches to this kind of assignment is to change the point-of-view character and see the events through the eyes of a different person. You may change the events themselves, but if you want a real challenge, keep the events the same and find a way to make your reader perceive them differently!

Examples of altered perspectives in retellings from history:
- In the *Aeneid*, Virgil retold the events of the *Iliad* from the perspective of Aeneas, a man on the losing side of the Trojan War, allowing us to see what the Greek "heroes" look like to those they conquer.
- In the *Heroides*, Ovid wrote monologues by wronged women in which they address the men who wronged them. For instance, Dido gets to confront Aeneas for jilting her in order to sail away and found the Roman Empire.

Questions you might take as your starting point:
- How does King Marsile feel about Charlemagne's campaign against Muslims in Spain in *Song of Roland?* How does he feel about having to deal with someone like Ganelon in order to have a hope of winning?
- What would the first half of *Beowulf* look like if it were told from the perspective of Grendel's mother, or the second half if it were told from the perspective of the dragon?
- How does Jessica feel about having to convert to Christianity to be an acceptable bride for Lorenzo in *Merchant of Venice?*

Include an **analysis of your work.** Consider questions like the following (you do not necessarily have to address each one):
- What problem or problems in the original does your fix-it fic address?
- Why did you choose to "fix" the problem as you did?
- How does your fix-it fic allow us to see the original in a new way?

You will be assessed based on the evidence of critical thought, creative effort, and cogent analysis of your own work, particularly in relation to how your work reflects on the original text.

Goals

- Students will confront and address features that they find troubling in a piece of literature from the syllabus.
- Students will be empowered to "talk back" to literature of the past by calling it out on its injustices.

Student Learning Outcomes (SLOs)

- Students will demonstrate creative thinking by producing a piece of fiction or poetry based on but differing from a piece of literature from the syllabus.
- Students will be able to analyze their own work and cogently explain its relation to the piece of literature they have chosen to retell.

Canon Fanfiction and Theory

The following assignment is geared toward higher-level students, or to a class that has incorporated instruction on literary theory. If time allows, having students read this book or selections from it (particularly the studies of published novels in chapter 2 or the case studies in chapter 3), will give students an inroad into the expectations for and possibilities of this kind of assignment.

Literary critics use particular lenses (theories) to bring out different aspects of any given piece of literature. A similar approach can be taken by a creative writer, setting out to retell, reinvent, or otherwise reimagine that piece of literature using a particular theoretical approach.

For this assignment, **select a piece of literature from our syllabus and a theoretical lens** through which you wish to look at it, and instead of writing an academic paper, write a piece of fiction or poetry that applies your chosen lens to that literature.

Examples from published authors of the twenty-first century:
- In "The Wife of Bafa," Patience Agbabi rewrote the *Wife of Bath's Prologue* as a persona poem, reimagining Alisoun through a postcolonial perspective by making her a Nigerian woman speaking from within her own cultural context.

- In *Vinegar Girl*, Anne Tyler retold *Taming of the Shrew* from Katherine's point of view, using a fourth-wave feminist lens to address the oppression of women implied in the original.
- Kazuo Ishiguro wrote a spinoff of the King Arthur stories in *Buried Giant*, using trauma theory to explore collective loss, violence, and memory in the context of Arthurian England.

Combinations you might consider (though you may choose others):
- *Völsunga saga* through a feminist lens
- *Beowulf* through an ecocritical lens
- *Egils saga* through a disability studies lens
- *Malory's Morte D'Arthur* through a trauma theory lens
- *Song of Roland* through a queer theory lens
- *Othello* through a postcolonial lens
- *Twelfth Night* through a Marxist lens

Include an **analysis of your work.** Consider questions like the following (you do not necessarily have to address each one):
- Why is your chosen lens a useful one for viewing the original work?
- How does your fiction or poetry demonstrate that theoretical lens?
- Does your work allow us to see the original in a new way?

Include a bibliography of at least **three secondary sources** (book chapters or articles) that you used as research to help you learn about your chosen theory or the original piece in the preparation of your project.

You will be assessed based on the evidence of critical thought, creative effort, and cogent analysis of your own work, particularly in relation to how your work applies your chosen theory.

Goals

- Students will engage creatively with otherwise academic subjects (literature of the past and literary theory).
- Students will learn how theory applies to real-world issues (social justice, ideology, etc.) and how literature, even literature of the past, reflects those issues.

Student Learning Outcomes (SLOs)

– Students will demonstrate creative thinking by producing a piece of fiction or poetry based on but differing from a piece of literature from the syllabus.
– Students will apply literary theory to their own creative work.
– Students will be able to analyze their own work and cogently explain its relation to the piece of literature they have chosen to retell.

Scoring Rubric

Creativity   Score out of 10 _____

> A high-scoring project will demonstrate an effort to think creatively and find an interesting, insightful, or unique approach to the assignment. A low-scoring project may simply have reproduced the original in different words or may have copied a well-known published approach (for instance, retelling *Jane Eyre* from the perspective of Bertha Mason as was done in Jean Rhys's *Wide Sargasso Sea*).

Understanding of original text   Score out of 10 _____

> A high-scoring project will acknowledge content learned in class regarding analysis of the original text, even if that is to disagree with that analysis. A low-scoring project will not make it clear that the student has studied the original work at all. (For example, randomly deciding to alter the setting of a work to present-day America without being able to explain why such a move is thematically meaningful makes the instructor suspect you did not have a grasp of the themes of the original.)

Analysis of creative work   Score out of 10 _____

> A high-scoring project will offer a cogent and thoughtful analysis of your own work, touching on the themes, issues, or theoretical insights you have applied. A low-scoring project may not recognize what is insightful or important in your own work, or it may offer haphazard or surface-level analysis.

Grammar and style   Score out of 5 _____

> A high-scoring project will demonstrate the level of writing expertise expected in a class of this level. A low-scoring project may not be proof-read or may demonstrate a distracting level of informality in writing style. Note: informality may be appropriate in your creative writing, but the analytical portion should be written in academic style.

Bibliography

Primary Works

Austen, Jane. *Pride and Prejudice*. London: Macmillan and Company, 1950.

Barker, Pat. *The Silence of the Girls*. New York: Doubleday, 2018.

Beowulf. Directed by Robert Zemeckis. Paramount Pictures, 2007.

Beowulf. Edited by Bruce Mitchell and Fred C. Robinson. Malden, MA: Blackwell, 1998.

Chaucer, Geoffrey. *The Canterbury Tales*, *The Riverside Chaucer*. 3rd edition. Edited by Larry D. Benson. Oxford: Oxford University Press, 1987.

Chevalier, Tracy. *New Boy*. London: Hogarth Shakespeare, 2017.

Datlow, Ellen, and Terri Windling, eds. *Snow White, Blood Red*. New York: Avon, 1993.

Green Knight, The. Directed by David Lowery. A24 et al., 2021.

Hamlet. Directed by Franco Zeffirelli. Icon Productions, 1990.

Hávamál. Eddukvæði: Sæmundar-Edda. Edited by Guðni Jónsson. Íslendingasagnaútgáfan, 1954; online text Heimskringla.no, 2019. https://heimskringla.no/wiki/H%C3%A1vam%C3%A1l.

Headley, Maria Dahvana. *The Mere Wife*. New York: Picador, 2018.

Homer. *The Iliad*. Translated by Robert Fagles. London: Penguin Classics, 1991.

Hornblower. Directed by Andrew Grieve. Meridian Broadcasting, 1998 – 2003.

Jacobson, Howard. *Shylock Is My Name*. London: Hogarth Shakespeare, 2016.

Kistiakovsky, Andrei A. *Khraniteli*. Moscow: Eksmo, 1982, 2003.

Laxdæla saga. Edited by Sveinbjorn Thordarson. Icelandic Saga Database, 2007. http://www.sagadb.org/laxdaela_saga.is.

Miller, Madeline. *Song of Achilles*. New York: HarperCollins, 2012.

Morrison, Toni, lyrics by Rokia Traoré. *Desdemona*. London: Oberon Modern Plays, 2012.

Napoli, Donna Jo. *Hush: An Irish Princess' Tale*. New York: Atheneum, 2007.

Nesbø, Jo. *Macbeth*. London: Hogarth Shakespeare, 2018.

Ovid. *Heroides*. Edited by William L. Carey and David J. Califf. The Latin Library, n.d. http://www.thelatinlibrary.com/.

Scieszka, Jon. *The True Story of the Three Little Pigs*. New York: Viking, 1989.

Shakespeare, William. *Macbeth*. In *The Complete Works of Shakespeare*. 4th edition. Edited by David Bevington, 1219 – 55. New York: Longman, 1997.

Shakespeare, William. *Othello, the Moor of Venice*. In *The Complete Works of Shakespeare*. 4th edition. Edited by David Bevington, 1117 – 66. New York: Longman, 1997.

Shonagon, Sei. *The Pillow Book*. Translated by Meredith McKinney. In *The Norton Anthology of World Literature, Volume B*. 3rd edition. Edited by Martin Puchner, 1127 – 53. New York: W.W. Norton, 2012.

Sir Gawain and he Green Knight. Edited by J. R. R. Tolkien and E. V. Gordon. Oxford: Clarendon Press, 1967; online text University of Michigan Library, n.d. http://name.umdl.umich.edu/Gawain.

Tempest, The. Directed by Julie Taymor. Miramax, 2010.

https://doi.org/10.1515/9781501515972-008

Valdimar Ásmundsson,[500] trans., and Hans de Roos, trans. *Powers of Darkness: The Lost Version of Dracula [Makt Myrkranna]*. New York: Harry N. Abrams, 2017.

Zarins, Kim. *Sometimes We Tell the Truth*. New York: Simon Pulse, 2016.

"Þorsteins þáttur uxa-fóts." *Íslendingaþættir*, Snerpa, May 1999. https://www.snerpa.is/net/isl/uxafots.htm.

Student Papers

Jeffs, Lucy. "Rewrite." 1 December 2016. World Literature to 1600. South Carolina: Erskine College. Student paper, used with permission.

Miller-Wells, Ani. "Modern Pillow Book Lists." 22 October 2018. World Literature to 1600. South Carolina: Erskine College. Student paper, used with permission.

Moody, Christopher. "The Soldier." 29 April 2019. Medieval Literature. South Carolina: Erskine College. Student paper, used with permission.

Secondary Works

"A Letter on Justice and Open Debate." *Harper's Magazine*, July 7, 2020. https://harpers.org/a-letter-on-justice-and-open-debate/.

Abercrombie, Nicholas, and Brian Longhurst. *Audiences: A Sociological Theory of Performance and Imagination*. London: Sage, 1998.

ADE Ad Hoc Committee on the English Major. "A Changing Major: The Report of the 2016–17 ADE Ad Hoc Committee on the English Major." The Association of Departments of English, 2018. https://www.ade.mla.org/Resources/Reports-and-Other-Resources/A-Changing-Major-The-Report-of-the-2016-17-ADE-Ad-Hoc-Committee-on-the-English-Major.

Adney, Karley. "Leon Garfield's *Hamlet*: Introducing Shakespeare, Reflecting on Contemporary Britain." In *Inhabited by Stories: Critical Essays on Tales Retold*. Edited by Nancy A. Barta-Smith and Danette DiMarco, 92–106. Newcastle upon Tyne: Cambridge Scholars Publishing, 2012.

Anderson, Greta. "Responding to Rise in Campus Anti-Semitism." *Inside Higher Ed*, 2020. https://www.insidehighered.com/news/2020/09/09/anti-semitism-rise-new-semester-starts.

Archive of Our Own (AO3), 2020. https://archiveofourown.org/.

Ármann Jakobsson, Anna Katharina Heiniger, Christopher Crocker, and Hanna Björg Sigurjónsdóttir. "Disability before Disability: Mapping the Uncharted in the Medieval Sagas." *Scandinavian Studies* 92, no. 4 (2020): 440–60.

Barry, Peter. *Beginning Theory: An Introduction to Literary and Cultural Theory*. 4th edition. Manchester: Manchester University Press, 2017.

Barta-Smith, Nancy A., and Danette DiMarco. "Introduction." In *Inhabited by Stories: Critical Essays on Tales Retold*. Edited by Nancy A. Barta-Smith and Danette DiMarco, 1–12. Newcastle upon Tyne: Cambridge Scholars Publishing, 2012.

---

500 In keeping with Icelandic practice, I cite Icelanders by first name.

Barthes, Roland. "Death of the Author." Translated by Richard Howard. *Aspen*, no. 5+6 (1967): section 3. www.ubu.com/aspen/aspen5and6/threeEssays.html#barthes.

Battis, Jes. *Thinking Queerly: Medievalism, Wizardry, and Neurodiversity in Young Adult Texts.* Kalamazoo, MI: Medieval Institute Publications, 2021.

Beidler, Peter G. *The Lives of the* Miller's Tale. Jefferson, NC: McFarland and Company, 2015.

Bennett, Andrew, and Nicholas Royle. *An Introduction to Literature, Criticism and Theory.* London: Taylor & Francis, 2016.

Berger, James. "Trauma without Disability, Disability without Trauma: A Disciplinary Divide." *JAC* 24, no. 3, special issue, Part 2: Trauma and Rhetoric (2004): 563–82.

Bergljót S. Kristjánsdóttir. "Introduction." In *The Saga of the People of Laxardal and Bolli Bollason's Tale.* Translated by Keneva Kunz. Edited by Bergljót S. Kristjánsdóttir, ix–xl. London: Penguin Books, 2008.

Binns, Alan L. "The Story of Þorsteinn Uxafót." *Saga-Book* 14 (1953–1955): 36–60.

"Biography." *Jo Nesbø*. Penguin Random-House, 2021. https://jonesbo.com/jo-nesbo/.

Black, David A. "Character; or, The Strange Case of Uma Peel." In *Cult Television*. Edited by Sara Gwenllian-Jones and Roberta E. Pearson, 99–114. Minneapolis: University of Minnesota Press, 2004.

Booth, Paul J. "Fandom: The Classroom of the Future." *European Fans and European Fan Objects: Localization and Translation.* Edited by Anne Kustritz, special issue, *Transformative Works and Cultures*, no. 19 (2015). dx.doi.org/10.3983/twc.2015.0650.

Bragg, Lois. "Impaired and Inspired: The Makings of a Medieval Icelandic Poet." In *Madness, Disability and Social Exclusion: The Archaeology and Anthropology of 'Difference.'* Edited by Jane Hubert, 128–43. London: Routledge, 2000.

Carney, Jo Eldridge. "'Being Born a Girl': Toni Morrison's *Desdemona*." *Borrowers and Lenders: The Journal of Shakespeare and Appropriation* 9, no. 1 (2014): 1–20.

Cartmell, Deborah. "Introduction." In *Adaptations: From Text to Screen, Screen to Text*. Edited by Deborah Cartmell and Imelda Whelehan, 23–28. London: Routledge, 1999.

Caruth, Cathy. *Unclaimed Experience: Trauma, Narrative, and History.* Baltimore, MD: Johns Hopkins University Press, 1996.

Cavicchi, Daniel. "Foundational Discourses of Fandom." In *A Companion to Media Fandom and Fan Studies*. Edited by Paul Booth, 27–46. Hoboken, NJ: Wiley Blackwell, 2018.

Clinton, Katie, Henry Jenkins, and Jenna McWilliams. "New Literacies in an Age of Participatory Culture." In *Reading in a Participatory Culture: Remixing Moby-Dick in the English Classroom*. Edited by Henry Jenkins and Wyn Kelley, 3–24. New York: Teachers College Press, 2013.

Coppa, Francesca. *The Fanfiction Reader: Folk Tales for the Digital Age.* Ann Arbor: University of Michigan Press, 2017.

Coppa, Francesca. "Slash/Drag: Appropriation and Visibility in the Age of *Hamilton*." In *A Companion to Media Fandom and Fan Studies*. Edited by Paul Booth, 189–206. Hoboken, NJ: Wiley Blackwell, 2018.

Crenshaw, Kimberle. "Demarginalizing the Intersection of Race and Sex: A Black Feminist Critique of Antidiscrimination Doctrine, Feminist Theory and Antiracist Politics." *University of Chicago Legal Forum* 1989, no. 1 (1989): 139–67.

Cucarella-Ramon, Vicent. "Decolonizing *Othello* in Search of Black Feminist North American Identities: Djanet Sears' *Harlem Duet* and Toni Morrison's *Desdemona*." *International Journal of English Studies (IJES)* 17, no. 1 (2017): 83–97.

Davis, Lennard J. "Crips Strike Back: The Rise of Disability Studies." *American Literary History* 11, no. 3 (1999): 500–512.

De Certeau, Michel. *The Practice of Everyday Life*. Translated by Steven F. Rendall. Berkeley, CA: University of California Press, 1984.

De Kosnik, Abigail. *Rogue Archives: Digital Cultural Memory and Media Fandom*. Cambridge, MA: MIT Press, 2016.

De Waal, Kit. "Don't Dip Your Pen in Someone Else's Blood: Writers and 'the Other.'" *Irish Times*, June 30, 2018. https://www.irishtimes.com/culture/books/don-t-dip-your-pen-in-someone-else-s-blood-writers-and-the-other-1.3533819.

Donaldson, Elizabeth J. "The Corpus of the Madwoman: Toward a Feminist Disability Studies Theory of Embodiment and Mental Illness." *NWSA Journal* 14, no. 3, "Feminist Disability Studies" (2002): 99–119.

Edwards, Alexandra. "Literature Fandom and Literary Fans." In *A Companion to Media Fandom and Fan Studies*. Edited by Paul Booth, 47–64. Hoboken, NJ: Wiley Blackwell, 2018.

Erickson, Peter. ""Late" Has No Meaning Here': Imagining a Second Chance in Toni Morrison's *Desdemona*." *Borrowers and Lenders: The Journal of Shakespeare and Appropriation* 8, no. 1 (2013): 1–16.

Everelles, Nirmala. "Race." In *Keywords for Disability Studies*. Edited by Rachel Adams, Benjamin Reiss, and David Serlin, 145–48. New York: New York University Press, 2015.

Falck-Ytter, Terje, and Sofia Loden, "The Perils of Suggesting Famous Historical Figures Had Autism." *Spectrum: Autism Research News*, 22 September 2020. https://www.spectrumnews.org/opinion/viewpoint/the-perils-of-suggesting-famous-historical-figures-had-autism/.

"Fan fiction." *Oxford English Dictionary: OED Online*. Oxford University Press, June 2019. oed.com.

Fanlore. Fanlore.org, 2019. https://fanlore.org/wiki/.

Fantuzzi, Marco. *Achilles in Love: Intertextual Studies*. Oxford: Oxford University Press, 2012.

Farley, Shannon K. "Versions of Homer: Translation, Fan Fiction, and Other Transformative Rewriting." *Transformative Works and Cultures* 21 (2016): n.p.

Farris, Sara. "American Pastoral in the Twentieth-Century *O Pioneers!*, *A Thousand Acres*, and *Merry Men*." *Isle: Interdisciplinary Studies in Literature and Environment* 5, no. 1 (1998): 27–48.

Fathallah, Judith May. *Fanfiction and the Author*. Amsterdam: Amsterdam University Press, 2017. https://www.jstor.org/stable/j.ctt1v2xsp4.

Felski, Rita. *The Limits of Critique*. Chicago: University of Chicago Press, 2015.

Fricker, Karen. "Creating the Space of Truth in the Make-Believe World of the Theatre: An Interview with Peter Sellars." *Journal of Adaptation in Film and Performance* 7, no. 2 (2014): 209–23. doi:10.1386/jafp.7.2.209_1.

Frus, Phyllis, and Christy Williams. "Introduction: Making the Case for Transformation." In *Beyond Adaptation: Essays on Radical Transformations of Original Works*. Edited by Phyllis Frus and Christy Williams, 1–18. Jefferson, NC: McFarland and Company, 2010.

Garland-Thomson, Rosemarie. "Feminist Disability Studies." *Signs* 30, no. 2 (2005): 1557–87.

Gilbert, Arthur N. "Buggery and the British Navy, 1700–1861." *Journal of Social History* 10, no. 1 (1976): 72–98.

Gilbert, Ruth. "'Strange Notions': Treatments of Early Modern Hermaphrodites." In *Madness, Disability and Social Exclusion: The Archaeology and Anthropology of 'Difference.'* Edited by Jane Hubert, 144–58. London: Routledge, 2000.

Gilroy, Amanda. "Our Austen: Fan Fiction in the Classroom." *Persuasions On-Line* 31, no. 1 (Winter 2010): n.p.

Goldenberg, Judi. "*PW* Talks with Madeline Miller: Love, Fighting, Death, Longing." *Publishers Weekly*, December 5, 2011, 56.

Gray, Jonathan, Cornel Sandvoss, and C. Lee Harrington. "Introduction: Why Study Fans?" In *Fandom: Identities and Communities in a Mediated World*. Edited by Jonathan Gray, Cornel Sandvoss, and C. Lee Harrington, 1–16. New York: New York University Press, 2007.

Greenblatt, Stephen. *Shakespearean Negotiations: The Circulation of Social Energy in Renaissance Europe*. Berkeley, CA: University of California Press, 1988.

Grossman, Lev. "Foreword." In *Fic: Why Fanfiction Is Taking Over the World*. By Anne Jamison, xi–xiv. Dallas, TX: Smart Pop/BenBella Books, 2013.

Guarracino, Serena. "Africa as Voices and Vibes: Musical Routes in Toni Morrison's *Margaret Garner* and *Desdemona*." *Research in African Literatures* 46, no. 4 (2015): 56–71. doi:10.2979/reseafrilite.46.4.56.

Gwenllian-Jones, Sara. "Virtual Reality and Cult Television." In *Cult Television*. Edited by Sara Gwenllian-Jones and Roberta E. Pearson, 83–97. Minneapolis: University of Minnesota Press, 2004.

Gwenllian-Jones, Sara, and Roberta E. Pearson. "Introduction." In *Cult Television*. Edited by Sara Gwenllian-Jones and Roberta E. Pearson, ix–xx. Minneapolis: University of Minnesota Press, 2004.

Hellekson, Karen, and Kristina Busse. *The Fan Fiction Studies Reader*. Iowa City: University Of Iowa Press, 2014.

Heng, Geraldine. *The Invention of Race in the European Middle Ages*. Cambridge: Cambridge University Press, 2018.

Hergenrader, Trent. "Genre Fiction, and Games, and Fanfiction! Oh My! Competing Realities in Creative Writing Classrooms." In *Can Creative Writing Really Be Taught? Resisting Lore in Creative Writing Pedagogy*. Edited by Stephanie Vanderslice and Rebecca Manery, 135–49. London: Bloomsbury Academic, 2017.

Herman, David. "Storyworlds." In *Routledge Encyclopedia of Narrative Theory*. Edited by David Herman, Manfred Jahn, and Marie-Laure Ryan, 569–70. London: Routledge, 2005.

Hestetun, Øyunn. "Palimpsest of Subjugation: Inscriptions of Domination on the Land and the Human Body in Jane Smiley's *A Thousand Acres*." In *Contesting Environmental Imaginaries: Nature and Counternature in a Time of Global Change*. Edited by Steven Hartman, 48–68. Leiden: Brill/Rodopi, 2017.

Higl, Andrew. "The Wife of Bath Retold: From the Medieval to the Postmodern." In *Inhabited by Stories: Critical Essays on Tales Retold*. Edited by Nancy A. Barta-Smith and Danette DiMarco, 294–313. Newcastle upon Tyne: Cambridge Scholars Publishing, 2012.

Hills, Matt. *Fan Cultures*. London: Routledge, 2002.

Hills, Matt. "Implicit Fandom in the Fields of Theatre, Art, and Literature: Studying 'Fans' beyond Fan Discourses." In *A Companion to Media Fandom and Fan Studies*. Edited by Paul Booth, 477–94. Hoboken, NJ: Wiley Blackwell, 2018.

Hills, Matt. "Media Academics *as* Media Audiences: Aesthetic Judgments in Media and Cultural Studies." In *Fandom: Identities and Communities in a Mediated World*. Edited by Jonathan Gray, Cornel Sandvoss, and C. Lee Harrington, 33–47. New York: New York University Press, 2007.

Hooker, Mark T. *Tolkien through Russian Eyes*. Zurich: Walking Tree Publishers, 2003.

Jamison, Anne. *Fic: Why Fanfiction Is Taking Over the World*. Dallas, TX: Smart Pop/BenBella Books, 2013.

Jenkins, Henry. "Afterword: The Future of Fandom." In *Fandom: Identities and Communities in a Mediated World*. Edited by Jonathan Gray, Cornel Sandvoss, and C. Lee Harrington, 357–64. New York: New York University Press, 2007.

Jenkins, Henry. *Convergence Culture: Where Old and New Media Collide*. New York: New York University Press, 2006.

Jenkins, Henry. "Fandom, Negotiation, and Participatory Culture." In *A Companion to Media Fandom and Fan Studies*. Edited by Paul Booth, 13–26. Hoboken, NJ: Wiley Blackwell, 2018.

Jenkins, Henry. "How the Extended Marvel Universe (and Other Superhero Stories) Can Enable Political Debates." *Confessions of an Aca-Fan*, May 6, 2015. http://henryjenkins. org/2015/05/how-the-extended-marvel-universe-and-other-superhero-stories-can-enable-political-debates.html.

Jenkins, Henry. *Textual Poachers: Television Fans and Participatory Culture*. London: Routledge, 1992.

Jenkins, Henry. "Youth Voice, Media, and Political Engagement." In *By Any Media Necessary: The New Youth Activism*. By Henry Jenkins, Sangita Shresthova, Liana Gamber-Thompson, Neta Kligler-Vilenchik, and Arely M. Zimmerman, n.p. New York: New York University Press, 2016. https://opensquare.nyupress.org/books/9781479829712/read/.

Jenkins, Henry, and Wyn Kelley, eds. *Reading in a Participatory Culture: Remixing* Moby-Dick *in the English Classroom*. New York: Teachers College Press, 2013.

Jenkins, Henry, with Sangita Shresthova, Liana Gamber-Thompson, and Neta Kligler-Vilenchik. "Important Reminder: Superman Was an Undocumented Immigrant." *Fusion*, n.d. https:// fusion.tv/video/103908/superheroes-are-undocumented-immigrants-and-the-other-way-around/.

Johnson, Eleanor. "The Poetics of Waste: Medieval English Ecocriticism." *PMLA: Publications of the Modern Language Association of America* 127, no. 3 (May 2012): 460–76.

Joyce, Ashlee. "Gothic Misdirections: Troubling the Trauma Fiction Paradigm in Pat Barker's *Double Vision*," *English Studies* 100, no. 4 (2019): 461–77. doi:10.1080/ 0013838X.2019.1601417.

Kelley, Wyn, Henry Jenkins, Katie Clinton, and Jenna McWilliams. "From Theory to Practice: Building a 'Community of Readers' in Your Classroom." *Reading in a Participatory Culture: Remixing* Moby-Dick *in the English Classroom*. Edited by Henry Jenkins and Wyn Kelley, 25–39. New York: Teachers College Press, 2013.

Kligler-Vilenchik, Neta. "'Decreasing World Suck': Harnessing Popular Culture for Fan Activism." In *By Any Media Necessary: The New Youth Activism*. By Henry Jenkins, Sangita Shresthova, Liana Gamber-Thompson, Neta Kligler-Vilenchik, and Arely M. Zimmerman, n.p. New York: New York University Press, 2016. https://opensquare.nyu press.org/books/9781479829712/read/.

Kohnen, Melanie E. S. "Tumblr Pedagogies." In *A Companion to Media Fandom and Fan Studies*. Edited by Paul Booth, 351–68. Hoboken, NJ: Wiley Blackwell, 2018.

LaCapra, Dominick. *History and Memory after Auschwitz*. Ithaca, NY: Cornell University Press, 1998.

LaCapra, Dominick. "Trauma, Absence, Loss." *Critical Inquiry* 25, no. 4 (1999): 696–727.

Lanier, Douglas M. "The Hogarth Shakespeare Series: Redeeming Shakespeare's Literariness." In *Shakespeare and Millennial Fiction*. Edited by Andrew James Hartley, 230–50. Cambridge: Cambridge University Press, 2017.

Lanier, Douglas M. *Shakespeare and Modern Popular Culture*. Oxford: Oxford University Press, 2002.

Leverage, Paula. "Is Perceval Autistic? Theory of Mind in the *Conte Del Graal*." In *Theory of Mind and Literature*. Edited by Paula Leverage, 133–51. West Lafayette, IN: Purdue University Press, 2011.

Linton, Simi. "Reassigning Meaning." In *Claiming Disability: Knowledge and Identity*. By Simi Linton, 8–33. New York: New York University Press, 1998.

Lopez, Lori Kido. "Fan-Activists and the Politics of Race in *The Last Airbender*." *International Journal of Cultural Studies* 15, no. 5 (September 2012): 431–45.

Mancini, John, "The Big 'Aladdin' Casting Reveal Doesn't Get Disney off the Hook on Race." *Quartz India*, July 16, 2017. https://qz.com/india/1030404/naomi-scott-mena-massoud-and-will-smith-aladdin-casting-news-doesnt-get-disney-off-the-hook-on-race/.

Mangels, Andy. "Lesbian Sex = Death?" *The Advocate*, August 20, 2002, 70–71.

McDermid, Val. "Review." *The Guardian*, May 15, 2014. http://www.theguardian.com/books/2014/.

Miller, Toby. "Trainspotting *The Avengers*." In *Cult Television*. Edited by Sara Gwenllian-Jones and Roberta E. Pearson, 187–97. Minneapolis: University of Minnesota Press, 2004.

Moonbeam's Predilections. "Fanfiction Terminology." *Angelfire.com*, September 2017. http://www.angelfire.com/falcon/moonbeam/terms.html.

Morimoto, Lori. "Ontological Security and the Politics of Transcultural Fandom." In *A Companion to Media Fandom and Fan Studies*. Edited by Paul Booth, 257–88. Hoboken, NJ: Wiley Blackwell, 2018.

Nepveu, Kate. "Diana Gabaldon & Fanfic Followup." Live Journal, 2010. https://kate-nepveu.livejournal.com/483239.html.

"Original, adj. and n." *Oxford English Dictionary: OED Online*. Oxford University Press, June 2019. oed.com.

Orr, Mary. *Intertextuality: Debates and Contexts*. Cambridge: Polity, 2003.

Ozdek, Almila. "Coming out of the Amnesia: Herstories and Earth Stories, and Jane Smiley's Critique of Capitalist Ownership in *A Thousand Acres*." In *New Directions in Ecofeminist Literary Criticism*. Edited by Andrea Campbell, 62–73. Cambridge: Cambridge Scholars Publishing, 2008.

Pande, Rukmini. "Who Do You Mean by 'Fan'? Decolonizing Media Fandom Identity." In *A Companion to Media Fandom and Fan Studies*. Edited by Paul Booth, 319–32. Hoboken, NJ: Wiley Blackwell, 2018.

Pande, Rukmini. "'You Do Realize *The Lion King* Is Set in Africa, Right?' Utilizing Fan Studies to Teach about Race and Racism in the University Classroom." In *Fandom as Classroom Practice: A Teaching Guide*. Edited by Katherine Anderson Howell, 96–112. Iowa City: University of Iowa Press, 2018.

Pearson, Roberta. "Bachies, Bardies, Trekkies, and Sherlockians." In *Fandom: Identities and Communities in a Mediated World*. Edited by Jonathan Gray, Cornel Sandvoss, and C. Lee Harrington, 98–109. New York: New York University Press, 2007.

Pratt, Murray. "Detective Harry Hole: Nationality: Norwegian/Creator: Jo Nesbø." In *Detective*. Edited by Barry Forshaw, 90–98. Bristol: Intellect Books, 2016.

Pugh, Sheenagh. *The Democratic Genre: Fan Fiction in a Literary Context*. Bridgend, Wales: Seren, 2015.

Racebending.com – Media Consumers for Entertainment Equality. Tumblr, 2017. https://race bending.tumblr.com/.

Ralph, Iris. "An Animal Studies and Ecocritical Reading of *Sir Gawain and the Green Knight*." *Neohelicon: Acta Comparationis Litterarum Universarum* 44, no. 2 (December 2017): 431–44.

Rich, Adrienne. "When We Dead Awaken: Writing as Re-vision." *College English* 34, no. 1, special issue: Women, Writing and Teaching (October 1972): 18–30.

Roll, Nick. "A Schism in Medieval Studies, for All to See." *Inside Higher Ed*, 2017. https://www.insidehighered.com/news/2017/09/19/one-professors-critique-another-divides-me dieval-studies.

Romano, Aja. "About." Tumblr, 2020. https://bookshop.tumblr.com/about.

Romano, Aja. "I'm Done Explaining Why Fanfic Is Okay." *Livejournal*, 2010–2013. http://book shop.livejournal.com/1044495.html.

Rosen, Jeremy M. *Minor Characters Have Their Day: Genre and the Contemporary Literary Marketplace*. New York: Columbia University Press, 2016.

Rosen, Jeremy M. "Minor Characters Have Their Day: The Imaginary and Actual Politics of a Contemporary Genre." *Contemporary Literature* 54, no. 1 (2013): 139–74.

Rourks, Camacho. "No Fantasy or Sci-Fi: Teaching Genre as Workshop." AWP Conference, 30 March 2019, Oregon Convention Center, Portland, Oregon. Panel Discussion.

Rubin, Daniel Ian. "Hebcrit: A New Dimension of Critical Race Theory." *Social Identities* 26, no. 4 (2020): 499–514. doi:10.1080/13504630.2020.1773778.

Rudd, Gillian. "Being Green in Late Medieval English Literature." In *The Oxford Handbook of Ecocriticism*. Edited by Greg Garrard and Cheryll Glotfelty, 27–39. Oxford: Oxford University Press, 2014.

Said, Edward W. *Culture and Imperialism*. New York: Vintage, 1994.

Sanders, Julie. *Adaptation and Appropriation*. 2nd edition. London: Routledge, 2015. doi.org/10.4324/9781315737942.

Sandvoss, Cornel. "Death of the Reader? Literary Theory and the Study of Texts in Popular Culture." In *Fandom: Identities and Communities in a Mediated World*. Edited by Jonathan Gray, Cornel Sandvoss, and C. Lee Harrington, 19–32. New York: New York University Press, 2007.

Schott, Christine. "How to Save Literary Studies." *The Chronicle of Higher Education*, January 3, 2016 (Web); January 8, 2016 (Print). http://chronicle.com/article/How-to-Save-Literary-Studies/234713.

Sellars, Peter. "Foreword." In *Desdemona*. By Toni Morrison, lyrics by Rokia Traoré, 7–11. London: Oberon Modern Plays, 2012.

Sellars, Peter, Toni Morrison, and Rokia Traoré. "*Desdemona*: Dialogues across Histories, Continents, Cultures." Townsend Center for the Humanities, 28 October 2011, University

of California Berkeley. https://townsendcenter.berkeley.edu/media/desdemona-dia
logues-across-histories-continents-cultures.

Seymour, Jessica. "Racebending and Prosumer Fanart Practices in *Harry Potter* Fandom." In *A Companion to Media Fandom and Fan Studies*. Edited by Paul Booth, 333–47. Hoboken, NJ: Wiley Blackwell, 2018.

Siebers, Tobin. "Disability in Theory: From Social Constructionism to the New Realism of the Body." *American Literary History* 13, no. 4 (2001): 737–54.

Stanfill, Mel. "The Unbearable Whiteness of Fandom and Fan Studies." In *A Companion to Media Fandom and Fan Studies*. Edited by Paul Booth, 305–18. Hoboken, NJ: Wiley Blackwell, 2018.

Stanhope, Kate. "Bury Your Gays: TV Writers Tackle Trope, the Lexa Pledge and Offer Advice to Showrunners." *The Hollywood Reporter*, June 11, 2016. https://www.hollywood reporter.com/live-feed/bury-your-gays-atx-festival-901800.

Thomas, Bronwen. "Canons and Fanons: Literary Fanfiction Online." In *Dichtung Digital: Journal für Kunst und Kultur digitaler Medien* 37, no. 9 (2007): 1–11. https://doi.org/10.25969/mediarep/17701.

Thomas, Bronwen. "What Is Fanfiction and Why Are People Saying Such Nice Things about It?" In *Storyworlds: A Journal of Narrative Studies* 3 (2011): 1–24.

Thompson, Allison. "Trinkets and Treasures: Consuming Jane Austen." *Persuasions On-Line* 28, no. 2 (Spring 2008): n.p.

Torfi H. Tulinius. "Re-writing the Contemporary Sagas: How Several Modern Novelists Use *Sturlunga Saga*." In *The Garden of Crossing Paths: The Manipulation and Rewriting of Medieval Texts*. Edited by Marina Buzzoni and Massimiliano Bampi, 193–208. Venice: Università Ca' Foscari, 2005.

Truskauskaite-Kuneviciene, Inga, Julia Brailovskaia, Yuka Kamite, Gabija Petrauskaite, Jürgen Margraf, and Evaldas Kazlauskas. "Does Trauma Shape Identity? Exploring the Links between Lifetime Trauma Exposure and Identity Status in Emerging Adulthood." *Frontiers in Psychology* 11 (2020): n.p. doi:10.3389/fpsyg.2020.570644.

Tulloch, John. "Fans of Chekhov: Re-approaching 'High Culture.'" In *Fandom: Identities and Communities in a Mediated World*. Edited by Jonathan Gray, Cornel Sandvoss, and C. Lee Harrington, 110–22. New York: New York University Press, 2007.

Turk, Tisha. "Metalepsis in Fan Vids and Fan Fiction." In *Metalepsis in Popular Culture*. Edited by Karin Kukkonen and Sonja Klimek, 83–103. New York: De Gruyter, 2011.

United States, Court of Appeals for the Eleventh Circuit. *Suntrust v. Houghton Mifflin Co.* 268 F.3d 1257, 10 Oct. 2001. *United States Court of Appeals for the Eleventh Circuit*. https://law.justia.com/cases/federal/appellate-courts/F3/268/1257/608446/.

Uprichard, Lucy. "In Defence of Call-Out Culture." *Huffington Post*, December 27, 2013. https://www.huffingtonpost.co.uk/lucy-uprichard/call-out-culture_b_4507889.html?guc counter=2.

Van Steenhuyse, Veerle. "The Writing and Reading of Fan Fiction and Transformation Theory." *CLCWeb: Comparative Literature and Culture* 13, no. 4 (2011). https://docs.lib.purdue.edu/clcweb/vol13/iss4/4/.

Wagner, Geoffrey. *The Novel and the Cinema*. London: Associated University Presses, 1975.

Ward, Sean Francis. "Erotohistoriography and War's Waste in Pat Barker's *Regeneration* Trilogy." *Contemporary Literature* 57, no. 3 (2016): 320–45.

"What We Believe." *Organization for Transformative Works*, n.d. https://www.transformative works.org/what_we_believe/.

Whelehan, Imelda. "Adaptations: The Contemporary Dilemmas." In *Adaptations: From Text to Screen, Screen to Text*. Edited by Deborah Cartmell and Imelda Whelehan, 3–19. London: Routledge, 1999.

"Who Killed Kennedy?" *Archieology101*, 2006. http://archieology101.tripod.com/whokilled. htm.

Windling, Terri. "White as Snow: Fairy Tales and Fantasy." In *Snow White, Blood Red*. Edited by Ellen Datlow and Terri Windling, 1–20. New York: Avon, 1993.

Zarins, Kim. "Intersex and the Pardoner's Body." *Accessus: A Journal of Premodern Literature and New Media* 4, no. 1 (2017): 1–63. scholarworks.wmich.edu/accessus/vol4/iss1/2.

Zinman, Toby. *Replay: Classic Modern Drama Reimagined*. London: Methuen Drama, 2015.

Index

https://doi.org/10.1515/9781501515972-009